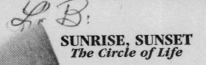

SUNRISE, SUNSET
The Circle of Life

Mother Nature
straining, exhausted;
One last push—finally,
first light!
Red-faced and
wondrous to behold.
She croons a lullaby, vowing
never to let this moment go.
Dawn.
Rekindled flame,
Slowly inching upward,
independent and strong;
Reaching fingers
of light across the sky,
Eager to fulfill
her destiny,
and become…
Today.

Father Time
reflective,
melancholy;
Once clothed in
garments of
fiery grandeur.
Now wearing a
cloak of dismal gray.
Singing dirges for
souls he's sent to rest.
Dusk.
Faltering light.
Seeking comfort and settling
into aching, empty arms.
Lovingly in the night, he plants
The seeds that become…
Tomorrow.

—*Kathleen Marie Marsh*

ISBN: 0-9760796-0-7

Published by Otter Run Books, LLC
16965 Nicolet Road, Townsend, WI 54175
www.otterrunbooks.com

Cover art by Betsy Popp
Book design by Printing Services Management, Madison, WI

First Printing October 2004
Printed in the United States.

SUNRISE
SUNSET

A novel that traces the circle of life
and the role that female friendships play in the
journey that, if you live long enough, often ends where it began.

Kathleen Marie Marsh
and Heather Sprangers

Otter Run Books, LLC

Acknowledgements

We wish to thank our team of
manuscript readers for invaluable feedback.

That includes our friend Angie Sanderfoot;
Kathie's sister, Carol Roche; Heather's mom, Nancy Dey;
and Heather's aunt, Sandy Weiland.

Of course we also acknowledge with
heartfelt appreciation our husbands, Adam and Jon,
whose support and patience during this project
have been nothing short of boundless.

We also wish to thank Julie and Linda
and the entire Paradise Island waitstaff!
Paradise Island, pictured on the cover,
is the place where we met
as this novel took shape and became a reality.

Dedication

We dedicate this novel to
Heather's son, Benjamin Sprangers,
her miracle baby. Ben is in the sunrise
of his life's journey, full of hope and promise
We watch with delight to see
what he will become.

We also dedicate this book to
Kathie's mother, Rose Mary Brantmeier,
now in her sunset years. Rose Mary is locked
in a courageous battle against the ravages
of Alzheimer's Disease.
Her heroic struggle is an inspiration to
everyone who knows and loves her.

CHAPTER 1

Thursday, March 6th

Janelle never saw it coming. The Medical Center elevator jolted and abruptly stopped, throwing her sharply forward into the rail. She was so thrilled to run into her former English teacher, Ellie Reed, that she hadn't noticed the elderly woman with her step forward and push the Emergency button. Janelle tried to break her fall by grabbing the arm rail with her left hand, instinctively shielding her stomach with her right.

"Mom! Don't do that again!" Ellie said sharply, removing the old woman's hand from the keypad and guiding her to the back of the elevator.

"You all right, Janelle?"

"Uh huh, no harm done." Janelle let go of the rail, still cradling her stomach protectively. *God, I hope my baby's okay! I wonder if Ellie knows. I bet I forgot to email her.*

"What was your floor, Janelle?"

"Three."

Ellie pressed Reset and then the right button, and the car moved up slowly once again. A tune Janelle vaguely remembered was playing softly, and the old woman began to fidget with the neckline of her jacket as she hummed along. *"Sunrise, sunset...swiftly go the years...one season following another...laden with happiness and tears."*

"Mom, now what're you doing? Leave your jacket on." Ellie gently held her mother's hands to her sides before refastening the top two buttons.

"I hate this jacket...it's too tight."

"You have to keep it on; it's chilly today. Besides, you've lost a lot of weight, so how can it be too small? We'll take it off when we get to Dr. Randolph's office."

"I don't care what you say, this jacket's too tight." The old woman's face was set in a determined frown and she looked rather confused. "Dr. Randolph, who's that?"

Ellie looked sheepishly at Janelle, as if she suddenly wished that she and her mother were alone. The elevator stopped and the doors opened. Ellie's mother stepped forward.

"No, Mom," Ellie said firmly, holding her back. "This isn't our floor. Janelle's getting off here."

"Janelle? That's a nice name. I'm Helen..." She pointed to Janelle's abdomen. "You're pregnant, aren't you?"

You're kidding...what is she, psychic? I didn't think I was even showing yet! Speechless, she stood with her mouth agape, astonished that Helen had noticed the small rounded swell of her stomach that she was still rubbing gently.

"Pregnant?" Ellie asked. "Wow! Congratulations!"

"Sorry...I forgot to tell you, Ellie! I'm seventeen weeks. Matt and I heard the heartbeat last month...I can't wait till I hear it again today." Janelle's sapphire eyes sparkled as she tucked her corn silk blonde hair behind her ears in a gesture of self-consciousness Ellie remembered so well.

Suddenly Ellie's face took on a worried expression. "That bump before...you sure you're okay?" She reached over and pressed the Door-Open button so Janelle could answer her question.

"Positive," Janelle fibbed. *I am definitely not positive! Please God, let my baby be okay, I feel cramps starting.*

"Are you sure?" Ellie asked. "I know you've gone through so much to make this baby...told you it would happen though, didn't I?"

"Happen, what happened?" Helen interrupted.

Janelle pointed to her stomach. "Baby..." she said and added, "Nice to meet you, Helen. I was Ellie's student in junior high; she was my favorite teacher."

Helen looked at her daughter blankly, "You're a teacher, Eleanor? What do you teach?"

"English, Mom. You know that."

Extremely distressed and wanting to be on her way, Janelle looked at her watch and then at Ellie. She noted with genuine surprise that her former teacher's hair was streaked with gray and the crow's feet lines near her eyes were deeper and more pronounced. Ellie appeared to have gained a little weight as well.

"My appointment's in a few minutes, Ellie, but let's get together soon and catch up."

"Sure thing," Ellie said, then whispered, "Sorry about my mother. It comes and goes; an hour from now..." Ellie was still pressing the Door-Open button and holding her mother back.

"Not to worry. I'll call or email you...I promise."

"Super, Janelle...take care of yourself...and that baby."

Janelle said her goodbyes with a big smile, but her face turned to a worried frown as she hurried down the hall.

CHAPTER 2

Thursday, March 6th

Janelle quickly passed the Family Fertility Lab to the Women's Health waiting area. The spacious room was quiet and relaxing. She noticed some toddlers playing in the far corner, a few moms with infant car seats—probably there for baby's first checkup, and several other pregnant women with their noses in baby magazines. She went straight to the registration desk.

"I have an appointment with Doctor Felding and I need to see him right away."

"Your name?"

"Janelle Spencer."

"What seems to be the problem?"

"An old lady started pushing buttons in the elevator and it stopped with a jerk. I fell forward and barely caught myself before my stomach hit the arm rail. I'm getting cramps now and I'm worried about my baby!"

"Any bleeding?"

"I don't really know; I haven't checked...but it doesn't feel like it."

"Doctor is running behind schedule, but we'll see what we can do."

"Look," Janelle glanced at the receptionist's nametag. "Penny, I've spent untold misery for almost two years, not to mention thousands of dollars getting pregnant, and I am not going to risk..."

"Please, just have a seat, Mrs. Spencer. As I already said, we'll see what we can do."

Seeing it was useless to argue, Janelle began steady rhythmic breathing, forcing herself to calm down. She hung up her coat and went over to look at the colorful fish in the aquarium. She loved the soothing bubbles and the fish seemed just as interested in her as she was in them. The brightest yellow fish swam up to the glass and it brought Janelle back to her seventh grade writing class. Mrs. Reed had a bright yellow sweater that always hung on the back of her chair. She never cared if it matched the outfit she was wearing or not. She'd tell her students, "This is my sunshine sweater. Some days it matches what I'm wearing, and some days it doesn't, but it always makes me think of warm happy things."

As she sat down in the chair closest to the fish tank, Janelle wondered if Ellie still had that sweater. *Surely it must be out of style by now.* Janelle let herself do the math and calculated that she was in Mrs. Reed's class over fifteen years ago. *How can that amount of time slip by so quickly when every minute now seems an eternity?*

Janelle's abdominal discomfort eased—conscious breathing was helping. Looking for anything to occupy her thoughts, she reached into the canvas bag she always carried and pulled out her pregnancy journal. As a seventh grader, Janelle had learned from Mrs. Reed the value of recording feelings on paper, and she wanted the journal to be a treasured keepsake, showing her baby how much she and Matt had wanted to become parents.

Right after she and Matt decided to start their family, Janelle's mother, Claire, had given her a cheerful diary to record her thoughts and feelings during this very special time in her life. At first the journal sat out on Janelle's nightstand, but after a year of trying, the book's empty pages mirrored her empty womb, and it became a wretched reminder of their failed attempts to conceive. One morning when she got up to find her period starting, Janelle angrily threw the journal on a bookshelf in one of the spare bedrooms so she wouldn't have to look at it. Now she carried it everywhere.

The front of the book was arranged by month for details about doctor appointments, prompting the writer to record important details by starting a sentence and then leaving the rest blank. The opening line said: *My initial reaction was:* Janelle read her response.

> *I couldn't believe it! I was actually shaking with excitement, and I couldn't wait until Matt got home! I looked in the garage three times before he actually got home because I thought I heard him pull in the driveway.*

Janelle turned to the back of the book where empty pages beckoned for her to journal the way she preferred, without prompting. She'd decided to write letters to the baby in that section; she had four so far. Just then the door next to the receptionist's desk opened and the nurse called out, "Janette Fink?"

Darn, Janette...I thought she was gonna say Janelle. I went to grade school with a Joe Fink...kids can be so mean. She recalled the teasing chant from the bullies on the playground. "Stinky, Finky! Your favorite color is pink. Stinky, Finky! You still take your bath in the sink. Stinky, Finky!" and on and on it would go. Janelle gently rubbed her tummy. *Hopefully, you're safe with the last name Spencer, honey.* She got out a pen to write but then decided to read her previous entries.

November 20th
Dear Baby,
> *I can't even begin to explain to you how I'm feeling! I hardly got anything done at work today because I was thinking so much about you. I can't believe I'm going to be a mommy! I've been waiting so long and your daddy and I are so happy! We thought we would keep the news to ourselves for a little while, but that idea went right out the window when the pregnancy test was positive! Hopefully, as each day*

*passes this will feel more real and I will be able to stop
pinching myself!*

I love you already...Mommy.

Janelle smiled, remembering the tears of joy spilling
down her mother's face when they announced that Claire
would finally become a grandmother.

December 21st
Dear Baby,

*I can't believe I'm 8 weeks pregnant! I'll be
holding you in my arms before I know it! Luckily I've
had only a little morning sickness, but as long as I eat
something, my stomach settles. Tuesday I thought I
would throw up, but it was just dry heaves (yuck!).*

*Daddy came with me to the first doctor
appointment, but we didn't even see the doctor—just
a nurse who did a family history. She was nice but
what a list of "No-No's!" No skydiving, bungee
jumping, snowmobiling, tuna, chocolate, caffeine,
alcohol, diet products, or over-the-counter medicines.
Would you mind telling me how I am going to live
without my diet soda and chocolate?*

*Grandma Claire came with me to the second
appointment, and we had a different nurse who was so
crabby. We really wanted to listen to your heartbeat,
but my uterus was tipped and we couldn't hear a
thing. Let's see if I can make you laugh. Afterward,
Grandma Claire was telling everyone that we heard
three heartbeats! Then she'd say: "Janelle's, the doctor's,
and mine!" We shocked a lot of people, especially your
daddy! Seriously, the doctor's sure there's just one
"you" in there. I had to ask because I used a medicine
to help me get pregnant, and it increases the chances of
having twins.*

*We haven't agreed on a boy's name, but if you're
a little girl...what do you think of the name Dana?*

*Everyone keeps asking what your name's going to be,
but it's a secret! I can't wait until you start moving
around in my tummy!*

Love, Mommy

*December 25th
Dear Baby,*

*Merry Christmas! We are having such a busy
holiday season! Daddy just got a nice Christmas bonus
so we should be able to pay down some of our bills. We
went to Aunt Christine's for the Knott's Christmas and
to Grandma Sandy's for the Spencer's. Everyone was
asking how I felt and the only thing I can complain
about is being so tired!*

*Grandma Claire kept apologizing because all the
presents she bought for us were actually for you! You
got a really nice baby swing that we know you're
going to love and Grandma Claire made you a
beautiful quilt with baby carriages on it! Daddy and I
are so happy and excited; you really are our very own
Christmas miracle!*

Love, Mommy
*P.S. Don't get too used to all the sweets I'm eating. It's
just a Christmas thing!*

Janelle looked around and saw that no one had moved.
Her stomach cramps had definitely subsided so she
repositioned herself in the uncomfortable chair and read her
most recent entry.

*February 14th
Dear Baby,*

*I'm on my lunch hour, sitting in Paradise Island,
eating a hot fudge sundae. Pure heaven. (I sure do
love ice cream these days!) We finally got to hear your
heartbeat...ka-thump...ka-thump...very impressive*

*first "words!" In April we'll have an ultrasound and
get our first pictures of you.*

*I want to start looking pregnant, but I'm still
wearing regular clothes. Everyone tells me that one
morning I'll wake up with a baby belly and my pants
won't fit. Grandma Claire and I are going shopping to
buy you a crib and pick out paint and wallpaper for
your nursery. I can't believe I'm almost fourteen
weeks...you're going to be here before I know it. I can't
wait to meet you! Will you be my Valentine?*

Love, Mommy ~☙

Janelle finished reading and tucked the journal back into
her bag, then turned her attention to the aquarium to look for
her favorite fish. As if beckoned by Janelle's attention, it
appeared from behind a brightly painted rock that paled in
comparison to the fish's brilliant canary-colored scales. Its
sunshine-yellow color made her think of Ellie again, and she
let her mind drift back to seventh grade.

A vivid memory filled her. Janelle was in Mrs. Reed's
class, working on a unit on the Alaskan Iditarod Dog Sled
Race. Each student was to predict the winner, follow that
musher's progress, and write a persuasive article related to
some aspect of the race. As an added incentive, the student
who wrote the best composition would be Mrs. Reed's
luncheon guest at Paradise Island.

A quiet, capable student, Janelle wasn't that interested in
the overall assignment, yet she was intrigued by the writing
component. Then to her chagrin, she was the only student to
choose Susan Butcher, a relatively unknown female
competing in a very grueling sport against some of Alaska's
toughest men. Some of the kids made fun of Janelle for
choosing Susan, but Mrs. Reed stopped the teasing with one
cold stare. When Butcher was first to cross the finish line in
Nome, Ellie allowed Janelle to gloat a little.

The next week Ellie announced that Janelle had won the
contest with an exceptional essay arguing that women can
display intelligence, composure and endurance as well as

men can. As promised, Ellie took Janelle to lunch and the young girl fell under her Socratic spell. Janelle read and wrote like words were facing extinction and cried on the last day of school when she hugged her favorite teacher goodbye. The next year she volunteered to be Mrs. Reed's student assistant, and they had floated in and out of each other's lives ever since.

We had lunch last summer and spent the whole time talking about infertility, Janelle recalled. Ellie was very empathetic, revealing that it had taken her five years to conceive her first child. Janelle was aghast. At that time she and Matt had been trying for almost two years and Janelle couldn't imagine going through even one more month of disappointment, much less several more years. *I remember we were even considering adoption then because I talked to Ellie about it, and she told me about several adopted students she'd had in class.*

After that day, Janelle emailed Ellie a few times about the infertility treatments, but eventually it was just too depressing to write about the failures. *I can't believe I forgot to let Ellie know we finally got lucky! Jeez…pregnancy must affect the brain too!*

Janelle stiffened when she felt another pelvic twinge, and anxiety gripped her once again. *Why is it taking so darn long? Please, God…I need to see the doctor now!* As if in answer to her prayer, Dr. Felding's nurse appeared, took a folder off the wall rack, checked the name and called out, "Janelle Spencer?"

The waiting room was crowded and stuffy as Ellie led her mother to the only two empty side-by-side chairs. The walls and low nap carpeting were mauve, off-white and gray, the color-du-jour of medical institutions.

"Sit here, Mom, I'll check you in. Want to look at a book?" She handed her mother a gardening magazine. Helen began to turn the colorful pages, casually glancing at them as Ellie approached the receptionist's window. "Helen Lowe to see Dr. Randolph," she said when the woman behind the desk looked up from a pile of folders. A copier behind her busily spit out papers.

"Fill out these forms, please," the receptionist said in a rather curt tone, handing Ellie a clipboard with a pad of documents attached.

Quickly skimming the papers, Ellie said, "Don't you already have all this? I spent thirty minutes yesterday answering these same questions during a pre-registration phone conversation."

"It's routine procedure, Mrs. Lowe," the receptionist replied with an air of dismissal.

"I'm not Mrs. Lowe," Ellie responded, her voice sounding a little more annoyed than she actually felt. "My mother is Mrs. Lowe. I'm Mrs. Reed."

"Well, then...Mrs. Reed, if you want your mother to see Dr. Randolph today, you'll have to fill these out. It's standard procedure." The tone of the receptionist's voice was as testy as Ellie was beginning to feel. She sighed and went back to her mother who was still just turning the bright pages.

Ellie noticed with a pervasive sadness how old and feeble her mother looked. Helen's once thick dark brown hair was now pure white and wispy, so sparse her scalp was easily visible beneath. Her frail neck curved forward as she bent over the magazine, her glasses slipping slightly down her nose. The veins in her neck protruded, her skin was sagging and wrinkled, and she looked thinner than Ellie could ever remember. She had a sudden urge to gather her mother in her arms, carry her back to the car and drive off somewhere, anywhere where her mother was young and healthy and vibrant again. *Why does her life have to come to an end like this—slowly but surely losing her grip on reality? I miss her quick wit and sharp mind...I wish she could simply go to sleep and never wake up, like Dad did.* Ellie determinedly shoved her morbid thoughts aside and went back to completing the forms.

FAMILY HISTORY:
Born: Helen Miriam Jackson; Bayeville, Wisconsin.
October 25, 1920.
Marital status: Widow. Husband of 48 years, Francis;
deceased, 1988.
Children: Frank, (57) accountant; Ellie (55) teacher;
Josie, (49) stockbroker.

Well, that's one good thing...at least Mom's failing memory means she won't have to deal with Frank's problems now. On second thought, she's always been in denial about Frank's problems—drinking, gambling, bullying...whatever other selfish, inconsiderate things he can think of...don't get me started! Ellie had admitted to herself years ago that she suffered from a severe case of The Middle Child Syndrome—especially where her mother was concerned. Frank was Helen's first-born and could do no wrong, and Josie was the baby so any mistake on her part was overlooked or automatically forgiven. *Dad knew Frank isn't the angel Mom thinks he is, but he's gone now so Frank could become MY problem.*

"Are you my mother?" an elderly man yelled at Helen.

"No! What's the matter with you?" Helen replied with a bewildered look on her face.

"Then where is she? What did you do to her? I want my mother!" The man was shouting now and approached the two women in a threatening way.

"Arnie, Arnie, it's okay. I'm right here; I told you I'd be right back," a gray-haired woman said as she guided the man firmly back to his chair. Ellie read the woman's sweatshirt, which said: *Great-Grandmas are the Greatest.*

"I'm so sorry," the woman said. "He thinks I'm his mother, but I'm actually his wife. He has Alzheimer's. It wasn't so bad in the beginning, but he's been really going downhill lately. Still, I just can't put him in a home. We promised each other..." Her voice trailed and she looked pleadingly for understanding. Arnie sat back in the chair, still muttering.

At the mention of the word "home," Helen put down her magazine and said in a self-righteous tone, "No, you can't. No one should ever have to go to one of those horrible places. My Francis and I promised each other we'd never...and I fully intended to hold him to it. Then he had to go and die on me. In his sleep...in our bed...imagine! I still can't believe he did that to me!" Then she added, "Alzheimer's. I hope I die before that happens to me. I don't want to be a burden to anyone, no sir, not me. Not like your Grandpa Jackson..."

"Mom, don't talk so foolish," Ellie scolded, ignoring her mother's reference to her grandfather's last years. It was too painful to discuss. Grandpa Jackson had always been so sharp, so alive...and the last time Ellie had seen him at the nursing home, he was incapable of recognizing anyone, curled in a fetal position and sucking his thumb.

Suddenly, the music from the television anchored on the ceiling blared. An elderly woman was aiming the remote squarely at the set and calling loudly, "It's time for my story!" She clung desperately to the remote, even as an elderly man tried to take it from her.

"Vange," the man Ellie presumed to be her husband, said firmly. "Give it to me. We'll watch your story when we get home." Vange stared at him blankly but finally let go of the remote and the man quickly lowered the volume.

Startled and annoyed by the sudden loud sounds, Helen looked at Ellie and whispered, "Take me home!"

"It's okay, Mom," Ellie soothed. "It won't be much longer. Here, look at your magazine...now doesn't this look just like Rebecca?"

Helen studied the picture Ellie was pointing to. From her blank expression, Ellie knew Helen had no idea who she was talking about. "You know, Rebecca. Your favorite, and only, granddaughter?"

"No, I think she looks like Janelle," Helen said. Ellie was flabbergasted...Helen seemed to have forgotten a granddaughter she had known and loved for twenty-seven years but remembered Janelle whom she had briefly met in an elevator!

"You know what, Mom? Rebecca called me last night. She said she loves her new law firm and Minneapolis...she wishes she had made the move sooner. She especially likes being closer to her brother. Can you believe it, Mom? Jonah's graduating from college in June."

"Jonah...such a big boy, always hungry. He loves sugary treats; why he can eat a plateful of cookies all by himself," Helen said. "And he's going to be a teacher." Ellie shook her head. *How can Mother not remember Rebecca, yet recall Jonah's sweet tooth and future plans?* "A teacher..." Helen went on. "Just like me. Just like my Eleanor. What grade do you teach again?"

"Seventh, communication arts and writing. I had Janelle in seventh grade. She was one of my more successful projects." Ellie always called her students her "kids" and tried to treat them all alike, but each year she selected a few who needed something extra in the way of attention. She called them her "projects" and worked especially hard to make a difference in their lives. It could be frustrating when a kid didn't respond, but in Janelle's case, it was just what she'd needed to blossom.

Helen scrunched her face, as if trying to focus, but Ellie could see by the blank look in her mother's eyes that the name Janelle no longer registered.

"I like it when you talk about teaching, Eleanor... makes me remember how much I loved it. I've been thinking about going back to subbing next year. Of course, your father won't like it one bit. He made me retire so we could spend more time together. I'm glad, but still, sometimes I really miss teaching..."

"Subbing is one of the hardest jobs in the world, Mom." Ellie laughed ruefully. "I think you should stay just where you are...retired and at home." She didn't mention that her father made her mother give up teaching because he hated his own cooking, or that subbing was hard enough when you were young and possessed of all your faculties.

For the past year, Helen had been what Ellie's husband Jack called "moving in and out," gradually losing her grip on reality. Now she pursed her lips and glared at her daughter. "I can still work with the best of them, and don't you dare forget it, missy! I remember how hard subbing is...did it for three years before I finally landed that full-time job." Her voice was getting louder as she became agitated and argumentative.

People in the waiting room were starting to stare. "Mom, I know, you were a great teacher...the best." Helen smiled and relaxed, pleased at the compliment.

"But I can't remember things as well as I used to. My memory's still good, just short." Her mother chuckled at what she thought was a little joke.

"Well, that's why we're here, Mom," Ellie smiled at her wearily. "To find out why and what we can do about your memory lapses."

"Right, we have to ask the doctor," Helen replied. "What's his name again?"

"Dr. Deborah Randolph. She's supposed to be the best."

"Mrs. Lowe?" a loud voice called. "Helen Lowe?"

"Let's go, Mom; the nurse is calling you."

"Well, it's about time," Helen looked around the waiting room and then at Arnie and Vange and whispered to Ellie, "Sitting here with all these crazy people is making me crazy."

CHAPTER 3

Thursday, March 6th

Janelle left the doctor's office feeling convinced that her baby was fine. *Thank God... after everything we've been through. I'm not sure what's up with that old woman, poor Ellie...she must be a handful!* She brushed her negative thoughts aside as she approached the same elevator she had ridden so often, fighting back tears after yet another failure. She let her mind skim over the timeline of disappointments. *By the time our baby's born, Matt and I will be just two months away from our fifth wedding anniversary. Could we really have had our third and fourth anniversary during the time we were trying to conceive?* On their fourth anniversary, Matt had sent her flowers at work. She still had one dried rose and the card on her desk that said it all: *I love you. Matt.*

As the elevator doors opened, she tried to recall their third anniversary. *Why can't I remember?* Every thought floating around in her brain seemed to be about infertility tests, labs, doctors and procedures. Now all of that was a world behind her. Finally, she was on the incredible, but a little frightening, journey to motherhood—a journey she had almost been convinced would always be just beyond her reach.

As she pulled out of the parking lot, Janelle reached for her cell phone. "Hi, could I speak to Claire, please? This is her daughter." As she waited for her mother to come to the phone, Janelle decided it would be best not to tell her about the incident in the elevator with Ellie's mother.

"Hello, this is Claire."

"Hi, Mom, it's me. I'm just leaving the doctor's."

"Janelle! Tell me...the heartbeat?"

"A lot louder and stronger than last time. I can't remember how many beats per minute the doc said it was, but it was fast! Mom, I think I'm finally starting to believe I'm really truly pregnant."

"And why not? You and Matt deserve this more than anyone I know. You're going to be such good parents."

"Thanks, Mom. Hey, guess who I saw at the clinic before my appointment?"

"Who?"

"Ellie Reed."

"Really?" There was an abrupt change in her mother's voice, which took on a slightly chilly tone. "How is she? She certainly must be excited to hear you're pregnant."

"Actually, I barely got to talk to her. She was taking her mother to an appointment and she had her hands full." Janelle's resolve to keep secret what happened crumbled. "Her mother was acting so weird—confused and childish. I don't know what she was thinking, but she pressed the emergency button...the elevator jerked to a stop...I fell forward and bumped my stomach pretty hard. I was so scared that something happened to the baby, Mom."

"Oh my God," Claire cried. "Are you...is the baby?"

Hearing the panic in her mother's voice, Janelle was immediately sorry. She decided once and for all to stop sharing bad news with her mother. "Mom, don't worry. It's okay; the doctor said we're fine."

Seemingly reassured, Claire told Janelle to rest when she got home and turned the conversation back to Ellie's mother. "Sounds like dementia," Claire said, her tone turning more sympathetic. "I certainly hope she has family to help."

Janelle knew her mom was speaking from experience with her mother-in-law, Grandma Knott. "I know she's got a brother and a sister, but I can't remember if they live nearby."

"Well, unfortunately they could live right in her backyard and still not pitch in. Your dad's sister was no use at all with Grandma Knott."

"Speaking of Grandma Knott, what was her middle name?" Janelle asked, deliberately changing the subject to avoid another sermon about selfish Aunt Christine.

"Madeline, why?"

"Madeline, huh? Too long. We thought if we had a girl, her middle name could be Grandma's middle name."

"Oh, your dad would really have liked that," Claire said. "But if it's too long, use Marie. That's Grandma Knott's first name and Grandma Keller's middle name."

"Ooooh, Mom, I like that." Janelle was quite sure that Marie was also Ellie Reed's middle name, and she felt a surge of happiness that she could use the names of three important people in her life. "But of course I have to talk to Matt."

"Are you sure you won't tell even me what first names you've picked out?"

"Mom, I can't. Matt and I promised each other...you sure aren't making it easy for me to keep my promise." Janelle secretly wondered if her mom would approve of the name Dana.

"Sorry," Claire said sheepishly, "I'm just excited to be a grandma, that's all. I want to know everything I can."

"I understand. Mom; sorry, I have to go. I'm in the driveway and I have no clue what to make for supper. Matt'll be starving when he gets home."

After parking her car in the garage, Janelle walked to the curb to get the mail. Shuffling through it as she walked into the house, she recited out loud to the baby, "Phone bill, credit card offer, parenting magazine, oh, and the Fertility Clinic, another payment due. I guess you and Mommy are going to have to pay some of these bills."

Janelle set the mail down, and taking the new baby magazine she'd ordered, walked down the hall to check out her changing figure in the full-length mirror. *Jeez...how did that old woman know I was pregnant? I can hardly tell myself and all my clothes still fit...okay, most of my clothes. Must be this face glowing with anticipation!* Tossing the magazine on the couch, she transformed herself into "wife mode." Twenty minutes later, Janelle found herself in the kitchen preparing dinner, after she'd started a load of laundry...folded the load left in the dryer...checked the answering machine...sorted the bills and gathered the garbage for Matt to take to the curb.

She opened the refrigerator and scanned the nearly empty shelves. *Jeez...how can it be so bare again? When am I going to find time to go to the store?* Janelle hated getting groceries and often wished she could afford to hire a grocery shopping service like some people employed a cleaning person.

"Well, I guess it's grilled cheese tonight," she sighed. "The question is," Janelle said, rubbing her tummy again, "what time will your daddy be home?"

As Janelle set out the ingredients for the simple meal, she decided to steal a few moments to write in her journal. Matt usually called on his way home, which would give her ten minutes to get started on the sandwiches. She snuggled down into the couch, knowing immediately that she should make more time to relax. *How am I ever going to have time to do everything I do now plus all I'll have to do once the baby is born?*

❧

March 6th

Dear Baby

I went to the doctor today and heard your heartbeat again...it was incredible! My eyes opened wider than they ever have before because it was so LOUD, so fast, and so strong! Next month I have an ultrasound—Daddy and I can't wait to get a glimpse of you! I haven't really "popped" yet. My tummy's getting bigger, but it's hard sometimes and soft at others. Every day I try to take some time to savor being pregnant with you, this is the most amazing experience. I am so honored to have you growing inside me. July feels like it's so far away. I can't wait to be finally become your mother!

Love, Mommy ❧

ack Reed came in late from a union meeting to find Ellie
sitting in her black leather chair, putting comments on the
final paper from a large stack of seventh grade book reports.
"Have dinner, honey?" he asked. Sometimes when Ellie got
into her schoolwork, she snacked on junk food instead of
making herself a healthy meal.

"Uh huh. Mom and I stopped at JR's for a turkey and
Swiss sub. You?"

"Pizza at the meeting," Jack said. As a Wisconsin union
official representing a wide variety of blue-collar workers, he
often ate dinner with local members he was representing.
"How'd things go today?" Jack poured himself a cup of
hazelnut decaf and brought the pot to refill Ellie's mug.

"Grueling. . .it took all day. This Dr. Randolph she saw is
supposed to be the best, but I can't say I like her. She gave
Mom a complete physical and ordered some other tests, like
blood work and an MRI. I thought Mom would have a tough
time with the MRI, feel claustrophobic or something, but she
was fine. Then we went to a clinic where they gave Mom some
mental exams."

"Like what?"

"Oh, math and memory, stuff like that. She's amazing,
Jack. She aced the oral math tests, answered some of the
calculations faster than I could. But the matching and
memory, well. . .she really struggled. A couple times she gave
me that glare, you know, like she was getting really teed off. I
just smiled and told her to keep trying. She didn't like it one
bit, but she did it." Ellie got up, straightening the pile of
papers before placing them neatly in her school bag.

"Sorry you have to go through this, honey," Jack said.
"Come here," He held his arms open wide and Ellie went to
him, melting into his strong, encircling embrace.

"You're my rock," she said.

He hugged her a long time and then drew back and
looked directly into her eyes. "I'll do what I can, Ellie. But

sooner or later you're going to have to realize you can't do everything for everyone. Sometimes you have to lean on other people, even, God forbid, your sister and brother. They're Helen's children too. Ask them...it's too much for one person."

"Asking them and not getting help would be worse than not asking and doing it all myself. And you know my sister; she and Carl can't even find time to come up to visit Mom. Besides, Josie's in complete denial that Mom even has any problem at all."

"And Frank..." Jack began.

"Frank! He'd just make things worse. The only time he calls or comes to visit Mom is if he wants money. If she says 'no' he makes-up some wild story and she caves. What he does amounts to emotional extortion, but she thinks she's being a 'good mother' by helping him out. Sometimes I get so mad I could spit nails, but what's the use? As long as Mom's considered legally competent, she can do what she wants with her money." Realizing that she was speaking in a strange voice that didn't even sound like her, she abruptly stuffed her anger and plunked herself down on the sofa. Jack sat on the side chair facing her, his face full of empathy.

Finally regaining control, Ellie continued. "Speaking of Frank and money, that reminds me, Jack. After Dr. Randolph's, we went to the pharmacy for Mom's heart medication refill. She didn't have any cash so she told me to write out a check. When I recorded it, I noticed that last week she sent Frank five *thousand* dollars. I asked her about it, but she just glared at me and said, 'Mind-your-own-business.' I brought it up again on the way home and she said Frank needed tuition money to take some courses so he can...what did he call it ... 'retool' and finally get a good job."

Jack chuckled ruefully. "Yeah, right. Tuition, huh? I'd wager your mother's last dollar that money went right to the blackjack tables."

"That's a sure bet. Anyway, I reminded her that Frank's been out of work almost a year. First, she told me again to mind my own business and then she said that since Frank had never been fortunate enough to find the right girl and have a family, he'd been 'shorted' gift-wise all these years, so he was entitled to a little extra. That's how she rationalizes sending him money...can you believe it?"

"A *little* extra?" Jack replied disdainfully. "Lord knows we don't need your mother's money, Ellie, but she's not helping Frank. I know he told us all he lost his last job in a company restructuring, but I heard something through the grapevine a couple months ago I haven't mentioned because I'm not sure if it's true. There was a rumor he had embezzled several thousand dollars from an elderly client. When the company confronted him, he returned all the money so they let him go quietly."

"Wouldn't be a bit surprised, Jack. With the high demand for accountants, there has to be a reason why he can't find another job. If only my parents hadn't spoiled him..."

"No, let's not go there," Jack interrupted. "We've been over this way too many times before. Frank's fifty-seven years old, for God's sake...he should be making plans to retire."

"He'll always be 'Mother's little boy,' and for her sake, I have to at least try to keep the lines of communication open."

"No, you don't, but I guess that's why I love you, babe. You've got a heart as big as Alaska. Turn around." He came over, sat down on the couch, and began massaging her back, kneading the tense muscles until she started to relax.

"Mmm, that feels good."

"Are you up for a little downtime tonight?" Jack asked with a twinkle in his eye. While the kids were growing up, downtime was their code word for making love.

"If you play your cards right," she said mischievously, "I think I can come up with an appropriate task." Even after all these years, making love with Jack was exhilarating, the best stress reliever she had ever found.

"Well, lead the way, Teach," he said. "I'm ready for any assignment you can think up."

CHAPTER 4

Friday, March 7th

Think you'll have to work late again tonight?" Janelle asked as Matt sat on the garage stoop while putting his muddy work boots on. It was 6:30, on another unseasonably warm, overcast March morning.

"Probably. Hard to say for sure. All this snowmelt, everything's so wet." Matt got up after securely tying the laces.

"Well, I'm trying to figure out if I can hold off grocery shopping until tomorrow, but there's not much food in the house...unless you want grilled cheese again tonight. You know," she added dramatically, "I really hate grocery shopping, and having to do it after work makes it even more despicable."

"Despicable, huh?" Matt laughed as he reached to give her a hug and goodbye kiss.

"It is, Matt," she whined. "I really, really despise it."

Matt kissed her forehead and then her lips. "I know...I think you may have told me that once or twice before. How about we make tonight a breakfast-for-dinner night?"

"I don't think we have any cereal you like and we need milk." Janelle was still lingering in his sweet soap-scented neck as his strong arms fell to the small of her back, pulling her slightly rounded tummy tight to his body.

"I'll stop at the gas station on my way home if you remind me when I call you, or we can have pancakes," Matt suggested. "Do we have any syrup? Last time we were out."

"You added it to our list so I bought it," Janelle said, trying to reinforce the helpfulness of adding items to a grocery list as they're emptied. "You'd better get going, it's twenty to already," she added, taking time for one more hug. She waved goodbye as he backed his pickup out of the garage and then hurried back to the kitchen to throw her own lunch together, along with her mid-morning snack of tomato juice and a cinnamon raisin bagel.

When Janelle first found out she was pregnant, she tried everything to make herself concentrate at work, but all she wanted was to go home and read baby books and magazines. Each workday seemed to drag on until she could get home again to read. Around the time her second trimester started, she stopped feeling queasy after taking her prenatal vitamins and was finally able to find a balance. Of course, she was always thinking of the baby, but she found ways to weave the task at hand into her thoughts too.

Janelle checked her rearview mirror as she signaled and slowed to turn into the parking area for Creative Solutions, Inc. *Mom usually calls by now, she must be running late this morning.* Janelle always rolled into the lot as close to seven as possible, which meant if anyone was behind her, that person was probably in a hurry too. She knew the chances of being rear-ended were great, and the growing life inside of her made her more cautious now. She drove defensively, sighing with relief each time she arrived safely in the lot as the cars behind her continued on to the different companies in the business park.

"Morning, Beth," Janelle greeted the receptionist as she walked by the front desk. "How're you this morning?"

"Hi, Little Mama! I'm feeling fine because it's Friday! The phones are crazy already, but that's okay because I'm wearing blue jeans today." Beth made her declaration like a proud second grader at show-and-tell.

"Agreed. If they'd just realize we all work better in jeans, they'd let us wear them every day instead of just Fridays."

"That would be so-o-o nice, but don't hold your breath."

"I can't wait to see my desk," Janelle said, rolling her eyes. "I had to leave early yesterday to see the doctor and I can only imagine."

"Oh, that's right," Beth called as Janelle headed down to her cubicle. "You'll have to tell me all about your appointment later. Have a marvy Friday!"

"You too, Beth," Janelle called back just before turning the corner to her small, ugly office. Creative Solutions had been built thirty-five years before, and thankfully there was no hideous carpeting on the walls anymore, as Janelle had seen in the alumni photo album, but the place had not been updated for at least twenty years. Janelle deduced that to be the main reason that whenever possible sales reps made their calls to the client's place of business rather than inviting clients to Creative Solutions.

Pumpkin orange and light green cubicle walls with chocolate brown carpeting weren't exactly the best decor for an advertising agency that preached the importance of company image. Some of their clients had similar phobias about interior design changes and they presented special challenges to Janelle if she was designing their websites. Often she had to crop every picture she'd been given and only place the object or product on the page. Then she'd use computerized backgrounds to pull the client's logo colors into the website to create the polished look that Creative Solutions boasted it could always deliver. Janelle still thought that their new company slogan 'Income Expansion thru Image Enhancement' was a bit much, but she had to admit it seemed to be bringing in the business.

Jeez...what a disaster! My desk never used to look like this...I wonder if being pregnant affects the neatness gene; either that or someone else is using my desk! She scrounged through the haphazard pile of papers that had accumulated, then reached under her pea-green banquet table, which served as her desk, to press the power button on her computer. She slid her chair backward to her tan banquet table and turned on her radio and printers, then quickly slid back to her computer to log in for email, simultaneously reaching for the phone to retrieve her voice mail.

She listened to the messages on the speaker phone, then stood up to take off her jacket and put her purse in the bottom drawer of the slate-gray filing cabinet. Finally she pulled out the to-do list she'd made the night before and skimmed it. *I feel like I have two jobs, but I only get paid for one. Matt helps a lot with laundry and general cleaning, but he doesn't have a clue about how much clerical work there is to running a household.*

Change Matt's dentist appointment
Make transfer from savings to checking
Send payment to fertility lab
Call to ask why car insurance went up again
See Accounting about changing W-4 withholding
Call day care; see if they offer direct withdrawal payment option
Send card to Cassie
email/call Ellie

Janelle always had her list with her. Sometimes she would stay at her desk during lunch to work on it, but that was counterproductive because then other people assumed she was available to help them and usually that's what ended-up happening. Instead, she relied heavily on the modern convenience of her cell phone and the privacy of her car.

After downloading her email, Janelle quickly sent a short message to Donna in Accounting, asking for a new W-4 form. Consulting her list again, she decided she could put stamps on the lab payment and on the card she had made on her computer last night for Cassie.

Janelle liked to send cards that said just the right thing, but she always added her own hand-written words to make sure the person knew she really cared. Cassie's card said "Thinking of You" on the front with a beautiful sunset in the distance. Inside it said: "My dear friend, I'm thinking of you the same way the sun rises and sets...again and again and again..." Janelle had spent a long time finding the right words to add after Cassie's tearful call describing how she and Jeff had finally made the decision to have an infertility work-up done. Remembering her own struggle, she knew there really wasn't a perfect thing to say. She finally just wrote: *Dear Cassie, whenever you need someone to listen, I'm here. Love Janelle,* and then went to bed with a very heavy heart for Cassie and Jeff and what potentially lay ahead.

By 7:15 most of her co-workers had squandered the early morning minutes on chitchat or walking down to the kitchen for a caffeine jolt. Janelle saw this as frivolous time-wasting, since just as everyone else was sitting down to assess the workday that lay ahead, she had already separated and prioritized everything.

There were twenty-five emails, but nine were spam, and she quickly deleted them. Next came interoffice memos; some announcements that could be read quickly and discarded too. The subject of one was *Kitchen Science Projects* from Beth. Janelle loved Beth's emails so she opened it.

Dearest Co-workers,

   There are some nasty science projects in the refrigerator. Please visit the 'lab' today and take what's yours. At 3:30 anything left that has fuzz growing on it is going in the garbage—container and all!

   Very sincerely, Beth

P.S. Check out the brown shriveled thing on the top shelf. Nasty! Could it be an apple?

Janelle laughed and then read an email from her boss. Larry needed help on a spreadsheet and wanted her to know that the deadline for the grocery store website was extended. The store manager had to get franchise approval, which was taking longer than anticipated. Also, the Cloth-Is-Best Diaper account rep was wondering when they would have a few layouts to look at since they had a grand opening in another state in three weeks, and would their website be up and running by then? Janelle found the Cloth-Is-Best account in the middle of her prioritized pile and set it on top.

How am I ever going to pull all this together so we can be on-line in three weeks? Due to the nature of the subject, Janelle had already gone over budget on the research portion of the project. She hadn't thought about using cloth diapers until she got this account, so instead of just visiting competitors' websites to make sure her client had a unique look, Janelle found herself reading every single word she could find on cloth diapers.

"Janelle?" Larry's voice asked through her speakerphone.

"Yes?"

"Did you get my email about Cloth-Is-Best?"

"Actually, I just finished reading it...their file's on the top of my pile."

"Good. With the way they're expanding, that's going to be a big account, and I want to keep them very happy. When will you have something for me?"

"Okay if I work on it this morning and answer that question after lunch?"

"Sure. I'll check with you then."

I hope there's nothing else too pressing. She checked the sender line of the rest of her email and opened one from Cassie. It was a brief message asking how her doctor's appointment went. *Oh jeez. How am I going to answer this? Last night we didn't talk about the baby or me at all. Does Cass really want to know the details of my pregnancy?*

That reminded Janelle she needed to email Ellie Reed. She decided to take care of that and then focus on Cloth-is-Best. She'd have to reply to Cassie's email later. *I've walked in Cassie's shoes; there's no right way for a pregnant woman to discuss her experiences with a woman coping with infertility. I need time to think about what to say.*

Arriving to school early as usual, Ellie looked around her classroom. Thirty metal desks with bright orange seats and wooden tops were crowded into square footage designed for twenty-four. Large poster pictures of her favorite authors like Jack London, Pearl Buck and Ernest Hemingway stared down at her from the tack strips lining the uppermost portion of the walls. A utilitarian table and chairs sat on one side of the room, three bookcases stuffed with trade books she herself had bought on the other. On the back wall was a huge bulletin board with a lifetime collage of photos of her classes, some of the pictures dating back over thirty years. Ellie's eyes lingered a moment there. *All these years people have entrusted me with their most precious possessions, their children. I know I should take the photographs down and preserve them in an album...no...seeing them there reminds me of the difference I've made in so many lives. God, how I love this job.*

Ellie had always preferred to teach perched on a simple three-legged wooden stool or roaming around her classroom, getting up close and personal with her "kids." Despite Columbine and other stories of dangerous schools, she had always felt safe and useful here, secure in the knowledge that every day she transformed this uninspiring room into an exciting place of teaching, learning and growing.

Ellie went to sit at her ugly green metal desk, but as she rounded the corner, a piece of jagged metal reached out to snag her hosiery. "Dammit," she fumed. "That's the second pair this week!" She took a bottle of clear nail polish out of her desk and carefully dabbed a tiny amount on the end of the run to keep it from getting worse; then sat down.

Funny how being gone just one day can mean so much work when I come back. There was a big pile of papers to grade, a stack of mail to go through and several announcements to read. She checked the substitute's report first: *No problem—great kids—call me again!* was written in big letters at the bottom of the report.

Thank God. At least I don't have a leftover mess of classroom infractions to deal with. Ellie sorted through and prioritized the rest of the pile. Seeing nothing urgent, she put the papers aside for later and continued her morning routine. She checked her lesson plan and wrote the day's schedule on the green chalkboard. Each morning she scheduled two or three activities designed to engage young adolescent minds. In no time at all she was done organizing everything for the day.

Next, it was time to check her voice mail. Ellie touched the star button and made a face as she recognized a voice that was becoming all too familiar.

Mrs. Reed, this is Mrs. Nielsen calling to let you know Henley will not be in school all next week. We are taking a family vacation. Of course this means we will need make-up work. Please have it in the school office by 2:00 P.M. today.

With an exasperated sigh, Ellie pushed the erase button and retrieved the second message:

It's Mrs. Nielsen again. It's 2:30 on Thursday and you didn't have any work for Henley in the office. How do you expect him to keep up if you don't give him make-up work? No wonder half the kids fail your class and none of them like you.

There was more, but without listening to it, Ellie pressed the retrieve button a third time.

Hi, Ellie. Janelle Spencer. It was so-o-o good to see you today. I apologize for not calling sooner, but running into you was like a sign. Hey, let's get together this week. I'll email you a place and time tomorrow morning before things get too crazy at work. Check your email and your calendar and let me know. We have so much to catch up on. See you soon.

Ellie smiled. *Well, well, Mrs. Nielsen. You are full of it. There is at least ONE student out there who likes me. True, Janelle's twenty-eight years old now, but she liked me when she was thirteen too. I'm definitely going to fit a visit with Janelle into my schedule. I need it.*

Next Ellie turned on her aging computer and clicked on the email icon. There were several messages, including a long one from Mrs. Nielsen chastising her for not calling her back with Henley's assignments. She read her principal's message, just a reminder about the faculty meeting Wednesday after school. She opened Janelle's email last.

Ellie, can we meet at Paradise Island for an hour Tuesday night around 7? We can do dessert if you like (I'm always up for ice cream — the baby loves it!). I'd really like to see you.
Janelle

Ellie quickly typed her response:

> Hi, Tuesday at 7 it is. Can't wait to reconnect. You know
> Paradise Island's ice cream is my favorite. I'm still
> wearing the two pounds I put on thanks to last month's
> Flavor of the Month, cherry cheesecake.
> See you Tues. E.

She had less than twenty minutes until she had to be in the hall supervising the students' arrival, and she still had to check her faculty "snail mail" box, get a video from the library and respond to Mrs. Nielsen's nasty messages.

As she gathered herself to walk down to the faculty workroom, a familiar face appeared. Almost in tears, the girl said pleadingly, "Mrs. Reed, can I come in at noon? I need to talk to you about something...it's personal. Please? You're the only one I can trust."

"Sure, Kaylie. I'll be here. Just come in right away because I have a phone call to make when we're done. Hey, you look pretty sad. Are you going to be okay till then?"

The girl smiled weakly. "Yeah, I think so. I can usually manage to make it through the morning if I know we'll talk at lunch. See you at recess." Kaylie took the tissue Ellie handed her and hurried to the restroom down the hall. *I don't mind helping kids with their problems, but why don't they go to the guidance counselor?*

Just then she heard her cell phone ringing. It was in her purse in the bottom drawer of her desk; she'd forgotten to turn it off. It rang four times before she got to it.

"Eleanor, this is your mother. It's getting late and we have to get to Mass. Why aren't you here yet to pick me up?"

"Mom, it's Friday and I take you to church on Sunday. I'm at school; I have to teach today."

"Friday? No, it's Sunday, Eleanor. And we always go to early Mass on Sunday," Helen said stubbornly.

"Mom, it's only Friday. Are you on the cordless? Look at the calendar I made for you." Ellie waited while her mother walked over to the kitchen wall calendar, where Ellie had clearly noted all her mother's appointments and activities.

"See...yesterday was Thursday. I crossed it out after we got back home. Remember? I took a personal day yesterday so I could drive you to see Dr. Randolph where you had all those tests. That makes today Friday."

"We went to the doctor yesterday?"

"Yes, Mom. So today's Friday. And I have so much to do here...I'll have to call you later. I also have a student here with me, Mom...so I'll call you tonight." Ellie's white lie caused her a momentary pang of guilt.

"Okay, Eleanor. Call me later...Friday. My, my...oh dear..." Helen hung up without saying goodbye.

Ellie turned the phone off, tossed it back into her purse and hurried to the faculty workroom. She returned in time to greet the kids as they entered. *So much for hall monitoring.* Some of her early arrivals were already seated at their desks, quietly writing in their journals. *I'm late for hall duty, I didn't get to the library or Henley's mother...more things to do during lunch.*

The last student to arrive for first hour was Henley Nielsen who handed her an envelope. "A note from my mother," he said smugly. "She's really mad at you."

Ellie took him out in the hall so the other students couldn't overhear. "Did you consider the fact that maybe the person she should be mad at is you, Henley?" He refused to look at her. "All right then," Ellie said, her tone caring but firm, "I'll tell you what I think. You're a very intelligent kid, but you're falling behind because you miss at least one day a week, you don't pay attention when you are here, and you don't do the assignments I give."

She reached up to put her hand on his shoulder so he would look at her, but he roughly pushed it away. "Don't touch me! If you try that again, I'm calling social services."

She backed off and took a different tack. "Henley...I care about you. I want to help..."

"Care about me? Nobody gives a shit about me."

"That's not true..."

"If you care so much," he said sarcastically, "then just leave me alone!"

"Sorry, I can't do that...but I have to start class now so we'll talk about this later." He brushed her aside, defiantly walked to his desk muttering curses under his breath, threw his books down, and sat, arms folded across his chest. Ellie sighed and went back to her desk, throwing the letter on top of her pile. She took off her soft walk-around-school-shoes, put on the navy blue heels that matched the conservative navy pinstripe suit she was wearing, and took a deep breath to compose herself before beginning class. Softly touching the bright yellow sweater hanging over the back of her chair, Ellie reminded herself that these students were not responsible for her family problems or the situation with Henley. She paused for a second and put on a sunny face. *I'll deal with you and your nasty letter later, Mrs. Nieslen! I'm not going to let you ruin my day.*

CHAPTER 5

Tuesday, March 11th

Ellie pulled into the Paradise Island parking lot Tuesday night ten minutes early. She carefully parked her new black Ford Thunderbird, which she had nicknamed "Blackbird," far away from all other vehicles to avoid any chance of nicks or scratches. Purchasing Blackbird had been a fiftyish whim. Ellie knew she probably shouldn't have bought the sleek retro sports car, especially when she wanted to retire in three years, but she loved the way she felt when driving it. Sometimes even young men whistled and waved at her. She also knew it wasn't good to get too attached to any one thing. Life was too precarious for such foolishness, but...well...she told herself she deserved the car because she had worked since she started babysitting at age twelve. Jack had agreed, but since his wife was a bit too heavy-footed behind the wheel, he worried that she would kill herself in a reckless dash of speed, trying to get somewhere ten minutes early, of course. Ellie's always-arrive-early habit was acquired from her father, but since, like him, she despised waiting, the two behaviors were a bewildering and irrational mix.

Entering the restaurant, Ellie waved to Linda and Julie behind the counter and selected the "Corner Tiki Hut" booth. Like all the tables by the window, it had a straw ceiling and a bud-vase made from bamboo sticks that held an artificial tropical flower. Ellie sat down, and as she pulled out her cell phone to make a quick call to her daughter, she noticed the decorative butterflies sitting on the outside of the neighboring tiki huts. *I love the atmosphere here. It's one of the few places a woman can feel comfortable dining alone.* Ellie surmised that Rebecca must have still been working because no one answered. She left a message: "I'm thinking of you and I love you. Call me when you can."

When Rebecca was born, Ellie called her a miracle baby. Two doctors had told the Reeds that due to Ellie's erratic menstrual cycle, they would probably never have children. When Ellie finally did become pregnant, she had read every single thing she could find on prenatal nutrition. She had finally settled on the gospel according to Adelle Davis's *Let's Have Healthy Children*, choking down horrible tasting things like brewer's yeast in tomato juice and high protein shakes made with eggs and soy powder.

But it paid off. Rebecca was a healthy, highly intelligent, congenial little girl. Ellie had not had time to practice the same regimen when Jonah came along, and she wondered if that accounted for the difference in her children's attitudes toward school. Jonah was certainly capable, but he preferred sports and hard-rock music to Ellie's passions—poetry and Broadway musicals. She cringed when he bragged that, despite turning in a slew of required book reports over the years, he had never actually read a single novel.

While Ellie loved both her children so deeply it made her heart ache, one of Ellie's favorite jokes was that if God had given her only Rebecca, she would have thought she was a perfect mother, so He gave her Jonah to keep her humble. Ellie was pressing the End button on her phone just as she saw Janelle enter the parking lot in her late model two-door coupe.

Funny, she mused, *Janelle's young enough to be my daughter and she's the one driving the sensible car.* A few moments later her former student entered the ice cream parlor. Scanning the room quickly, their eyes met and Janelle smiled broadly, rushing over to give Ellie a warm, affectionate hug. Ellie noticed Janelle's snug-fitting clothes and grinned. Then both of them started talking at once.

"It's so good to see you, Janelle," Ellie said, laughing as Janelle deferred to her to begin. "We have so much to catch up on, I don't know where to begin."

"That's for sure," Janelle replied brightly. "Should we order now or wait? I see there's a long line at the counter."

"Let's wait. I'll keep an eye out and when the line's gone, we'll go up. I already know what I want. Blackberry Swirl's their Flavor of the Month. Jack and I stopped here Sunday after taking my mother—you met her the other day in the elevator—out to eat. I indulged, of course, and decided right then and there that blackberry swirl is my second favorite, right behind cherry cheesecake."

Janelle winced at the mention of the elevator incident, but she covered her discomfort with a mischievous grin. "I distinctly remember when we came here after I won the contest in your class that you liked Rocky Road best."

"I haven't eaten chocolate in years," Ellie replied. "It makes me break out in fat."

Both women laughed. "But, to tell the truth, if it comes from a cow, I'll eat it." Frozen dairy treats and cheeses of all kinds were Ellie's downfall and probably accounted for most of the extra twenty-five pounds she carried on her five foot three inch frame, as well as the elevated cholesterol problem she had yet to seriously address.

"So besides ice cream, any other cravings?"

"Hmm, I drink tomato juice every morning. I always liked it, but now I feel like I need to have it every day."

Ellie laughed. "It's pretty strange the things your body—and your mind—for that matter, go through when you're pregnant."

"So far I'm hanging in there. Tell me about your mother, Ellie. How is she?" Janelle deftly changed the subject, but Ellie knew she was just being polite; the younger woman was obviously bursting with news about her pregnancy.

"Well, I have to go back to her doctor Friday after school for the test results from the day we ran into you in the elevator, but I think she's in the early stages of Alzheimer's. Most likely she inherited it from her father's side of the family."

"I'm so sorry, Ellie," Janelle said sympathetically. "My Grandma Knott had it and I know this is going to be rough...caring for her and everything."

"I guess so," Ellie replied, determined to hold back the tears that glistened in the corners of her eyes despite her best efforts. "But let's talk about this later. Right now I want to hear all about your new little Spencer. When is he or she expected to arrive?"

"Well, not until July; I'm only eighteen weeks," Janelle said, tucking some loose strands of hair behind her ears. "It was such an ordeal getting pregnant."

Ellie gave Janelle an exaggerated quizzical look, which caused both of them to giggle like schoolgirls. "Well, not that part, of course——the whole fertility thing."

"What was it that finally worked?"

"We used a process called Intra-Uterine Insemination, IUI for short. I charted my monthly cycle with a fertility monitor, which told me when I was ovulating, and the doctors had me on medication to promote the production of eggs so we could be sure we'd have at least one egg each month."

"Do you mean you could be having more than one?"

"No, the doctor already said my uterus is too small for me to be carrying twins, but the drug could've increased my chances for multiples."

"Okay, once you ovulated, then what?" Ellie was fascinated; if IUI had been available when she was first trying to conceive, she might have had a child years earlier.

"Then Matt made some sperm...we called it a donation. I took it to the clinic and the lab tech separated out the most active swimmers...we called them baby-makers...and the doctor used them to inseminate me."

"What did they use, a syringe?"

"Yes, but it had a skinny eight-inch straw that they used to push the sperm all the way up so our baby-makers had less distance to swim. It may sound cold and clinical to some people, Ellie, but it's allowing me the opportunity to carry a baby——grow a baby——inside of me for nine months."

"Plus, it's your own baby," Ellie added.

"That didn't matter as much to us as it does to some people. Trying the IUI was the most affordable option to start with and even that was expensive enough. We were both ready to start the adoption process if it didn't work."

"Good for you, babies are miracles, no matter what."

"In my pregnancy journal I told the baby that being pregnant's the most profound experience I've ever had."

"So you're keeping a journal?"

"I'm not writing in it everyday, just after each doctor appointment, but I reread my early entries that day I saw you and I like it. I want the baby to read it someday," Janelle said wistfully. "What about you? Are you keeping a journal of your experience with your mom's illness?"

"I know I should, but I never find time. Teaching my classes and seeing to Mom's needs is more than I can handle right now. Caring for an aging parent is a lot like taking care of a baby; there's no instruction book," Ellie said. "My mom took care of Grandpa Jackson until he died, but I was so young, I just remember the bitter end...I honestly don't know how she did it."

"I worry that I'll get Alzheimer's someday since my Grandma Knott died from it. Do you?" Janelle asked.

"I try not to worry about it. I just pray that I die in my sleep like my father did. If I get Alzheimer's and Jack's still alive, well, I don't think he could deal with it. If Jack's gone, it would fall to Rebecca...Jonah wouldn't know...anyway, in my experience, it's the women who carry these burdens."

"Don't you think Rebecca would want to take care of you as long as she could?"

"I don't want her to have to. Like I said, there's no instruction book—no formula or recipe. But like it or not, my already full life has to make room to take care of Mom."

"Well, there you go," Janelle said.

"What?" Ellie was confused.

"I'm writing my journal for the baby. You should write one for Rebecca. Record all the steps of your journey...that way if you do get Alzheimer's, Rebecca would have what you so desperately need, an instruction book."

Ellie had to admit Janelle's idea was a good one. "I don't think I ever mentioned it, but I kept a journal when I was pregnant with Rebecca...it's in my safe for her. But I was so busy that I didn't write one for Jonah. I was determined not to give my second baby short shrift, but it just happened."

"Well, I might not have to worry about that," Janelle said, her hand on her tummy. "This little one might be an 'only' like its mommy."

"You and Matt don't want more?"

"Well, if we do try for a second, we'll most likely have all of the same fertility issues and BILLS."

"I know lots of happy families where there are just you, me and baby makes three. Whatever happens... happens."

"I'm not sure I could do it again, even if we could afford it. After each try with this one, we had to wait two long, long weeks——I think the waiting was the worst part."

Ellie reached across the table to touch Janelle's hand. "It always is. Janelle, please forgive me for saying this, but you need to stop this senseless fretting. I heard or read somewhere that ninety percent of the things you worry about never happen, and ninety percent of the bad things that do occur happen so fast you haven't got time to worry about them. Don't borrow trouble, honey. Let the future take care of itself."

"I know you're right. Matt says when I try to control everything, I'm just asking for it," Janelle replied. "And as things turned out, I suffered needlessly the first three times the procedure failed. Jeez...how I hate that word...procedure."

Ellie nodded. She, too, despised the word.

"In the beginning, when we first started trying...the old-fashioned way..." Janelle and Ellie shared another little chuckle, "I dreamed a lot about having a baby. But then, when all the infertility stuff started and the depression set in, I told myself not to get too far ahead of things because it only made the failed attempts that much harder. I remember that even though I knew other people went through the same things, I never felt so alone. I had a constant dialogue going on in my head... about God, money, how some women get pregnant on their first try, how this just had to work this time, whether it was all worth it, adoption, unwanted teen pregnancies...confusing and irrational stuff like that. I was *so* depressed."

Ellie smiled sympathetically and Janelle went on.

"Even though I was busy and by every other standard time was going fast, for me the days crawled by because I couldn't get away from that dialogue in my head...I couldn't get away from myself."

"You've always been your own worst enemy with all that worrying you do," Ellie said gently.

"I know. Believe me, I tried not to think about it, Ellie. I really did, but it was impossible. Everywhere I looked there were babies or pregnant women, and here I was, waiting to see if it was finally safe to start dreaming of my own baby. It was awful." The painful memory brought tears to her eyes.

"And now you're one of those pregnant ladies," Ellie said, brightening the mood. "And if my math calculations are correct, you got pregnant in November, just a few months after we had lunch, right?"

"Uh huh, we had the fourth IUI on November 6th."

"November 6th? Janelle, that's my birthday!"

"Are you serious? Your birthday must've brought us luck because two weeks later the pregnancy test was positive. Matt and I were so afraid to believe it at first. Sometimes I still can't believe I'm actually going to be a mother. I think I felt the baby fluttering last night. Matt said it was probably just a gas bubble, but I know it was the baby. I felt it on my left side, right under my heart—it's early, but I felt it, Mrs. Reed...I mean Ellie." Even after all these years, Janelle still had trouble breaking the habit of calling Ellie Mrs. Reed. Even though they were friends now, part of their relationship would always be student and teacher.

"Well, I felt that fluttering with both of my children at four months, so I agree it's most likely the baby and not gas," Ellie responded, grinning at Janelle's look of self-satisfaction.

"Any names picked out yet?"

"Yes, but we aren't telling anyone until the baby's born; that way no one can talk us out of a name we like." Janelle said, deciding to surprise Ellie with her choice for a middle name if she had a girl.

"Good thinking, but then you always were a good thinker, Janelle. I bet your mom and Matt's parents are so excited to have a grand baby!"

"My mom is beside herself; she can't wait. And Sandy's excited too," Janelle said. She decided not to dish the dirt on Matt's mother to Ellie. This wasn't the time, and she was too tired to even bring it up.

"What about Matt's dad?" Ellie asked.

"His dad was never around when he was growing up—he was always on *business trips*, if you know what I mean," Janelle said, making quotation marks in the air. "The business trips started before Matt was born. His mom had gained a lot of weight with her first two pregnancies, and when she found out what was going on, she proceeded to starve herself for months trying to compete with the other women. She must have had success in getting her husband back because she got pregnant with Matt." Janelle sighed and finished the story. "Unfortunately, it didn't last. They finally divorced when Matt was a freshman and his dad pretty much vanished. I think the last we heard he's living in Nebraska."

"Ouch! A classic dead-beat, huh? How does Matt feel about that?"

"He hates what the whole mess has done to his mom. Having an absentee father left a huge impression on him in regards to the kind of husband and father he wants to be."

"Good for Matt. All too often they repeat the cycle."

"You mean sort of like kids who are abused who grow up and abuse their own kids?" Janelle asked.

"Yes, sort of, but abuse is much harder to stop. Over the years I've seen it with my own students. A very small percentage manage to break the cycle. If I could bottle up a cure for abuse, I'd do it in a heartbeat."

"Matt's two brothers seem to be following their father's example. They both moved out of state when they graduated and took jobs that require a lot of traveling. His oldest brother is divorced—luckily they didn't have any kids. His other brother is still playing the field, but I'm sure he's broken plenty of hearts along the way," Janelle said.

"I didn't have either of his brothers in class, but I wonder how they were different from Matt at that age," Ellie said, looking up at the counter. "I see the line's gone now. Let's pay the rent on this booth and do dessert."

"Oh, but I haven't even looked at the choices yet," Janelle said, grabbing the menu. She opened onto a picture of a glorious-looking strawberry concoction and instantly decided. "I'm ready." She grinned and the two women walked together to the counter. Unwilling to waste a single minute of their precious time together, they continued their conversation as Linda prepared their order.

After chitchat between mouthfuls of the sinfully delicious treats, the tone of the conversation took a serious turn. "Ellie, about your mom. Don't you have a brother and a sister who can help?" Janelle said tentatively, not sure if asking was appropriate.

Ellie laughed wryly. "Josie would never take a day off work unless it was for a golf outing or a political fund-raiser," she said, her voice laden with more than a touch of resentment. "Besides, she's so impatient with Mother. She corrects her mistakes and gets more than annoyed by her inability to carry on a normal conversation."

"And your brother?"

"Frank? We don't have enough time for me to tell you why any help Frank would give would be quite the opposite. He's a compulsive gambler...he drinks...I think he steals! Trust me when I say, Frank is more in need of professional help than Mom is."

The look on Janelle's face showed clearly that the younger woman hoped she hadn't touched on too sensitive a subject, but Ellie added reassuringly, "I'm going to figure out how to handle this, Janelle. Jack helps me...when it gets too much, I dump my fears and frustrations on him. The only real casualty in my life has been my own personal time. I've had to neglect most of my friends. They understand though."

After a pause during which the younger woman seemed to be carefully choosing her next words, Janelle said, "That makes me feel guilty, asking you to spend time with me."

"Don't you dare," Ellie said reprovingly, hearing Helen's voice echoing in her head, "this friendship is part of what keeps me sane."

Janelle's look of apprehension turned to a smile. "I think of you as my friend too, Ellie. How's school going?"

"One of my more difficult students this year has a mother that's actually more of a pain than he is. She told me on voice mail last week that none of the kids like me. I know in my heart that's ridiculous, but a remark like that really cuts deep, anyway...I thought of you when I listened to her nasty comments, so don't you dare feel guilty about tonight. Besides, you rescued me from grading papers."

"Okay then, no guilt," Janelle said as she looked at her watch. "Oh jeez, Ellie, it's quarter to nine and I promised Matt I'd be home by nine." The two women hurriedly cleaned up their mess and headed for the door. They exchanged a quick hug and promised to get together again soon. Janelle smiled and waved as she sped away.

Ellie stood in the parking lot for a moment, wondering how she could be so lucky to have this young woman as her friend. Seeing Janelle always made Ellie feel good, but it also made her miss Rebecca more. She suddenly felt that longing again, wanting to hold her daughter in her arms, wishing Rebecca lived closer so that they could get together for an ice cream treat like she and Janelle had just done.

Everything in life's a trade-off. I raised my daughter to be successful and independent, I'm proud of her achievements, but I sure miss her being a part of my everyday life. She sighed as she sank into the luxurious leather seat of her beloved Blackbird, popped in a Suzy Bogguss CD and pressed the forward button until she got to track 5, her favorite. "It's never easy...letting go..." she sang softly as she drove home to Jack.

CHAPTER 6

Friday, March 14th

Cee you later, honey. Cassie's here," Janelle said before she
Splanted a kiss on Matt's lips. "We shouldn't be too long."

They were going to meet Lisa and Tracy for a "girls night
out." Janelle always felt better if she could schedule time with
her friends when Matt was busy doing something else, but
tonight he had no plans. He was vegging, clad in sweats and
sprawled out on the couch watching TV.

"No kidding," Matt teased. "Your bedtime's eight-thirty
now, isn't it?"

"Stop it, Matt. I can't help it I'm tired."

"Okay, just so you can get us up in the morning." He
knew Janelle hated that he could sleep through the alarm and
needed her to wake him.

Chilled by the brief walk from her house, Janelle
welcomed the heated air pouring out of the vents in Cassie's
fun, little car.

"Burrr, it's cold out!" Janelle shivered. "What happened
to our warm weather?"

"I know," Cassie said. "I'm ready for spring, but in
Wisconsin, winter isn't over till it's over."

Janelle shuddered and changed the subject. "What time
are Lisa and Tracy getting there?"

"Lisa made reservations for six-fifteen, so we should be
good. Janelle, you never replied to my email last Friday. Is
everything okay with the baby?"

"Oh, I'm sorry Cass. Everything's fine, we heard the
heartbeat again. I didn't reply because the night before you

had called and told me you and Jeff were going in for the work-up. I knew how upset you were and I didn't want to make it worse by writing something that might bother you."

"You think I'd be jealous?" Cassie asked, a hint of anger in her voice.

"Maybe. I can only go from my own experience. I have to admit I was jealous of every pregnant woman I saw. I couldn't stand to be near one."

"Janelle, I know how long you waited. You have to believe me when I say I'm genuinely happy and excited for you and Matt."

"I do believe that. But when it comes to the emotional roller coaster of infertility, I also know that it's possible for you to be happy and jealous at the same time."

"Okay, you could be right," Cassie admitted, "but you have to tell me about your appointments; otherwise I start to worry that something's wrong. Promise me."

"I promise. I'm sorry, Cassie," she paused. "Do you have any answers yet?"

"Answers? What are answers?"

"What do you mean? What's wrong?"

"It seems our infertility is neither a male nor a female factor. As of right now, they just have a big fat question mark on our file."

"So are they going to do more tests?"

"Maybe, but they told us that a large percentage of couples never know the medical reason for their...how did one doctor say it?...difficulty to conceive."

"It's has to be tough not knowing, but keep in mind the flip side. If it's a male factor, that could lead to Jeff feeling like it's his fault or you feeling the same if they say it's female."

"Did you and Matt go through that?"

"No, we were very open and talked a lot. But I joined an infertility support group called SOS, Saving Our Selves, and some of the other members said it happened to them."

As Cassie pulled into the restaurant parking lot, she asked Janelle for a favor. "Lisa and Tracy don't know, so don't say anything in front of them, okay?"

The hostess greeted them like they were old friends and led them right to the table where Lisa and Tracy, who had left a good description of them with the hostess, were already munching on appetizers.

The four women were exchanging their hellos when Lisa blurted out, "I'm glad you're finally here, I can't wait any longer! I have great news, I'm pregnant!"

Cassie froze and Janelle felt trapped between her empathy for Cassie and her excitement for Lisa. She watched as the color drained from Cassie's face. Tracy let out a squeal of excitement. "No way! We didn't even know you were trying!"

"That's the amazing part," Lisa said. "We thought it would take a while because of everything that happened with you, Janelle, but it didn't! We just started trying last month and well—we're pregnant!"

Ellie sat in Dr. Randolph's office, listening carefully to the specialist interpret Helen's test results. As Ellie expected, the cognitive tests showed her mother to be "all over the place." In math and order of operations, Helen had scored amazingly high, probably due to her innate aptitude for calculation. But her answers on the association and quick recall portions of the test had been erratic. She was confused and couldn't put the simplest of logical connections together.

"To summarize, Mrs. Reed," Dr. Randolph said with absolutely no emotion in either her light-gray eyes or carefully modulated voice, "the MRI results confirm my preliminary assessment, atrophied brain cells in the cortex. In layman's terms, your mother's brain is shrinking. Given the family history, test results, and current behavior, the inescapable diagnosis is Alzheimer's Disease."

Ellie swallowed hard. "What's her long-term prognosis?" *You may be the best doctor, but you could certainly stand to work on your bed-side manner.*

"Your mother has entered what is called retrogenesis, a steady, gradual return to the state of infancy. Her short-term memory center is already severely compromised. If we do nothing, she will decline rapidly."

"I see," Ellie said, but she wasn't referring to Dr. Randolph's answer. What she could see was Grandpa Jackson in that nursing home bed. She had to force herself to listen as the doctor continued in her business-like tone.

"Fortunately, there are medications available that may slow down the progression of the disease, allowing her perhaps another year of some quality-of-life. There's one I'd like to try—it's shown promise in patients like your mother."

Ellie brightened. "Of course. Then there's some hope..."

"Mrs. Reed, I apologize, but I must be blunt. Families need the truth if they are to adequately cope with what's ahead. A cure, or even the potential for remission for Alzheimer's, is a long way away."

"But I've seen so many specials on TV lately," Ellie couldn't stop from blurting out.

Dr. Randolph brushed her off. "Regardless of what you see on television, such treatments are too far off to be of much help. For the short term—medication may slow down the deterioration of her brain function; however, if she lives long enough, as I said before, she will regress to the earliest stages of infancy."

Dr. Randolph took out her prescription pad and scrawled a few lines. "Here." She tore off the top page and handed it to Ellie. "I've prescribed a three-month supply. It's quite expensive, but her supplemental insurance should pick up most of the cost. It can work well with patients who tolerate it, but you must make sure that she takes it faithfully. I want to see her again in three months for a follow-up assessment."

Ellie took the paper, her hand shaking slightly. "Is there anything else I can do?"

"Perhaps. We have an in-house social worker, Sharon Kelly, who handles those details. Her office is just up the stairs on the left. My nurse made an appointment for you for next week Friday at four-fifteen. If that doesn't work, stop at the desk on your way out to re-schedule. Good luck, Mrs. Reed. See you in three months."

Ellie sat there for a moment...stunned at the brusque attitude. *Did she just instruct me to be here next Friday in much the same way I would tell a student he needed to stay after school for tutoring? Who the hell does she think she is anyway?*

Dr. Randolph hurried out, taking her insensitive manner with her. *She's probably on her way to confirm the worst fears of yet another family. What a job...at least in teaching I can always justify sugarcoating negative assessments—parents seem to never accept the unvarnished truth about their kids—they invariably blame me or the school. After all, we're talking about children and their potential for growth... for learning... for change...which isn't quantifiable. So what if I don't like this doctor's personality? I have to admit she's honest... brutal, but honest.*

CHAPTER 7

Thursday, March 20th

> *Dear Ellie,*
>
> *I just need to vent. I thought people said dumb things to me when I was trying to get pregnant. I had no idea it would continue now!*
>
> *If it's not my beloved oh-so-perfect-mother-in-law commenting on my weight gain, then it's this flakey girl in marketing telling me about a friend of hers who had a friend who had a sister who went in for an ultrasound at twenty weeks and found out the baby had serious birth defects and her doctor recommended that she abort it. Do these people think I need more to worry about?*
>
> *Sorry to leave this in your email...I sure hope everything's going well with your mom.*
>
> *Talk to you soon. Janelle.*

Just before she left school Thursday, Ellie had read Janelle's distress email. Unfortunately, she had problems of her own to deal with before she responded. She'd finally had the time at lunch to finish entering her students' grades into the computer and tally the third quarter results. They were mostly A's and B's, a few C's and D's, just three F's: Suzanne McNeal, a habitual truant who was in police custody for breaking and entering; Justin Langer, a severe case of unmedicated ADHD who rarely even brought a pencil to class; and Henley Nielsen.

She had asked Justin and Henley to stop by her classroom after school to discuss a plan to do make-up work so they could pass. She had managed to nab Justin as he rushed by her in the hall—he promised to come in for extra help, but Henley made her sorry she'd even bothered.

"Go to hell, you fat old bitch," Henley said when she caught up with him at his locker. "Kiss this," he said, pointing to his left buttock, "or maybe you'd rather perch," he added, his middle finger raised in an obscene gesture.

Ellie wrote him a detention for disrespect, which he defiantly crumpled up and threw on the floor. She shook her head in frustration as she returned to her desk and recorded the incident in her daily log before attacking a huge pile of character sketches that needed grading. It was almost six when she finally packed up and headed for home.

Ellie settled into Blackbird, found her cell phone and checked her voice mail. The only message was from Jack, wondering what time she would be home and telling her not to worry about him for supper because he'd had an early dinner during his weekly department meeting at work. Ellie pressed seven to delete Jack's message and made a spontaneous decision, pressing two for speed dial home. "Hi, Jack, it's Ell."

"Hey, babe. How'd your day go?"

"I'll fill you in when I get home, but since you already ate, would you mind if I call Janelle to see if she can meet me somewhere for a bite? Sounds like she had a rough day."

"Go ahead. Have fun."

"Thanks Jack; you're my silver lining...love you."

"Love you too, babe. Later."

Ellie dialed Janelle's number. By the fourth ring she began to lose hope, but she waited so she could at least leave a message. On the fifth ring, Janelle answered.

"Hi, it's Ellie. How're you feeling now?"

"Ellie! Thanks for calling."

"Did you eat yet?" Ellie asked.

"What? No, Matt's working late and I haven't decided what I'm hungry for."

"How about meeting me at Paradise Island in about twenty minutes?"

Janelle obviously didn't have to think about it. "Sounds great! I can't wait to see you...I'll get us a table if I get there before you do."

Arriving first, Janelle found a window seat on the side facing the driveway and sat so she could watch for Ellie's new little black sports car. She and Matt intended to buy a different vehicle, something with four doors, but they were waiting until next summer when the fertility bills were paid. Janelle had been driving her eleven-year-old car since she was seventeen. Everyone kept telling her it was going to be an inconvenience to have a two-door after the baby came, but for the sake of their budget, she was determined to make do.

Janelle decided to look at the dessert specials while she waited. Opening the menu, she thought of her mother-in-law's snide remarks regarding her weight. *Funny...my dear perfect mother-in-law...with your surgically enhanced lips, chin, cheeks...God only knows what else...oh, don't let me forget...your ever-so fashionably-thin body. Funny how all you have to do is open your mouth and poof—all your physical allure evaporates!*

"You know, Janelle," she had said, her eyes slowly scanning Janelle's full face and snug pants, "I only gained fifteen pounds with Matt. Have you asked your doctor about your weight gain?"

"Sandy, you only gained fifteen pounds because you were trying to lose weight. Thankfully, that didn't hurt Matt. Fifteen pounds isn't enough for an entire pregnancy. My doctor said thirty to thirty-five pounds is healthy."

"Healthy? I should say so," Sandy said sarcastically.

"Well, I've only gained eight so far," Janelle assured her.

"Really? I'd have guessed a LOT more than that. If that's all you've really gained so far, I'd be even more leery about thirty to thirty-five."

Janelle's unpleasant thoughts were interrupted when the familiar black T-bird pulled up. Ellie looked just plain worn out as she approached the restaurant.

"Janelle, sweetheart," Ellie said with open arms and a huge smile when she reached the table.

Janelle rose to Ellie's embrace. She hadn't realized how much she needed a hug until she found her face buried in Ellie's cushiony shoulder.

"Oh, Ellie. I'm so sorry to bother you with my trivial worries. I know how busy you are."

"I can't argue that...things do seem to be in overdrive," Ellie agreed, "but you are not to be sorry for sharing your worries with me. I love that we can get together and, as you say, vent. Let's order our food first so we can unload on each other, okay?"

Ellie ordered with ease...her usual: honey mesquite turkey with bacon, two bags of chips, a strawberry shake. Janelle hemmed and hawed about what to have, partially because of Sandy's comments, but also because she was hungry and yet nothing really appealed to her. She decided on the crab salad special. Thinking again of Sandy, she skipped the chips.

"Thanks again for calling me, Ellie," Janelle said. "Before I elaborate on my distress call, I insist that you go first; you look like you've had a long day."

"What do you mean? I'm fine. Let's talk about you..."

"C'mon, Ellie. I saw you get out of your car. You looked so sad and tired. You transformed yourself, for my sake, I'm sure, the second you came in here. So I insist...you first."

"Oh, all right...this whole week has been one thing after another. I'm having serious problems with a student and his mother, whose parental involvement borders on harassment. I told you about her last week."

"Are you serious? What's she doing?" Janelle asked.

"Every time I turn around, that woman is in my face about something. And now today he..." She told a shocked Janelle about the incident. "So I gave him a detention, which he promptly tore up... he'll be getting an "F" on his report card. I can just imagine what she'll do when she sees that."

"I don't get it," Janelle said, "the problem is obviously the kid's. What's with her?"

"Beats me, but I think she wants me fired. She's constantly sending emails or leaving voice mails telling me what a terrible teacher I am and how much all the kids hate me. It's unnerving to say the least."

"Oh, so she thinks her son's issues are the same as the entire student body?"

"I guess she must," Ellie answered. "Part of me can't help wondering if *his* problems may be related to *her*..." Ellie shook her head and went on. "To top it off, there's my mother. Dr. Randolph quite bluntly told me Mom definitely has Alzheimer's. We went over the test results last Friday. I think the woman knows her stuff, but I guess I just expected her to be a little more empathetic."

"Instead she gave you the cold hard facts and then moved on, huh?"

"Pretty much, but she did make me an appointment with a social worker."

"Social worker?"

"Supposedly 'to handle the details' as she put it."

"Well, if you ask me, it sounds like your Dr. Randolph has a poor bedside manner." Janelle found herself getting more than a little agitated. "I realize doctors, nurses, even lab technicians, must walk a fine line to stay objective, but there's a distinct difference between being objective and being as downright insensitive as she sounds."

Ellie shook her head in agreement, not quite sure what to say since Janelle was getting visibly upset. "When we first started trying to get pregnant," Janelle went on, her voice getting tight, "I had this absolutely wonderful nurse who specialized in infertility. She was the sweetest woman! She told us she had personally gone through some of what we were experiencing. Then our insurance changed and now I have this battle-ax named Trudy who barks orders and makes me feel like I'm intruding on her busy day. Even though I've seen the doctor three times, she still has to check my chart to see what my name is."

"I know exactly what you mean," Ellie said. "When I got pregnant with Rebecca, I remember one of the nurses always called me Elaine, even though I'd correct her every time. I can't imagine not bothering to learn my student's names."

"I can relate... Trudy is a doozy. I've decided she'll never warm up to small talk so I've stopped trying."

"Still, I do know some wonderful nurses," Ellie countered. "Jack always says you should walk two moons in someone else's moccasins before criticizing them." She smiled and changed the subject. "Let's see though, according to your SOS earlier, that nurse isn't the only insensitive person you're dealing with."

"You're so right. Like I told you in the email, I thought people said dumb things to me when they knew we were trying to get pregnant. Like, 'if it's meant to be, it'll happen' or 'look at all the practice you're getting...that's the best part' or 'there's a reason for everything...maybe God has different plans for you.' Some days I could have just screamed at the things I had to listen to."

"So now you're pregnant and everyone feels the need to share a favorite having-a-baby horror story, right?"

"Exactly. A girl I hardly know in marketing decides to tell me an awful story. She overheard me telling Beth, the receptionist about the ultrasound..."

"Ultrasound?" Ellie interrupted, "I had one of those when I was pregnant with Rebecca. I'm sure they're much improved these days...and it's certainly not a risky pro-ce-dure." She drew out the word and the two women laughed.

"Well, after what Donna felt the need to tell me, I'm a little scared about the whole thing," Janelle admitted.

"It'll be fine. People are born ignorant and some can't seem to get over it...that's why they need teachers." They both laughed at Ellie's teasing. "You just have to file-thirteen the dumb things they say or your stress level'll go sky-high. Just let it roll like water off a duck's back."

"I know you're right, Ellie, and I manage to do that with most people, but how do I cope with Sandy, my runway-model mother-in-law? At my seventeen-week appointment, I had gained eight pounds. Nurse Battle-Ax grunted something about that being close to normal, and my doctor said it was borderline low. He said I should make sure not to skip any meals, yet my mother-in-law keeps letting me know that she thinks I'm gaining too much."

"You're almost half-way through your pregnancy and you've only gained eight pounds? I'd be doing a little dance if I were you! When I was five months along with Rebecca, I'd already gained almost twenty! I was much smarter the second time with Jonah, but I wouldn't change a thing about my first time."

"How much did you gain?"

"Almost fifty," Ellie admitted sheepishly. "See," she pointed to her girth. "I'm still carrying twenty of that today."

"Well," Janelle blurted out resentfully, "according to Sandy, my fat must be larger than her fat, if she even has any, because to her, my eight pounds looks like fifteen. She said from the looks of my face and derriere, I should check with my doctor to make sure it is only eight pounds!"

"Save us from stereotypical mothers-in-law," Ellie said, rolling her eyes, "but Janelle...she's wrong, and you need to find a way to control this."

"I know, Ellie," Janelle said, almost in tears. "With all Matt and I've been through...whenever the slightest thing goes wrong...I get positively irrational." She intentionally didn't mention the incident with Helen in the elevator. "Plus I'm worried about my friend Cassie. She and her husband are having infertility problems too."

"Cassie Kingsford? What's going on, Janelle?"

"What do you mean?"

"Years ago, two women might've become friends because they shared the same heartache of infertility. Maybe they'd meet at a support group or something. But...you and Cassie have been friends since elementary school...and you *both* have issues with infertility?"

"I have another friend, a co-worker from a previous job, she has one baby but now she's having trouble conceiving a second," Janelle said.

"I think it has to be environmental, Janelle. Every time I turn around, someone seems to be having fertility issues."

"Maybe, but are there really more cases now or is it that people just didn't discuss it?"

"Sure, people talk more than they used to, but...I'm sorry Janelle, you were talking about Cassie."

"Yes, a bunch of us got together last week for dinner and we weren't there two minutes when Lisa announced she was pregnant after her first month trying," Janelle shook her head, remembering the pain that flashed in Cassie's eyes.

"Oh, poor Cassie."

"I felt so bad for her, Ellie! She kept it together pretty well during dinner; Lisa and Tracy were so excited, they didn't notice anyway, but on the way home, with me, Cassie lost it."

"Thank God she has you, Janelle. You can be there for her, but you can still be happy for *you*. And another thing, you can't let your mother-in-law stress you out so much. It's not good for you or the baby," Ellie said firmly.

"I know," Janelle said.

"Does Matt know his mother's talking to you like this?"

"He knows she has issues about her weight. He blames his dad and his 'business trips' for messing her up."

"That's right, you said that last time," Ellie said sarcastically. "He went for younger, thinner women."

"I'm not sure about younger, but certainly thinner— Sandy used to be about a hundred pounds heavier."

"A hundred pounds?" Ellie asked incredulously.

"Unbelievable, isn't it? She lost some while they were still married by starving herself, even while she was pregnant with Matt; then after the divorce she hired a personal trainer."

"I'm going to do that someday, maybe when I retire." *Yeah right...like my retirement check'll cover that!*

"Well, apparently she didn't see results fast enough so she had her stomach stapled and a tummy tuck."

"So her husband's unfaithful and she blames herself. Why do so many women do that?"

"She thinks being thin means being happy and loved."

"Ahh, like *The Portly Princess of Thynneland*—the queen believes the only happy people are thin people."

"I haven't heard of that book, what is it?" Janelle asked.

"I've added a new segment to my curriculum to include writing by local authors. This one's a grown-up fairytale about childhood obesity. It's pretty good, the kids are really enjoying it. Anyway, Sandy's thin now. So...is she happy?"

"Who knows, she sure seems to get a great deal of pleasure out of commenting on *my* weight gain."

"Janelle, just remember it's *her* problem, not yours. When Sandy looks in the mirror, she probably still doesn't see thin. There are lots of women like that."

"I know Ellie, but I really thought that after all the time it took for me to get pregnant and everything we went through that she wouldn't be this way. I mean, what is she thinking? She knows all the hurdles we encountered. I'm not asking her to celebrate my weight gain, but at least she could keep her mouth shut if she can't say something nice."

"You're pregnant and that's a very wonderful thing! I *personally* think we *should all* celebrate your weight gain."

Janelle chuckled.

"I'm serious. Gaining weight means a healthy baby and that's the most beautiful thing you could ask for. Speaking of beautiful things, do we have time for dessert?"

Janelle looked at her watch. "Matt should be home soon, but I think I have time for an ice cream cone."

Janelle ordered a small blackberry-vanilla twist; Ellie a large vanilla dipped in sprinkles. As they savored their cones, the conversation turned to less serious things.

"My mom and I went shopping last night. We ordered a convertible crib for the baby and I bought teddy bear wallpaper border for the nursery."

"I bet the nursery'll be something else. Pardon me, I'm usually up-to-date on teenage stuff, but baby stuff...what's a convertible crib?"

"Oh, they should have thought of that a long time ago. It starts out as a crib, converts to a day bed, then to a full-size sleigh bed—it's gorgeous solid oak. You should see it. I can't wait until they deliver it."

"So your baby can use the bed from birth all the way through high school?"

"Uh huh, isn't that neat?" Janelle was starting to feel better about everything. "I'm so glad you called me, Ellie. This was just what I needed."

"Good," Ellie said as she retrieved a piece of waffle cone that had fallen onto her sleeve and plopped it into her mouth, "Isn't it great we both love ice cream?"

"It's certainly my main weakness, but doesn't everyone?"

"No, but that just means there's more for us!" Ellie laughed. Then she checked her watch. "Sorry, Janelle. Wish I could stay longer, but I promised Jack I'd be back..."

"Why didn't you say something? I feel so..."

"Remember what I said last time?" Ellie scolded. "No guilt. Besides, I needed this as much as you did."

"Okay...so when do we do this again?" Janelle said as she put her coat on and they headed to the door. "Oh, I forgot to tell you...the weekend after next I have an overnight seminar for work."

"Well, let's keep in touch...we'll work something out," Ellie said as they walked out to the parking lot and she hugged Janelle goodbye.

"Sounds great. Good luck with the social worker," Janelle called over her shoulder as she unlocked her car and got in.

Ellie pressed the unlock button on her remote and called back to Janelle, "Make sure you email me about your ultrasound..."

"Will do!" Janelle said as she drove off with a big wave. Ellie responded by throwing her a dramatic kiss and Janelle drove home feeling revived and full. She wondered why she got along so well with Ellie. *She's older than my mom, but it feels like we're the same age when we're together. She shares her wisdom with me, but she doesn't talk down to me. I was really lucky to have her as a teacher. Who would have ever thought I'd be fortunate enough to still have her as my friend?*

CHAPTER 8

Friday, March 21st

The next day, Janelle stood discreetly off to the side as Bradley, the company computer tech, installed her new sound card. The unsettled weather had continued and a midday thunderstorm came up without warning while Janelle was running errands at lunch. Luckily, she had an umbrella in the car and didn't get soaked, but when she returned to her desk, she found lightning had struck nearby and fried her computer's sound card. She'd been forced to call Bradley and beg for assistance, knowing she was in for a scolding because she thought it a waste of time to turn off her computer when she was only going out for such a short time.

Janelle, like most people at work, considered Bradley the ultimate geek. Betty in Human Resources wisely advised everyone, "Never, ever piss off the computer tech."

"Thanks, Bradley," Janelle said. "Hope I don't have to see you again for a while." He made sort of a "fat chance" snort and put his tools back into his shopworn leather satchel.

"You'll see me the weekend after next at the seminar."

"I will?" Janelle was completely surprised. "Why are you going to a desktop publishing workshop?"

"If you'd read the memo, Janelle, you'd have seen that desktop publishing is only one session...there's also web hosting and intranet cabling."

"Intranet cabling? Why would I want to attend that?"

"If you remember, the company goals for this year include cross training. I'll be gone the beginning of May, and according to Larry, you'll be in charge of some of my work."

"You're kidding, right?" Janelle started to laugh but stopped when she saw the look on his face. "But that's less than a month after the seminar. I don't know anything about your job; and I have enough on my plate already. I'll have to train someone to do my job when I'm off with my baby."

"I am definitely not kidding," Bradley said, his nose in the air. "Larry also mentioned that when you're gone, they'll need me to maintain your accounts, so I guess we'll be training each other."

Janelle was visibly miffed. *How could I have missed this? Larry told me he might go to the seminar, but he never said anything about anyone else. Cross training? I don't have time to learn Bradley's job. I'm having a baby in July...what a crock!*

"Who's handling new accounts while I'm gone?" Janelle was furious that she was getting more information from the company nerd than from her own boss.

"I got the impression Amy and Larry will cover those while you're out...on maternity leave." Bradley said it in a tone Janelle thought implied it was a wonderful fringe benefit.

"Maternity leave...you make it sound like I'm getting paid time off and I'm not," Janelle snapped, feeling her cheeks getting red. "At this company I don't even get short-term disability. I do get twelve *unpaid* weeks off, but that's only because the Family Medical Leave Act says I'm entitled to it and can't lose my job if I take it."

"Really," Bradley said as if genuinely surprised, "I thought maternity leave was paid...like vacation."

"Not here...my husband's working as much overtime as he can to pay our fertility bills and cover my salary so I can take off the full twelve weeks." Janelle blushed and wished she hadn't mentioned the fertility bills; she didn't want to get into personal issues with Bradley. Luckily, the tension of the moment was broken when the intercom crackled: "Bradley, you have a call on line one, Bradley, line one."

Instead of going back to his own office, Bradley pushed his heavy-rimmed glasses up his nose and reached for her phone. "Do you mind?" Before Janelle could object, he was already sitting in her chair saying, "Good afternoon, this is Bradley...Oh, hi Beverly." Janelle noticed his leg start to bounce up and down nervously under her table-desk as she turned away and tried to work on some filing.

"What?" he asked. "Oh, um, I'm at Janelle Spencer's phone...what do you mean...of course I have a good reason. She needed me to replace a sound card. The storm knocked hers out." Bradley was still fidgeting nervously. "Milk? Sure...anything else?" Since the phone call was so obviously personal, Janelle felt annoyed he had taken it at her desk—she had tons of work to do.

Milk...sounds like a wife's request. Is he married? Anxious for him to leave, Janelle slammed a file drawer shut. Startled, Bradley turned to look at her, and when he did, she saw a thin gold wedding band she'd never noticed before.

"No, Beverly, I'm not. I'm going back to my desk right now." He looked away from Janelle as if embarrassed.

"Okay, I'll see you when I get home. No, I won't forget." Bradley hung up. Picking up his leather satchel, he said, "Make sure you shut down your computer properly tonight...we're supposed to get more storms."

"Wait, shouldn't we make sure it's working before you leave?" Janelle sat down to open a test website.

"No, I gotta go. Call me only if there's a problem!" He hurried down the hall, his damp sneakers squeaking loudly.

What's with him? He gets a call from his wife...acts as if he's doing something wrong and then practically sprints back to his office. Weird.

It took Janelle the rest of the day to wrap up the Cloth-is-Best account. It must have been her new-found personal interest in the topic because it looked to be some of the best work she had ever done. Once the client had seen the logo—an adorable baby swathed in a pure white cotton cloth diaper, supposedly saying: "My parents found the secret to an improved bottom line, Cloth is Best!"—everything else just seemed to fall into place. *Ellie was right. I foolishly worried I wouldn't be able to deliver this project on time. I'm in control...no problem, I even have a few hours to spare.*

Janelle spent the rest of her afternoon putting the finishing touches on the *Pure-as-Snow* detergent website... the best type of soap to wash cloth diapers. She finished the last link and checked the clock: 3:59. "Time to go home, little baby," she said to her stomach, then remembered Bradley's strict order.

Being a person who knew lightning *could* strike twice in the same place, she shut down the computer and then just to be safe, decided to actually unplug everything. She pulled back her chair and reached under the table-desk to pull the CPU and monitor plugs from the wall outlet. It was a tight fit and she couldn't reach the electrical cord without getting down on the floor and crawling halfway under the table. She was still not close enough to the outlet, so she grabbed hold of the cords and yanked. Without warning, her desk came crashing squarely down on top of her.

She cried out in pain as it hit her backside and she heard her computer monitor bounce heavily on the floor. Startled, she rose in surprise, shifting the heavy weight of the table from her butt to her shoulders. Hearing more things teetering and falling, she tried to lift her head but hit it hard on the slanted leg brace. The pain of the blow took her breath away and she fell to the floor. Suddenly, a sharp pain shot from her stomach and she felt something wet and sticky under her.

Somehow she managed to look back and saw a red spot spreading on the carpet under her pelvic area. "My baby," she cried. "Someone help me, please help me! I can't lose my baby!" The last thing she was aware of was the sound of footsteps running toward her.

Ellie trudged wearily up the carpeted stairs, dreading her appointment. Coming slowly down was a very overweight woman carrying medical folders and a jumbo plastic cup of soda. Ellie read her nametag: Marsha Small, RN. *She certainly isn't "small." Why doesn't the doctor she works*

*for tell her what a burden it is to carry around all those
extra pounds? Oh for God's sake...you should talk...you
could stand to lose twenty yourself!*

Ellie entered Sharon Kelly's office, announced her arrival
as directed by ringing a bell on the desk, and sat with her
glum thoughts in the tiny waiting room area. Ten minutes
later, two women about her age, obviously sisters, emerged
from the office. One wiped away a tear as the other said
something to her that Ellie didn't catch. Then the older one
put her arm around her sister as they left. *Oh...so that's how
sisters are supposed to be to each other; I'll have to let Josie
know. Oh...aren't you the funny one!*

"Mrs. Reed?" asked a heavy-set woman with short-
cropped black hair. Ellie guessed her to be in her mid-thirties.
"I'm Sharon Kelly. Come on in." Sharon was wearing navy
blue knit stretch pants that showed her panty line and a
multicolored filmy shirt that was at least two sizes too big. But
her welcoming smile and melodic voice were as attractive as
her clothing wasn't.

"Mrs. Kelly," Ellie began as the woman sat down on the
skimpy gray seat cushion of a utilitarian chair positioned
next to a huge window overlooking the parking lot.

"Please, call me Sharon, Mrs. Reed," the social worker
replied, directing Ellie to sit opposite her in a matching chair.

"Okay, then call me Ellie," she said as she sat down and
pulled a yellow legal pad out of her "medical bag" which held
all her reading material regarding her mother's illness.

"As Dr. Randolph may have told you, Ellie, her role in
this process is to slow down the medical progression of the
disease. Presently there is no reversing the effects of
Alzheimer's. My job is to help the patient and family adjust
and cope with the deterioration that the progressive stages of
the disease will bring." She said the words matter-of-factly,
yet with a warm voice that seemed to make them easier to
accept. "By the way, I took the liberty of going through your
mother's medical file during lunch. My current caseload
can be unmanageable so I do what I can to be prepared for
my appointments...it saves everyone time."

Ellie was getting more impressed by the minute. Sharon reminded her of a younger version of herself who had chosen the only other profession besides teaching Ellie had considered during her college years.

"Why don't we start by looking at your mother's current living situation?"

Ellie gathered her thoughts and began. "Mother lives alone in the same house she and Dad bought when they got married after he came back from World War II. A next-door neighbor, Carolyn, checks on her several times every day. She won't take money for helping...anyway, I'm only twenty minutes away and my husband Jack and I spend almost every Sunday with Mom—we take her to church, out to brunch, grocery shopping, whatever she needs. I've also been seeing her at least once during the week because of medical appointments and such."

"I noticed that there are two other children, a sister and a brother. Where do they come in?"

"Let's not even go there," Ellie responded, her voice betraying some of the bitterness she felt. "The burden for Mom's care will probably be all mine."

"I see," Sharon said, "but I do hope we can get them into the loop so they will be able to provide some assistance in the future. Alzheimer's caretakers need every bit of help they can get. In my experience, siblings who aren't involved can be in denial or even question the caretaker's actions or motives. And if I may coin a phrase, if they aren't part of the solution, they will definitely be a part of the problem."

"I'll try. Just know that I will probably be the one who has to, as my husband so aptly puts it, do all the doing."

"Okay, then let's get started on the 'doing.' First of all, you'll want to get power of attorney and take charge of her finances as soon as possible. Alzheimer's patients are easy targets and there are dozens of clever, fraudulent schemers out there. Make sure you put your name as co-signer on her investments, bank accounts, tax forms, things like that, and instruct the statements be sent to you. Financial institutions are usually very cooperative. It prevents bad publicity for them if there's a breakdown in the system. Family members can usually convince Alzheimer's patients to give them co-signing rights if they approach it as a security issue."

Ellie nodded but wasn't thrilled about the prospect of getting her mother's cooperation in anything financial. Sharon waited for Ellie to finish jotting down her first "to-do" item before continuing.

"Does your mother still drive?"

"No, thank God," Ellie responded, looking out the window at the parked cars. An ambulance was pulling into the parking lot, its lights flashing but its siren silent. *I hope it's no one I know. Oh for God's sake…how could I think that? It's always someone that somebody knows.*

"Good, taking a car away from them is the most difficult part, except for the eventual nursing home placement."

Dragging her attention back to the task at hand, Ellie grimaced and said, "Well, Mom isn't really aware that she doesn't have a car anymore. A few months ago she had a fender bender. Luckily, the attending officer happened to be a former student of mine, so he knew to call me at the school. By the time I got to the scene, he had already called to get the car towed, telling Mom it couldn't be driven. He mentioned that his grandfather had Alzheimer's and that he *understood.* I remember at the time, his reference ticked me off. All I could think was, *cripes she's just losing her license, not her mind!*"

"I know this sure can be difficult. The most important thing is to keep them safe from themselves. How about the stove? Is she still using it, or does she have a microwave?"

Ellie nodded. "Yes, we bought her one last year that's very simple to operate. She uses it all the time."

"Great. Find a way to disable her stove so she can't use it. Tell her it's broken, which will force her to use the microwave. She'd be much more likely to start a fire with an unattended pan on the stove or to start her clothing on fire by leaning over a lit burner than to get into trouble with a microwave. Buy easy to prepare, nutritious meals that she can reheat quickly. Many older people don't eat right, especially Alzheimer's patients."

As Sharon continued to rattle off the steps necessary to allow her mother a few more months of independence, Ellie summarized each item. "You might want to ask that neighbor to help make sure she eats regular meals and takes her medication. Also, your mother needs lots of stimulation; I'd seriously consider a senior day center for her. Sounds like she's alone an awful lot."

Ellie nodded again. She felt stupid just writing and nodding, but these rapid-fire directions were making her head spin and it was hard for her to think. She decided to just write it all down and process it later.

"Where is her mail delivered?"

"To her mailbox, in a cluster of four or five at the end of the drive. Why?"

"Change her address to yours so that you get her first class mail. If the neighbor is willing, have her watch your mother's mail, incoming and outgoing, and give her permission to intercept any suspicious-looking letters or packages. People with Alzheimer's are very vulnerable to mail fraud. They've been known to 'mail' the grocery list or family photographs. Sign your mother up for the 'do not call' telemarketer's list today. Unfortunately, questionable charities and the like will still be able to call. Remember, women like your mother are easy targets."

Alarmed that she had not thought of this herself, Ellie put a star next to this item. "Usually, Ellie, I suggest a family meeting to set this plan in action. You might want to at least try to get your siblings on the same page."

The task ahead seemed so daunting, her eyes welled up with tears, and Sharon empathetically reached over to pat her hand. *Better start working on your back muscles...you know who'll be carrying the load...and for God's sake— wipe those tears off your face!*

"You aren't alone, Ellie. Call me if you need to. I'm usually good at returning phone calls within a day or two, emergency ones as quickly as possible. Here...this blue folder contains some literature for you to read. My direct line number is on the brochure inside."

As Ellie got up and thanked her, Sharon reached out and warmly shook her hand. Then Ellie took the folder, tucked it inside the manila one and left. She heaved a deep sigh at the thought of the road ahead, wondering if her mother had felt the same way upon hearing her own father's diagnosis.

The big difference is that by the time Grandpa needed a caretaker, Mom was retired, with the time to care for him. Who am I kidding? Who ever has time to care for an ailing parent? Ellie squared her shoulders and tried to be positive. *You can do this...it's a matter of making time, not having it.* Unsuccessful in her attempt, she felt totally overwhelmed. *Yeah, right! Now, who am I kidding? I can barely manage everything I have to do now!*

On the brink of tears as she left Sharon Kelly's office, she was so lost in her own miserable thoughts that she took a wrong turn at the end of the corridor. Walking around for a few minutes, she somehow ended up in the emergency room waiting area. As one often does, she scanned the room. *Omigod...there's Janelle's husband, Matt!* He was sitting slumped over with his head in his hands—she didn't know if she should speak to him or not. *What if something terrible has happened to Janelle and the baby?* She knew she really should get home to make dinner for Jack, but she couldn't leave without first finding out what had happened.

"Matt," she said as she approached him. "What are you doing here?"

"It's Janelle," he said, confirming her worst fear that it actually *had* been someone she knew in that ambulance. "She had an accident at work. I don't know what happened, but they have her in emergency right now. I just got here and they won't tell me anything. I can't get in touch with her mom. And my mom's out of town with Roger, her new boyfriend. I feel so helpless!"

As they spoke, a nurse approached. "Are you Janelle Spencer's husband?" Matt nodded. "Janelle's going to be fine. She needed a couple of stitches for the deep cut on her head, and she'll have a very large bruise on her bottom which will make sitting difficult for a while."

"The baby?" Matt asked, as if afraid to hear the answer.

"Your baby's fine too. Babies are very insulated in a mother's tummy and it would take more than this to dislodge your little tyke. But the biggest problem is your wife's state of mind. We just can't get her to calm down. You see...a can of tomato juice spilled on the carpet...she thought it was blood...well, you can imagine...between that and the nasty bump, she's convinced there's something wrong with the baby. The doctor's hesitant to give her a sedative, and she just won't believe us when we try to tell her everything's all right."

"Thank God, I don't know what I'd have done if..." He turned to Ellie. "I know you must be busy, but would you have time to come in with me? You know how she is when she gets an idea in her head. Janelle trusts you. Maybe she'll believe you if you tell her what the nurse just said."

"Of course, if you think it'll help."

"Are you Janelle's mother?" the nurse asked.

"No, just an old friend," Ellie replied with a smile, noticing the nurse's raised eyebrows. "Is it okay?"

"It's really up to Matt," the nurse said. "If he thinks you can help, then by all means..."

"Matt, go on in; I'll be there in a second...I just need to make a quick call to my husband."

"Thanks, Mrs. Reed. I'll tell her you're here. I know it'll make her feel better," Matt said as the nurse led him away to the recovery room.

CHAPTER 9

Friday, March 21st

Janelle was sitting up in her hospital bed, gently pushing on her stomach. "Matt, I wish I could just feel the baby move," Janelle said anxiously.

"Janelle, the nurse said..."

"Which one did you talk to? The short blonde one or the tall one with olive skin?"

"I don't know if she was short, but the nurse I talked to had blonde hair. Why?"

"Because," Janelle said, sounding very agitated, "the one with the blonde hair is just training and the tall one doesn't even have any kids of her own."

"Why does it matter if the nurse has kids or not?"

"How can she be sure if she hasn't ever been pregnant?"

"Janelle, calm down and think this through. Nurses have medical training. The blonde one told me it would take a lot more than what happened to you to affect the baby."

"A lot more than a rickety old banquet table, supposedly my ergonomically correct workstation, falling on my backside?" Janelle redirected her anger to her employer.

"I suppose you'll have to fill out a workman's comp claim," Matt said.

"Damn right! I mean really, Matt, how many times have I complained to you about the unorganized office set-up and the incredibly ugly, old...*unsafe*... furniture?"

"I remember you almost didn't take the job because you thought the burnt orange and pea green walls would stilt your creativity."

"Matt, this is no time to joke around," Janelle said. "If something happens to our baby because that stupid table fell on me, how will I ever forgive myself?"

Just then the tall nurse with olive skin came in with Janelle's chart. Ellie was following right behind her.

"Ellie!" Janelle cried. "How did you know I was..."

"Now, Mrs. Spencer," the nurse interrupted, "Susan mentioned you are concerned about your baby. I assure you...everything's fine. The paramedics checked the baby's vitals on the way here and I rechecked them after you were admitted. Everything's perfectly normal."

"I know you did...Nancy," Janelle said, looking at her nametag, "but you don't understand everything we did just to get pregnant...I would feel so much better if I could see my own doctor. Can you *please* call Dr. Felding?"

"Normally, yes, but he's on vacation this week and unavailable. We have perfectly competent..."

"I don't mean to intrude," Ellie interjected, "but I have a suggestion."

The nurse turned around on her heel. "Who are you?"

"My good friend," Janelle said. "What's your idea, Ellie?"

"Well, you told Janelle the baby's vitals were checked and everything was fine?" Ellie began.

"Yes...so?"

"Well, why not let Matt and Janelle hear the baby's heartbeat? That's not too hard to do, is it?"

"Yes!" Janelle said. "That's a great idea, Ellie. Why didn't I think of that? Please?" Janelle begged. "I'm so afraid something's happened...I haven't felt anything that seems like the baby moving since I've been in here."

"And you probably won't until later, after you've gotten some sleep and relaxed a little. Your blood pressure's borderline and the doctor would like to see that come down.

"It would help relax me to hear our baby's heartbeat."

"All right then," the nurse said as she walked over to the cabinet to get the Dopler.

Ellie arrived home from the hospital exhausted and in need of a hug. Jack was sitting at the kitchen counter on the phone. Ellie surmised he was going over the volunteer blood drive Jack's affiliate was sponsoring the next week. Jack was deeply engrossed in the conversation and engaging in a habit she detested—picking at the hair of his full gray mustache. She walked over and put her arms around him and nuzzled his neck, which smelled faintly of his favorite cologne, a smell that always made her feel safe and loved.

"Well then," Jack said into the receiver, "we'll meet for breakfast at seven on Monday the 31st. The director of the Blood Center will be there to help work out the details. See that you get all your guys there...tell them we need them *all*...starting with the line crew at eight sharp." Grunting a note of thanks, he hung up.

"How's Janelle?" he asked, turning to wrap her in his comforting arms. "Everything okay?"

"She had to have stitches in her forehead, but she's going to be fine. What a freak accident. Her desk collapsed on her when she was trying to unplug her computer. She was so sure she'd lost the baby...some tomato juice had spilled and she thought it was blood. The nurses couldn't convince her otherwise. Finally, I suggested they let her listen to the baby's heartbeat. That worked like magic to settle her down. Honestly, Jack, why didn't the nurse think of that herself?"

"C'mon, Ellie. Nurses are as overworked and stressed out as teachers. Hospitals keep cutting staff at the same time they raise the number of patients they're supposed to take care of. Something's gotta give somewhere. Our union represents a lot of health care workers; we try...but the regulations and budget cuts make it almost impossible. Unfortunately, because nurses are caretakers—they don't like politics. They feel their profession looks bad if they organize into unions." Jack's voice kept getting louder as he spoke about issues that meant so much to him. "We're losing the fight to assure decent nurse-to-patient ratios…which equates to decent health care. It's no wonder hospitals have a bad rap."

Ellie recognized the familiar signals of Jack climbing on his soapbox, speaking out on behalf of working class people. *Here we go again…but it's funny how I never get sick of listening to him. Ellie, you're a pretty lucky woman to have such a passionate man—always fighting for the underdog—not to mention the fire he has for you, even after all these years. Thank you, God, I'm not sure what I would do without him.*

"Remember Leah, that nurse's assistant our union lawyers represented in that malpractice case? You know, the one who was so exhausted from working double shifts she mixed up a couple of patients' meds at County Medical? Well, she tried to commit suicide last week. Said she couldn't take the stress anymore. Now she's in the hospital, on the other side of the needle."

Agitated and on a roll, Jack continued, "Yesterday our union office got a response from the proposal we sent to the legislature asking them to rescind mandatory overtime for our nurses. They gave our ideas lip service but nothing's going to change. A few more years of 'compassionate-conservatives' and we'll all be…" Catching the intent look on his wife's face, he abruptly stopped his ranting.

"Of course, you're right," Ellie admitted, ashamed of herself for being so judgmental about Janelle's nurse.

"Sorry for the liberal speech," Jack said sheepishly. Ellie smiled indulgently. She felt her heart swell with love for this man who put so much energy into helping people, unlike so many politicians who talk endlessly at election time about making the world a better place for "working families" but then seem to do nothing once they're actually in office.

"What about your appointment with Sharon Kelly? How'd that go?" Jack said, needing to change the subject.

"She gave me a list of things to do, starting with calling a family meeting. You'll be at the Blood Bank on Monday the 31st, right? I'll call Josie and Frank to set up a meeting with Mom's attorney on that day."

"Good idea. I hope for your sake they'll want to become involved. This is going to be pretty hard on you, isn't it, hon?" He gently touched the side of her mouth that always twitched when she tried not to cry.

"I doubt Josie will come. She'll just say I should do whatever I think is best, and of course...then I'll worry that if something goes wrong, she'll blame me," Ellie said. "And Frank...we both know Frank resents the fact that Dad and Mom appointed me executor of their estate. Frank thinks because he's the oldest and the only male in the family he should have final say on family decisions. No matter what, this is going to be touchy. I've always been convinced Dad knew he was irresponsible and had a gambling problem." Jack nodded in agreement.

"The social worker said it'll be easier to get things settled legally if they're on board," Ellie continued, "so I'll call them and see what they say, even though I know..."

"Hey, did you eat dinner yet, hon?" Ellie shook her head. "Then let's order one of those deep dish pizzas. We had one last week at a union meeting. They're really good...I'm starving...you're stressed... it'll be quick and easy."

Ellie knew they shouldn't eat such high calorie food, but her stomach was growling and Jack always seemed to know when she needed some "comfort food." Thinking guiltily of the badly neglected treadmill in the den, she said, "Okay, sounds good; I guess my diet can wait until Monday."

Sensing her hesitancy and knowing exactly what she was thinking, Jack said, "Don't worry about it, I love you just the way you are—little love handles and all."

Ignoring his "compliment," she replied, "I love you too. I'll call for the pizza, but I think I'll wait until tomorrow to call Josie and Frank. I don't have the energy to talk to either of them tonight."

CHAPTER 10

Saturday, March 22nd

Oh, Matt. I'm so unbelievably stiff," Janelle said as he helped her out of the car.

"Remember what the doc said, it'll hurt for a few days...especially sitting. Here, take my arm; you're going straight to the couch."

Obeying Matt's orders, Janelle stretched out on the sofa and tried to take a nap. She slept poorly, awakening after an hour. Matt was sitting in a nearby chair, just watching her.

Seeing love and concern on Matt's face, Janelle was determined to show him she felt okay. "I'm feeling much better, Matt...do you think we can get started cleaning out the nursery today so we can paint it before Easter?"

"Janelle, we have plenty of time for that," Matt said. "I've been sitting here thanking God you and the baby didn't get hurt. I was so worried...anyway, you're staying right where you are."

"Okay, Dr. Spencer, if you prescribe rest on the couch for the patient...then it's rest on the couch. I have a few baby magazines I can look through. Would you mind getting them? They're on the nightstand in the bedroom." Matt headed for the bedroom and she snuggled down into the cushions, wrapping her feet in the folds of her favorite blanket. Just as she was finally comfortable, she felt the baby kick her sharply.

"Matt, come quick! Hurry!" Janelle yelled. He rushed from the bedroom to Janelle's side, a panicked expression on his face.

"What? What's the matter, Janelle? What's wrong?"

"Nothing. The baby's moving. Come here Daddy…see if you can feel it!" Janelle guided Matt's hand to a spot on her right side just under her ribs. When nothing happened for a few seconds, Janelle pressed firmly on Matt's hand.

"Janelle, don't push so hard!"

"It's okay, just wait…"

"Janelle, I don't…" Feeling uncomfortable, Matt started to pull his hand away just as the baby gave another kick.

"Oh! Oh God, I felt that…was that?…I think I felt our baby!" Matt's dark brown eyes grew wide with wonder.

"Wow, I think that's the hardest one yet," Janelle said as Matt laid his head on her tummy.

"That's because our baby was saying 'hello' to his daddy for the first time," he said with a proud grin.

Their tender moment was interrupted by the doorbell. "Who could that be?" Matt asked, sounding very annoyed.

"Yooo…whooo! Hello-o-o, Matt…Janelle, it's just me," Claire said, letting herself in.

Jeez…not again…she always picks the wrong time to walk in on us! Here we are having our first real baby moment and she has to barge in! I'll just have to make it up to Matt later…anyway, I want her to feel this too…it's so cool! "Mom, come feel my tummy, the baby's kicking!" Janelle called into the kitchen. Claire approached her daughter and gently put her hand on her stomach.

"Oh, Janelle, your dad would have loved this. Rich would have been such a good grandpa."

"I know, Mom," Janelle lied. She didn't really know what kind of grandfather her dad would have been; he had died when she was so young, she really didn't have any vivid memories of him. There were two pictures of him holding her and it looked like he loved her, but she couldn't remember.

"I was frantic when I got home and got Matt's message," Claire said, "I wish you'd have let me come to the hospital."

"I'm sorry, Mom. But I was so exhausted by the time I finally believed the baby was okay, all I wanted to do was sleep," Janelle explained.

"And she needed it," Matt added. "I finally persuaded her to rest after Mrs. Reed left."

Claire's blue eyes flashed. "Ellie Reed? Why on earth would you let her come and not me?"

Janelle was taken aback...her mother sounded like a jealous eighth grade girl. "Mom, it's not like I called her and asked her to come...she was there to see a social worker about her mother and happened to see Matt in the emergency room...and, well...it turned out to be a very good thing she was there."

"Well, how nice she could be there for you, Janelle. I do hope everyone there knew she was just an old friend and not your mother." Claire saw Janelle's frown and caught herself, obviously embarrassed that she had let mother-envy capture her tongue. She gently touched the stitches in her daughter's forehead. "Oooo, honey, this must hurt!"

Janelle thought it best to ignore her mother's adolescent reaction to the news that Ellie had helped her through her crisis. "Not near as much as my butt and lower back. I haven't looked, but I'm told there's a huge bruise from the table falling on me. I either have to stand up or lie down; sitting really hurts."

"I just can't believe this," Claire said, her envy changing to indignant anger as she paced the room. "A table fell on you at work? Creative Solutions better take this as a wake-up call. This could've been really...what if the you or the baby'd been seriously hurt?"

"Let's not go there again," Matt said firmly. "It took long enough to convince Janelle the baby wasn't hurt. Her blood pressure sky-rocketed and we don't need her worry-machine-brain to kick into high gear again."

"Matt, Mom's right," Janelle noted with relief as the fire in Claire's eyes softened when her daughter took her side in the matter. "It's ridiculous that a table fell on me."

"I know...I know...but you need to relax, Janelle."

"Now Matt's right," Claire said, assuming the role of referee. "You get your 'worry-machine-brain' from me, Janelle, and I know it doesn't do any good to over-react... just being pregnant...is stressful enough. All I have to say is Creative Solutions better come up with a 'creative solution' to keep you safe."

"I'll talk to Larry about it Monday," Janelle replied.

"Do you think you should go to work on Monday?" Claire asked.

"Maybe not, I think I'll wait to see how things go today and tomorrow."

"Good idea," Claire agreed. Then, feeling the work issue was resolved, she changed the subject. "Did you show Matt the adorable border we found for the nursery?"

"Uh huh. I picked up the paint on my lunch hour Friday. I really was hoping to get it done before Easter, but now I don't know."

"Matt, are you still doing the base coat?" Claire asked.

"That's the plan."

"If you could do it this week, Janelle and I can do the decorative painting the Monday after Easter. We both have the day off, right Janelle?"

"Right. Larry told me I could take off a couple days since I have to go to that weekend seminar." Janelle turned to Matt. "Do you think you can get the base coat done before Easter?"

"Sure."

"Okay, kids," Claire said as she reached down to gently kiss Janelle's forehead. "I'm gonna get out of your hair. Get some rest, Janelle. I'll talk to you tomorrow. See you Easter."

"Sounds good Mom, love you," Janelle responded, suddenly feeling very tired.

Matt saw Claire out. As he closed the door, the phone rang. "Now who?" he asked. Janelle secretly hoped it would be for him; she was tired and didn't feel like talking.

"Hello," Matt said. "Uh...hi, Mom, yeah...Janelle's fine and so's the baby."

Thank God he answered—she's the last person I want to talk to—even when I'm not tired!

"Uh huh...uh huh." Matt was saying. "No, we came home this afternoon, about an hour and a half ago. I know...I was worried too, but everything's fine."

Matt looked over at Janelle. "Sure, she's right here."

Janelle shook her head, but it was too late. Matt held the phone out to her.

"Hi, Sandy," Janelle said in a quiet monotone, hoping Sandy would keep the conversation short.

"Hi, Janelle. How're you feeling?"

"Pretty sore and really tired," Janelle answered honestly.

"Matt tells me everything is fine though. What a relief! By the way, did they check your weight when they admitted you?"

Janelle couldn't believe her ears and felt her cheeks getting hot. "No, Sandy, they don't weigh people in the emergency room."

"Oh, of course not," Sandy said. "I just thought since you were there you might've asked them to double-check; the other scale might be off, you know."

Matt had left the room. Janelle could hear him opening their nearly empty refrigerator in search of something to eat. She wished he had stayed in the living room to hear her side of this ridiculous conversation. Resisting the urge to yell at her mother-in-law, she took a deep breath, *I'll try to follow Ellie's advice...just let it roll like water off a duck's back.* She sweetly said, "No, I had more important things on my mind. I'll just wait until my next appointment when we have the ultrasound."

"Well, I just hope that this accident won't keep you in bed for any length of time...it's hard enough to control your weight during pregnancy when you're active."

"Don't worry, Sandy, I'll be up and around in a day or two. Thanks for calling. See you next weekend for Easter," Janelle said in as sweet a voice as she could manage through her clenched teeth. She clicked the cordless phone off and muttered angrily, "She is some piece of work!"

Matt was still rifling through the fridge. *Good*, she thought, perturbed at his mother and taking it out on him. *He's going to have to go grocery shopping tomorrow. I bet he won't like it any more than I do!*

It was Saturday afternoon before Ellie finally reached Josie on her cell phone. "March 31st?" Josie asked. "Just a minute, let me check my organizer." Ellie heard a few electronic buttons being pushed and waited patiently, quite sure that her sister would not be able to make it.

"I'm afraid I can't, Ellie...I have one of those must-attend things. But you go ahead, make the arrangements; I'll support whatever you decide."

"But I need you there, Josie, in case Frank makes things, you know...difficult."

"I know you can handle our big brother," Josie said brightly with her usual air of dismissal. "Carl and I will come up to visit soon. We really wanted to come for Easter, but his pharmaceutical company is sending us on a short cruise to Bermuda. We've both been working ourselves to a frazzle lately and need to get away."

Ellie wanted to scream. *You need to get away! I'm the one working...taking care of a household and looking after mother! You...you have a cleaning lady...a shopping service...a masseuse...I could go on but what's the use?* Instead, she quietly said, "Okay then, Josie. Have a good trip. I'll let you know what happens with the attorney." *Like you didn't know that would be the case.*

Ellie dialed Frank's number. He never answered his phone, so she expected it when a disembodied voice said: "You have reached 521-3440. Leave a message."

"Frank, this is Ellie. Mom is having some medical problems and we need to set up a family meeting with her attorney. It's scheduled for Monday, March 31st at ten-thirty with Ray McCarthur at the Wallace Law Office. Please let me know if you're coming."

Ellie had no idea if her brother would call her back or show up for the meeting, but she hung up satisfied that she had done her best to do what Sharon Kelly had suggested. Now the ball was in Frank's court.

CHAPTER 11

Monday, March 24th

Janelle rolled out of bed Monday morning with a very sore lower back and a dull ache from the bruise on the top of her left butt cheek. Easing herself into the shower, she looked down at her stomach as the soothing water splashed on her back and noticed her navel—as she had been taught to call it—was starting to stretch. *Jeez...I wonder if I'll get one of those funny-looking "outy" belly buttons. I've seen them on some women...they look so weird! Maybe if I get one I'll try to tape it down or something.*

Remembering she'd been a little uncomfortable in her snug dress pants Friday, she decided that today would be as good a day as any to wear maternity clothes for the first time. Luckily, she had a nice wardrobe to choose from, thanks to a friend of her mother's who was done having babies and happy to give her maternity clothes away. Janelle had sorted through the garments right away, washing everything she liked and hanging things in matching outfits in her closet. She chose a pair of black dress pants and a cute black shirt with cheerful daisies around the bottom edge.

Looking at herself in the full-length mirror, Janelle decided she looked "sort of" pregnant. She pulled the shirt tight and wondered how long it would be before her tummy wasn't hidden by the generous folds of maternity shirts. She debated taking the outfit off and putting some regular clothes on, but decided it was better to be comfortable and look a little sloppy than to be uncomfortable and look as if she was gaining weight.

Pulling into the parking lot at 6:59, Janelle glanced in the rearview mirror to make sure her hair was still covering her stitches and wondered if she'd make it through the whole day—it was still painful to sit. The phones were already ringing when she walked in, so Beth gave her a big thumbs up as she walked by. *I wonder if I'll need a new computer monitor. What if the mess is all still there... would anyone have come in on the weekend to clean up?* "I don't believe it!" Janelle said in amazement when she walked into her office cubby.

"Does that mean you like it?"

"Larry! You scared me," Janelle said, seeing her boss staring at her with a big grin on his face. "Like it? I LOVE it! Who had time to do this? It's incredible...a brand new desk, a REAL desk...and new filing cabinets!"

"I went to that office furniture place on the Avenue Saturday and asked what they had in stock. Then yesterday, Bradley and I set it all up," Larry said, obviously proud of their accomplishment.

"I don't know what to say," Janelle replied, looking around at her transformed office. "What happened to the ugly green and orange walls?"

"We used this cool clingy stuff, sort of like wallpaper, but no messy paste; we just stuck it on the walls," Larry explained. "Actually, it worked pretty slick."

Janelle walked around one wing of her new desk to check out her new burgundy chair, and she noticed a bouquet of huge red tulips next to a new seventeen-inch flat panel monitor. "Oh, now I do feel spoiled. A new chair, a flat panel monitor, *and* flowers?"

"Well, usually the computer guys get the new stuff...that monitor was supposed to be Bradley's, but he decided to give it to you instead. And the flowers are management's way of sending an apology. To tell the truth, remodeling this place is long overdue. We're actually going to do the entire office while you're on maternity leave."

"Well, thank you. I never expected anything like this. I'm really glad you did it, but I never thought..."

"So, you like it, huh?" Bradley asked, as he walked into the room with a self-satisfied expression.

"I love it! You gave up your flat screen for me? You came in on a Sunday to set this up? Thank you so much, both of you. It's absolutely perfect!"

"Good. By the way...I'm glad I've got you both here," Larry said, switching to a more business-like tone. "Janelle, Brad tells me he talked to you about our cross training idea."

"Yes, he mentioned it," Janelle said as she took off her coat, watching their faces closely to see what their reaction to her outfit would be.

"Well, I'd like you two to start working together today," Larry said, glancing quickly at her stomach and then back at her eyes.

"Today?" Now Janelle wasn't sure how to react.

"Right. Amy and I'll take care of all new clients, but I want you to bring Brad up to speed on your existing accounts so he can service them after you have the baby. Oh...and he'll be out of the office the first week in May...I'd like you to cover for him." Seeing the look on her face, he added, "Don't panic, he'll be reachable by phone and should be able to talk you through any problems that come up."

Janelle looked at Bradley, wondering why he always stood with his shoulders slouched and why he didn't get a decent haircut. *He's such a geek. How will I do this?* Then remembering he had gone out of his way for her, and feeling a little guilty for her nasty thoughts, she smiled brightly and said, "Okay, Larry, we'll do the best we can," sounding more confident than she felt.

"Great, I'll let you two get to work then," Larry said as he turned to leave. "And Janelle..."

"Yes?"

"I'm really glad you and the baby are okay."

"Me, too, Larry. Me, too."

Ellie slept fitfully and groaned when the alarm rang. She stumbled to the kitchen, where she dumped fresh water into the coffeemaker—specifically purchased because it delivered her the necessary jolt of caffeine, hot and black, in three minutes flat. Ellie poured two glasses of tomato juice; set them on the counter, and doled out the vitamin supplements she and Jack downed every morning. Just as the pot sputtered to signal the coffee was ready, she took their favorite stoneware mugs out of the dishwasher. Ellie poured herself and Jack generous mugfuls and carried them to the bedroom where he still lay snuggled under the covers.

"Coffee, honey," she said, setting the mugs down on their dresser. Ellie peeled off the lightweight nightgown she had to wear the last few years...*darn hot flashes and night sweats...they seem to be getting worse...I wonder if it's all the stress?* She downed another big gulp of coffee and forced herself into the shower. Hot coffee and hot water did the trick; an hour later, groomed and dressed, she climbed into Blackbird feeling more relaxed than she had in days. She even felt like singing along to the showtune from *Fiddler on the Roof* that she'd retrieved from the CD stack in her living room—after hearing it in the elevator the day she ran into Janelle. "Sunrise, sunset, quickly go the years... one season following another, laden with happiness and tears..." *Life isn't so bad, the sun's shining...*

Arriving at her classroom door, Ellie saw a green note from the principal hanging from the clip where she put out the hourly records of class attendance.

See me right way, as soon as you get here.
It's important! Tom

Tom was far and away the worst principal Ellie had ever worked for. A good-looking, but not very bright, man, he had used his charm to move up the administrative ladder. But Ellie knew he was a classic case of the Peter Principle...

promoted to his level of incompetence. Tom had failed to keep up with the changes occurring in education, and he easily caved in to parents whenever they called to complain about the smallest thing, somehow always assuming it was the teacher's fault.

"What is this?" Ellie wondered aloud. She unlocked her door, set her book bag down and hurried to Tom's office. A strong proponent of the open-door policy herself, she found Tom's door shut, as usual. She knocked softly.

"Oh, Mrs. Reed. Come in." The tone of his voice was unmistakably frosty. "I'm afraid you have a problem." He handed her a thick folded document. "You have a student, Henley Nielsen...Mrs. Nielsen has filed a formal complaint against you for educational malpractice."

"What?" Ellie asked. *This has to be a bad joke.* She had taught for thirty years and had always been considered one of the best, hardest working educators in the district. She had, in fact, won several awards for excellence. True, she was often called "mean" by some students, but what they really meant was that she was tough and strict. Ellie had always thought teachers who were too lazy to hold students accountable, and tried to be popular by being easy, were the ones who should be sued for malpractice.

Tom went on. "She came in yesterday after school. It seems the state test scores were mailed to parents last month. When Mrs. Nielsen saw that Henley's scores had actually declined since last year, she blew up. She's asking fifty grand as compensation for outside tutoring to bring the boy up to grade level, and also for your immediate dismissal. According to the complaint, you don't teach basic skills, refuse to communicate with parents, intimidate students and play favorites. She also claims you called Henley 'stupid' in front of the class, ridiculed him on a number of occasions, and even raised a hand to him last week."

Ellie felt her face flush and turn hot and she needed to sit down. "What is happening in your room, Ellie? I thought I told you when I moved him into your class at semester to watch it with this kid."

"Are you blaming me for this, Tom?" Ellie asked incredulously. "Do you actually think I would call a student stupid...that I would ever humiliate any student? The truth of the matter is his parents split up last year after his father allegedly had an affair with his secretary. Quite a nasty divorce from what I hear, and Henley's caught right in the middle. Is it any wonder he's having big-time attitude problems and refuses to do the work I assign? I think he's playing his parents...one against the other, and I'd be willing to bet he ditched the test on purpose...I wouldn't put it past him, at this point."

"Nevertheless, we'll remove him from your class."

"And put him where? You already moved him into my room after neither Carrie nor Judd could handle him. I was the last English teacher left when you sent him to me."

"Well, since there are only eight weeks left in the term, we'll put him in the library on independent study. I know it's extra work for you, but if you will send his assignments every day, one of the aides will work with him. In the meantime, gather any information you think pertinent to the case, write out your recollection of what has happened in your room, and get it to me ASAP."

Ellie's shoulders sagged. She did not have the time nor the energy for this. "The woman is a vindictive lunatic, Tom. Why must this be given any credence? Are you...is the district...going to stand up for me?"

"Now you know we don't automatically do that, Ellie. In this district, we consider the parents to be our customers, and you know the customer's always right."

"Should I consult a lawyer, Tom?" Ellie's voice was tight.

"It's probably not a bad idea for you to get legal advice."

"Great. I'll call WEAC today...they must handle this kind of thing on a regular basis."

"Fine, but get me Henley's assignments before the end of the day. I'll be the go-between until some acceptable arrangement is in place." The principal got up and headed for the door in a gesture of dismissal. "By the way, Ellie, how's your mother doing?" Tom asked, attempting to end the meeting on a personal note—something he probably picked up at his latest administration workshop.

"Just fine, Tom," she lied, not wanting to share any personal issues with the man. "She's fine. Thanks for asking."

Ellie returned to her classroom with a heavy heart. Her usual light steps were plodding and she wondered how on earth she would summon the energy needed to teach. "Oh, no," she said to herself. At her door stood Kaylie, the girl she had recently counseled at lunch.

"Mrs. Reed?" Kaylie said. "I brought you something." She held out the most perfect yellow delicious apple Ellie had ever seen. "I know you like this kind...you ate one the day we had lunch. I just wanted to thank you for being there for me the other day. I took your advice and wrote that letter to my mom about how her boyfriend creeps me out. She read it and promised I don't have to do stuff like watch TV with them unless I want to. Anyway, now us two...we're getting along better. Well, I just wanted to say thanks."

Ellie took the apple and hugged the girl warmly. Each year the state association sent out a memo warning teachers never to touch their students, but Ellie routinely ignored the advice, figuring her grandmotherly persona made her safe from THAT accusation.

"Kaylie, this is the nicest thing a student has done for me in a long time. You have no idea how much it means to me...and you chose the perfect day. We two," she said by way of correcting the girl's grammar error without drawing embarrassing attention to it, "can have lunch again sometime soon, okay?"

"You know, some kids say you're mean, Mrs. Reed," the girl said with an open honesty only adolescents can display. "And Henley Nielsen...he's supposed to be my friend, but I don't like it that he's always making fun of you." Ellie smiled weakly, her stomach turning at the mention of Henley's name. "But I think you're tough on us because you want us to learn, and I don't care what Henley says...you're my favorite teacher." Kaylie uttered the words with defiant emphasis and then walked away with a wave and a smile.

Ellie glanced at her watch. The bell was about to ring, so she took the apple and went to her desk. Kaylie's gesture had touched her and renewed her. She vowed not to let one bad apple spoil her barrel. The result was a great lesson where she guided her students into the magical world of the 1897 Klondike through a wonderful story by Jack London.

The day passed quickly as Ellie once again lost herself in the turbulent world of adolescence. She met Tom's deadline for turning in Henley's assignments and as she drove home, promised herself an indulgent treat—she would lie down for an hour before preparing a nice dinner for Jack. She wasn't sure if she should tell him about the Nielsen complaint... he'd react with anger and all kinds of advice... the last thing she needed tonight.

After hanging up her coat, she checked the answering machine: two new messages. Ellie pressed the Play button.

This is Frank. I definitely plan to be at that meeting on the 31st. Someone has to look out for Mother's interests.

Click. The icy tone of the message meant trouble. Ellie frowned. *Yeah... right... Frank! Whose interests will you really be looking out for?* She listened to the second message, which turned her frown into a smile.

Hi, Ellie. It's Janelle. I'm feeling so much better. Thanks for being there for me at the hospital. It really helped to hear the baby's heart. I just wanted to wish you a Happy Easter... will see you soon! Call or email me. Love ya. Bye.

The sound of Janelle's voice was like a tonic, and Ellie decided she didn't need a nap after all. She went into the kitchen, took a package of round steak out of the refrigerator and gathered the ingredients for Jack's favorite meal: a big salad, beef stroganoff over wide noodles, and broccoli in cheese sauce. For dessert she'd serve his favorite ice cream. She decided to put on a CD while she cooked. "Why *should* a woman be more like a man?" she sang out, freely editing the lyrics of her least favorite song from *My Fair Lady*.

CHAPTER 12

Friday, March 28th

Janelle found herself daydreaming as she drove her familiar route to work. She was feeling conflicted. Fridays were always good because she could dress down and today she was wearing a very stylish pair of maternity jeans. "But where did the week go?" she asked the windshield of her car. *Yesterday, I was officially twenty-weeks along...half way. I waited and prayed so long to get pregnant...now, in a blink it's half over.* She made a left turn and the morning sun reflected off her wedding ring, throwing a prism of light. She loosened her grip on the steering wheel to complete the turn and rubbed the underside of her ring with her thumb so the light would make it sparkle again.

She and Matt had looked at rings before he asked her to marry him. Like a lot of men, Matt hated shopping unless it involved hunting, golf or grown-up-kid stuff like video games or trampolines. Janelle teased him all the time, because not only was he allergic to shopping, he got what Janelle called "Buyer's Remorse Disease." The first time she witnessed it was after he purchased a motorcycle that Janelle assured him he could afford if he followed the budget that she put together.

"Janelle, I can't believe I bought myself a motorcycle," he said. "Maybe I should've waited till I got my raise."

"Matt, you told me you wanted this motorcycle, and I showed you how you can afford it. I included an extra seventy-five dollars a week in your budget for 'extras.' Think of the budget as a recipe, all you have to do is follow it."

"I know, I'm just not used to buying expensive things for myself. I wish I was as good with money as you are."

"Well, it would be one thing if you were stashing all your money in the bank to build a nest egg for a wonderful future with me, but I know you aren't. So at least this will be better than spending the money and not knowing where it went."

Little did Janelle know that this second-guessing would become a ritual. When he started talking about going shopping for rings, she told him she would look with him so he knew what she liked, but she would not talk him through it. She knew she couldn't happily accept an engagement ring if she was witness to his Buyer's Remorse after its purchase.

They went to the mall and visited a half dozen jewelry stores. Janelle found the perfect ring at the second shop. When they left the mall, after stopping back to peek at the one she liked best, Janelle told herself not to hold her breath. *It might take a while for Matt to cope with his "disease" on his own.*

One week later Matt placed that engagement ring on her hand and it had been there ever since. Janelle told him she had expected it to take him a lot longer to figure things out, but he replied, "Janelle, I love you. I decided a long time ago that I wanted you to be my wife. So I made up a 'recipe' and called it Operation Nest Egg." He beamed at the look of surprise and adoration in her eyes.

"So you knew last week, when we were looking at rings that you..."

"It depended on what we found, but I was sure hoping so. By the time we left the mall, yeah, I knew."

Janelle's ringing cell phone interrupted her thoughts.

"Hi, Mom," Janelle said without even looking at the caller number.

"Hi, Janelle. How're you doing this morning?"

"I'm good. We should be all set for Monday. Matt finished the base coat last night," Janelle was still rubbing the backside of her wedding ring.

"Great, I'm planning on it."

"What time are we supposed to come over on Sunday for Easter?" Janelle asked.

"We're going to eat at noon, but you can come over whenever you want. Around ten or eleven."

"Okay, sounds good. I'm at work now. Talk to you later, Mom." Janelle rushed by Beth who wished her a "Happy Good Friday." She didn't stop to chitchat because she wanted to get a few things done before Bradley arrived. She hung her coat on her new hook and booted up her computer.

"Janelle, pick up your phone," Beth's voice said through the speakerphone. Janelle quickly reached for her phone, knowing Beth was about to say something confidential.

"What's up?" she asked in a hushed tone.

"What's going on with you and Bradley?"

"Nothing, I'm training him. Why?"

"Well, yesterday was the first time I've ever seen him without a pen-protector shirt on; now today he walks in without glasses and a new hair style! And let me tell you, he doesn't look half bad."

"Really," Janelle said as she typed in her login. "I don't know about the shirt thing, but the other day he took off his glasses, and I noticed he had nice eyes...so I asked him if he'd ever considered getting contacts."

"And he said he would, for you?" Beth teased.

"What do you mean...*for me*? I'm happily married and in case you forgot, I'm starting to look like a house."

"I know. Just teasing. But you don't look like a house; you look like a cute little mama!" Beth chirped. Then her voice turned serious. "But if I were you, I'd be careful. The way I hear it, his wife is something else."

Janelle recalled Bradley's strange behavior the day he fixed her sound card.

"What exactly do you mean, Beth?"

"Gotta go, phone's ringing. Bye."

Jeez, I wonder what the heck the story is with Bradley and his wife. Janelle pulled out her to-do list. She was about to search for Ellie's school district's website, hoping to find a bio that would show her full name so she could confirm that her middle name was Marie, when Bradley walked in.

"Morning, Janelle," Bradley said from behind. Janelle spun her chair around, rendered speechless with the change in his physical appearance. *He really doesn't look half bad...okay, he looks pretty darn good!*

"Umm...morning, Bradley," Janelle said, looking away.

"So...what do you think?" Bradley asked hesitantly.

Janelle was hoping he wouldn't ask. "I think, like I said, that you look good without glasses."

"Thanks, and can you call me Brad?" he asked as he pulled up a chair and sat down. The implication was unmistakable...he wanted a more casual relationship.

"Okay...Brad," Janelle said. Then she assumed a business-like tone. "We still have seven more accounts to go through today."

"And then we'll have half of them covered, right?"

"Uh huh. That was my goal...to be half done by the end of the week."

"You always meet your goals, don't you?" he observed, looking directly into her eyes.

Janelle felt a little uncomfortable with his look so she quickly averted her eyes. "Well, I try," she said, thinking about her "goal" of getting pregnant years before she did.

"Good; then let's get started," he replied with a big smile and a twinkle in his brown eyes.

E llie spent all day Good Friday with Helen. Under the pretext of "spring cleaning," she managed to find and organize most of her mother's personal and financial records. Jack helped by distracting Helen long enough for Ellie to surreptitiously gather the documents and get them out to their car. Then Ellie kept Helen busy while Jack sneaked into the basement and turned off the breaker switch for the stove, taping over it and writing DO NOT TOUCH on it in case a Good Samaritan unwittingly tried to fix the stove.

They took Helen to Good Friday services, then out for fish. At dinner, Helen asked Ellie at least three times what grade she taught and could not seem to remember her grandchildren's names or what they were currently doing. Amazingly though, she told Jack a funny story about her experience as a teacher in a one-room schoolhouse and went into great detail about the privations caused by sugar and tire rationing during the 1940's. Helen then surprised them by saying she wanted to go home early because she was having company the next day.

"Really, Mom. Who's coming over?" Ellie asked.

"Why, your brother, Frankie. I thought you knew that. He called yesterday. He's taking me to Easter Sunday Mass." Helen then went on and on about how proud she was of Frank's excellent academic performance in high school, his graduating magna cum laude with an accounting degree and his landing a position in a Fortune 500 company.

Ellie and Jack listened politely, but gave each other a "look." Those particular achievements had occurred decades ago, and Jack and Ellie had endured the boring recitation countless times before. "And he has a job interview next week," Helen added.

Ellie and Jack exchanged another glance, and Ellie carefully processed this bit of news. *This means Frank will actually be at the meeting like he said in his message. I'm not sure if I'm happy about that or not, but at least I won't be caught off guard if he's his usual obnoxious self and tries to make trouble.*

CHAPTER 13

Easter Sunday, March 30th

Since she would be seeing Sandy on Easter, Janelle had hoped she would still fit into her regular clothes, but she was sadly disappointed. She had four different outfits suitable for the occasion, but each one was tight in places she didn't think very flattering. She looked through her maternity wardrobe with a critical eye and settled on cream-colored dress pants and a hip-flared pastel printed top, with three-quarter length sleeves and a white satin baby ribbon stitched at the neckline.

Hauling herself into the shower, Janelle relaxed and tried not to think about Matt's mother as the warm water soothed her still sore lower back. She looked down at her tummy, deciding that sometime between last weekend and today, she had popped. She hadn't noticed it from one morning to the next, but when she forced herself to consider what Matt would think if he saw her naked, she realized her body had changed remarkably in the last few days. The last time they'd made love was the weekend before Janelle's accident.

It wasn't that Janelle felt limited physically, but Matt seemed to move slower and touch softer for fear of hurting her and the baby. Afterwards, wrapped in each other's arms, Janelle tried to talk about it, but Matt denied that he acted any different than before she was pregnant. Janelle recalled reading several articles about how a husband might react sexually to his pregnant wife's changing body. She was hoping Matt would be in the category of men that were turned-on rather than off by their wives emerging motherhood. *The next time we're together, I'll definitely know what category Matt fits in.*

They arrived for Easter dinner at Claire's at ten-thirty. The morning had started out gray and raw, but it was rapidly turning into a bright sunny day with a crisp wind that failed to steal the warmth the sun was trying to provide. "Hello, Happy Easter!" Claire said, opening the front door and beckoning them inside.

"Hi, Mom...Happy Easter," Janelle said as Matt helped her take off her coat.

"Janelle! You look so cute in maternity clothes!"

"Jeez...Mom, I was hoping to wear regular clothes today, but nothing fit." *So...is cute a good thing?*

"Why? You said you couldn't wait to look pregnant."

"I know, it's just I have this outfit that I thought would be perfect," Janelle lied. She was not going to tell her about Sandy's obsession. After exchanging Happy Easters, Matt went into the living room with Uncle Rick to watch TV while Janelle went to help Claire and Aunt Christine in the kitchen.

"I said church was just so beautiful this morning," her aunt said as she sliced the ham. "I was just gonna say I don't understand why you and Matt didn't go."

Jeez, that's annoying! Why does she talk that way? For as long as Janelle could remember, Aunt Christine said the words "I said" or "I was gonna say" in almost every sentence.

"Aunt Christine," Janelle said with a sigh, unable to avoid the conversation she and her devout Catholic aunt had engaged in several times before, "it isn't that Matt and I don't believe in God; we just don't feel we have to go to church to proclaim it."

"Well, I said what will you do when your baby's born? Will it be baptized?"

"Of course," Janelle said, hoping that would satisfy her.

"I said where?"

"Christine, why does it matter to you where their baby's baptized?" Claire asked, trying to rescue Janelle.

"I was just gonna say I just don't understand why they don't go to church. I said how will the baby learn about God?"

"What was that email I got the other day?" Claire countered, trying to remember. "Oh yeah, going to church doesn't make you a Christian any more than standing in a garage makes you a car."

"That's a good one, Mom. I like that. The only thing I've learned from Catholic churches over the last few years," Janelle turned to Christine, feeling frustrated that religion was once again the topic, "is that it seems there are a bunch of priests having a very difficult time with their vows of celibacy and no child is safe because of it!"

Christine looked at Janelle as if she had sinned by even mentioning the well-documented sexual abuse scandals. "I said, so where did you say you'll have your baby baptized then?" Christine asked again.

"Matt and I are having the pastor that married us come to our home to baptize the baby."

"Oh, Janelle, Pastor Patson," Claire said. "He did such a great job at your wedding—what a great idea!"

"Thanks, Mom," Janelle said, but noted the look on her aunt's face that meant the discussion was not over.

"I said, so your baby won't be baptized Catholic?" There was obvious dismay in her aunt's tone.

"Our baby will be baptized a *Christian* and will learn about God from us," Janelle said firmly.

Claire, sensing they were approaching dangerous territory, deftly changed the subject. "Speaking of the baby, we need to talk about the shower. Does June 14th work for you?"

"Mom, the only plan I have for this summer is to have this baby sometime in mid-July," Janelle said, rubbing her tummy. "Whatever date you pick will work fine for me."

"I think you should have the shower in May, Claire. I said what if Janelle goes early?"

"What!" Janelle exclaimed. "My due date is July 20th; how early do you think I would go?"

"Well, doctors aren't always right about due dates, Janelle. I said, a girl at work went into labor eight weeks before her due date so everyone was worried, I said but it turned out the doctor was off on the due date by six weeks."

Christine had a point, but Janelle knew, in her case, a miscalculation on due date was not possible since the doctors knew the exact date and time of the insemination. However, Christine knew nothing about the IUI. Claire and Janelle never discussed her struggle to become pregnant in Christine's presence—they knew she would throw a negative slant on it and probably suggest it wasn't 'God's will' for Matt and Janelle to have children if they couldn't do it naturally.

"Oh, Dr. Felding is quite sure about my due date and my ultrasound should confirm it."

"Okay, then it's settled," Claire said. "June 14th is the date of the shower. Mark your calendars."

"Done. I'll tell Matt's mom tonight when we go there."

"Great, why don't you go get Uncle Rick and Matt? It's time to eat."

After they said a prayer of thanks for the Easter message and the feast spread out before them, Janelle silently added: *Thank you, Lord, for giving Matt and me this special blessing—our baby.*

Later, Janelle couldn't help but compare the difference between the gathering at her mom's and the one at Sandy's. From the moment Janelle took off her spring coat, everything immediately went south—beginning with Sandy scanning her from head-to-toe with an apparent look of disdain and asking, "Janelle, dear, do you really need to be wearing maternity clothes already?"

Janelle didn't quite know how to respond and was grateful when Matt wrapped his arms around her from behind. "Isn't she gorgeous, Mom? I think what they say about pregnant women glowing is true. It makes the baby seem real, now that Janelle's starting to show."

"Well, she certainly *shows*," Sandy replied in a overly-concerned tone. "Aren't you worried that she shows so much already? We all know how hard it is to lose the extra weight."

Janelle's blue eyes flashed with anger and she didn't let Matt answer his mother. "What shows is that I *am* pregnant, and proud of it...and in the next few months...I hope it shows a lot more! Have you forgotten all that we went through to get pregnant? I'd appreciate it if you'd keep your comments about my weight to yourself, Sandy."

Sandy reacted as if Janelle had slapped her. She stood, mouth wide open but speechless.

"Janelle, go get me a candy bar from my Easter basket," Matt said, shoving her toward the living room, "and get yourself one too." Janelle saw the look on his face and did as he asked. As she walked away, she heard him trying to smooth things over. *Jeez, will he ever just set her straight? Her obsession about gaining weight is beyond ridiculous! Pregnant women are* supposed *to gain weight!*

Easter Sunday Mass was a ritual Ellie had cherished since childhood. The church was overflowing with worshippers, many of whom she hadn't seen since Christmas. The sacristy was adorned with a huge display of white trumpet lilies, sweet-smelling flowers that proclaimed not only the resurrection of Jesus, but heralded all the promise of another resplendent Wisconsin spring. She inhaled the incense; for some reason that pungent smell always made her feel sanctified. She noticed most people were dressed in fancier clothes than usual and decided it was time to buy herself something new, maybe something in yellow, her favorite color. Turning her thoughts back to the service, she was thankful for so much this day, and especially grateful that her parents had raised her to be a practicing Catholic.

As they knelt to pray, Ellie looked down the pew at her husband and children. Jack was reciting along as the priest intoned the verses, but Jonah busied himself by re-setting his watch for Daylight Savings Time. Ellie knew her son went to Mass only when he couldn't get out of it, but she had been just as indifferent to her faith when she was in her twenties. She didn't nag Jonah about it; he had grown up to be a good man, kind, honest, hard working and decent. *Give them wings and teach them to fly—I think I accomplished that.* She noticed Rebecca was also not paying attention, instead reading the

Old Testament *Book of Ruth*. "Naomi, wheresoever you go, I go," Ruth had said in complete submission to her mother-in-law. *I'm sure Rebecca would never have such devotion to me...and I'm her mother...but then I guess I don't have it for my mother either. After all, I did leave her with Frank today, didn't I?*

Since neither of her children had a "partner" and there seemed to be nothing promising on either horizon, Ellie often wondered if she'd ever be blessed with grandchildren. *But Janelle's baby is due in July...I'll just have to "practice" with the new little Spencer, just in case I get to be a real grandma someday.*

The service ended with a rousing rendition of *I Know That My Redeemer Lives* sung by choir and congregation and the Reeds filed out of church and headed to brunch at the Downtown Hotel. At over fifteen dollars per person, this was the most expensive, and exquisite brunch in town, but the Reeds thought it worth every cent. The fresh fruit table, omelets made to order and sinfully rich pastries were "coronary counter food," according to Rebecca, who insisted on picking up the check for the meal.

After a chilly start, the day turned out to be unseasonably warm, blue skies and highs in the low 60's, so they sat in the sunroom when they got home. By 4:00 they had exhausted every topic from the economy to politics to the lack of any real entertainment on prime time television.

"Well, it's time to hit the road, little bro. I want to get home before ten," Rebecca said as she got up to pack her things for the long ride to Minneapolis. She had picked up Jonah Friday night in LaCrosse and would drop him off on her way home.

"I guess so, but as much as I want to get back, I hate to leave...the food's so good around here," Jonah replied in a transparent hint. Ellie gave him a wry smile and went to the kitchen to put together the leftovers of last night's dinner in a "care" package for him. She also wrapped up what was left of the pecan sticky rolls she had baked especially for Rebecca, and filled two tins with homemade peanut butter cookies.

"Here...for the ride, in case you get hungry," she said, handing over the packages of goodies.

"Thanks, Mom, you're the best," they recited in unison. Ellie laughed and hugged each one tightly as she said goodbye and then waved lustily from the sidewalk until their car disappeared down the street.

What a wonderful family I have, she thought, turning toward the house. Then something made her look back and she blinked twice as she watched a car coming down the street toward her. *It's Frank and Mom!* Frank parked the car and was helping Helen out before Ellie's shock subsided. *I wonder what's going on...Frank never comes over, even when we invite him!*

"We thought we'd drop by, it being Easter and all," Frank said as if it happened every holiday.

"Happy Easter," Ellie was dumbfounded. "This is a quite a surprise."

"I told you she wasn't going to like it if we came," Helen said reprovingly to her son.

Well, if we're putting you out, Ellie..."

"No, not at all, come on in."

Jack, who had spread out on the sofa to take a nap, sat up groggily when the trio entered the living room. He too, was blown away by the unexpected guests but shook hands with Frank and made small talk with Helen as he ushered her to her favorite chair. The tension in the air was so thick it was palpable, but things loosened up once Frank and Jack had each downed a double scotch on the rocks, and Ellie had herself drained a large goblet of white merlot.

"Well, Frank," Jack said in an effort at making polite conversation with a brother-in-law he despised. "Mother tells us you have a job interview this week."

"No, that wouldn't have been a good fit for me. I've decided instead to open a consulting business here in town."

"A consulting business?" Ellie asked.

"That's correct. I'll be assisting small businesses, setting up their accounting systems online, helping them improve their net profit by taking advantage of tax code loopholes.

Some of us have to keep up with emerging technology, right?" As usual, his tone was condescending, as if Ellie and Jack had never touched a computer. "I've already arranged to lease an office. It has an apartment upstairs so I'll be moving in a couple weeks. I should be up and running the first of May."

Ellie was alarmed and wanted more information. "Sounds like an interesting idea...but who did you say was financing all this, Frank?"

"Oh, would you like to meet my financial backer? I think you already know her." He pointed to Helen who smiled proudly at her son.

Ellie's stomach lurched. Part of her regretted drinking the wine and part of her wished she had chosen vodka instead. Still, she had the liquid courage to ask, "How, Frank...and how much?"

"Simple, we just used technology. Surprisingly, those online home equity loan ads are for real...the money is amazingly easy to get. It took less than two hours to get Mom qualified and another ninety minutes to cement the deal."

"Home equity loan?" Jack's voice displayed the surprise and concern Ellie was feeling.

"Yeah, would you believe they gave us seventy-five grand at six percent, sight unseen?"

"You borrowed seventy five thousand dollars—using Mother's house as collateral, Frank?"

"Right. With all my contacts, I figure I should pay off the loan in less than a year."

"All your contacts? Frank, you haven't lived in this area for twenty-five years," Ellie's voice raised in alarm. Jack shook his head in disbelief at what Frank had managed, yet again, to pull over on Helen.

"I figured you two would rain on my parade. You make me sick with your superior attitudes," he said petulantly. "I'm going to finally make some real money, and I won't have to do it by putting up with other people's spoiled brats..." He looked straight at Ellie, then he turned toward Jack. "Or kissing up to mill workers reeking of sweat or nurses smelling like bedpans."

"At least those stinking mill workers and nurses make an honest living," Jack replied, trying but failing to reign in his temper, "and one of them is worth a hundred frickin' bean counters working an angle."

"You liberals," Frank said with venom, as if it were in the same class as perverts or terrorists, "you just don't get it, do you? You're a dying breed and you better wise up because the world has gone conservative, folks. It's all about money now...our brave new world is made of the money, by the money, and for the money. That's the 21st Century Golden Rule...he who has the gold makes the rules."

"If that's the case, Frank," Ellie said, her voice shaking in outrage, "we can all kiss our democracy goodbye."

Helen, who had been silent during the entire exchange, had obviously heard enough. "Don't you ever stop, Ellie? All you ever do is argue. I'm sick of it and I'm tired. Frankie, take me home."

CHAPTER 14

Monday, March 31st

Janelle returned to bed after her seventh trip to the bathroom. Between getting up to empty her bladder and replaying the Easter dinner disaster at Sandy's, she wasn't getting any sleep. She looked at the clock: 2:12. Matt's alarm would be going off at 6:00 and Claire was coming at 6:30 to get started on the baby's room. She tried to delicately arrange herself in her pregnant-sleep-position without success. She placed her heavy soybean pillow behind her lower back, easing herself from a sitting position at the edge of the bed down onto her left side. She propped her five-foot body pillow next to her and reached her right hand out to pull up the covers. Finally comfortable, she drifted off to sleep.

It was nearly dawn when Janelle awoke again, this time with a powerful leg cramp. Involuntarily, she cried as the pain shot up her calf and settled into a lingering ache. "Owweeee, Owwee," she whimpered, hushing herself so she wouldn't wake Matt. She tried rolling onto her back, pushing her tummy toward the ceiling as she arched.

"Another charlie horse?" Matt mumbled.

"Uh huh. God, they hurt," Janelle groaned.

"You need to drink more water."

"Matt, I already have to pee every five minutes. Drink more water...do you want me to live in the bathroom?" Janelle resisted the urge to point her toes because Ellie had told her it would just make the cramp worse.

"If you did, at least one of us would get some sleep," he muttered as he sat up to help her massage her leg.

"I'm sorry, Matt. I've been restless all night. I can't stop thinking about the fight with your mom. I shouldn't have blown up at her like that."

Matt pulled her close. "Don't be sorry that you stood up to her, honey. She had it coming, I told her to knock it off when we first got there." Janelle wanted desperately to roll to her side and lie in the spoon position with Matt's arms around her, but the spasm in her leg had still not subsided.

"I know she did, but now she's mad at us."

"Janelle, stop worrying. Mom never stays mad long, especially when she realizes it's her fault."

"And what makes you think she will?"

"Common sense will tell her it's wrong to nitpick someone about gaining weight, much less her own daughter-in-law who's pregnant with her first grandchild."

"What? You seriously think she's just going to wake up one day and realize that?"

"No, when she sees her therapist again, she'll be able to figure it out."

"So her therapist will help her find her common sense?" Janelle highly doubted it.

"Exactly," he said smugly. "Now let's get some sleep; one of us has to work in the morning." He rolled back to his side of the bed after kissing her cheek. The pain in her leg finally ebbed and she drifted off to a light dreamy sleep.

In her dream, she and Matt were walking through a park, enjoying a warm summer breeze and the sound of kids playing on the swings. Janelle looked down and realized Matt was pushing a baby stroller. *The baby's here? Is it a boy or a girl? What does it look like?* She was reaching down to pull the canopy of the stroller back for a look when the B52's "Love shack! Baby, love shack!" blared out of the clock radio.

"Jeez," Janelle said, snoozing the alarm, "that's an obnoxious song so early in the morning."

"Whadaya mean?" Matt mumbled, sounding hurt. "That's our song."

"It's our fast song; our slow song would be much nicer to wake up to."

Rolling over, Matt began singing huskily, "Lady in Red...is dancing with me...cheek to cheek....da da da da...this beauty by my side, Lady in Red."

Janelle laughed at the part where he forgot the words and Matt reached over to tickle her.

"Matt, please stop. I'm sorry, I didn't mean to laugh."

"Laughing is good for you," he tickled her more. "This is for your own good."

"Tickle torture is still torture, Matt, so stop," she giggled, trying to sound angry.

"Okay, fine. But only because I gotta get in the shower. What time's your mom coming over?"

"She said six-thirty, but knowing her, she'll be early." Janelle went to the kitchen to pack Matt's lunch while he showered. She cored and sliced a Granny Smith with her apple slicer and put it in a plastic zipper bag; then grabbed two ham sandwiches she had made the night before from leftovers her mom sent home with them. She piled the apple, the sandwiches, two 16-ounce bottles of water, a granola bar and two bags of chips in Matt's red and white lunch box. *I wonder what Sandy would say if I ate like he does?* she mused as she packed two twenty-ounce bottles of soda and ice in the matching small cooler.

The doorbell rang at 6:25, just as Matt was heading out. Janelle asked him wait a second and went to the front door wishing her mom could have arrived just five minutes later like they agreed. She let Claire in and rushed to say goodbye to Matt. Then she went to her closet to find something old and comfortable to wear.

Five minutes later, she found Claire in the nursery. As promised, Matt had already done the base coat, taped the baseboards, and covered the carpet with plastic.

"So, what do you think, Mom?"

"Oh, Janelle, I love the yellow. It's cheerful and bright, just like a baby's room should be." Claire stood in the middle of the room, slowly turning on her heel. Noting that two of the walls had windows and one contained the closet, she asked, "Now where are you going to put the crib?"

"I like the color too, but it will look even better once we paint on the stripes. Even though there's room on the outside walls for the crib, I'm thinking this inside wall would be better." Janelle walked over to where the crib would stand.

"I agree," Claire said. "Then what else goes back in here when we're done? A dresser, a bookshelf, a rocking chair. What about a changing table?"

"The dresser's wide enough so we bought a pad for the top; we'll use that as a changing table. We might put the matching nightstand in here just because we have it and there's room."

"There's definitely room," Claire said looking around. "All three bedrooms in this house are good size."

"The only reason we were able to build this house is because you bought the lot for us, Mom."

"When you were little, your dad and I thought it was really important to put money away each payday for your future. When he died, I took a chunk of the life insurance and set it aside for you. I used it to pay for the wedding and give you this lot as a wedding present." Growing up, Janelle had known her mom had money from a life insurance policy, but she had no idea how much, and until now, she didn't know that a portion of it had been set aside for "Janelle's Future."

"Well, Matt and I really appreciate all you've done for us. I won't lie, it's been tough making ends meet, with the house and the infertility bills...but we love it here, Mom. It's the perfect place for our baby to grow up," Janelle said, patting her tummy.

"It sure is," Claire said approvingly. "Well, let's get started. What's the plan? How're we going to do the stripes?"

Janelle explained they would run tape vertically up each wall in six-inch stripes, alternating dark yellow with rag-rolled lighter yellow all the way around the room. The taping was very time consuming because of all the measuring, but luckily, they only had to tape to the top of the door and window trim rather than all the way to the ceiling. They were going for the "dropped ceiling" look so the eight-inch teddy bear border would be hung level with the door and window trim. Janelle helped Claire tape one wall, then stopped so she could follow behind Claire and do the rag-rolling.

"So when do you get the stitches out of your forehead?" Claire asked as she carefully measured and applied tape.

"I don't. They're supposed to dissolve after two weeks, but they itch and I'm already sick of trying to fix my hair so they don't show."

"I can't believe they completely remodeled your office in one weekend. By the way, how's the cross training going?"

"Really well. We got halfway through my client accounts last week, but the others are more complicated so they'll take longer. I just want to get the easy stuff done and out of the way before the seminar next weekend."

"Didn't you say the guy you had to cross train was a real nerd? What was his name...Brant or...?"

"It's Bradley, actually Brad, but I shouldn't have been so judgmental. He used to look the stereotype—high water pants, pocket protector shirts, heavy framed glasses—and of course he's really into computers."

"Sounds like he's just your type," Claire teased.

"Funny you should say that, Mom," Janelle said with a look of amusement. "You should hear the new office gossip. Brad did a complete one-eighty in the appearance department this week. Beth told me that by the end of the day Friday everyone was buzzing about Bradley-the-Geek turning into Bradley-the-Babe, and she couldn't resist asking me if there was something going on between us."

"Well, how different can he possibly look?"

"He got a really flattering haircut and contacts, plus he's wearing clothes that fit and dress shoes instead of those ugly sneakers. He does look a lot different, especially without the glasses...he has nice eyes."

"People don't really think there's anything going on between you two?"

"Some of them think he's got a crush on me...he's made all these changes in his appearance since we started cross training."

"Is he single?"

"No, married...and apparently his wife is *super* jealous. Beth said I'd better hope she doesn't hear the office gossip...she might go psycho."

"Be careful, Janelle. Maybe you shouldn't be working so closely with him...with all the office buzz and his wife acting so...maybe you shouldn't be going to the seminar this weekend since he's going..." Claire said with concern.

"Mom, that's ridiculous. Brad hasn't done or said a single thing that I would call inappropriate. I've already got him half-trained to take over for me when I have the baby. Besides, why would he have a crush on me, we're both married...and he never says anything like..."

"It usually isn't what a guy says, it's how he acts and what he doesn't say that leads people to fill in the blanks. There are enough scary stories about jealous husbands *and* wives..." Claire warned.

"Either way, I'm not changing things at work. I just want to get Brad trained and survive the first week in May when he's gone. Then I can stay home with the baby and not worry about work."

"Well, just make sure you set him straight if he does make a pass," Claire said as she applied another piece of tape.

"I will; don't you worry. I'm taking Ellie's advice..."

"Oh, really?" Again, there was an unmistakable chill in Claire's tone. "And what would that be?"

"She told me not to let anything interfere with my happiness now."

"Good advice, the kind a mother should give," Claire said a bit too smoothly. "It's wonderful, if a tad unusual, that you two are such good friends. By the way, have you heard from her since the hospital?"

"What did you just say?" Janelle asked. Something in Janelle's tone caused Claire to stop taping and look at her.

"I said, it's wonderful that you two are friends."

"No...let's see...you called it 'a tad unusual.' Do you think it's wrong that I have a friend older than you?"

"No, why would I? You've been casual friends with Mrs. Reed for years," Claire said defensively.

Janelle needed to put out this smoldering fire once and for all. She had an idea; she knew her mother well enough to know if Sandy took one position where her daughter was concerned, Claire would most likely take the other.

"I'm so glad to hear you say that, Mom," she replied. "Sandy thinks it's...what did she say...*twisted*, that I'm friends with a woman twice my age." Janelle crossed her fingers, hoping that Claire would take the bait.

"Twisted?" Claire raised her eyebrows and sniffed derisively. "Well, I'd say Sandy's the one who's twisted for thinking such a thing. You know what I always say, a person can never have too many friends."

Janelle saw her mother's self-righteous expression and congratulated herself on tying up this loose end.

"So...how's Ellie's mother?" Claire changed the subject.

"Unfortunately, she does have Alzheimer's, and Ellie's having a tough time. She's got a brother and a sister, like I thought, but it sounds like they aren't going to help at all."

"Uh, oh. Been there, done that with Christine and Grandma Knott. Speaking of Christine, I had to bite my tongue when she was harassing you about religion yesterday. How hypocritical can a person be?"

Janelle could see the vein in her mother's neck starting to bulge. "I mean, what kind of a Christian lets her dead brother's wife take care of their dying mother and does nothing to help?"

"Maybe it was just too hard for her...watching her mom deteriorate," Janelle offered.

"And it wasn't hard for me? Then she gets up on her high horse and chastises my daughter for not going to church? Who does she think she is?"

"Chill, Mom. Let's not talk about her. You did a great job with Grandma. Dad would've been proud of you."

"You're right, honey," Claire said as she patted the last piece of tape in place, "and he would've helped. It's gotta be lunch time. You hungry yet?"

"I'm famished," Janelle said. She knew she better eat pretty soon——even the carefully measured stripes were starting to look crooked to her. Then she felt the baby moving around and patted her stomach. "Actually, we both are."

Claire's face lit up with a smile. "Then it's lunch...party of three."

"Okay if we nibble on leftovers from yesterday?" Janelle asked as they walked to the kitchen. "How about a ham sandwich with mustard and a large glass of milk?"

"Sounds yummy...is this some of the ham I sent or did Sandy have leftovers too?"

"No, there wasn't much left," Janelle said.

"By the way, I never asked...how is Sandy and how was her Easter dinner?"

Uh, oh, I knew she was going to ask me that...there's no way I can tell her about Sandy's ridiculous obsession with my weight or the ham incident. "Um...she's fine...good food...you know, the usual." Janelle fibbed, afraid to give her the details of what had actually transpired.

Even after Matt asked his mother to quit bugging Janelle about her weight, Sandy started in again—apparently wanting to make sure Janelle didn't eat too much. Treating her like a small child, she'd taken her plate from her and filled it with very small portions—intentionally avoiding the bread, potatoes and ham. When Janelle asked her to pass the ham, Sandy acted as if she hadn't heard her. Then when she asked Matt to *please* pass the ham, Sandy had interrupted, "Janelle, dear...I gave you some turkey; ham is really too fattening for you right now." Having had enough, Janelle stood up, slammed down her silverware and reached across the table for the platter of ham.

"I'm *sorry*, Sandy. I thought we came here to *eat* tonight...my mistake! I guess if this is a bad time for *me* to eat ham, then maybe it's a bad time for *everyone*. Maybe...maybe it's a good time for you to *wear* the ham instead! God knows you could use some meat on those bones!" Janelle marched to Sandy's side of the table and dumped the entire platter directly onto Sandy's lap. The thick slices of ham landed with a wet plop and splashed all over her mother-in-law's designer dress. Everyone had sat in stunned silence for a moment or two, then Matt slowly stood up, cleared his throat and said, "Uhhh...well, then...I guess we'll be going now..." He was grinning as they walked out the door.

Remembering Sandy's and Matt's looks of utter astonishment, Janelle smiled to herself. *No...I can't tell Mom about the incidents with Sandy...she's too protective of me...better keep my complaints to myself...when Sandy finds her "common sense" I'll have to forgive and forget; Mom might not be able to.*

"Is June 14th good for Sandy for your baby shower?"

"Sorry, Mom, I completely forgot to ask." Knowing her mom so well, she knew exactly what Claire would say next. She felt her stomach begin to churn.

"Well, you have her number at work. Call and ask her."

Ellie arrived for the meeting fifteen minutes early. Frank was nowhere to be seen, so she checked in with the receptionist and sat down in a comfortable black leather chair to wait. She set the bulging folder of documents containing Helen's financial profile on the table beside her and looked around. The office was attractively decorated in a tasteful but not extravagant style, the waiting room exuding the desired law office aura—solid, classic, portraying an image befitting trusted legal professionals.

At 10:40, Ray McCarthur, their family attorney and another of Ellie's former students, popped into the waiting area and announced that he had to take an important conference call. Ellie was a bit miffed...her appointment was for 10:30. *Funny, other professionals like doctors and lawyers have no problem making clients wait. But if I'm even a minute late for class or a school meeting with these same people now acting as parents, my professionalism would be called into question and there'd be hell to pay.*

Ellie hid her annoyance, faked a smile and said, "No problem. My brother's supposed to join us and he's not here yet." Ray ran his fingers through his thinning hair and disappeared, leaving Ellie alone with her thoughts. She amused herself by studying the other two clients in the waiting room.

People-watching was one of her favorite pastimes. When the kids were little and they were forced to wait somewhere, they would make time pass more quickly by secretly signaling each other if someone interesting caught their attention. The game required that a "selection" be observed without catching on that the three were examining his or her every feature. Then later, usually at mealtime, they would make up some wildly imaginative story about the "subject." Jack, when he made it home in time for dinner, would end up adding details even though he hadn't even seen the individual. Rebecca and Jonah both enjoyed the game so much that sometimes even now at holiday celebrations, they retold their favorite stories until they were laughing so hard their sides ached.

Finally...Ray returned and led her into the small conference room, and asked, "Are we still waiting for Frank ?"

"Unfortunately, I haven't been able to reach him anywhere. I tried his cell and Mom's number, thinking he might be there. I have to admit I'm a little worried that no one answered at Mom's; I hope she's okay."

"I understand, I would be too. Anyone you'd like to call?"

"Well, Mom's neighbor knows where I am."

"Then, let's keep this short." Within a half hour, Ray, who was very efficient and experienced in this area of the law, had gone through the folder of documents, had his secretary make three copies of those he needed, prepared a standard power of attorney and durable power of health care for Helen to sign, and given Ellie a checklist of several other things that needed to be done. Gathering the papers together, he said, "That should do it for now—let me know if there's anything else you need my help with."

Even though she was in a hurry, Ellie thought she should tell him about Frank's getting Helen to apply for a loan.

"Frank's behavior borders on illegal," Ray said, "but we'd never win this one in court. Until Helen is declared incompetent, she's in charge of her own finances and there's not much we can do."

"Can't we just cancel the loan?"

"Sure. Did you say he applied over the weekend? At farm&home-equity-loans.com?"

Ellie nodded.

"Wisconsin cancellation laws apply here, so I'd better take care of it right after you leave. I'll call their office and speak to their corporate counsel." He shoved back in his chair. "And it might be a good idea to keep copies of any paperwork this whole incident generates. I think it's wise to keep that kind of documentation on file... in case he makes another similar move. Of course, after Thursday, he'll have to have your approval for anything involving your mother's finances. I only wish we had gotten together on all of this sooner."

"Me too. I had no idea my brother was capable of doing something like this."

"Nothing surprises me anymore, especially when it comes to relatives and money. Anyway, I'll get this going right away, because under the circumstances, it needs to be done ASAP. I think I can have an answer for you within an hour. Want me to leave a message on your machine to let you know it's done?"

"I'd rather you called my cell phone." She reached in her purse for one of her personal cards and handed it to him.

"Sure, no problem. I'll call you as soon as I find out anything." He finished gathering Helen's papers together and placed them in a neat pile. "And as for the rest of this, my secretary can have the crucial documents ready by Thursday. I know you can't get away during the day, but the office is open until 7:00 p.m. on Thursdays. Why don't you bring your mother in for the necessary signatures? That will avoid the slightest chance of anyone suggesting any impropriety here."

"Good idea, Ray. I'll pick Mom up after school and we can be here by five-thirty. If I promise to take her out for supper, she'll come willingly."

"Perfect," the lawyer replied, getting up to re-button his capacious suit jacket over his substantial stomach. The gesture reminded Ellie of a little joke she shared with her students at the beginning of the school year. "I know lots of your fathers because I had them as students," she would say, "and of course they've changed. Many of them now have less hair and more tummy."

"Thank you, Ray, this has been a big help. I'd better get going." Ellie rose to leave.

"No problem, Mrs. Reed...Ellie. That's what we're here for...I'll see you Thursday at five-thirty." Then he added, "Enjoy the rest of your day off. You teachers are so lucky, short workdays, long vacations, summers off..."

Ellie bristled but didn't say anything. She had heard this mantra so often she was sick of it. She herself never had a weekend or vacation during the school year when she didn't have tons of schoolwork to do. And she had never taken a summer off, always teaching summer school, or tutoring remedial students to bring in badly needed extra money, or taking courses to earn her master's degree, or attending staff development classes because it was the only way to move up on the salary schedule.

"Well, you're lucky I took the time to help you after school during seventh grade English," she teased. "Your spelling was despicable."

"Yeah, yeah," he said with a smile as he put an affectionate arm around her. "And then they invented computers with spellcheck and grammar check and all that techno stuff that makes spelling irrelevant. Irrelevant...i-r-r-e-l-e-v-a-n-t." he said, spelling the word carefully, letter by letter, just as he had done dozens of times many years ago as a seventh grader. Ellie nodded in teacherly affirmation, and Ray's face lit up in a self-satisfied grin as she left the office.

Ellie cranked up the volume on the CD playing in Blackbird and sang along to *If Ever I Would Leave You* from *Camelot* as she drove south on the busy highway. She eagerly anticipated the delicious pampering that lay ahead. Insuring optimum use of her precious afternoon off, she had made an appointment to check out a new local women's health club and booked a soothing full-body massage. She planned to serve something take-out on her best table service that evening for dinner. The accompanying bottle of her favorite bubbly was currently nestled in her refrigerator wine basket, cooling to just the right serving temperature.

Thinking of her health club appointment caused Ellie to remember her promise to get back into shape for summer. *Naturally, all I have to do is just* think *about beginning an exercise program, and my stomach starts to growl.* She looked at the clock on the dashboard—even though she could have almost guessed the exact time. *Funny...during the summer my body adjusts easily to the change in routine, but during the school year...11:56 and forget it...I'm famished!*

"If ever I would leave you, it wouldn't be in springtime," she sang along to the CD. Suddenly, a spontaneous and crazy thought seized her. It was the end of March. Springtime. She picked up her cell phone, fully aware she shouldn't be using it in the fast and heavy traffic of Eastern Wisconsin's busiest highway. Ignoring her own safe driving admonition, she pushed speed dial for Jack's office.

"Jack Reed," his deep resonant voice said after one ring.

"Hi, honey."

"Hey, babe, what's happening?"

"I just finished with Ray McCarthur, the meeting left me famished and since we haven't had lunch together in months, think you can get away to meet me at the club?"

"Perfect timing! We just wrapped up at the Blood Bank. If you get there first, order my usual: rib-eye steak sandwich on sourdough with hash browns."

"Ten-four. Love ya." *Maybe I should check on Mom again...oh for God's sake...you know Carolyn would've called if there was anything amiss; can't you ever relax?*

Fifteen minutes later Ray called to give her a heads-up on canceling the loan. Ellie thanked him profusely, getting the impression Helen's attorney didn't think it was any big deal. Ellie did. She winced when she considered how ticked off Frank was going to be, but pushed those ugly thoughts away. *Not today...today is my day to do what I want.*

Ellie saw her exit and turned off the highway into the completely deserted club parking lot. *Duh, it's Monday... they're closed.* Exasperated, she reached for her cell to call Jack. Just as she did, the phone rang.

"Eleanor Reed?" an unfamiliar male voice asked when she answered.

"Yes? This is Ellie Reed...who's this?"

"Good. You don't know me, but my name's Russ Paalman. My wife, Olivia, and I belong to the same church as your mother. Matter of fact, we think we've seen you there with her occasionally over the years, although we usually go to early Mass and you go to the later service."

Ellie wondered what all this had to do with her. "What can I do for you, Russ?"

"Well, Ellie. I'm not sure just how to explain this. We're at your mother's house. We brought her home a little while ago. We had stopped at the bakery, you know, right near the football stadium, and noticed her sort of wandering down the street. She was acting really strange and when we asked her if we could help, she burst out crying and said she was lost."

"Oh my God! Is she all right?"

"She seems fine now. In fact, she went right to bed when we got here. Luckily, we managed to get her address out of her. I know this neighborhood pretty well so we decided to just bring her home."

"Did she say how she managed to be there?"

"She said something about her son taking her to the casino, but she had lost all her money, gotten bored and wanted to go home. Apparently when she found him at a card table, he told her he wasn't ready to leave. She said she didn't want to bother him and had decided to walk home."

"But where you found her is miles from the casino..." Ellie said. "And miles from her house."

"I know. Good thing we spotted her. That's a really busy part of town. Who knows what might have happened...well, the thing is...Eleanor, we have to be in Escanaba for dinner with our grandkids by five. Is there someone who can come to stay with her? We don't feel right just leaving her here alone."

"I'll be there in fifteen minutes. Is that okay?"

"Sure, I'll fill you in on all the rest when you get here."

"Russ? Thanks...I can't imagine if you hadn't...we're so lucky you happened..."

"No problem. We're just glad we stopped there today. We hardly ever go out for donuts anymore. But the grandkids love their cherry-cheese coffeecake."

"Thanks again, Russ. See you in fifteen."

Ellie pressed End to complete the call just as Jack drove into the parking lot in his pick-up. He rolled down his window, seemingly ready to tease her about choosing a restaurant that was closed on Mondays, but he stopped short when he saw the look on her face.

"Jack, it's Mom...some people found her wandering around way on the other side of town. It sounds like Frank took her to the casino and wouldn't leave, so she tried to walk home. I have no idea how they got my cell phone number, but thank God they did. I have to get over there right away." Ellie was working herself into a complete panic.

"No...we *both* have to get there right away," Jack said, well aware of the fact that Ellie was not in any shape to be driving. Taking complete control of the situation, he parked his truck, ordered her to move over to the passenger side of Blackbird, and got behind the wheel. He then pulled out his company cell phone—within minutes, he had directed his secretary to re-route his calls to his mobile phone, reschedule his afternoon staff meeting to later in the week, and asked her to fax him the AFSCME report on the current understaffing of correctional officers at state prisons to their home fax.

Once they were on the freeway, he turned to Ellie and said, "Start from the beginning..."

Ellie quickly filled him in on the few details Russ had given her. The ride seemed to take forever. Jack held Ellie's hand, sensing her distress. Finally she spoke, very quietly, her anger like white-hot embers.

"When Frank didn't show at the law office this morning, I should've known something like this was going to happen." Then she began to chastise herself. "I should have guessed,

I should have driven there right after the meeting with Ray. I should have known..."

"You stop that right now," Jack's voice reverberated through the small interior of the sports car. "You are not responsible for your brother's irresponsibility!"

"But to leave Mom alone to her own devices in a casino, how could he?" Ellie asked helplessly.

"Ell...not everyone is as responsible...why I heard about some guy in Vegas," Jack said. "Apparently he left his little girl unsupervised in a casino. Some sicko came along, took her into a restroom...drugged her, put a wig on her and kidnapped her...the video cameras later traced it...they found her a few miles away...raped and murdered. Then the a-hole of a dad had the audacity to tell the casino he wouldn't tell anyone about *their* negligence if they gave him ten grand...unbelievable!"

Ellie shuddered at the thought of the horrendous things some people could do. *Frank's bad, but not that bad. Still, I wish I knew how to confront him. Good God...you have no problem setting anyone else straight—what's your problem with big brother?"* Frank had always wielded the power in their sibling relationship. He always managed to put her on the defensive and make her feel insecure. Part of it was his being older, part of it the verbal cruelty that used to reduce her to tears when she was younger. *But this time...this time he's gone too far...and I have Jack along to back me up.*

Ellie's heart pounded and her mouth was dry as they pulled up in front of the small story-and-a-half frame house she had grown up in. They parked in the street because an immaculately clean, shiny red SUV occupied the driveway leading to the two-car unattached garage.

"That must be Russ's vehicle," Ellie said. "Thank God for people like him."

A sixty-something thin man with a great shock of white hair came to the front door to greet them. He was wearing a wildlife print flannel shirt with brown denim jeans whose loops held a belt secured by a huge belt buckle that said *Grand-Pa* on it.

"Hi, I'm Russ Paalman," he said with a friendly smile and a firm handshake. "This is my wife, Olivia." Olivia, a large woman almost twice the size of her husband, was sitting on the sofa in the small living room watching television.

"I'm so pleased to meet you," Olivia said with a smile as broad as her bosom. Russ sat on the couch with his wife; Ellie and Jack sat down in the only other two chairs. The four adults made the small room seem even smaller than Ellie remembered it. *How did my parents manage to raise a family of five in this little house?*

"Is that coffee I smell?" Jack inquired.

"It is; we made a pot of decaf when we got here," Russ said. "I hope you don't mind. We needed a little something to wash down the cookies Helen insisted we try. A little on the dry side...but quite delicious," he added.

"Absolutely no problem; I'm glad you did," Ellie said as Jack went to the kitchen. Ellie and the Paalmans sat in silence for a moment, and when Jack came back munching on a cookie and sipping from a large green and gold Super Bowl Champions mug, Ellie excused herself to look in on Helen. She was napping peacefully, almost childlike in her repose.

Ellie carefully closed the door to Helen's bedroom and rejoined the group in the living room. "Just to be sure I have it all straight, tell me again what happened today," she said.

Russ cleared his throat. "Well, as I told you over the phone, we stopped in at the bakery on our way to Escanaba. We came around the corner and noticed an elderly woman walking in a kind of zigzag fashion. We slowed down as we passed and the wife here," he gestured to Olivia who smiled broadly, "recognized her as Helen Lowe from church. We parked and walked back to see if she was all right. She sat down on a planter by the side of the street and started to cry, saying she was lost and that two different times a man had tried to give her a ride. She said she knew better than to get into a vehicle with a stranger, but when we convinced her that we were from her church, she came with us. As I said on the phone, after a little prodding, she gave us her address. I know the neighborhood so we brought her home."

"You forgot the part about calling the casino, dear," Olivia interrupted.

"Oh, that's right. When we first got here, we thought maybe someone at the casino might be looking for her so we called their customer service number. After what Helen had said about being there with her son, we asked them to page a Frank Lowe. They did, several times; I could hear it in the background, but no one took the call. So then we did a little detective work and found a calendar in the kitchen with your phone numbers. When no one answered at your home, we decided to try your mobility phone."

Ignoring his misuse of the word "mobility," Ellie smiled politely as he said, "We tried the casino again, just before you drove up. I would imagine whoever took her there must be out of their mind with worry."

Ellie had put the whole thing together, but she had no desire to get into that, so she made up a plausible story.

"We just found out that Mom has Alzheimer's," she said. "We knew this 'getting lost thing' was a possibility but didn't expect it to happen so soon...anyway, there's a casino shuttle bus stop right down the street at the convenience station. She used to ride it to play bingo every week when she...well, she stopped going a couple years ago because she couldn't keep up with the numbers." Ellie knew she was rattling on but couldn't stop herself. "Anyway, Frank was here yesterday for Easter dinner. She probably took the shuttle this morning, got confused about how she got to the casino, and well, thank heavens you came along. The Lowe family can never thank you enough, but..." Ellie reached into her pocket and extended a crisp twenty-dollar bill to Russ.

"No, oh, no, we're just happy to help," Russ said, refusing the money. "Besides, who knows what we'll pull when we're old."

Olivia smiled sweetly but reached over to take the bill. "Thanks," she said. "I know you won't stop insisting until we accept something for all our trouble."

Ellie smiled back as Olivia took the money. "I know this isn't much but..." She realized she just wanted the

Paalmans to be on their way. Getting up, she politely said, "Now we don't want to keep you from your day any longer; you have given the Lowe family enough of your precious time." She could feel a tension headache coming on and her stomach was letting her know it was long past time to eat.

Getting the hint, Russ retrieved their jackets from the hall tree and helped Olivia squeeze into hers before putting his on. "And thanks again," Jack said as he escorted them to the front door.

"See you in church Sunday, then?" Russ asked as they walked to their SUV.

"Right, Sunday, church," Ellie said and waved as they drove off.

"Thank God for people like Russ and Olivia," Jack said. "Ellie, I'm starved. I wonder if Helen has any real food in her fridge. Let's see what we can rustle up to eat."

After a make-do meal of tuna salad sandwiches, cottage cheese on peach halves and caramel delight cookies he found in the freezer, Ellie looked in on her mother once again.

This time the creak of the door awakened Helen who sat up with a start.

"Who's there?" she called out in alarm. "Francis?"

"No, Mom. It's me. Ellie." Helen faintly grunted in acknowledgment, then lay back down on her pillow while Ellie came and sat down on the edge of the bed.

"What are you doing here?" Helen asked.

"You gave us quite a scare, Mom."

"What, am I sick?"

"No, but you did have quite an adventure this morning. Remember?" Ellie asked, as her mother looked at her in complete bewilderment. "Frank...the casino...."

"I haven't been to that place in years," Helen replied angrily. "The machines are so tight you can't win a nickel and the bingo games are rigged so the same people win all the jackpots." Abruptly Helen changed her direction. "Where is Frank? Is that lazybones still in bed? He said he was going to take me someplace special today. I want to go someplace special, he promised! Eleanor, go get Frank up, it's late!"

"No, he's not here, Mom. Did he go back to Milwaukee?"

"Of course not. He took me to Easter brunch. He wanted to pay, but he forgot his wallet and so I wrote a check. Good thing I had my checkbook in my purse. I don't always remember it." Helen seemed to recall nothing about their visit to Ellie's yesterday.

Ellie's brain processed this information and reacted with suspicion. "Mom, where's your checkbook now?"

"It's where it always is, in my purse," she said defensively. "I cashed a check at the casino so Frank and I could play a while." Helen was clearly upset that Ellie was asking these questions, unaware that she was contradicting what she'd previously said. "I better get dressed," she started to say and then realized that she was already in street clothes. "I guess I must have fallen asleep last night on the sofa and your brother must have helped me to bed. What a wonderful son I have." Her face glowed with affection and pride.

"What time is it?" she asked, putting on her glasses that lay on the nightstand and squinting at the clock nearby. "Two-thirty? Oh my, no wonder I'm hungry. I usually have a snack about three. Will you be a good daughter and fix me a piece of toast with strawberry jam and a glass of milk? I always drink milk. No coffee or soda for me. No sireee. My father was a dairy farmer and milk is what I always drink."

As Ellie went to the kitchen to fetch her mother's snack, Jack looked up quizzically. "She can't remember a thing about getting lost," Ellie told him softly. "Or yesterday afternoon either, for that matter. Talk to you later," she whispered when Helen appeared in the living room.

"What are you doing here, Jack? Is it Sunday? Is it time for church?"

"No, it's Monday, Helen. Ellie and I had the day off so we decided to pay you a surprise visit."

Just as the toast popped up, Ellie thought she heard a noise outside. *If that's Frank, I swear I'll kill him!* She quickly spread the jam, put the toast on a plate, and carried it and a glass of milk to Helen, who sat at the table making small talk with Jack.

As Helen took her first bite, the front door opened and Frank's voice called out, "Mom, are you here, Mom?"

"In the kitchen, Frankie," Helen called warmly. Frank came in with a big smile that faded immediately into a scowl when he saw Jack and Ellie sitting at the table with Helen.

"What are you two doing here?" he asked coldly.

"As if you didn't notice my car on the street?" Ellie snapped, barely controlling her anger.

"I know you think your precious sports car is quite the eye-catcher, but did you ever stop to think that maybe everyone is secretly laughing at the old lady driving it?"

"Where have you been?" Ellie asked, pointedly ignoring his question.

"It's really none of your business," Frank said, "but if you must know, I went out to get some groceries for Mom. There's nothing to eat in this house. Obviously you never make sure she has any good food to eat." He opened the sack he was carrying to reveal a six-pack of beer and a large bag of cheese curds.

Ellie regarded his "groceries" with disgust. "Stop with that already. We know where you were," she said as Frank opened a beer and took a long drink.

"Yeah? Where?"

Helen interrupted. "Now stop this right now, Ellie. Can't you ever be nice to Frank? Why must you always talk to him like that?"

Ignoring her comment, Jack broke in. "Cut the crap, Frank. We know you went to gamble this morning."

"And we know you took Mom along because you needed her to cash a check," Ellie added. "We don't know how much you managed to get from her this time, but we'll find out..."

"So what? Mom's a big girl who can take care of herself. She wanted to go to play some bingo and last time I checked we were both twenty-one. Those are the only legal requirements they have at casinos."

Helen took a drink of milk and a big bite of strawberry toast. Then she put her hands over her ears like a small child to block out the argument.

"And the check was only for a grand," Frank said derisively when he noticed his mother was shutting out their words. "It's not like she isn't loaded."

"What do you mean...*only a grand*? How could you? That's more than half her income for an entire month! You...you self-centered, rotten..."

"Careful, little sister. Don't have a conniption fit; might have the big one right here and now and miss out on your inheritance." Frank's words dripped with sarcasm.

Helen threw up her hands in disgust and took her snack into the living room, turning up the television volume to cover the loud voices in the kitchen.

Ellie plunged ahead now with reckless abandon as emotion trumped intellect. "And then you ditched her. You left her to fend for herself. Did you know she left and decided to walk home after you wouldn't take her? That two men tried to pick her up? That some nice people from her church found her lost and wandering around miles away from the casino...and you never even asked how she got home? God knows what might have happened..."

Frank's face showed absolutely no remorse. "What might have happened, happened," he said glibly. "She looks fine so no harm done."

Jack, who had watched in quiet fascination as his wife actually stood her ground in the presence of her older brother, now entered the fray.

"No harm done, Frank? For starters, you ruined the one day Ellie has off until Memorial Day. You put your mother through a harrowing experience, needlessly putting her in harm's way, not to mention losing a thousand dollars of her hard-earned money."

As Jack spoke, Ellie suddenly remembered the forgotten health club and massage appointments. *Now I have to make embarrassing apology phone calls...so much for doing something just for me.*

"It's none of your damn business, Jackie Boy," Frank replied, "so butt out! It's a business deal between my mother and me—she knows I'll win it back and then some."

Ellie snorted in disbelief at her brother's cavalier attitude about losing that much money. *There's no reasoning with him—he's not only compulsive...he's delusional!*

"Well, I hope you had fun because there isn't going to be a next time," Jack said.

"What do you mean? You can't stop me." Suspicion dripped from Frank's eyes.

"Starting tomorrow," Ellie said, massaging the truth a little, "Mom's checks will need my signature." Frank's expression turned to hatred and Ellie's voice shook as she continued. "And by the way, don't be expecting any start-up funds for your consulting business. Mother's lawyer cancelled the loan this morning."

"Why you greedy, conniving, fat bitch..." Frank began.

"You ever say anything like that to her again, in or out of my presence," Jack said in a voice Ellie had never heard come from him before, "and you will be in immediate need of serious medical attention."

"This conversation is over," Frank said. "I was planning to stay here until my new apartment's ready. Give Mom a chance to have some family around for a change. But I can see I'm not welcome." He went into the spare room and threw his things into a suitcase, slamming it shut. He carried it into the living room where Helen was watching a game show, answering questions aloud while no one listened.

"I'm leaving, Mom," he said, giving her a pat on her hand and a kiss on her cheek.

"Why?" she cried out. "Don't go. You just got here, Frankie. Why are you leaving already?"

"Ask Ellie, she's the one with all the answers," he yelled over his shoulder as he slammed the front door behind him.

CHAPTER 15

Wednesday, April 2nd

The calendar on the refrigerator read: Wednesday, April 2nd–*Ultrasound 3 PM!* Janelle noticed it each time she opened the door to get different items for Matt's lunch. She remembered she had the option of taking an appointment the day before, but superstition prevented it. *I'll let someone else take the April first appointment. I can wait one more day…no reason to do anything to jinx myself now that I'm finally pregnant.*

Matt came into the kitchen to talk with Janelle as he put his socks on. "So the appointment's at three?"

"Yes, but we have to be there at two-thirty because I have to drink a bunch of water first. You should leave work by two. You won't forget, will you?"

"Stop worrying! We're actually going to see our baby today; this is too important to forget."

"Well you forgot that I don't tell my mom when I'm having problems with yours," Janelle said bluntly.

"Janelle, I really don't get what the big deal is. So I told your mom we had a fight with my mom at Easter and we left early. Who cares? It's not like I told her the 'juicy' details," he said, pretending to dump the ham on her head instead of Sandy's dress.

Janelle ignored his feeble attempt at humor. "Matt, the big deal is I spent all morning trying very carefully not to mention it and then you walk in the door for a surprise visit at lunch and you blab away. Now she's upset because she thinks I tell her everything and I obviously don't. She's also ticked because your mom's on my case about gaining weight and to top it off she thinks it's *twisted* that I'm friends with Ellie Reed."

"I didn't tell your mom anything about Ellie," Matt interrupted. "You must've told her that. And why do you always have to say Ellie Reed? It's not like we know any other Ellies. The next thing you know you'll be spelling it; Ellie R-E-E-D. It's completely unnecessary to always say her last name. I know who Ellie is."

"Sorry! I didn't know that bothered you. I did tell my mom about Ellie, but it wasn't a big deal until after you told her about the Easter fight. Then she decided I talked to Ellie about Sandy instead of her." Tears were forming in her eyes.

"So now we're fighting," Matt said.

"I know I'm making mountains out of mole hills, but I have a very good female-worrier role-model to emulate in my mother. And your mother's common sense hasn't seemed to kick in here yet...we haven't heard from her in two days. She knows the ultrasound's today; I thought she'd call. So your mom's not talking to us, my mom's feeling hurt, we're fighting...the only decent relationship I seem to have right now is with Ellie."

"Then take her advice, Janelle! Remember? Water off a duck's back...you've got to stop worrying about this stupid stuff and focus on the baby. You're way too stressed."

"How's that supposed to help? If I focus on the baby, I'll get so nervous I'll just freak. What if something goes wrong? What if all of this is just too good to really be true?"

"Come here, babe," Matt said. Recognizing her need for a hug, he put his strong arms around her. "I don't know why God made us wait so long, but I know in my heart He's not going to change His mind now."

"I want to believe that, Matt. I try to believe it, but..." Janelle said into his chest.

"Hey, it's going to be okay...are *you* going to be okay?" She shook her head. "Good...I'd better get going; after all, I have a family to support." He gave her another reassuring kiss before heading out the door.

On her way to work Janelle got her usual morning call. "Hi! You excited about the ultrasound?" Claire seemed unable to hide the excitement in her own voice.

"I'm a nervous wreck."

"Has Sandy called you?" Claire probed carefully.

Janelle still hoped that eventually she and Sandy would be back on speaking terms, but she knew her mom might still harbor ill feelings. She wanted to say, "Mom, please don't ask me about Sandy," but instead she found herself tearfully saying, "No, I thought for sure she'd call last night. She knows my appointment's today."

"Are you crying? Stop it, Janelle. If the woman's that stupid, she certainly isn't worth crying about."

"Mom, see, this is why I tried not to tell you about our fight. You get so mad and that just makes things worse."

"What do you want me to do? Of course I'm mad. She's so fixated on having a perfect body that she has a problem with anyone who doesn't."

"The thing is, Mom, she's always going to be in my life and I'd rather we got along, especially with the baby coming. So I don't want you to be mad at her."

"What difference does it make?"

"It just makes things harder for me when I know you're upset, Mom," Janelle said again.

"Janelle, you worry too much."

"That's original, Mom. I've never heard that before...I wonder where I get it from."

Claire ignored Janelle's sarcastic tone and changed the subject. "So your appointment's at three? You have to call me as soon as you're done."

"I don't know how long it'll last, but I promise I'll call. I'm at work now; I have to go in," Janelle said grabbing her things and checking her face in the mirror.

"Okay, honey, have a good day...everything's going to be just fine, you'll see."

"Thanks, Mom. Talk to you later." Janelle wiped the streaked mascara from under her puffy eyes. *My God, I look like something from a freak show. Puffy, red eyes, pale as a ghost, stitches in my forehead.* She checked her watch: 6:59. *How will I ever have time to get the baby ready and to day care and still get myself to work by seven?*

Beth was already talking to two other co-workers and the phone was ringing when Janelle walked in, so all she did was wave hello, which was completely fine with Janelle. She didn't need Beth to notice she'd been crying and ask why.

Janelle arrived at her cubicle hoping for some time alone, only to find Bradley and Larry in her office discussing the weekend seminar.

"Oh, here she is," Larry said, glancing at his watch. "I was just telling Brad that I'll drive us to the seminar since we're leaving from here anyway." Janelle carefully slipped behind them both to get to her desk.

"That's fine with me. I hate driving in unfamiliar areas and I wouldn't trust my car to make the trip anyway." Janelle busied herself with her normal morning routine so she could avoid making eye contact with either man.

"Good," Larry said. "I'd like to leave early afternoon to avoid rush hour traffic, so both of you need to wrap up by two on Friday, okay?"

"No problem," Brad said. Janelle just nodded as Larry left, then turned to check her email, wishing Bradley would leave as well to give her a few minutes alone, but he sat down and began flipping through his yellow legal pad of notes. "Let's see, I had a question on one of your accounts and now I can't seem to find it," he said, going back to the beginning to look again.

"Was it about billing? Logos? Design? Layouts?" Janelle listed possibilities as she glanced in his direction to see he was still looking down.

"Oh, now I remember...Cloth-Is-Best. I was telling my wife about the potential savings over disposable diapers. She thinks we're crazy to think any parent would go back to the Dark Ages and deal with soaking and washing soiled diapers. I was just wondering how much business this company does, cause I gotta admit, cleaning diapers doesn't sound like fun to me either."

"Well, apparently there are people—environmentalists mostly, who go this route. My contact at Cloth-Is-Best sent me a complimentary start-up set after we launched the website. I considered cloth because of the cost savings, but the day care requires disposables so I couldn't use them there, even if I wanted to. I might try them on weekends, but I don't relish the idea of cleaning them. I doubt the babies care one way or another, so long as they're dry and comfy."

"Speaking of babies..." Bradley looked at her quizzically, "how're things going?"

"I have an ultrasound today...I'm excited, but nervous and scared too," Janelle wondered why she found him so easy to talk to. Last week, when the rumors started, Janelle vowed not to get too friendly with Bradley. Unfortunately, that was a promise she was finding difficult to keep.

"Don't be scared," he said. Then, looking at her wistfully, he added, "I remember when Beverly had an ultrasound. It was incredible. You know, Beverly was never more beautiful to me than when she was pregnant. All women have such an amazing radiance when they're pregnant."

Janelle blushed and he quickly looked away. "I really can't believe that when I leave my appointment today, Matt and I will have the first pictures of our baby."

"Take a video tape with you and you might leave with your first home video."

"Really?" Now Janelle was intrigued.

"Yeah. Depending on the lab and who does the ultrasound, some of the machines have a tape deck."

"Did you get a video of your daughter?"

"No, The technician asked if we'd brought a tape, but we didn't because no one told us and the hospital doesn't provide them. I don't know why not. The procedure's not exactly cheap or anything. It wouldn't hurt their profit margin to provide one measly tape to each expecting couple. Anyway, we were really disappointed, so now we tell everyone we know to take one along just in case."

Janelle pulled a sticky note out of her dispenser and wrote "Video Tape" on it, then stuck it on her purse. Even before she was pregnant, she'd always written herself reminder notes and made countless lists, but she found since she'd been pregnant she needed to rely on them more than ever. *I wonder if I'll get my memory back after the baby is born?*

"Let's get started," she said, turning her attention back to work. "But first, give me a few minutes to browse through my inbox. And remember, I need to leave by two, so let's just work until lunch, and then we'll have time to get some of our own stuff done too." Bradley nodded and stepped down the hall to get a refill on his coffee.

Just as Janelle finished her email, her phone rang.

"Hello, Creative Solutions, this is Janelle."

"This is Sandy." Janelle felt her heart begin to race and her face flush.

"Sandy, hi. What's up?"

"What's Matt's number at work?"

"541-1476; is something wrong?"

"No, I just need to talk to him, that's all. Thanks."

"Sure, you're welcome," Janelle said, stunned that Sandy had hung up before delivering the apology Matt was so sure would be forthcoming. She slammed the receiver down and felt her face get even hotter. "You're welcome! Goodbye! Whatever!"

"Ah hem…" Bradley cleared his throat as he came around her office door with a fresh cup of steaming coffee, obviously startled by Janelle's angry outburst. "Is everything all right?" he asked timidly. Janelle wanted to lie, but what was the point, he must have heard her.

"No, *nothing's* all right, Brad. Things are such a mess!"

"Is it something you want to talk about, Janelle? I'm a really good listener."

Ellie always slept fitfully, but on Tuesday night she had awakened around midnight, shaking and sobbing. It was the same bad dream she'd had on and off ever since she could remember. In her recurring nightmare, she was a little girl, probably just six or seven, on vacation at her great-grandpa's farm. She was alone, and for some inexplicable reason wearing her beautiful white first communion dress and happily dancing around on an empty hay wagon. Suddenly a pack of hungry wolves surrounded the wagon. She could still see their murderously cold eyes, saliva dripping from their lolling tongues. She could actually smell the fetid odor of their carnivore breath; feel the air generated by the snapping yellow teeth coming closer with each second. But as always, just as they jumped up onto her platform and closed in for the kill, she awoke.

Numbness usually accompanied the feelings of terror and helplessness in the dream, but eventually Ellie willed herself to awaken more fully. She shuddered and crawled over to Jack's side of their king-size bed to snuggle. Startled by her unexpected presence, he gave a small involuntary snort, then turned and enveloped her in the strong, loving arms that had comforted her for over three decades.

"That hay wagon dream again, babe?" he asked in a husky, sleepy voice.

"Uh huh," she said. "But I don't think it's ever been this vivid. I could almost feel their teeth crunching into my body."

"Oh, honey," Jack said with such sympathy and love that Ellie started to weep. Ellie was positive it was the incident with Frank on Monday that had caused her to have the nightmare and she was sure Jack was thinking the same thing, but they didn't talk, they just held each other. Then somehow, probably from complete exhaustion, they both fell back to sleep.

When the alarm went off again, Ellie awoke—feeling like she had been run over by a hay wagon. Everything hurt, especially her massage-starved upper torso. She stretched out and forced herself from the warm bed. Her recollection of the terrifying dream faded as she slipped into her daily routine.

Jack had asked her at bedtime to make sure she woke him so they could have breakfast together. He was going to the other side of the state to present a session called "Halting the Erosion of Wages and Benefits for Union Members" at the annual American Federation of State, City and

Municipal Employees seminar, and they wouldn't see each other for nearly a week. Ellie was happy and jealous at the same time because as part of the trip, Jack was going to spend some time with their son. Jonah had even arranged for Jack to visit the high school where he was student teaching to "observe" him. Just thinking about Jonah following in her footsteps made Ellie's heart sing. She only hoped he would love teaching as much as she did and would find the same glorious fulfillment and satisfaction in what she called the M&M's of education: managing, motivating, and molding young minds.

As always, Ellie made coffee, showered, brushed her teeth, did her hair and makeup and got dressed as Jack grabbed an extra half hour of sleep. Then, in a half-hearted attempt to improve her cholesterol numbers, she quickly assembled the ingredients for oatmeal and poured Jack a cup of coffee to take to him when she woke him with a kiss. As she filled his mug, she noted the pot was only three-quarters full. This morning she hadn't been able to even wait the three-minute brewing time and had already "stolen" a cup to see her through her morning grooming.

Uncharacteristically, Jack was already awake when Ellie took him the steaming liquid. Her husband liked both his coffee and his beer rich and dark, and she liked to tease that Jack never drank water unless it was perked or brewed.

Jack quickly got ready for his day and joined Ellie at the breakfast table. She divided the cooked cereal into the waiting bowls, sweetening hers with sugar substitute and his with brown sugar and cinnamon. As always, they started the meal with a short prayer and then proceeded to wash down a small mound of vitamins with a glass of tomato juice. For each: one multivitamin—general health maintenance; one complete B complex with added Vitamin C—to fight infections and viruses; two 333 mg calcium with magnesium and zinc added—for strong bones, proper digestion and male prostate maintenance; plus 400 mg folic acid, 1000 mg Flax oil, 400 mg Vitamin E and a low-dose baby aspirin—all for optimum heart and circulatory system function.

Once Frank had watched this ritual and commented they were just "pissing away money" because most of the supplements were uselessly flushed out of the body. But neither Ellie nor Jack had been sick in over a decade, coinciding pretty much with when they had started on the supplements. They had considered that Frank might be right for a change, but decided not to mess with success.

Thinking of Frank made Ellie shudder again. Monday had been one of the worst days of her life. After Frank had left in a fit of self-righteous rage, Helen had been in such a state that Ellie's heart ached for her. Helen blamed the entire situation on Ellie and at one point accused Ellie of starting the fight because she was jealous of Frank spending time with her. Then, abruptly, as she had done on several occasions before, Helen had changed the subject completely and seemed to forget everything that had happened.

Amazed and relieved by the sudden about-face, Jack and Ellie had stayed the rest of the day. They played a good game of cards, with Helen being sharp as a tack and winning the entire jackpot in less than two hours. She happily raked in her jackpot of pennies, nickels and dimes. Jack and Ellie shuddered as she exclaimed, "Aahh, if Frankie could see his mama now...he'd be soooo proud!"

At dinnertime, while Ellie scrounged around for the makings of a passable meal, Carolyn from next door came over. Helen was in the living room and warmly greeted her neighbor when Jack let Carolyn in and then ushered her into the kitchen to talk with Ellie.

Ellie didn't think it a good idea to share the story of Helen's "casino adventure," so she said nothing about it. Carolyn did mention that she and Frank had conversed the day before and she was under the impression that he was staying for a few days. She explained that she just happened to look out the front window earlier and had seen him throw a suitcase into his car and leave. She said she had noticed Ellie's car on the street in front of the house, so she had decided to come over to touch base with her, mainly to get an update on the results of Helen's tests.

Jack was in the living room talking to Helen about the new wildlife print by an amazing local artist named Betsy Popp that he and Ellie had given her mom for Christmas, so Ellie filled Carolyn in on Dr. Randolph's assessment of Helen's condition. Ellie lied then, saying her brother had gotten an emergency phone call from work and had to go home to take care of urgent business. Carolyn seemed to accept Ellie's explanation of Frank's sudden departure and promised to continue to check on Helen and to make sure she was eating and taking her medication.

After Carolyn left, Ellie proceeded to prepare a tasty impromptu meal consisting of canned beef stew she "doctored up" with mushrooms, buttered wide noodles and a blend of frozen cauliflower, broccoli and carrots in cheese sauce. They finished off the rest of the cookies with mint chocolate chip ice cream and chocolate topping for dessert. At 7:30 Helen went to her bedroom and got into her nightgown, announcing it was time for them to go home because she was going to bed. Ellie tucked her mother in and kissed her on the cheek. Five minutes later Helen was fast asleep and Jack and Ellie had taken the opportunity to go to the basement to check the kitchen stove breaker switch. At her suggestion, he put another larger piece of duct tape over the switch and wrote *Danger-Do Not Remove* on it before going back upstairs. Ellie checked one last time on her mother. Helen was snoring loudly so they decided it was safe to leave.

They hashed over the day's events in the car on the way to pick up Jack's truck. Ellie drove and Jack navigated. They had almost slipped into an argument over Frank's outrageous behavior, but Ellie decided it best to be silent and let Jack rave. There wasn't much she could do to soften Jack's anger, and since she knew its source to be the love Jack had for her and his sincere affection for Helen, she let him rant and gesture until his anger dissipated. By the time they were pulling into the club parking lot, Jack had cooled down and was now trying unsuccessfully to assuage Ellie's undeserved guilt about what happened. They had toyed with the idea of stopping for a nightcap somewhere, but decided it was not a good idea and that they should just go back home. Jack pulled into their driveway a full five minutes after Ellie had parked Blackbird in the garage, and since they were both too exhausted to do anything but read the paper, they had gone to bed right after the late-night news.

"Thinking about Frank?" Jack asked when he saw the expression on his wife's face.

"Of course, what else?" Ellie responded. "But let's not talk about it anymore, okay?"

As they finished their oatmeal over chitchat about Jack's trip and his accompanying visit with Jonah, Ellie lost track of time. When she finally looked at the clock, she panicked. "Yikes! It's almost five after seven! I'll go get the goodies I put together for Jonah, and you can finish packing your things after I leave. I really wish I could go with you. Sometimes I miss the kids so much I feel like a part of me is missing."

"Then Janelle Spencer calls, you go see her, and you somehow come back all complete again," he teased.

As usual, just thinking of Janelle brightened Ellie's mood. "Oh, that's a great thought, hon. I'll have to call her and see if we can get together sometime next week when you're out of town."

The look of delight on his wife's face made Jack smile. "I don't quite understand this friendship you have with her, but I'm glad you've got it, Ellie." Then he reached out to hug her goodbye. Suddenly, a thought seemed to strike and he grew serious. "Just be careful to keep this friendship thing kinda low-key, Ellie. It's possible her family may misunderstand your relationship."

"What on earth does that mean?" Ellie replied, once again melting into the embrace of the only man she had ever loved. She was already looking forward to the next time they would enjoy the almost sacred ritual of entwining their bodies and souls in pleasure-filled moments celebrating how deeply fulfilling long-married love can be.

"It's just that you act sometimes like she's your daughter, and when women are involved, feelings can definitely be…complicated. Janelle's real mother or even, for that matter, Janelle's mother-in-law…could get jealous or something." Ellie looked at Jack with a mixture of surprise and bewilderment, wondering where on earth this unlikely observation had originated.

"Don't look at me like I've lost it, Ellie. I've listened to my share of talk radio, you know."

Ellie responded now by laughing out loud. "Now that's as far-fetched as it can get. Besides, you know I've always maintained that no one can ever have too many people love you." Then she added, "I'll always love you, no matter what."

Jack repeated, "I'll always love you too, no matter what." Then he was laughing and kissing his wife goodbye.

"And speaking of love," she said as she reluctantly disengaged herself from Jack's embrace, "I'd love to stay right here, but my seventh grade darlings await me. I won't get to school as early as usual today, but who cares?" She put on her jacket and picked up her book bag, her briefcase, her lunch and her purse.

"You do, Ellie, so get going. I'll just have to survive the next week without you, your great cooking, and your great loving," Jack said with a twinkle in his eye as he shooed her toward the door.

"You know how time flies when you're having fun. I love you, and don't forget to tell Jonah I love him and miss him." Ellie replied with a big smile. "You'll be home before you know it. Well…back to the salt mines," she said in jest as she closed the door behind her.

CHAPTER 16

Sunday, April 6th

At 3:06 in the morning, Janelle finally gave up. She never slept well in hotels, and without Matt, it was even harder. She was exhausted but tossing and turning was getting old. She turned on the wall-mounted lamp next to the bed, squinting until her eyes adjusted, and then reached over to retrieve the ultrasound pictures from the nightstand. She rubbed her growing belly as she examined the grainy photos.

"Hi, baby. Mommy can't sleep. I can't get comfortable. Are you?" The soft white skeleton in the pictures seemed to resonate a serenity Janelle wished she could feel as her thoughts drifted back to Wednesday afternoon. She had arrived home from work a little after two, and Matt was just getting out of the shower. She could hear him whistling as she entered the master bedroom.

"Hi, beautiful," he said cheerfully. "Mom said she called you at work. Feeling better now?"

"No, why would that make me feel better? She only called to get your work number."

On his way into the walk-in closet, Matt stopped in his tracks and turned on his heel. "You're kidding, right? You mean you guys didn't make up?"

Janelle laughed. "Now you're kidding, right?"

"Seriously, Janelle, what did she say when she called?"

"Matt, we were on the phone for less than twenty seconds. She asked for your number at work. I gave it to her and asked if there was anything wrong, hoping she would want to talk, but she said no, she just needed to talk to you. That was it. I was so upset I was a blubbering idiot afterward to Brad...Bradley. Believe me, with that and leaving early, my day wasn't very productive."

"That just doesn't make any sense, Janelle. She apologized to me for the other night, and when I asked her if she talked to you, she said she called you at work."

"Well, that's true. She did call me and she did talk."

"Here I was thinking all day that things were patched up between you two." Matt had tenderly drawn her in for a hug. Needless to say, one thing led to another, and they were almost late for her appointment.

Janelle smiled, remembering how she had surprised herself by actually relaxing and giving in to Matt's spontaneous desire. "Your Daddy," Janelle said to the white shape on the ultrasound picture as she recalled how tenderly he had made love to her, "is very good at alleviating stress, but your grandmother is just the opposite. She's forever saying I'm gaining too much weight and the doctor says I'm not gaining enough. That sure puts Mommy in a tough spot. What do you think, sweetie?"

She knew there was no question as to whom she should listen to, but it helped to talk to the baby. Janelle carefully examined the picture that showed its profile, trying to decide if the baby would have Matt's nose or hers. Her mother had concluded it was definitely the Spencer nose.

Thinking of Claire, Janelle drifted back once more to Wednesday. As promised, Janelle had called her mother on her cell phone after the ultrasound, and Claire had begged them to come over before they went home.

"Please, please, please! You have pictures of my first grandchild! Janelle, please? You have to stop."

"Okay, okay, we'll be there in a little bit, Mom. Calm down," Janelle said, amused by her mother's enthusiasm and excited to share the experience.

"Good, but hurry up. I'll be waiting!"

"My mom's so funny," Janelle said after hanging up. "She's really excited to see these pictures. She'll probably wet her pants when we pop this tape into the VCR!"

"Yeah. It's so cool that we got that. I'm even excited to watch it again. Make sure you thank that guy..."

"Bradley...Brad," Janelle said, using the abbreviated name as he had instructed and feeling grateful for his advice about taping the ultrasound.

"Yeah, Bradley, make sure you thank him for telling you about the tape."

"I will. Hey, we can't stay at Mom's long. I have to start packing for the seminar, there's laundry to finish, and I want to get on the computer to scan the ultrasounds. I told Ellie I'd email them and I should also send a set to Cassie. By the way, is it okay if I invite Ellie to meet me for dinner next week?"

"Sure. Ah, Janelle..." Matt hesitated before speaking again, "ah, could you email them to my mom too?" Janelle could see the pain in his eyes and knew it came from the fact that they weren't going to be visiting Sandy to show off the first pictures of her grandchild.

Janelle had to say it. "Matt, should we just go see her? I'll apologize for the mess I made at Easter and we can put this all behind us."

"No, Janelle, my mom owes you the apology. That's all there's to it. If she can't figure that out, then I guess she won't see us, or the baby."

"Whatever you say," Janelle replied. She was partly glad that Matt felt that way, and partly disappointed because she was sick of waiting for Sandy to make the first move. "But instead of me emailing her the pictures, why don't I print a copy and leave it with you this weekend in case you see her?"

Matt nodded in agreement as they turned into Claire's driveway. Claire came running out in her stocking feet, her face radiating with excitement.

"Mom, we're coming in...you shouldn't be outside without shoes."

"Don't tell me what to do, Janelle. I want to see my grandchild. Where are the pictures?" Claire grabbed them from Janelle's hand as they headed into the house. She oohed and aahed over the photos, but when Matt discretely put the tape in the VCR and pressed play, something happened that

Janelle knew was rare; her mother was speechless and tears rolled softly down her cheeks.

They watched the five-minute video three times. After the first time, Claire babbled, "There wasn't any of this amazing technology when I was pregnant." After the second time, she said, "Oh, I feel like I noticed stuff this time that I missed before. Let's watch it again!" On the third time, she decided the baby was going to have Matt's nose, which was a bit longer and thinner than Janelle's little button nose.

"I wonder why I can't tell," Claire hinted openly, "if it's a boy or girl."

"You know we want it to be a surprise, Mom," Janelle responded, "so we asked the sonographer to avoid the groin area completely."

Remembering again how Claire had smiled broadly to hide her obvious disappointment, Janelle shifted around, trying one last time to find a comfortable sleeping position on the sagging hotel mattress. "No dice, little baby," she finally said aloud. "Well, if I can't sleep, I might just as well do something useful." She dug around in her overnight bag for her pregnancy journal, found a pen and began to write.

❧

April 6th
Dear Baby,

We had our ultrasound and you are adorable! The most amazing part was when you started sucking or chewing. The doc said you're about ten inches long and weigh less than a pound, but we saw all your fingers and toes and your heart looks so strong!

You're due to make your appearance into the world around July 20th, but I wonder if the fireworks on the Fourth might scare you into coming sooner? I signed your Daddy and me up for a massage class because my back is really sore and I want him to learn how to give me a massage without hurting you.

By the way, your nursery is all decorated and it's gorgeous. The only thing it needs now is YOU! ❧

As she signed *Love, Mommy,* the words started to blur and dance on the page. It was 4:00 now and she was beyond exhaustion. She set the journal down on the nightstand, pulled the lightweight hotel blanket up under her chin, and finally fell off to sleep.

At 7:30, the phone next to her head began its annoying clatter. It rang three times before she groggily lifted the receiver a few inches, then noisily let it drop back into the cradle. *Jeez…why do the stupid voices on wake up calls have to be so damn chipper? "Good morning! This is your seven-thirty wake-up call. Thank you for staying with us. Have a great day!" Why not a soothing voice, "Good Morning Sleepyhead, we know you're tired so we'll let you sleep a little longer and call you back in ten minutes."*

Janelle wanted to snuggle a little longer, but she only had a half-hour to get ready. Her normal efficient morning routine was completely upset due to how bruised and tender her entire body felt. She forced herself out of bed and into the shower, hoping the last session would end early so she could just go home.

"Housekeeping," Larry said in a high-pitched female voice. Janelle could hear Bradley chuckling as she answered.

"Hi, guys, I should've set an earlier wake-up call. I didn't sleep very well…I ache even more after dancing last night." She looked sheepishly at Bradley who just grinned. He had managed to drag her out onto the dance floor, in spite of her protests, determined to get her out of her mother-in-law funk.

"I'm not quite ready," she added, pointing to her freshly scrubbed face and wet, tangled hair. She saw embarrassment register on their faces, surmising their discomfort was a reaction to seeing her "in the rough" for the first time ever.

"Oh, um, we'll just go check out and meet you down in the breakfast room," Larry said politely. "We'll wait to take the bags out to the SUV until after we eat, okay?"

"Great. Thanks, guys. I'll hurry; I promise." Even as Janelle closed the door, she wondered how she could possibly get ready in such a short time. She hated to rush, but by 8:15 she was walking into the dining room, wearing a very flattering ankle-length navy blue denim dress and sandals. She'd managed to twist her hair up, holding it in place with a sapphire-blue clip that matched her eyes. Her makeup was understated but made her look very put-together. Bradley smiled appreciatively, and she blushed beet-red when he complimented her. They made small talk as she ate a light breakfast while Larry went to get the vehicle.

Both men accompanied her to the wrap-up session, which ended early as Janelle had hoped. Even the instructor seemed ready to be done with hotel living—mentioning several times how much he was looking forward to seeing his family and sleeping in his own bed tonight. Janelle couldn't agree more. She hadn't ever felt so tired in her life, and the persistent headache that had plagued her on and off for days was definitely *on* today.

The two-hour ride home seemed to take forever. She sat in the back seat while Larry and Bradley sat up front, discussing the seminar and other work-related topics. She contributed just enough to be polite, but was really preoccupied with thoughts of Matt and the baby. *It'll be so nice to get home to Matt…and our king-size bed is such a luxury; I don't stop often enough to appreciate all I have.*

On a whim, she pressed firmly on the right side of her stomach, hoping to identify the baby's body part that was wedged tightly under her rib cage. The baby responded by moving! Janelle applied pressure to various places on her belly and the baby responded each time, sometimes kicking hard. She wasn't able to determine the weapon of choice, perhaps a heel or a knee, but a few times the movement was so dramatic she could only imagine the baby doing a compete somersault in her womb. *If only Matt could feel this…I hope the baby's this active when I get home!*

Even though they didn't know the baby's gender and hadn't decided on a name yet, they were no longer just Matt and Janelle. They were Matt, Janelle and the baby; they were a family. Tears welled up in her eyes as she thought about that, but she quickly dabbed them away so Larry wouldn't spot her in his rear view mirror and ask if she was okay.

Larry pulled into the Creative Solutions parking lot as his overhead console clock read 12:54. Due to the session ending early, skipping lunch—a decision Janelle was beginning to regret as she felt nauseous and a little wobbly—and her boss's great confidence in his radar detector, they arrived an hour earlier than expected. Larry dropped his passengers and their luggage off in the otherwise deserted parking lot. "See you tomorrow," he said as he drove away.

Don't remind me. Tomorrow's Monday. Talk about a short weekend.

"Need some help?" Bradley asked as she started to retrieve her luggage.

"Sure, thanks." *I can do it myself but why turn down the help? Go ahead pamper me, I'm pregnant!*

"There you go; you're all set," he said after securing her small overnight bag and overstuffed duffel bag and closing her car's trunk. "Guess neither of us knows how to pack light," he teased.

Janelle smiled sweetly and thanked him, then unlocked the car and heaved her purse onto the worn and faded passenger seat, already feeling more at home here than she had at the pricey hotel. She got in and fastened her seatbelt, automatically pulling out more belt than she needed, then gently releasing the slack to rest under her growing waistline.

"I wonder if Matt had a breakthrough with Sandy while I was gone," she said out loud as she fumbled with her keys. She glanced over to make sure Bradley hadn't seen her talking to herself, but he was too busy rearranging things in his hatchback. Janelle gathered he wasn't any too happy because he tossed things this way and that to make room for his luggage and the new high-tech computer he'd bought at the seminar.

Janelle slid her transmission into reverse and continued to watch Bradley fight with the large white cardboard box. She was just going to get out to help him when she heard, and felt, her car backfire. Startled, she screamed and then yelled, "Oh my God, what the hell..." Before she realized what was happening, her entire car was enveloped in acrid, thick black smoke. In her panic, she gulped in several big breaths of the toxic air. She began coughing and retching from the fumes as her empty stomach convulsed from the smell. Instinctively, she closed her eyes against the smoke and somehow shifted the car into park. Blindly groping for the door handle, using all the strength she could muster, she pushed the door open and fell out onto the cement. "Oh my God," she cried out as the fresh air hit her face. "Please...please don't let anything happen to my baby!"

Still retching, she tried to force herself up as she heard Bradley shouting and running toward her, but she couldn't see anything. Then she felt him pulling her up and dragging her away from the car to safety.

With Jack gone all weekend, Ellie had managed to get so much done. She had spent Friday night cleaning. First, she put on old comfy sweats, opened all the windows to let in the fresh April breezes, and assembled all her cleaning supplies. Then she stacked several of her favorite Broadway musical soundtracks on the CD player. As always, she had sung along to *South Pacific* as she cleaned her bathroom. "I'm gonna wash that man right outa my hair," she sang, only this time she thought of Frank as she sprayed cleaner on the commode in a swoosh of disinfectant foam. *I wish getting rid of you was this easy...hmmm...kind of ironic...I'm cleaning the toilet and wishing I could flush you down and watch you disappear like the little turd you are,* she mused with a grim smile as she wiped away the germs and flushed the toilet.

Feeling only slightly guilty for having such destructive daydreams, Ellie lukewarmly regretted the nasty things she was working over in her mind, forcing herself to think of something else before thoughts of Frank ruined her evening. No one in the family had heard from him in a week and that was fine with her. She finished the bathrooms in a flourish and then vacuumed the living room and bedroom carpets to

West Side Story, moving her vacuum back and forth as she sang, "Someday there'll be a new world, a world of shining hope for you and me," all the while thinking of how much she needed the massage she had rescheduled for Saturday.

Four hours later, her entire house was gleaming and smelling like vanilla from the candles burning on the polished oak coffee table. She was glad she didn't have to do a thing in the spare bedrooms that her children still considered theirs, but she did sit on the bed in each room for a few moments to soak up a bit of family nostalgia provided by the left-behind mementos of her daughter and son still lingering there. She was just leaving Jonah's room when she heard the CD changer click and the *Fiddler on the Roof* show tune, *Sunrise, Sunset*, began playing. She never sang the lyrics without wanting to shed a tear or two—the words a poignant reminder of how quickly children grow up. "Is this the little girl I carried...Is this my little boy at play...I don't remember growing older...when did they? When did she get to be a beauty? When did he grow to be this tall? Wasn't it yesterday when they were small?"

Suddenly she had realized something else. Janelle's baby would soon be starting its life journey while Helen was in the process of ending hers. *Time passes so quickly; when we're young we think we have all the time in the world, then before we know it our children are grown and leave home...our parents get old...heck...we get old...where does the time go?*

Refusing to let herself become melancholy, she grabbed her favorite pillow and blanket and reclined on the living room sofa to watch her favorite teacher-movie for the fourth time. In the middle of the film, sometime around midnight, she fell asleep on the couch and stayed there, not opening her eyes until the next morning.

By mid-morning she was luxuriating in the long overdue full-body massage. Her masseuse remarked three times that she seemed extremely tight—forcing her to admit it was high-time she stop by the health club for the free tour. An hour later she headed directly there. After a quick orientation,

Ellie decided to take out a trial membership. Doing something just for her left her feeling a little guilty. *What is so wrong with being good to yourself? You read about it, you tell others to do it, and yet you can't do it yourself.*

After an early lunch of a grilled chicken sandwich without mayo, a garden salad with fat free dressing, and a diet soda, Ellie went shopping for new workout clothes at the mall. She bought cross trainers at a discount shoe store and then spent the rest of the afternoon window-shopping. For supper, she made herself a package of low-fat microwave popcorn to munch on as she watched a country music channel.

Afterward, she made several phone calls to the people she loved. She tried Jonah's apartment; no answer. She called Rebecca's cell because she was in New York on business, but only got her voice mail. She called Jack's room at his hotel, and his cell phone, but he didn't pick up either so she assumed he was out for dinner with his fellow union staffers. She tried Janelle, Matt answered, reminding her that she was out of town for work. Embarrassed to have forgotten Janelle's plans, she did however, remember to compliment Matt on the ultrasound pictures of baby Spencer. She asked him to tell Janelle that she was looking forward to their dinner on Tuesday night. Matt promised to deliver the message.

Ellie decided to try and reach Josie one more time—she had called her sister every night for the past week to tell her about what she now referred to as the "Frankie Fiasco," but Josie had not returned any of her calls. It mystified and annoyed Ellie that Josie could be so unconcerned about something as significant as Frank's taking advantage of their mother, but, short of driving to Chicago to meet with her sister face to face, there was nothing much she could do.

Finally, after numerous unsuccessful attempts to reach people, Ellie was able to connect directly with Helen to remind her to be ready on time to go to Mass Sunday morning.

Then she scanned all one hundred fifty channels they paid forty-five dollars for each month, noting with disgust that there was nothing of interest so she read her *WEAC Journal* before going to bed right after the local news.

Up with the birds and feeling wonderfully refreshed on Sunday morning after two consecutive good nights of sleep, Ellie finished her schoolwork in no time at all. She showered and was amazed when she managed to fit into a dress she hadn't worn in several years. *I feel thinner already! Hmmm...you're actually starting to look better too, aren't you?* It was a chilly, rainy morning, but she was in such a good mood that she sang show tunes as loud as she could as she drove to spend the entire day with her mother.

As soon as she arrived, Helen began complaining that she had wanted to bake cookies, but her stove wasn't working. Ellie just smiled and promised that Jack would check it out next weekend, suggesting that Helen use her new microwave in the meantime. This seemed acceptable and Ellie changed the subject, carefully probing to see if her mother had heard from Frank. Helen was vague, so Ellie took that as a no and left it at that.

After Mass, they went out to breakfast, then to a folk music concert. Helen even clapped and sang, enjoying herself immensely. Mother and daughter ended the day with a light supper and Ellie felt content as she drove back home.

This was a good day. Mom was almost her old self. It must be Sundays—they've always been her favorite day. I'll have to tell Janelle Tuesday that I'm handling things just fine. With everything else that's happening in her life, it will give her one less thing to worry about. Thank you God, for deciding to give us all a day off...and what an appropriate name...Sun—day!

CHAPTER 17

Janelle spent Sunday afternoon and evening in the hospital. All her tests were negative so she was released after supper and sent home to rest. She went right to bed, not awakening until almost noon on Monday. Insanely, she dreamed about work. She couldn't bear to think of what her desk would look like on Tuesday. She had left early for the seminar on Friday and Dr. Felding's orders were emphatic. "No work tomorrow. Stay home and rest," adding, "aside from the accidents that keep landing you in the hospital, your blood pressure is up and you're still not gaining enough weight. You can go back to work Tuesday, but I don't want to see you back here until the baby is ready to be born."

As the mild sedative Dr. Felding had prescribed began to wear off, Janelle woke to find Matt standing by her bed.

"Good morning, babe. I love you so much," Matt said, kissing her hand.

"Matt, are you *sure* the baby's all right?" she asked him for the tenth time.

"Yes, Dr. Felding said so and we have to believe him," he assured her once again. "But YOU gave us quite a scare."

"This time I scared myself. You wouldn't believe how the smoke from the car blinded me. I felt like I was suffocating, and I was throwing up. I could hear Bradley running toward me, but I couldn't see a thing..."

"You passed out?"

"No...I never lost consciousness. Ask Bradley. I just couldn't see. Then I started worrying about the baby."

Janelle's head still ached slightly and her breath caught as she remembered her panic.

"Did you know Bradley called me at home once you were admitted?" Matt asked. Janelle shook her head. "Well, he said that on the way to the hospital you were kinda out of it so I figured that meant you fainted."

Aside from the day her desk fell on her, Janelle had never lost consciousness. She had often wondered what it would feel like to actually pass out ever since she watched Charlie Joslin faint during their third grade Christmas recital. They had been singing *Little Drummer Boy* when out of the corner of her eye she saw Charlie weave back and forth, then fall backwards off the top riser. Luckily, he had landed on the thick blue gym mats and hadn't been hurt.

"I wish I would've fainted, Matt. I think it would've been better than thinking I was going blind."

"Well, it's probably good that you didn't pass out; I doubt it would be good for the baby. Make sure you tell Dr. Felding about what's going on with your eyes," he instructed. Then he added, "I called and ordered our favorite subs—they should be ready now so I'm going to pick them up. I won't be gone long, hon...by the way...my mom and yours are in the living room. Is it okay if I send them in?"

"Your mom's here?" Janelle's voice was quivering.

"Yes, she's worried sick about you."

"She is? You didn't tell her she had to apologize..."

"Actually it was kinda funny. Mom was there when Dr. Felding came to tell me you were gonna be okay, and to make sure you take it easy...*then* he asked me if you're eating right because you hadn't been gaining enough weight!"

"And that made her common sense kick in?"

"That, and I told her I wasn't like my dad. I'm not going to leave you or cheat on you if you don't lose all your baby weight after the baby is born. Be nice to her, Janelle, she really does love you. I'll be back in ten minutes."

What happened next came as a complete surprise. Sandy came into the bedroom first and immediately walked over and took Janelle's hand. "I'm so sorry, Janelle. I know I've been awful and I'm going to do my best to be more positive and supportive. Can you ever forgive me?"

Janelle glanced apprehensively at Claire who was standing behind Sandy with an incredulous look on her face, then lifted her arms to offer Sandy a hug.

"Oh, thank you, Janelle! I promise to be less critical if you promise you'll ignore me if I slip, okay? Don't let my problem become your problem."

"Your problem?"

"Yes, I know I have a problem. I shouldn't be so obsessive about my weight but I am. Still, we can't let that hurt you or this little baby..." Sandy gently touched Janelle's tummy.

"I'll second that," Claire said with a look of satisfaction. Janelle was glad her mother was a witness to the scene; it saved her from having to decide how much to tell her later.

They all relaxed a little and Janelle related the entire story once again. Then she attempted to lighten the mood by saying: "Before I was pregnant, all I had to do was look at food and I'd gain weight."

"Well, looking at food isn't good enough, Janelle," her mother said, sternly. "You have to actually eat it."

Janelle was miffed that she was being scolded for no reason. "I'm telling you that I *do* eat, Mom. I'm not sure why I haven't been gaining, but I can assure you it sure isn't because I'm trying to lose weight by starving myself!"

"Did somebody say starving?" Matt asked as he came into the bedroom, followed closely behind by Cassie who carried a large bag of subs in one hand and a six pack of soda in the other. Cassie and Matt had run into each other at the sub shop where Matt had briefly explained what happened. Cassie insisted on coming right over to see Janelle.

"Well, I'm starving, so let's eat," Cassie said, passing around beverages and turkey mozzarella subs.

"Right here...in the bedroom?" Sandy asked. The look on her face was priceless.

"Sure, just like old times, huh, Janelle?" Cassie said with a twinkle in her eye. "Remember when we used to sneak out of high school at noon and eat lunch in your bedroom?"

"I have no idea what you're talking about, Cassie." Janelle grinned at the look on her mother's face as she learned about this decade-old secret. Then she turned to Matt. "Can you bring some folding chairs? We're having a picnic."

"Hmmm...a picnic in the bedroom," Claire said, recovering from her surprise and commandeering the side chair as she sat down with her sandwich. "I love it. We haven't done this since you were a little girl, Janelle."

Sandy daintily took a small bite of her sandwich. "You know, a lot people have lost an enormous amount of weight just eating subs," she observed.

"Mom..." Matt said reprovingly.

"Oops, sorry," Sandy replied, a guilty blush spreading across her face.

"This is yummy," Janelle said, ignoring Sandy's slip and diving into her sandwich. "I can see why Ellie likes this kind."

At the mention of Ellie's name, Matt hit his forehead with his hand. "Janelle, I completely forgot. Ellie called Saturday night while you were gone. She said something about you two getting together tomorrow night?"

"Oh, that's right," Janelle replied. "First, we need to find a new car...I'll call her to reschedule...she'll understand."

When their impromptu picnic was over, Claire and Sandy left to give Cassie and Janelle some time alone.

"Looks like I missed something major...Sandy was downright pleasant, and even she and your mom seem to be getting along."

"Amazing, huh? Sandy apologized and I feel like a weight's been lifted now that we're talking again."

"Pardon the pun, right?" Cassie said giggling.

"Too funny..." Janelle grinned. "Anyway, Mom and Sandy must've cleared the air."

"You're kidding! Really?"

"Unbelievable, isn't it? They're even working out the shower details together."

"So did you start a list for the shower?"

"I plan to start this afternoon, but I still have this darn headache..." Janelle dug for the crumbs in the bottom of her chips bag. "I just need to look up a few addresses. Good thing I only have to provide names of friends and co-workers. Ellie Reed will be at the top of my list—I can't believe I forgot to tell her I was pregnant. I'm sure looking forward to getting my brain back once the baby's born."

"You going to register somewhere? They'll want to put that in the invitations," Cassie advised.

"Yes, I'm making Matt go with me. He hated doing it for our wedding, but I don't care. This'll be more fun."

"I'll have to call your mom and see if I can help."

"By the way...how are *you* doing, Cass?" Janelle asked. "You're such a good friend...this has to be hard for you."

"It's a little tough..." Cassie said, closing her eyes for a moment, "but I'm thinking positively and my day will come...I know it will."

Ellie opened her classroom door Monday morning and went straight to work. She had come in early to take down the Jack London bulletin board and put up her colorful Elements of Poetry display. She loved teaching poetry and remembered Luanne Johnson's remark from *My Posse Don't Do Homework:* "Poetry makes exceptional use of words; words are thoughts and we can't think without them." *I wish I'd written that,* she thought as she lovingly removed the large letters J-A-C-K L-O-N-D-O-N from the tack board.

As she replaced the old items with the new, it occurred to her that it was already the fourth quarter, her favorite time of the school year...not because summer vacation was coming soon...because her seventh graders were more mature now, acting more grown up, and capable of much deeper thought processing as almost all of them had now passed from concrete into operational thinking. Ellie often said that if she ran the educational system in America, she would promote kids to the next grade level in the spring, when nature decreed that kids were a year older and ready for a new challenge, not after Labor Day, as was the custom. The current system made no sense to her, especially in light of the fact that it was based on a tradition dictated by an agricultural economy that no longer existed, even in Wisconsin.

The poetry bulletin board was almost complete when she was interrupted by a sharp knock on her already open door. She turned as Tom said, "I just found out that Mrs. Nielsen will be at the school board meeting tonight. I have an idea about what she'll say; just thought you might want to be there." Ellie looked at him with a quizzical expression and he continued, "She's supposedly going to present a copy of her official complaint against you."

"But, Tom, why would they put her on the agenda? Shouldn't personnel issues be dealt with in private?"

"Yeah, sure, normally, but she can speak about anything she wants to during the public portion of the meeting."

"Who told you about this, Tom?"

"Henley," he said sheepishly. "Last Friday...he was bragging that his mother was going public with her complaints about you. He told me she was going to see that this was your last year of, as he called it, torturing kids. I didn't tell you because I didn't want to ruin your weekend."

"Gee, that was thoughtful," Ellie said with a touch of sarcasm. "And just what *did* you tell him?"

"I said that school board policy prohibits citizens from addressing a concern unless it's on the agenda; however, anyone can talk during the public portion of the meeting."

"I see. You just *had* to tell him that."

"Of course, because it's the truth. Now don't go blaming me; you're the one she's got the complaint against."

"Isn't there any way to stop this?"

"No, the board president said our hands are tied."

"Well, that's great, because the local papers love this kind of stuff. They'll put the story on the front page, destroy my reputation and then later when my exoneration comes, they'll bury the story on page eight in tiny typeface."

"Is it necessary to paint the worst case scenario, Ellie?"

She ignored his question. "And of course Mrs. Nielsen will do interviews, just in case the television stations pick up on the story," Ellie went on with unrestrained bitterness. "What's even worse is I can't defend myself. The attorney told me I can't talk to anyone about this or I could potentially lose the right to their free representation."

"Now don't let this unfortunate situation interfere with your classroom performance," Tom warned her as he walked out the door. "We don't want more ripples in the pool," he said in an ominous tone.

"What is that supposed to mean?" she called after him as he hurried down the corridor. Ellie grew brazen. She had never taken this tone with a superior before in her life, but now her anger and frustration made her reckless. "It just so happens I have a meeting with my attorney after school today," she spat out. "Hopefully my lawyer can do something to keep this crazy woman from doing a complete character assassination on me. It doesn't sound like anyone else around here wants to help!" He stopped...held up his hand; then shaking his head, simply continued on his way.

Ellie's dinner meeting with her WEAC counsel, Stacey Fletcher, made her feel a immensely better. Stacey was not only highly intelligent, she was stunning—tall and beautiful with intricate corn-row braids wound tightly and pulled back to show off her perfect ebony skin and shining, heavily-lashed dark eyes. Being from a very under-represented ethnic minority in east central Wisconsin, she drew a few stares, but everyone was polite and friendly. Both women ordered a diet soda and the chef salad. Ten minutes after ordering, they were presented with a gigantic platter heaped high with fresh greens, ham, turkey, hard-cooked egg, cheese, tomatoes and croutons and a gravy bowl full of peppercorn ranch dressing.

A friend had once told Ellie, an empathetic and active listener, that she had a cup-of-coffee-face and people just naturally trusted her. This gave her free-range to ask personal questions in a genuinely innocent manner that flattered rather than offended.

Upon embarking on just such a conversation during the meal, the two women were amazed to discover that Stacey and Rebecca had both not only attended UW-Madison Law

School, but actually knew each other. They had even been casual friends until graduation took them on their separate ways. Stacey told a few stories about wild parties Rebecca had attended during law school, information Rebecca had conveniently forgotten to share with her mother. She asked for Rebecca's phone number and said she planned to reconnect and hopefully reactivate their friendship. Stacey's wit helped the knot that had been sitting in her stomach all day relax a little.

When the check came, Ellie insisted on paying. Stacey objected, but when Ellie told her the entire amount, including a very generous tip, came to fifteen dollars, she acquiesced, remarking that in her home town of Chicago their bill would have been three times that much.

Ellie and Stacey left the warmth of the family restaurant and drove to the board office. Stacey cautioned Ellie not to react to things Mrs. Nielsen might say, to let her do the talking. "That way it won't sound like a cat fight and hopefully the newspaper reporter will see the woman is a nut case," she said optimistically.

A few people were already seated when Ellie and Stacey entered and took chairs in the back. Tom came in right behind them so Ellie introduced them. Tom had quite an eye for the ladies and could not keep his eyes off Stacey.

A few minutes before the meeting was to begin, Tom caught Ellie's attention and pointed——Mrs. Nielsen had arrived. Ellie had never met the woman so she wasn't sure what to expect. What she saw was an obese, dishwater blonde, clad in a sweatshirt and tight-fitting blue jeans that made her rear look "two ax-handles wide" as Ellie's Grandpa Jackson might have said. She was wearing no makeup, and it looked as though she hadn't combed her hair. When Mrs. Nielsen sat down at the end of the row of folding chairs, Ellie's face puckered with disgust. *The woman's jeans are too short and her pink socks are supposed to be white...her broken-down running shoes are full of grass stains...If I wasn't the object of the woman's witch-hunt, I'd feel sorry for her.*

As usual, at exactly 7:00 the meeting was called to order with the reading of minutes and routine reports. When the president called for "items from the audience," Mrs. Nielsen heaved herself up with a grunting effort and loudly cleared her throat. She began reading from a sheet of paper on a clipboard, her tone high-pitched, making her voice sound slightly hysterical. She was obviously nervous, but self-righteous, like a woman on a holy pilgrimage who was going to complete her mission no matter what.

"My name is EvaLynne Nielsen and I live at 1211 Oak Street. I am here tonight to present a formal complaint against Ms. Eleanor Reed, a seventh grade teacher at the middle school. During the past three months, Ms. Reed has been my son Henley's English teacher, if you can call her that." Ellie grimaced as she saw the reporter, who had almost fallen asleep, sit up and turn on his tape recorder.

"My son tells me that their class spent January and early February 'studying'——if you can call it that——the elements of drama, including a play called *David and Goliath*. Could you explain why a public school teacher is teaching Bible stories? My son also tells me she showed the class a scene from a violent gang movie called *West Side Story*. Of what possible use is this material to impressionable seventh graders?"

Ellie felt her face redden as Mrs. Nielsen went on. "After six weeks of meaningless junk, Henley says they spent late February and March on some ridiculous unit on dog mushing in Alaska. As if any of these kids care about some stupid dogs running a thousand miles pulling a sled." Ellie was getting angry now, appalled that the school board president, whose own three daughters had thrived on those high interest, skill-building units, was letting Mrs. Nielsen trash the seventh grade curriculum she had spent two decades perfecting. Incensed, she started to rise to defend herself, but Stacey put a beautifully manicured hand on her trembling shoulder and Ellie managed to hold steady.

"And if all this is not enough to show Mrs. Reed's total incompetence, she doesn't have make-up work ready when a parent requests it. She talks about inappropriate things in class and calls students stupid and lazy. She yells at them when they come back after being absent, forcing them to miss lunch to come to her room to make up work. Yes! She actually yells at kids for being sick!" Her voice rose and cracked, and she took a deep breath before continuing.

"In conclusion, Eleanor Reed is obviously unfit to be a teacher. I wasn't there, but I know for a fact she told the parents at Open House last September that she doesn't believe in praise or rewards. She obviously prefers to rely on threats and intimidation as motivational tools..."

"Mrs. Nielsen," the school board president interrupted in a calm voice, "we can see that you have some concerns about Mrs. Reed's instruction methods and curriculum choices. This is a serious matter that I assure you will be taken up at a future meeting." The woman started to speak again, but he held his hand up to stop her. "The board has noted your remarks, Mrs. Nielsen. Thank you." Reluctantly, she sat down, giving Ellie a look of self-satisfied triumph.

The president then went on with the meeting. "Does anyone else wish to speak?"

Stacey, who had been taking notes during Mrs. Nielsen's tirade, rose and spoke, her voice clear, her inflection strong and her diction perfect. "My name is Stacey Fletcher and I am Mrs. Reed's legal counsel. First, we wish to voice strong objections to the public airing of what one might call Mrs. Nielsen's dirty laundry. Mrs. Reed has been a hard-working, effective educator in this district for over three decades. We certainly wish to speak to Mrs. Nielsen's concerns. Please let us know when the next session will be held so that we may adequately prepare our rebuttal."

Ellie saw the reporter turn off his recorder and slip out of the room. Something in the way he glanced at her as he left made her knees weak. *Everyone knows his newspaper and a local television station are owned by the same company and often share "human interest" stories. Dear God, don't let this story be on the ten o'clock news.*

As the board took a five-minute recess before beginning its previously published agenda, Stacey and Ellie decided they had stayed long enough. Ellie felt as if she'd been kicked in the gut but held her head high as they left the room.

"Well, the worst part is over...and you did a great job of holding yourself together in there," Stacey said as they walked along in the cool evening air. "My advice is not to discuss this with anyone, except your husband, of course. It'll be hard to keep quiet, but it's very important...especially to the press— they can, and often do, misconstrue things. If you have to talk to someone, call me," Stacey said firmly. "It's going to take a while, but we'll settle this by the end of the year."

"Part of me is so angry and part of me is completely embarrassed...will my exoneration be public, like the flogging I just took?"

"I'll do my best," Stacey promised. "I know how much a teacher's reputation means in a community like this."

"I hope so because teaching isn't just a career for me— it's a huge part of my life, Stacey. I'm fifty-five years old... only three years away from retirement. I can't go out on this sour note. It'd destroy me."

"Then trust me, Ellie. I specialize in these icky-sticky cases. Consider me your guardian angel of defense."

"Deal," Ellie said, hugging the young woman before sending Stacey off with a brave smile and wave. As she walked the block back to where she had parked Blackbird, her shoulders slumped and her heart ached. *God...it was just a few hours ago that I was feeling so great about life...how can a day which started out with such promise end on such a negative note?* As she shook her head in dismay, she caught sight of well-known bumper sticker on the car near Blackbird—"Life's a bitch and then you die." *Well, that's just a little ironic isn't it? No, Mrs. EvaLynne Nielsen...you are the bitch...not life!*

The first thing Ellie did when she got home was check messages on the answering machine. There was only one.

> Hi Ellie, Janelle. I won't go into details, but my car died so Matt and I have to go car shopping tomorrow night. Can we reschedule for next Tuesday? Let me know. Talk to you soon! Bye!

Ellie quickly checked her wall calendar and penciled in *Janelle–PI–7:00.* Then she called Janelle to confirm. The answering machine picked up after five rings. She left a message, sighing with fatigue as she hung up. Remembering the mail, she walked wearily out to the mailbox by the curb. Sorting through the large stack of junk——mostly credit card applications and colorful advertising pieces, she returned to the kitchen. As Sharon Kelly had suggested, Ellie had routed all of Helen's first-class mail to Ellie's home address. Two letters——one from Frank to her mother and the other from Rebecca's law firm——caused her to raise an eyebrow.

Looking at the letter from Frank, she didn't know if she should open it or not so she put it on the kitchen table. Her bladder was bursting so she took the other envelope into the bathroom with her——curiosity getting the best of her. Ellie was still using the toilet when she tore it open. *What on earth…why would she write on office stationery…* inside she found another smaller envelope and a note that read:

> *Surprise! Happy Anniversary, Mom and Dad.*
> *We love you. Jonah and Rebecca*

Excitedly tearing the smaller envelope open, Ellie discovered five mezzanine seat tickets to a Milwaukee Brewers baseball game. Each ticket had a yellow note attached with a family member's name on it.

> *Dear Mom and Dad,*
>> *We invited the whole family to a baseball outing in honor of your 33rd wedding anniversary on Saturday, April 19th. It's all confirmed with Aunt Josie, Uncle Carl and Uncle Frank who already have their tickets. Let's meet by the statue of Robyn Yount in front of Miller Park at 11:15. We have lunch reservations for 11:30. Please bring Grandma with you.*
>> *LOVE, J and J*
> *P.S. We know how much all of you love the Brewers!*

Ellie's heart, so heavy just minutes before, soared at this unexpected and deeply touching gesture of affection. She knew Helen, who had followed the Milwaukee Brewers faithfully for decades, would be positively thrilled. The mention of Frank in her children's note reminded Ellie that his letter lay unopened on the kitchen table. Unable to resist the temptation, she decided to see what her brother was up to.

Feeling more than a little guilty, Ellie took a sharp cutlery knife, and running it along the flap, opened the envelope carefully, trying to do as little damage as possible so that she could get away with re-sealing it again if necessary. The one-page letter was written on lined notebook paper, exactly the kind Ellie's seventh graders used in school. Frank's scrawl was undisciplined and lazy. It might have been difficult for a layperson to make out some of his words, but Ellie had been reading papers done in marginal penmanship for years and she quickly digested the contents of the letter.

Dear Mom,

Sorry for leaving so fast the other day, but I could see that you were getting upset because of Ellie's negative feelings for me. She's always on my case lately, probably because she's jealous of my close relationship with you. Mom, I hate to ask, but I could sure use a little cash to tide me over until I get a job. When I was home at Easter, I found a book of checks in the desk in the spare room. I know you have strangers like that nosy neighbor coming and going there all the time, so I decided to take them with me for safekeeping.

Anyway, the easiest way for you to send me some money is this: there's a check already written out in the small envelope; just sign it, put it back in the envelope, seal it, and put it out in your mailbox for the postman to pick up. I've already addressed and stamped the envelope to make it easier for you. I know I just asked for money a couple weeks ago, but let's call this a down payment on my future. You know I'll pay you back.

All my love, Frank

P.S. Ellie told me she co-signs your checks now, but you can just write both names. It's your money, Mom!

Ellie was trembling with anger by the time she finished reading. She looked at the check; it was written for thirty-five hundred dollars! Her mind raced. *This has to be illegal... he virtually stole her checks...my brother's a criminal.* Her thoughts turned blood-red, anger rising like a bitter bile in her throat. She sat down at the table and tried to regain control *Breathe...just breathe!* After several moments, she began to calm down. Shaking her head to dispel her desperation and realizing it was getting late, she forced herself to get ready for bed. *I can't even bring myself to watch the news. I wonder if my face will be plastered all over the screen like some kind of criminal? God...what a day...was it just this morning that I was feeling so great?*

Feeling like she needed some kind of sedative before crawling under the covers, Ellie went back to the kitchen to get the anniversary surprise. She took the letter and set it on the nightstand, turned back the hand-made comforter, fluffed up her king-size feather pillows and got into bed. Then she tenderly reread the note, savoring the affection displayed by her children through such a wonderful gesture.

Suddenly it dawned on her that Frank would be at Miller Park on the 19th! She decided she was not going to spoil the occasion by confronting him. *What makes him think he has the right to take advantage of Mom like this! God only knows. No...I won't mention it and ruin the day.* She got out of bed, found the letter still lying on the kitchen table and quickly made a photocopy of it in Jack's home office. Then she carefully refolded it and placed it, along with the smaller envelope, back inside. She managed to re-seal the envelope with such expertise that no one would ever suspect she had opened it. She went back to bed, undecided whether or not to tell Jack about what she had done.

CHAPTER 18

Tuesday, April 15th

Ellie arrived at Paradise Island early so she occupied their favorite tiki hut booth and forced herself to work on the set of questions Stacey had sent. Janelle arrived promptly at seven and squeezed into the seat opposite Ellie.

"You are definitely beginning to show," Ellie said with an approving smile. Janelle had that pregnancy "glow" that made her attractive features even more striking. Ellie also couldn't help but notice that Janelle looked more and more like Claire, who had been in Ellie's English class her first year of teaching. In her mind's eye, she still could see Claire as a teenager—shoulder-length blonde hair, flawless skin, and the same sapphire-blue eyes—a real babe, as Jack would say.

"I know…it's good to finally be showing. My doc thinks I'm a bit behind schedule in the weight gain department. Sorry about canceling last week…hey…check out my new set of wheels…" she pointed to a four-door burgundy sedan in the parking lot. "Like it?"

"It's perfect for a growing family," Ellie replied.

"I know! The problem is Matt's having major Buyer's Remorse. It's more money than he's ever spent on a car, but I want something *safe* and big enough for a family. No more junk cars for me now that we have someone special to protect," Janelle said as she patted her expanding stomach.

"Good for you! You always were the practical one in the finance department. Hey, I don't know about you, but I'm starving. Let's order right away. I'm having the taco salad, a diet soda, and blackberry swirl fat-free yogurt.

"Sounds like something both baby and mama would enjoy," Janelle answered. "But I'll have a milkshake...no sense in eating fat-free at this point."

"Right, you stay here...relax...my treat," Ellie said and went to the counter to order. Linda gave Ellie her change and told her to have a seat; she'd take care of everything so Ellie happily rejoined her young friend.

"Ellie," Janelle started tentatively, "I saw the article in the paper about the school board meeting, *if you can call it that*. Are you okay? Want to talk about it?"

Ellie winced. The paper had covered the ugly details of Mrs. Nielsen's complaint. All Ellie had dutifully said when the reporter called was "no comment," grateful that at least there had been no television coverage. "Yes to both questions. Unfortunately, Stacey...she's my WEAC attorney...says I can't discuss it with anyone. What you read pretty much sums up one side of the issue."

"WEAC? What's that?"

"Wisconsin Education Association Council—my teachers union. Anyway, Stacey and I are preparing our rebuttal for the May meeting. I was working on that when you came in."

"Let me know when the meeting is, Ellie. I want to be there for you."

"Really?" Ellie was deeply touched. Janelle was not political in any sense of the word, and Ellie knew it would most likely be the first school board meeting she had ever attended. "It would make me feel better to know there was some support in the audience."

"I'm also working on another idea, but, like you, I am forbidden to discuss this with anyone at the present time," Janelle said with a secretive grin.

Ellie's curiosity was piqued, but just then the food arrived. They didn't waste any time; neither one had eaten anything since lunch so they savored every spicy bite.

"How are things at work, Janelle?" Ellie asked as they ate.

Janelle still hadn't told Ellie about the car fire, so she went over the whole story.

"Good God!" Ellie exclaimed when Janelle explained that Bradley had pulled her away from her burning car. "You're so lucky someone was there to help."

"Yes, I know, thankfully the baby and I are fine, the only downside is car payments we really didn't need right now," Janelle said. *I shouldn't have waited so long to eat.* Her head was throbbing and Ellie's face looked crooked.

"If it wasn't for these headaches..." Janelle massaged her right temple where the ache always seemed to originate.

"Headaches?"

"They're like sinus headaches, lots of pressure behind my eyes. They come and go. I'm sure they're nothing...really. It mostly happens when I get hungry. I just need to keep something in my stomach."

Despite Janelle's reassurance, Ellie was alarmed. "Could this be related to the car fire or your other accident? I see your stitches are gone."

"Uh huh. They dissolved like they were supposed to, but this area is still tender," she said as she rubbed the thin line of scar tissue on her forehead. "Oh..." she said, deliberately changing the subject, "there's something else I forgot to tell you about. Brad, you know, the guy who rescued me, well...he has this very possessive, jealous wife—Beverly. He lied to her about who was at the seminar with him and now she's on the warpath."

"Wait...wait...you lost me. Start from the beginning."

Janelle decided to give Ellie all the details. "Well, it all started right after Bradley had to learn my job—so he could cover for me when I'm off with the baby. I made an innocent suggestion that he should try contacts instead of his thick black glasses...well...for some reason he decided to also change his hair *and* the way he dressed. Of course everyone in the office had to tease me about my 'influence'...then on Tuesday, when I went back to work after the fire, Beverly came in to have lunch with him. Beth sent her back to my office thinking he was back there," Janelle paused to stir her milkshake and take a long sip.

"Yes?"

"Well...he was with Larry so I made small talk with her. I told her how grateful I was that Bradley had been there and able to take me to the hospital."

"And?"

"Evidently Brad had told Beverly that only men from the office would be going to the seminar and...."

"Oh, oh," Ellie said. "Then what happened?"

"She didn't say much to me, but when they came back from lunch Brad went straight to his office, even though we're supposed to be training. I found him sitting there with his face buried in his hands. When I asked what was wrong, he looked at me with this god-awful expression and said in a choked voice, 'You told her we went to the seminar together...and well... let's just say she's pretty upset.' Jeez Ellie..."

"So-o-o," Ellie said, "what's the big deal?"

"I know this sounds stupid...the thing is I really like Brad...he listened to me when I was upset about Matt's mother and we had a lot of fun at the workshop, especially Saturday night."

Ellie raised her eyebrows.

"The hotel had a lounge band," Janelle explained, "we danced a few times and had a really great time, as *friends*!"

"Be careful, Janelle—my advice is to stay as far away from him as you can," Ellie warned.

"That's easier said than done; we work together. Besides I'm happily married *and* happily pregnant," she said defensively. "Matt thinks the whole thing is insane; *he* trusts me! It's so frustrating because the whole thing makes me feel uncomfortable around Brad."

"Don't let this get to you, Janelle. This is supposed to be the best time of your life. Remember, don't give anyone permission to get in the way of your happiness."

"Thanks, Ellie. You're right. You always say just the right thing," Janelle said, relieved to have Ellie understand. Her headache was finally beginning to subside, and her eyes seemed to be focusing properly again. "And speaking of feeling better, how's your mother?"

"Well, she gave us quite a scare recently," Ellie said and proceeded to fill Janelle in on the "casino adventure" and the subsequent scene with her brother.

"He sounds like a real winner," Janelle said. "Maybe being an only child has its little rewards."

"Good point," Ellie said. Then without knowing why, she confessed, "I did something I'm a little ashamed of, Janelle. I haven't even told Jack about it. I'm afraid of what he'd say."

"Well, sounds like you'd like to confess something."

"You're right...just promise to keep this between us."

"Of course."

"Well, my mother's social worker told me to take over her accounts and have her first class mail forwarded to me. It wasn't easy convincing Mom that she's vulnerable to being scammed, but she finally agreed that I should co-sign her checks. Then...last week in her mail there was a letter from my brother and...well...I opened it, Janelle."

"So..."

Ellie described Frank's request for the "forged" check.

"I see," Janelle said. "What did you do?"

"Nothing yet, I did make a copy before resealing the envelope and giving it to Mom. I'm not sure what to do..."

"What a rat! I think it's okay you opened the letter and good that you gave it to your mother—she's not incompetent yet! It sounds like she still has some good days...I just hope she's capable of figuring out what he's up to. What a jerk! Taking advantage of his own mother."

"Jerk's too nice a word. I was thinking more of an acronym, like SOB."

Janelle laughed, delighted to discover that her former English teacher used profane language the same way she did when she was upset. *I wonder how many students have the opportunity to discover their teachers are "normal" people.* Then she listened intently as Ellie filled her in on more of Frank's stunts. "Between my WEAC lawyer and Ray McCarthur taking care of mother's legal issues," Ellie concluded, "I feel like I spend more time talking to attorneys than I do anything else."

"Ray McCarthur? Matt and I just met with him last week to do our wills."

"Really? You two are even smarter than I thought, Janelle. Our kids were in grade school before Jack and I got around to having our wills done. When I think about what might have happened...well, every couple should make a will...especially if they intend to have children."

"Absolutely," Janelle said. Then she asked, "Ellie, please don't feel you have to answer this, but what is your mother's financial situation?"

"That's okay, I don't mind telling you. She's comfortable, but certainly not wealthy."

"Do you think she sent Frank the money he asked for?"

"I know she did. He cashed the check Friday."

"What are you going to do?"

"I don't know, Janelle. Part of me wishes I didn't have to deal with it at all. I simply don't know what to do. This must be why they say 'ignorance is bliss.' A little knowledge can be an uncomfortable thing."

CHAPTER 19

Friday, April 18th

Janelle was really looking forward to the weekend. Bradley had taken the day off, probably to perform damage control with Beverly, and Janelle got a taste of what it would be like when she'd have to fill in for Bradley. Three people in accounting called with complaints about programs performing illegal operations; one graphic artist demanded that a flickering monitor be replaced at once; and several administrative personnel needed help writing equations. She handled everything efficiently. *I better be careful...if people realize I'm so proficient, I might "inherit" this part of Bradley's job. I'm busy enough.*

Luckily, she didn't have any emergencies requiring her to call him at home. Since the day she had spilled-the-beans to Beverly, working together had been difficult enough. The last thing she wanted to do was stir things up. She shut down her computer and grabbed her short grocery list. *Good thing the day's over,* she thought as she headed out the door, *I have a splitting headache...these groceries are gonna have to wait until morning. I need a nap.*

She arrived home fifteen minutes later, not remembering much about the drive because she'd been thinking about baby names. They both liked "Dana Marie" for a girl, but couldn't agree on a boy's first name. All they knew was that the middle name would be Owen—after Janelle's grandpa.

She decided to change into more comfy clothes and curl up on the couch with a few of her baby-name books, hoping something would strike her this time.

"I don't know what everyone's so worried about," she said out loud as she caught a glimpse of her naked self in the mirror. "I'm *obviously* getting bigger." She threw on a pair of Matt's sweatpants and a long sleeve maternity shirt, feeling more relaxed at just the thought of lying on the couch. She eased herself into a comfortable position and immediately felt the baby shift, putting intense pressure on her bladder. "Jeez! I just went to the bathroom before I left work," she said aloud as she navigated her way to the bathroom. Just as she made it back to the couch, the phone rang.

"Hi, honey, it's Mom. How are you?"

"I'm good. Trying to fit in a nap before Matt gets home," Janelle answered, feeling another headache starting.

"Oh, I'll let you get to your nap. I just wanted to check with you for your shower list. You almost done?"

"I need a few more addresses. You aren't sending invitations out already, are you?"

"No, just trying to get a count for food, invitations, stamps...do you have a guesstimate how many?"

"Maybe about fifteen or so."

"I talked to Cassie and we decided we should mail them out a month before, three weeks at the latest."

"So by May 14th? I'll for sure be able to have the list to you by then."

"Great. With Memorial weekend, school ending and graduation parties, that's a busy time of the year, so we'll want to get on everyone's calendar," Claire explained.

"Speaking of Memorial weekend, Matt and I are going to have our annual get-together on Monday. I'm not doing invites this year, just telling people. Plan on noon." Janelle tried not to think of how much work it was to entertain her family and Matt's mom at the same time.

"Okay, sounds good. I wrote it on my calendar. So, will you be registered by May 14th?"

"I guess I'll have to be, won't I?" Janelle didn't want to think about adding another deadline to her to-do list.

"Janelle, I thought you'd be excited to register." Claire sounded puzzled and disappointed.

"I am. I just want us to register together. Matt's working later...I'm going to bed earlier...and you know how short the weekends are already."

"This is important, you'll find time. Do you have any idea where? We should include it on the invites."

"Baby Village."

"Okay...Baby Village it is..." Claire repeated slowly, obviously writing it down. "Anywhere else?"

"No, just Baby Village. We did two stores for the wedding and it was tons of work. One store is fine," Janelle said firmly, knowing Matt would agree.

"Okay, honey. You get back to your nap. Talk to you later. Love you."

Janelle returned to the boys' section of the baby name book and started reading the names out loud, ignoring spelling variations and deviations of each name: "Aaron, Abbott, Abdul, Abe, Abel. Hmmm, let's try a different letter." She randomly chose a different page and began again: "Dacey, Dag, Dale, Dallas, Dalaston, Dalton. Let's try again," she said turning a chunk of pages, "Napoleon, Nat, Nathan, Nathaniel, Neal."

She rubbed her tummy and asked the baby, "Why is this so tough? Mommy wishes you could tell us what you'd like us to name you."

Janelle once again turned her attention to the book. For some reason, the words on the page blurred. *Jeez, this headache is really bad!* She shut her eyes, hoping they just needed a quick rest. When she opened them again, her heart started to pound; *Oh my God...everything's blurry!*

"What's going on?" she said aloud. Fear gripped her and she began to feel nauseous. She took a deep breath and tried to focus, but it made her head hurt even more. *I better rest a little...it's just a bad headache...don't panic. Lots of pregnant women get migraines.*

Janelle forced herself to relax and managed to doze off. Twenty minutes later, the doorbell rang and she woke with a start. *Oh, jeez! I must've fallen asleep. I wonder who that could be?* She sat up slowly, noting that her headache was gone and her vision was crystal clear. Relieved, she went to answer the front door, carrying the baby book with her.

"Cassie! Come in. What a nice surprise! What's up?"

"Oh, not much. I just thought I'd stop by for a while."

Janelle followed Cassie into the living room, knowing something wasn't right. Cassie never just "stopped by."

"What're you reading?"

"This? Oh, I was trying, without luck, to find a boy's name," Janelle smiled. "I had no idea picking out names would be so difficult."

Suddenly Cassie burst into tears and buried her face in Janelle's shoulder. "I got my period today!"

"Oh, Cass," Janelle dropped the book to put her arms around her best friend, "I'm so sorry."

"This is ripping my heart out," Cassie sobbed. "How did you do this for over two years?"

"It helped to have good friends like you, Cass. You'll get through it too, I promise," Janelle said, hugging her friend.

Pulling herself out of the comforting embrace, Cassie said in an unbearably sad voice, "I thought I knew...I thought I understood..."

"What?"

"When you were trying to get pregnant and you talked to me, I thought I could feel your pain," Cassie explained.

"Cass, you must have. You were the best friend I could've hoped for. You always made me feel better."

"But Janelle, I was so wrong," Cassie said hoarsely as she choked back more tears. "I really had no idea...until now."

Because it cut a half-hour off the drive to Miller Park, Ellie and Jack picked up Helen on Friday night so she could stay over. Helen hadn't spent an overnight at the Reeds for quite some time, and with Jonah also home for the weekend, Ellie had a houseful. She was glad her home was still tidy from the thorough cleaning she had given it two weeks before. With just Jack and her there, things didn't get as messy as when the children were growing up. Still, she sometimes missed the activity and clutter that were a natural side effect of four people living in a modest-sized ranch home. The lyrics of a Doug Stone song popped into her head as she guided Helen to Rebecca's old room. *Love grows best in little houses...few walls to separate...when you live so close together...you can't help but communicate.*

Then another thought occurred to her. *I wonder if things would have been different if Klebold and Harris, the Columbine shooters, had lived in small houses...If Jonah had a stash of guns here, we certainly would've known.*

"Eleanor, did you bring my pillow?" Helen hadn't wanted to leave her house for an overnight; she only agreed because they were going to Miller Park. "You know I can't sleep unless I have my pillow. And why is this bed so hard?"

"Your pillow's on the chair, Mom. And you know you like a firm bed." Jack had brought in Helen's things, then rejoined Jonah in the living room where Ellie could hear them laughing and talking sports.

"I can't get this sweater off; it's too tight," Helen whined, having trouble getting undressed. Ellie went to help. She noticed with some surprise that her mother smelled awful, like she hadn't had a bath in a while and hadn't done a good job of cleaning herself after using the toilet.

One of the pamphlets from Sharon Kelly said lack of proper hygiene, especially bathing, is common in Alzheimer's patients. *I thought Mom would be exempt...I never thought in a million years she would fit the mold.* Then Ellie had a brainstorm.

"Why don't you take a warm bath before bed, Mom? It'll help you sleep."

"Oh, no, I don't dare get in the tub," Helen replied. "I might fall and hurt myself. A woman in the neighborhood fell just that way last month and now she's in a nursing home. I'm not taking any chances so don't you dare even suggest it."

"Well then, let's use the shower in my bathroom."

"You know I never take showers; I don't even have a shower at home."

"Well, we have one here, so let's go," Ellie said firmly.

"I don't want to take a shower. My hair will get all wet. I just had it set..."

"I have a shower cap, Mom; your hair will be just fine."

Ellie didn't give her mother any more chances to object. She just ushered her down the hall to their master bathroom. She turned on the overhead heater and fetched her blue terry cloth bathrobe hanging on the door.

Helen seemed completely at a loss as to what to do so Ellie instructed her, just as she would a child. "Take off your clothes, Mom, put on this robe, and call me when you're ready. I want to make sure the water temperature's comfortable for you."

Ellie closed the door to give her mother privacy and went to the linen closet where she rummaged around until she found an old shower cap, a washcloth and a big fluffy towel. After waiting several minutes for Helen to call out and tell her she was ready, she knocked on the door.

"Mom, are you ready?" Hearing no answer, she opened the door to find Helen standing there, stark naked, her frail body covered in goose bumps.

I guess Mom's obviously not as concerned with her modesty as I am...she looks so old and withered.

"What do I do?" Helen asked, looking around as if she was lost. She had pulled open the shower door and was standing there, just staring at the nozzle.

"It's easy, Mom. First, we put your shower cap on." She guided the plastic cap, securing the elastic snugly in place to protect her mother's hairdo. "Now we turn the water on." She turned on the faucet and felt the streaming water, adjusting the temperature until it seemed right. "How's this, Mom?"

Her mother put her hand out and pulled it back at once. "Ouch, that's too hot!" she said in a petulant voice.

Actually it's quite tepid...I get the feeling it doesn't matter what I do...it'll be wrong. After a few more adjustments, Helen was finally satisfied. *Well...that's pretty much right where it was when we started!* Ellie handed her a bar of soap and a washcloth. "Just put the soap on the washcloth, Mom, and clean yourself all over. Be sure to scrub your bottom, and then rinse all the soap off, otherwise you'll itch."

Helen made a clucking sound as if to say she knew how to wash herself, but Ellie stayed just to make sure. Five minutes later Helen was out of the shower and squeaky clean, Ellie patting her dry with the soft towel. It was getting too warm in the bathroom for Ellie, so she wrapped Helen in her robe and led her down to the guest room, where she helped her mother into her nightgown and tucked her in.

"That shower was nice, Eleanor. I haven't felt so clean in months. Maybe I do like showers."

Ellie nodded approvingly.

"Tell me a story, Ellie," her mother said, pulling the covers tight up to her chin. "Do you remember the one about the fairy princess?"

Ellie smiled. Even as a young child, she had been the family storyteller. As a four year old, she was already making up far-fetched tales to entertain everyone. Her mother looked at her expectantly. Ellie began, "Once upon a time..." and then related a treasured story she had made up in third grade. It was about a spoiled, selfish princess who had to exchange places with a real child for a day, learning that a person had to be willing to share in order to experience the delight of making a friend.

By the time the story was ending, Helen's eyes were droopy and she was close to sleep. Feeling an ache in her heart, Ellie realized that their relationship was becoming full circle role reversal. She took an extra moment to hug her mother tightly and kiss her forehead gently.

"Good night, Eleanor," Helen said.

"Night, Mom, I love you."

Helen nodded but said nothing. Ellie had realized long ago that her mother simply could not say those three precious words. Not once in her entire life had Ellie heard her say "I love you" to anyone. *I can't imagine not telling my kids or Jack how much I love them...or not giving them a hug every time I see them.* Ellie sadly shook her head and lightly touched Helen's cheek. *I know you love me, Mom...even if you can't say it.*

Ellie closed the door quietly and went into the living room to spend some time with her son. Jack had told Jonah earlier about the "Nielsen Problem." Not wanting to ruin the evening thinking about her troubles—there was nothing new to report anyway—she asked that they not even discuss it. Jonah told her about his student teaching experience. Ellie was full of advice on how to handle two difficult students he was working with and assured him it was early yet to hear anything on his resumes—so far he didn't have any bites on his applications for a full time job next fall. It was midnight before they realized how exhausted they were, so with hugs and I love you's, they finally went to bed.

The next morning Ellie served a delicious breakfast of French toast, sausages and orange juice. Then the family piled into Jonah's SUV and headed south. Everyone, especially Helen—who said she'd slept just like a baby—was in high spirits. The plan was to meet up with Rebecca at the ballpark. She was only able to stay the day because her firm was swamped with work. Ellie was disappointed because she'd been hoping Rebecca could spend at least one night at home.

Jonah had insisted on stopping for a newspaper to see who was pitching. Everyone was delighted that it was to be Jon Arhmon—the Brewers' young right-hander. Jonah told them there was a kid on the baseball team he was coaching that reminded him a lot of Arhmon.

"Wouldn't it be wonderful if you hadn't torn your rotator cuff in college, Jonah? You could've become a major league player instead of a high school teacher and coach," Helen observed as she picked at some lint on her pants.

Jack, sitting in the front passenger seat, looked back at Ellie, amazed that Helen remembered their son's tragic dream-shattering injury.

"You know Grandma...I don't think you ever missed one of my games," Jonah said, glancing into the back seat. "I always looked for you in the crowd, and I think I put a little something extra on my fastball, knowing you were there."

Helen smiled proudly at Jonah's comment. "And here I thought it was the cookies I always brought," she teased.

The family spent the rest of the drive talking, laughing, and singing along to country and western songs on a local radio station.

They arrived at Miller Park with plenty of time to spare. Off to the left, where the old stadium had been was Helfaer Field——one of the finest Little League ballparks in the country. As they pulled into the parking lot, everyone agreed that the Brewers' organization had made excellent use of the vacant space. Together, they walked up the long entrance, marveling at the beauty of the Miller Park structure. It was a sunny, but quite cool, mid-April day in Milwaukee, so the dome over the stadium was closed and would remain closed until the end of the game. A highlight of going to a Brewer game was the opening and closing of the roof while music was played. Ellie said she thought the ritual was worth the price of admission alone.

Finding their way to the huge bronze statue of Robyn Yount——the Brewer Hall of Famer, they spotted Rebecca waving enthusiastically. Beside her stood Josie and Carl, her godparents. Frank was nowhere in sight. *Good! Frank's not here yet…maybe with any luck he won't show up at all…I'm not sure I'd be able to bite my tongue…and that'd wreck the day for everyone.*

They took the elevator up to the restaurant for lunch. It was a splendid, traditional affair of bratwurst on a semmel bun; garnished with onions, sauerkraut and secret stadium sauce, accompanied by thick steak fries and cabbage slaw, all washed down with a large cup of beer. Frank arrived just as they were getting their food and the waitress hurried away to get another order. He seemed very upbeat and solicitous of Helen, helping cut her brat into more manageable pieces and getting a straw for her carton of milk.

Josie and Carl spent a lot of time talking about their cruise. Everyone joined in the conversation, mainly catching up on things that had occurred since Christmas——the last time they were all together. Everyone enthusiastically agreed the outing was a great idea, with Jonah admitting it actually had been Rebecca's idea (and cash) that made the day possible. Conceding as much without boasting, Rebecca said that her seventy-hour workweek came with one redeeming feature—a princely salary, and she insisted on picking up the tab for lunch also. Frank, in an attempt to appear gallant, objected, but deferred quickly when he saw that the bill was well over a hundred dollars.

A few minutes before game-time, they were all in their seats, just a few yards down from the press box. Helen stood up, turned around and waved. Jonah did the same, pointing to Helen, and shouting up that she had listened to almost every game broadcast over the past two decades. The announcers smiled widely and waved back enthusiastically.

The game started off on a bad note as the Brewers' arch-rivals took an early lead on a two run homer, but Arhmon regained command and shut down the opposition for the next seven innings. It was obvious the Brewers had come to play—they scored seven runs, including a 375-foot grand slam in the sixth inning by their rookie sensation, Hillard Brant.

To celebrate his favorite player's success, Jonah went to the concession stand and returned with several huge pretzels, dripping with mustard. Ellie and Rebecca passed, but everyone else indulged and Helen ate almost all of hers, washing it down with another carton of milk.

The game ended with the Brewers notching an 8-3 win. A few fans, including Carl and Josie, left as soon as victory was assured, but most stayed for the finale. Even though the Reeds had seen the spectacle before, it still filled them with awe. Helen especially sat rapt as the space-movie-theme played loudly over the PA system and the roof opened to reveal a cloudless azure sky.

Ellie gestured to the rest of the family to look at Helen who was smiling in childlike delight as she watched the pivots swing and the roof sections move slowly apart. The stadium roared with applause when it was fully open. Finally, it was time to close the structure until the next game. As the sections came together, it seemed to Ellie that it signaled the closing of a wonderful time for all of them. Everyone thanked the kids again for the great time. Frank kept repeating how great it was to spend the day with family.

Wow...Frank was great today. I'm glad I gave the letter to Mom last week and didn't confront him about it. I can't help wondering if there's something else going on or if he's finally beginning to grow up and realize how important family is...

They gathered their belongings and made their way out of the park. The women took the opportunity to make one last "pit stop" as they were leaving the stadium, in case it took a long time for the parking lot to empty. After using the restroom, Helen said she had an unsettled stomach from all the rich food. She wanted milk, but Ellie convinced her to try something carbonated.

Insisting that she could do it herself, Helen marched over to the vending machine. She was just taking her wallet out of her purse to find some change when it happened so fast that no one, including Helen, could have prevented it. A boy of about seven had apparently lagged behind his father on the way to the car and was running to catch up. With a full head of steam and not watching where he was going, he hit full force into Helen, who tumbled headlong to the cement walkway. The boy had not been hurt in the collision, simply yelled, "Sorry!" and disappeared into the crowd.

Helen tried to get to her feet, saying she was all right, but a nearby security guard insisted staff paramedics be called to examine her. The family stood by helplessly. Frank took off his jacket and covered his mother with it, taking the wallet that was still in her hand and tucking it into his jacket pocket. Within a minute or two, the paramedics arrived and took over. Handing Frank his jacket back, they checked Helen's blood pressure and pulse and gave her a thorough examination to determine if she had broken any bones. She appeared to have a pretty nasty scrape and a couple of bruises. After they put a bandage on her scrape and checked the contusion on her left arm, they released her with the advice that she check in with her family doctor if she felt the need.

Jonah went to get the car and the Reeds said their goodbyes to Frank. Ten minutes later, they were taking Rebecca to the airport. When her flight was announced, Rebecca hugged her grandmother gingerly, afraid she'd hurt her. Helen insisted she was fine and scolded the family for making such a fuss. After Rebecca left, Helen admitted her head did hurt a little. Wanting to use the small mirror in her wallet to check if she had a bruise on her forehead, she searched through her purse. That was when she realized her wallet was missing.

"Ellie, my wallet...I lost my wallet," she wailed.

At first Ellie was alarmed, then she remembered. "Frank put it in his jacket when you were on the sidewalk, Mom. In all the excitement, he must have forgotten to give it back to you. I'm sure he has it." Even though she spoke in her most reassuring tone, she couldn't help thinking, *Oh no...not her wallet...great...here we go again.* "He must be home by now; I'll call him and see if we can stop by on our way out of town to get it."

Ellie tried several times to reach Frank. Finally, she left a message saying that he should call her cell phone right away.

"Frank isn't home yet, Mom, but I told him to mail the wallet to you. You should have it by Tuesday at the latest." Helen set her lips in a frown of disapproval so Ellie went on, "You don't need money anyway, Mom. We'll take care of you, don't worry."

Jack and Jonah agreed and Helen accepted their reassurances. "Well, thank heaven my Frankie found the wallet," she said. "What if some criminal had picked it up? Then I'd really be upset."

CHAPTER 20

Friday, May 9th

After Matt left for work, Janelle stole a few minutes to re-read yesterday's journal entry:

Thursday, May 8th
Dear Baby,

I went to the doctor today. I've gained twelve pounds, but my blood pressure is still too high. I'm having a really tough time at work these days. It's hard to focus on anything but you. You'd laugh at the Old Wives Tales I'm hearing. Beth is saying you're a girl because my tummy is shaped like a basketball. She says if it looked like a football, you'd be a boy. Amy and Donna disagree and say she has it backwards! The best one I've heard is that if the hair on my legs is growing slower, I'm having a girl; faster if you're a boy! That's no help because I can't remember how fast it grew before!

I'm so excited for you to get here, I can hardly wait. I am excited and at the same time stressed—I have so much to do! We didn't end up taking the massage class I told you about, but we start Lamaze classes soon…maybe they'll teach us some relaxation techniques! Heaven knows I need them. I can't wait to hold you in my arms for the first time!

Love, Mom

Janelle closed her journal and checked the time. It was 6:38. She had seven minutes before she had to leave for work and she wasn't about to leave early; she already had enough overtime this week with Bradley gone. Things were going fairly well, even though she'd had to stay late every night to catch up on her own work. There were only a few times she'd had to wing it. Unfortunately, one of them was the flickering-monitor-complaint filed in person by a whiny graphic artist named George. "I put in this request two weeks ago. Didn't you tell Bradley?" Janelle had smoothed things over by trading monitors with him. Of course, George was more than happy to have her flat panel monitor. When Bradley called in, she planned to ask him how to order new equipment so she wouldn't have to use the flickering one for too long; it seemed to make her headaches worse.

Janelle decided to use her seven minutes to start the laundry. She dumped the towel load into the washer first and then hunted for stray socks; sometimes Matt's socks found their way into the wrong "pre-sorted" load. She sighed and shook her head as she rescued a pair.

As she added detergent, Claire's words rang in her head, "Janelle, I can't believe you run the washer and dryer when you aren't home. What if something happens and you have water damage...or even worse, a fire!" Janelle's response had been an exasperated, "que sera, sera."

"Please God," Janelle prayed quietly, as she left the house promptly at 6:45, "watch over my laundry while I'm gone."

Bradley called at 9:00 to check in. Janelle explained the George-monitor situation and sensed he wasn't overly thrilled with her decision to purchase a new one. She assured him that she'd checked the cord connections and the Internet for any updated drivers with no luck. He finally conceded and gave her the information she needed to place the order.

Shortly after hanging up, Donna from accounting beeped her. "Janelle, can you please come to my desk? Something weird is happening to my computer."

"Sure," Janelle sighed. *So much for a quiet day and leaving by 4:00.* "I'll be right there." She arrived at Donna's office, which was still in need of redecorating, to find Kim from accounts payable standing behind her, watching the screen and shaking her head in disbelief.

"Okay, now watch what happens...oh...Janelle, come see this," Donna beckoned. Janelle took a spot next to Kim. "Now look, I just typed this letter to Foot Works, Inc. Watch what happens when I print." Donna's printer spit the letter out and she whisked it off and handed it to Janelle. "Look at the customer's name."

Janelle looked at the letter. "What the..."

"What in the world could cause that?" Kim wondered aloud. "I've never seen anything like this...ever."

Wherever Donna had typed the letter "f," it was replaced with the word "fool." In this case, the customer's name was now *Fool*oot Works, Inc.

"What does it look like on the screen?" Janelle asked.

"Normal," Donna said, exasperated. "It just doesn't make sense!"

"Well, let's not panic. We'll try a reboot first." But before it was complete, the loud speaker crackled. "Janelle, please call Larry at 3-5-1, Janelle 3-5-1."

"Yes, Larry."

"Janelle, something really weird is happening in my spreadsheet. I'm working on my list of customers to invite to our annual golf outing. Everything looks fine on my screen, but when I print..."

"All the f's become fools."

"Why would that happen?"

"Not sure yet, but the same thing's happening to Donna. She's in a word document though; you're in a spreadsheet?"

"That's right, working on my Gol-fool list," Larry joked.

"I'm afraid this may be more than I can handle, Larry," Janelle admitted reluctantly. "I'll call Brad. Maybe I can catch him on his cell."

On the way back to her office, two more co-workers flagged her down...same problem.

When Brad didn't answer his phone, Janelle began to panic and left a frantic message. "Brad, this is Janelle. I need you to call me right away! It's urgent! We have some kind of fool virus here or something and I don't know what to do. Please call as soon as you get this!"

Janelle was just calling Larry to let him know that she hadn't been able to reach Bradley when Beth beeped in. "Janelle, I must be a fool today; even my computer's trying to tell me so."

Janelle buried her face in her hands. "You too?"

"Aww, you mean I'm not the only one? Here I thought I had a special relationship with my PC."

"I'm betting it's some kind of virus, Beth. I'm waiting for Bradley to call back."

"Okay, I'll just hang in there. Thanks, Little Mama!"

Janelle filled Larry in, then checked every resource she could think of for information on "fool virus." Out of options, she decided to wait for Bradley's help. Even though her desk contained several organized piles of things to work on, she couldn't muster the energy to start any one of them. She checked her inbox, seeing an email from Claire. *Good, I need a distraction.* She clicked on it.

Hi, Janelle,

Thanks for the shower list. Do you happen to have the file at work that you can email me? Not a big deal if you don't, I can retype it if I have to. We're going to print address labels (2 sets - 1 for the invites and 1 for your thank you cards—good idea, huh?)

Let me know! Love, Mom

Janelle grabbed her shower list disk from her canvas bag and clicked it into the drive. She attached the list that was on the disk to an email and replied:

Hi Mom,

Here's the file. Love, Janelle
P.S. Sorry so short - MAJOR problems here. XOXOX.

Just as Janelle pressed Send, the flickering started again. "C'mon," she hit the side of the monitor, "I already have a headache. Don't do this to me now!" When the image continued to flutter and roll, she knew trying to work at her computer was futile. What she really needed was some "mindless" work to do, so she decided to shut down her computer and catch up on her filing. As she opened her filing cabinet, she overheard several co-workers conversing at the copy machine. One suggested if they couldn't print anything, they might as well go home early. *I wish I could,* Janelle thought enviously, *I'm stuck here until we figure out this fool-thing, hopefully it won't be a big deal to fix.*

Looking at her file drawers, Janelle decided it was way past time to purge them since they were beginning to bulge. This was something on her get-done-before-the-baby-comes list. *Well, since I can't do much else...guess there's no time like the present.* She grabbed a stack of empty file folders and assembled a banker's box.

As she set the box on her desk, the phone rang. Thinking it was Brad, she picked it up on the first ring.

"Hi, Janelle, it's Mom."

Janelle hoped her mother wouldn't be hurt by the obvious disappointment in her voice. "Sorry, Mom, I can't talk now. We're having major computer problems and I'm waiting for Bradley's call."

"That's why I'm calling; are all the letter "f's" turning to the word fool?"

"Yes! Is it happening to you guys too?"

"Only since you sent me the shower list. I'm on my break so I opened it and started working on the labels. They looked fine on the screen, but not when I printed them."

"Oh, my God, Mom! I should've known better! We have a virus here and I sent it to you! What was I thinking?"

"Oh, sweetie. Don't worry. I've already reported it to our IT Department—they're good, they'll figure it out."

"Mom, if they do, will you call me? Maybe they can help us stop it here too. I have no idea when Bradley'll call in."

"Sure, I'll call if I hear anything. Now keep calm...for you and the baby, okay?"

"Okay Mom. Don't worry. I'll be fine. Call me if they figure anything out."

Janelle hung up and looked at the clock; almost noon. She decided to leave another message for Bradley and dialed his cell phone again.

"Hello, this is Bradley."

"Bradley! Didn't you get my message?"

"Janelle, what a nice surprise. Yeah, I sent you an email about twenty minutes ago."

"An email! Why?" Janelle was baffled. She spun her chair around to face her computer. "I said to CALL me right away."

"Chill, Janelle. I sent you a patch."

"Well, how would I know that? I shut down; this stupid frickin' monitor is driving me crazy! You should've called me!" Janelle felt her heart beating high up in her chest.

"Sorry. As soon as I got your message, I left the meeting and started working on a fix."

"A fix?" Janelle repeated. "How can you fix this without seeing it?"

"Just boot back up and open the email, Janelle," Bradley commanded. "I wrote clear directions...as long as you're on the phone, I'll walk you through it."

Janelle complied as ordered and then clicked on the "Fool Fix" attachment in the email. He had her save it to the desktop and move it into a specific directory before executing it by double clicking. Her monitor continued to flicker as the percent complete bar climbed and paused on its way to 100%.

"Done," she said after five minutes. "Now what?"

"Duh...print something. Everything should be just fine now, you'll see."

Janelle printed her mom's email. "Looks perfect," she squealed in delight. "You're a genius, Brad!"

"Okay, now print out my email so you remember how to get the file into that specific directory because you have to do that at every person's computer,"

"Ooooh," Janelle whined. "You're kidding, right?"

"No, I'm not. Just look at the email, it's all there. Just print it out and take it to every person's office."

"Thanks, Brad. You saved my life. Did I mention that we...that I miss you?" *Jeez, this is NOT going to be fun.*

"Well, it's nice to hear that," Bradley said. "I'm sure I'll miss you too when you're gone," Janelle could almost see Brad smiling as he repaid the compliment.

"That's not the same. I haven't had training for this stuff. At least you'll know my accounts. Everyone was coming to me to fix this thing; I didn't have anyone to go to."

Bradley ignored her comment. "Oh, by the way, ask everyone if they emailed outside the office. If so, tell them to send the fix to those addresses," Bradley instructed.

"I'll do that right away because I sent a diseased file to my mom. Her IT Department's trying to fix it now."

"So send her the new file and have her just forward the fix to her IT guys; they'll know what to do with it."

Suddenly, Janelle remembered. "You never answered me. How were you able to write a fix without even seeing it?"

"I, uhhh...I gotta get back to the seminar. Email me at the end of the day and let me know how everything went."

"But Bradley, I..."

"Gotta go. See you Monday. Call if you have any more problems...I'll do whatever I can from here."

Janelle went from computer to computer all afternoon, quickly becoming the office hero. Larry was especially grateful because, thanks to her, the day didn't turn out to be a total loss. At 3:45 she returned to her office. *I didn't finish any of my own work today. Oh well, I'm not staying late tonight. I need to get outta here!*

Before leaving, she took the time to sit down to write a short email:

Hi Brad,

    It's the pits here without you, but I'm managing somehow. I think everyone is up to speed now on our 'foolish' situation. Thanks for being there—I don't know what I'd have done without you!

    Janelle

P.S. Please come back soon, I miss you!

When she awoke early Friday, Ellie looked over at her solid white oak dresser. There sat three Mother's Day cards—one from Jonah, who had wanted to come home but was with his baseball team in LaCrosse making up a rain-out, one from Rebecca, who was in San Antonio on business, and one, a complete surprise, from Janelle, telling her how much she cherished their friendship. Sitting on the coffee table in the living room, there was also a small but lovely bouquet of yellow roses from Jonah. Next to the roses sat her gift from Rebecca, a copy of one of her favorite poems, *Chicago*, by Carl Sandburg, framed in sterling silver. She realized with longing that three weeks had passed since she had seen her children.

Ellie thought back. She had spent those weeks teaching, seeing to Helen's needs and preparing for the school board meeting. Taking a huge chance, she and Stacey had decided to speak publicly in answer to Mrs. Nielsen's complaint. Her principal was against it and tried to persuade Ellie to forget about the "whole mess" because Mrs. Nielsen had offered to withdraw her complaint if the matter could be settled without further publicity. She said Henley had admitted to fabricating a lot of his "grievances" and was under so much "negative peer pressure" that he was seeing a psychologist for post-traumatic stress disorder. She also indicated that if Ellie didn't agree to settle this quietly, she would pursue her complaint, as well as withdraw Henley from the school and "home-school" her son, thus costing the district several thousand dollars in lost per-pupil state school funding.

Ellie figured her professional reputation was worth a lot more than several thousand dollars and moved forward. As explanation for her final decision, she told her principal a story she had once heard about Winston Churchill. It seems that one morning a political opponent had mercilessly attacked Churchill's character in open Parliament. The two met later that day in the adjoining washroom, where the man apologized for his harsh words and praised Churchill as one of the greatest British prime ministers ever. "Next time," Churchill is reported to have said, "could you please insult me in private and praise me in public?"

Her decision made, Ellie relaxed and enjoyed herself Friday evening as she and Jack joined friends for the traditional fish fry at a local pub. They spent Saturday working out in the yard, a guaranteed elixir for the most bruised psyche, and went to a movie Saturday night before going to bed for some downtime.

Ellie got up early Sunday morning feeling incredibly rested and ambled out to start the coffee. There sat an exquisite card from Jack, telling her what a wonderful mother she was. She brushed away "tears for happy" as Jack called them, reading the lovely words that touched her heart deeply.

She and Jack didn't need to be at Helen's to take her to Mass until later, so Ellie retrieved the paper from the front porch, noticing that the sun was rising gloriously in a cloudless sky, promising a warm, lovely setting for Mother's Day family get-togethers. May was one of Ellie's favorite months because it was a time when, almost overnight, the northern Wisconsin landscape shook off its monochrome winter blanket and burst alive with color. Recent temperatures in the 70's had encouraged the lawns to trade their dead brown mantles for lush new green growth. Noise across the street caught her attention and she waved to a neighbor who was already breaking the morning peace with his bright orange lawn mower.

The warm spell had also set the trees and flowers blooming, and Ellie appreciatively drank in the view. The next-door neighbor's magnolia tree was covered with gigantic pink-edged white blooms, a few of which had already climaxed, the tongue-like petals scattered haphazardly on Chuck's perfectly manicured lawn. She decided to walk around the house, taking a stroll through her backyard where three flowering crab trees proudly displayed a breathtaking profusion of dark pink blossoms. Two apple trees on the far side of the yard provided the perfect backdrop as their buds were just opening, still green but with a tinge of white that promised their own splendid show within the week. A sweet smell of lilac from the adjoining yard wafted on the breeze. *No place is prettier than Wisconsin in May. It must be our reward for enduring the long winter months here.* Returning to the kitchen, she poured herself a cup of coffee and went out to their four seasons room to enjoy the early morning solitude. She sat down on the cushioned rattan loveseat to read the newspaper.

A short time later, Jack, still clad in his idea of pajamas, a white T-shirt and briefs, came out to get the sports section. Coffee in hand, he bent over to kiss his wife and said, "Happy Mother's Day, Ellie. Of course you aren't my mother," he teased, "but. . ." She shushed his nonsense with a kiss.

An hour later they were dressed and on the road. The twenty-minute ride was more enjoyable because of Blackbird. They usually took Jack's truck to Helen's on Sundays, since Blackbird was only a two-seater, but today Josie and Carl, who were driving up from Chicago, would chauffeur them all to brunch in their roomy mini-van. *I wonder if Frank will make an appearance today. . .Mom said she didn't know if he was coming or not. . .*

"It would have been nice to stay home today," Ellie mused as they sped north. "I think we've gone this route so many times my Bird knows the way by heart. But it'll be like old times, with Josie and Carl there. When Josie called to say they were actually making the trip, we agreed we don't know how many more Mother's Days we'll have with Mom."

"That's for sure," Jack agreed. "No matter how you feel about your folks, you'll miss them once they're gone." Ellie looked at Jack whose hand shook a little as he turned the radio up. She knew the story well. Jack's parents and younger sister had been killed in a freak accident when he was sixteen. A workman repairing a water main break in front of their home had unknowingly punctured a nearby gas line, and natural gas had slowly seeped into their basement. When the furnace ignited sometime during the night, the house exploded, instantly killing his entire family as they slept. Jack regretted that he, like most teens, had taken his parents being there for granted. Worse, the relationship had been stormy and the night of the accident there had been a huge fight. His father had ordered him to stay home until his chores were done, but Jack had left in a defiant huff to attend a party at a friend's house. He would never get over the fact that the last thing he had said to his father was, "Go to hell, it's my life and I don't need you to ruin it for me!"

Living on his own after that, Jack went to school days and worked nights and summers in a relative's landscaping company. He worked his way up to foreman by the time his firm was hired to update a yard adjoining Francis and Helen Lowe's property. That was how he met Ellie. It was a warm July day and she was reading in a chaise lounge out in the yard under a giant oak tree. Jack asked her if his crew could eat lunch in the shade and she said, "Sure, shade's free...I can share."

They struck up a conversation and he realized he had never met anyone like her. She was smart, funny and pretty—it took all his courage to ask her out. He admitted to being totally surprised when she actually said yes...then on their first date, even more surprised when he saw her pray before they ate. He had mildly rebuked her, telling her about his family, saying if there really was a God, it's hard to believe He'd allow something as terrible as letting an entire family die in a fire...it just didn't make any sense to him. He said he quit going to church and quit believing in God after the "accident." Ellie had tears in her eyes when she answered. "First of all your entire family didn't die—you're still here and I believe there's a reason for that. I believe God give us all challenges in order to teach us important lessons—many, many people face terrible situations...I believe it's how we respond to these situations that ultimately makes each and every one of us a better person. You say you gave up on God...well, I believe He never gave up on you... and He has given you an opportunity to test your faith and ultimately find peace and happiness in this world...if...if you put your trust in Him." Jack couldn't resist this young woman who thought so deeply and made more sense than anything else in his life.

They dated for four years while he worked nights to finish his degree in labor relations and she got her teaching license. While he wanted her with a fire that was only stoked higher by their heavy make-out sessions, she insisted on being a virgin on their wedding night. She was, and Jack told her she was more than worth the wait.

Ellie pulled into Helen's driveway and parked the car, noticing that the yard had not been mowed. Helen had insisted she would cut the lawn whenever it needed mowing. Because it was a small yard and Helen had an electric-start mower, they had reluctantly agreed. "After brunch I guess I'll have to get out the lawnmower," Jack said. "Good thing I have some old sneakers here." While Ellie definitely agreed the yard needed cutting, she wasn't sure the neighbors would like it if they fired-up the mower on Mother's Day afternoon.

Church was only three blocks away and the weather was perfect, so when Helen said she felt up to it, they walked to Mass. The church was crowded, with almost every woman wearing a corsage. Helen and Ellie were each sporting a white orchid—a surprise Jack had arranged by hiding the two cardboard flower boxes in Blackbird's trunk on Saturday evening. Mass was lovely, with a particularly beautiful rendition of *Ave Maria* and an inspiring, if somewhat rambling, sermon on the joys and sorrows of motherhood as portrayed in the life of Mary, the mother of Jesus.

On the way home, Ellie saw Carl and Josie drive up and park next to Blackbird. She grimaced when she heard a chink as Carl opened his door and nicked her car with it. "Dammit, that's a dent for sure," she whispered angrily to Jack. "We should've parked in the street."

"Ellie, chill out," he shot back. "It's just a car, for God's sake. Besides, we just came from church."

Angered by his comment, she gave him "the stare" and ushered her mother over to greet her sister and brother-in-law. Big hellos and hugs were exchanged in the front drive and Ellie gradually got over her snit. Since it was already after noon, they decided to head straight to the restaurant so they'd be there in plenty of time for their reservations.

Ellie groaned when she saw the buffet table piled high with all her favorite foods. She had been working out faithfully three days a week and following a low carb diet for almost a month. She had already dropped twelve pounds and lost thirteen inches, and even Josie, a perennial size six, had commented favorably on Ellie's "new" sleeker body. However, since it was Mother's Day, Ellie decided to splurge. Maneuvering past the tempting sweet rolls and pastries, she piled her plate high with roast chicken breast, scrambled eggs, cold shrimp, lean ham, a generous slice of prime rib, tomato slices, celery sticks, half a dozen radishes, and a crunchy dill pickle. She noticed Helen was eating mostly carbohydrates—the foods Ellie was strictly avoiding. *Mom's so skinny no matter what she eats. I wonder if someday it won't matter how many sweet rolls and desserts I eat...*

She pushed that thought out of her mind and indulged in a glass of merlot, then decided to have a refill. The wine went down easily and she said "yes" when Carl filled her glass a third time. She was feeling comfortably full and fantastic by the time Josie said "my treat" and gave the server her credit card to pay the check. Helen insisted on leaving the tip, opening her wallet and getting out three one-dollar bills. Ellie exchanged a look with Jack—he took the hint and fished a five out of his pocket and threw it on the pile.

"You finally got your wallet back, Mom," Ellie said.

"Yes, your brother brought it back yesterday," Helen said.

"Really? Frank was here?" Carl asked. This extraordinary bit of news stunned all four of Helen's brunch companions.

"Well, of course he came to see me," Helen said. "He would never forget me on Mother's Day." She looked at the skepticism on their faces and went on defensively. "We went out to dinner last night and had a lovely meal. He's such a wonderful boy, evidently I'm the only one here who can see that. Maybe it's because I...I prefer to concentrate on his good qualities...all of *you* focus on his faults," she added, pursing her lips like a defiant child.

Finding it hard to believe Frank had actually taken Helen out to dinner, Ellie thought maybe the wallet had come back in the mail and her mother had mixed up the dates of Frank's visits so she decided to change the subject. "Was everything in the wallet, Mom?" she asked carefully.

"And what do you mean by that?" Helen snapped. "If you are asking if money was missing, it wasn't! Frank would *never* steal from his mother," she said in a loud, angry voice.

Ellie saw that people were beginning to stare and was relieved when Jack offered Helen his arm and gallantly ushered her outside into the warm sunshine. Ellie rushed out behind them and attempted to take Helen's other arm. Still outraged by Ellie's question, Helen shoved her away and then freed herself from Jack. She marched to the car with her nose in the air. Carl and Josie gave Ellie a dirty look as if it was her fault for spoiling the occasion. They began their drive home in thick, tense silence, but when they passed the Nightingale Dance Hall, Helen did a complete change of face and began to recite the well-worn story of how she and Francis had met there on a lovely summer evening so many years ago.

The mood in the car changed as quickly as Helen did, and they were all laughing by the time they got home. Helen even reached for Ellie's steadying arm as she walked up the cement stoop to the front door. Josie tagged along behind while Carl and Jack went out to the garage to see if there was any gas in the lawn mower.

As the three women walked into the living room, to their complete surprise, there sat Frank, watching the Brewers game on television.

"Hi, Frankie," Helen said sweetly. "Did you have a nice time at the casino? Are we rich yet?"

"No, not yet, Mom. Maybe tomorrow."

"Frank...this is a surprise." Ellie managed to stay polite.

"Not to me, I knew you were all going to be here."

"Then why didn't you come to brunch with us?" Josie said as she went over and gave her brother a perfunctory hug.

"Wasn't hungry. I had a big dinner last night...also had a few errands to run."

Ellie could only guess what he meant by running errands. Then she saw the pile of discarded beer bottles and empty pizza box on the floor near the sofa. "He's disgusting," she muttered under her breath as she picked up Frank's garbage and carried it to the kitchen. She was putting the rinsed glass bottles into the recycling bin when a stack of junk mail on the counter caught her eye. Ellie picked up the pile, intending to recycle that too when a white business envelope tucked inside one of the papers fell on the floor. Ellie was confused for a moment because she was sure it was a credit card bill, and she knew her mother had never used a credit card in her entire life. Suddenly, Frank came into the kitchen. The way he looked at the envelope confirmed her suspicions.

"Gee. . . I wonder what this is, Frank," she said, holding up the letter.

"Looks like a piece of Mom's mail to me." He grabbed for it, but Ellie was faster. She ripped it open and read: *Your card has reached the maximum amount allowed and no more cash advances will be given until payment is received. Balance Due immediately upon receipt. . . $7000.*

"What is this, Frank? Mom doesn't have a credit card. She pays cash or writes a check for everything. Always has."

Their eyes locked and Ellie finally realized what was happening. "You opened a credit card using her name?"

"No, I did not. She opened that account herself." Frank's demeanor and tone of voice were threatening—daring Ellie to make something of it, just like when they were kids. "If you must know, little sister, she's had that card since Christmas, long before you took over her life. I just pointed out to her when I was here for the holidays that everyone should have a credit card. . . for convenience, for emergencies like being caught without enough cash. She told me to help her fill out the application. I repeat, she opened the account herself. That card's been in her wallet for months."

Her wallet. . . that explains it. . . he must have taken it out of her wallet after the Brewer game.

"But this bill says she owes them seven thousand dollars! Do you really think I believe for one second *Mom* spent. . ."

"Yeah, so what? Mom said I could use it to get back on my feet. Mind your own business, Eleanor."

"You bastard..." Ellie began.

"Keep your voice down. It upsets Mom enough when you insist on meddling in her affairs. It's Mother's Day...why not let her have a nice Sunday for a change?"

"You jerk! You run up seven-grand in cash advances on a credit card account...you basically tricked Mom into opening...and you have the nerve to tell me to mind my own business? Well, this IS my business. I am Mom's personal representative and I want to know how YOU plan to pay this."

"ME pay it? I don't think so, Sis, I'm a little short. And we both know whose fault that is, don't we? I'd be on easy street by now if you'd kept your nose out of my business. Besides, Mom's legally responsible for the debt. So YOU pay it, Miss Personal Representative."

Ellie opened her mouth to argue, but she heard Josie's voice say, "Frank's right, Ellie. If Mom opened the account and gave him permission to use the card, she's obligated to pay the bill." Ellie turned around. Josie had obviously heard almost their entire conversation.

"But this is wrong, Josie, Frank's stealing from Mom, and this isn't the first time..."

"Stealing? From my own mother? How dare you call me a thief," Frank said viciously. "I've never stolen a dime from her; she's *given* me every cent. In case you've forgotten, it's *Mom's* money—she can do with it what she likes. I've had it with you interfering in my life, telling me what I can and can't do...you and your moral outrage...you make me sick. So, Miss Power-of-Attorney, you go right ahead and take responsibility...*you* pay the bill!"

Frank took another beer from the fridge, smiled smugly at his sisters, and went back to the living room. Ellie and Josie knew they were defeated. For their mother's sake, they kept up pretenses for the rest of the afternoon, but Ellie fumed.

I'll pay the bill, but I'm closing the account. Hopefully, that will stop you from stealing any more money from her. Still, with two or three credit card applications coming in the mail each week...what's going to stop you from doing this again?

CHAPTER 21

Monday, May 12th

Janelle arrived at work feeling relaxed and happy that Bradley would be back so she could do her own job. *Darn! I never got a chance to order a new monitor on Friday!*

"Hi, Janelle! How was your Mother's Day?" Beth asked.

"Actually, it was extra-special this year," Janelle said, stopping to talk. "We went to my mom's for a couple hours in the morning and then Matt took me out to lunch. Then we stopped at his mom's."

"Sounds great...my day was crazy like all the rest. Get any Almost-A-Mother gifts?"

"How did you know?" Janelle stepped closer. "Matt gave me two yellow rose bushes for the yard and this necklace." She pulled at the chain around her neck. "It's the birthstone for July."

"Ooohhh, how sweet!" Beth said, touching the tiny gold cross pendant. "Hey, what if you have the baby early? The birthstone'll be wrong."

"Matt said he already checked. If I have the baby in June, he can exchange it, but we should be safe, I'm due the twentieth of July."

"What if you're late?"

"Bite your tongue, Beth! I better not be!"

"My birthday's in August. That makes it a good month," Beth laughed, seeing the look on Janelle's face. Then the switchboard beeped and they heard Larry's agitated voice.

"Beth, when you see Janelle, tell her I need to see her immediately, please?"

Surprised by Larry's request and especially by the tone of his voice, Janelle signaled for Beth not to tell her boss she was standing right there. "Okay..." Beth said, "as soon as I see her."

"What do you think that's all about?" Beth asked.

"I don't know, but I may as well go find out. Talk to you later." Janelle gathered her lunch, purse and canvas bag to drop off in her office first. When she got there, she saw a note taped to her computer screen:

Janelle, See me right away. Very important. —Larry.

Now Janelle really began to worry. *Did I do something wrong? Maybe I forgot someone's computer and the virus isn't gone.* She hurried down the hall.

"You wanted to see me?" Janelle said, nervously standing in Larry's doorway.

"Hi, Janelle. Come in and shut the door, please." He gestured for her to sit in the guest chair.

Janelle closed the door and sat down, trying to look as relaxed as possible. She couldn't ever remember Larry's door being closed for any reason.

"Janelle, I really don't know how to tell you this so I'm just going to say it."

"Okay," Janelle was positive she'd never seen Larry at a loss for words before either.

"I got a phone call at home yesterday afternoon from Bradley's wife. She thinks there's something going on between you two."

"What!" Janelle said incredulously. "Are you serious?"

"As serious as a heart attack."

"That's ridiculous! What did she say?"

"She said you sent Bradley an email on Friday saying you missed him."

"I don't believe this," Janelle sputtered. "You know what Larry? I don't need this. I'm having a baby in two months and I'm happily married. I don't need Bradley's wife making up stories and calling my boss at home on Sundays. Why did she call you in the first place?"

"Truthfully? She wanted me to fire you."

"Unbelievable!" Janelle said, propelling herself up from the guest chair to pace the room. "Larry, the email was completely innocent. She took it totally out of context. You have to believe me. You do, don't you?"

"Of course. Hey, don't worry—your job's not in question here. I just wanted to give you a heads-up because she also said she's going to call your husband."

Janelle's jaw dropped and she sat back down. "Call my husband? Why?"

"Quoting her, 'to make sure he knows what kind of wife he has,'" Larry said, imitating a snotty, female voice.

"Did you talk to Bradley about this?"

"I'm not even sure he knows."

"You think he doesn't know she reads his email?"

"Oh, I'm sure he knows that now—she told me they were fighting about it. I doubt he knows she called me or that she plans to call Matt."

"Well, what else did she say?"

"She just kept rambling on and on. I tried to hang up, but she was completely hysterical; I thought it best to listen."

"So what did you tell her you'd do?"

"Talk to you and tell you to be more careful about what you write."

"Larry, I can forward you the email; there's absolutely nothing suggestive about it." Janelle held the side of her stomach. The baby was wiggling around and delivered a sharp kick to her ribs. "This woman gives new meaning to the word psycho," she fumed.

"I can't disagree," Larry said, then suddenly changed the subject. "Janelle did you do something to your eye?" He leaned forward to look closer.

"What? Uh, no, it's nothing," Janelle replied, reaching up to touch her right eyelid. "I think I got bit by a mosquito Saturday night."

"I thought it looked a little puffy," Larry said, rocking back on his chair, apparently more relaxed now that Beverly's message had been delivered. "Email me that message. I want to document it in case there's additional trouble ahead." He got up, a signal that the meeting was over. "And Janelle, a word to the wise. You may want to screen your calls at home for a while...and for now, the cross training's on hold."

"Fine. Right now I couldn't care less if anyone learns my job." Janelle felt tears coming. "I just want to have my baby and get out of here for a while. I don't need this!"

"Janelle, please. Everything'll be fine. I wasn't even going to tell you until she mentioned calling your husband."

"Larry, did you know Bradley deceived her about the seminar? She didn't know I went along until I told her how grateful I was that her husband took me to the hospital. Why didn't he tell her? And why is this all *my* fault?" She grabbed a tissue from Larry's desk, angry with herself for getting upset.

"It's not. Bradley and his wife obviously have issues," Larry said, attempting to calm Janelle down. "At first I tried to explain that people often say or write things that can be misinterpreted. I told her about that time last spring when you were talking to Matt on the phone during lunch. When I interrupted to ask you a question, you called me 'honey'... remember? You were so embarrassed!"

"Oh jeez, I bet she had a field day with that one!"

"Well, in hindsight, I probably should have used a different example, but I can't change it now," Larry said, shrugging his shoulders.

Janelle grabbed another tissue and wiped as close to her eye lashes as possible to fix her smeared makeup. She got up and went to the door. "All I can say is I hope my baby comes early. In fact, any day now would be perfect."

"Janelle, stop it," Larry said. "It's too early. Please don't worry about this; it'll all work out."

"Don't wish this...don't worry about that...you sound like every other person in my life right now. I thought last Friday, dealing with that stupid virus, was a day from hell, but compared to this shit, excuse my choice of words, Friday doesn't even come close."

"Janelle, maybe you should take off at noon today. You don't have to use vacation, just take the time; I insist."

"I might just do that," Janelle replied, already thinking an afternoon nap would be heavenly since she and Matt were planning to attend the school board meeting tonight to support Ellie. "I didn't get anything done Friday though, so I'll wait and see how the morning goes and decide later. Thanks for the offer."

Janelle walked stiffly back to her office, careful not to make eye contact with anyone because they'd surely see she'd been crying. She booted up her computer, mouthing a short prayer that the monitor wouldn't act up this morning. *Thank you, God. With this headache, I don't think my eyes or my stomach could handle the flickering right now.* She decided to email Bradley about ordering the new monitor before she forgot again.

Bradley:
Please order the new monitor. I didn't have time Friday.
Janelle.

Short and to the point, she thought as she moved her cursor over to the Send button. *Nothing a wife could misinterpret. Jeez…what a bitch! Who does she think she is? She wants to call Matt and tell him what kind of a wife he has? I should write: P.S. I'm soooo glad you're back. I wonder what she'd think of that?*

Janelle clicked her mouse without editing the curt message and started on her pile of neglected work. She was mixing color combinations for a new FootWorks logo when her direct line rang. Still concentrating on finding eye-catching but complementing shades of purple and burnt orange, she picked up the phone.

"Hello, this is Janelle."

"Is this Janelle Spencer?"

"Yes…who is this?" Janelle was sure she'd heard the voice before.

"Bradley's wife, Beverly."

Janelle carefully placed her mouse beside the keyboard and sat back in her chair, her mouth suddenly very dry and her heart pounding.

"Yes, Beverly; how can I help you?" Janelle tried to sound as business-like as possible.

"I'm just calling to let you know that Bradley and I had a very interesting weekend. I saw the email you sent him last Friday. I assume by now Larry has spoken to you?"

"About what?" Janelle asked, evading the question.

"The inappropriateness of it, of course."

"Inappropriateness?"

"Don't play dumb with me, Janelle. I know what's going on with you and Bradley."

"Going on?"

"Stop the games. Ever since you and Bradley started cross training, all he ever talks about is you. His entire personality has changed, the way he dresses...everything! It's upsetting our whole family and I don't like it."

Janelle could feel her courage growing from the pit of her stomach. "I don't know what you're talking about."

"*I miss you, please come back,*" Beverly spat out the words. "Unfortunately, our daughter, Meredith, of all people, found it on the computer and saw it before I did. Can you imagine the damage that you have inflicted here?"

"I find that hard to believe," Janelle almost laughed.

"Believe what you want, Janelle. Bradley is married. This needs to be over."

"It was an innocent comment, Beverly..."

"Innocent? I think not," Beverly shot back. "For all I know, you begged Larry to take you along to the seminar so you could be with my husband. You must know he's one of those men who find pregnant women very appealing."

Janelle decided not to take the bait. "You'll have to trust me when I say there's absolutely nothing going on between Brad...Bradley and me. I am very happily married. The only thing I'm interested in doing with Bradley is training him to fill in for me while I'm off on maternity leave."

"I don't trust you at all, Janelle, but I do trust my husband...implicitly!"

Janelle just rolled her eyes. *Sure she does. She obviously doesn't even know what 'implicitly' means.*

"I just wanted to make sure that everybody was on the same page here. Bradley and I have had lengthy conversations about this, and I just don't want it to take up any more of my time. Frankly, it's beneath me and I want to just remove myself from it."

"Beverly, I..."

"Enough! This is it, Janelle. I don't want to get defensive, and I don't want you to get defensive either. In fact, I don't really want to spend my time and energy on this at all." Beverly's voice had gradually become louder and sounded ominous. "I wanted you to know that I'm well aware of the situation now..."

"There is no situation..."

"And for your sake, you'd better be careful in the future how you act with other women's husbands."

"Consider the message received," Janelle said softly, realizing it was pointless to argue with someone who refused to listen.

"I didn't hear you, Janelle. What?"

Sounding like a robotic machine, Janelle said louder, "Your message has been received."

"Good. Have a good day, Janelle."

Kill her with kindness, Janelle thought. "I certainly will. And you have a good day too."

Janelle hung up, stunned. *Unreal. No one's going to believe this, I can't even believe it!* She shook her head to clear the cobwebs. *How can I try to work now? What will Matt think when I tell him? I wish I could tell Ellie tonight, but I can't—tonight's all about Ellie and her problems with the school...my Beverly-Bitch story will have to wait.*

Ellie both looked forward to and dreaded the upcoming meeting. Stacey and she had agreed the rebuttal, like the original complaint, should be given at the regular board session. Ellie felt she was prepared, but lately things never seemed to go the way she anticipated. In the end, she decided to "give the problem to God" and spend the day enjoying her students' reactions to personal poetry.

For years Ellie's favorite mini-unit had been *Poems About Family Members*. She loved introducing the students to the wonders of poetry, but her favorite part of the course was when the kids finally put pen to paper and wrote their own poems—as tributes to a chosen family member. Year after year, she noticed many students elected to write about a grandparent. This exercise had taught Ellie the profound effect grandparents have on their grandchildren's lives—a role she just knew would be perfect for her.

The day went well, especially when Kaylie asked if she could write hers to her "third grandmother." Ellie had asked what on earth that meant and Kaylie just smiled and said, "Duh, you, Mrs. Reed." Her remark had renewed Ellie's faith in herself and her chosen profession. She glanced at the calendar on the wall. *Omigod...there's only two and a half months until Janelle's baby is due. It'll be so wonderful to hold a baby again.*

Ellie finished preparing for the next day, packed up and walked out to Blackbird. She was meeting Jack and Stacey for dinner. At first Ellie didn't like the idea because she thought he might get angry and use some "blue collar" language if he went to the board meeting—then she decided she needed him for emotional support regardless.

Stacey had picked up Jack at his office and they were already seated in the dining room when Ellie arrived. The two women briefly went over their presentation before ordering, Stacey explaining a few minor changes she had made. Ellie would have liked a cold mug of beer, but she settled for club soda with lime. The bar and dining room were packed—unusual for a Monday night—and Ellie recognized almost everyone as a former student, parent or colleague. Several people waved when she looked around, surprised and yet relieved that nobody came over to chat. All three diners had the tenderloin steak special with twice-baked potatoes and salad bar. They laughed and made small talk, declaring the subject of Mrs. Nielsen off-limits until seven.

Midway into the meal Stacey said, "You know, Ellie, I finally got in touch with Becca. She's going to be in Chicago this weekend; we're meeting Friday night at a sports bar near Wrigley. I'm not very interested in sports, but she insists she'll make a Cheesehead out of me yet!"

Ellie smiled, pleased that her troubles had rekindled one of her daughter's lost friendships. *That's the wonderful thing about life; everything's a trade-off... out of negatives come positives... sometimes greater than we can ever imagine.*

When dinner was over, Stacey picked up the check. The entire meal plus the tip came to forty dollars. "This was absolutely delicious, and I have more than enough left for supper tomorrow," Stacey said, pointing to the "doggy" bag sitting by her plate. "That bill would be over two hundred dollars in Chicago. I'll probably spend this much on a round of drinks Friday night."

"Well, we do enjoy great food at great prices here," Jack agreed, ready to mount that soapbox again, "but the average working guy's wages aren't keeping up with inflation..."

"Not tonight, Jack," Ellie said, noticing that it was time to leave for the school board meeting. "Save your moral outrage for the meeting."

As they walked to their cars, Jack ushered Ellie over to Stacey's car. "You have a hard enough time obeying the speed limit when you aren't nervous, Ellie, so I'll drive Blackbird. You and Stacey follow behind." For once, she didn't argue.

Pulling into the board office parking lot fifteen minutes early, Ellie noticed a lot more cars than usual. She looked at the marquee sign and was baffled when she read:
SCHOOL BOARD MEETING
MOVED TO CITY AUDITORIUM
MONDAY 7:00 P.M.

Why on earth would they hold the meeting in the auditorium? It's huge!

Stacey parked her car one slot over from Blackbird and Ellie joined her husband while Stacey fetched her expensive leather briefcase. It was a warm, invigorating spring evening and the sun was just setting—the sky a spectacular showcase. Surrounding the sinking bright yellow orb were the most intense shades of orange Ellie had ever seen. In breathtaking contrast, the sky behind presented a dazzling display in every imaginable red of the color spectrum—from the palest pink to the deepest purple. Keeping the sun company as it went to its rest were a few cottonball cumulus clouds.

What a beautiful sky...I so love the sunset...I only hope the sun isn't setting on my career.

Arriving at the meeting site, Ellie saw dozens of people milling about and dozens more already filing into the auditorium. She felt there must be some other event scheduled or they had mistakenly come to the wrong place.

Then she saw Tom come rushing over. "I thought you'd be here fifteen minutes ago. Amazingly, the Nielsens are no-shows so far; maybe this'll all just go away. You better get in there right away. I saved some seats down in front."

"Why so many people?" Ellie asked in wonder.

"Must be because the board's opening discussions on the budget cuts tonight. By six the boardroom was already full so they decided to move the meeting over here."

"Great news, Ellie," Jack said enthusiastically. "Whether Mrs. Nielsen shows or not, now the whole community can hear your side." Stacey gave him a thumbs-up response, but Ellie said nothing, managing only to produce a weak smile.

The trio walked down the aisle and took their reserved front row seats. Ellie turned around to see the room filling up quickly. Almost all the faces were familiar: colleagues, former students, parents whose children she now had in class. Kaylie and a large group of Ellie's current students waved enthusiastically when Ellie glanced in their direction.

She saw a reporter sitting off to the side, fiddling with his tape recorder. On stage, a TV news crew was noisily testing sound equipment. *Cripes...the sign says Maximum Capacity 600—Tom must be right; people really are upset about the budget cuts.* Ellie saw Mrs. Nielsen and Henley sit down off to her right, causing her heart to race and her mouth to go dry. Then she caught sight of Janelle and Matt

Spencer with a group of late-twenty-somethings and her panic subsided.

People were still coming in when the meeting began a full ten minutes late. By the time the board president rapped the gavel on the podium, every seat was filled and people were standing in the aisles. "Wow...money issues sure can bring out the crowds," Jack whispered.

As customary, the minutes of the last meeting came first. When the secretary read that Mrs. EvaLynne Nielsen had presented a formal complaint against middle school English teacher Eleanor Reed, the crowd stirred and burst into applause. Ellie felt her face turn bright red and she wanted to run from the room, but she held her head high as Jack gave her hand a reassuring squeeze.

"Before we begin the published agenda, is there anyone from the audience who wishes to speak?" the board president asked, looking around the room.

Several hands went up. Unsure how to handle the unusual situation, the board president cleared his throat nervously. Then a man Ellie had taught her first year in the district, Jim VanHueckel, rose and walked to the microphone. A local car dealer who did his own commercials, Jim's face was very familiar to all.

"Mr. President, some of us have remarks we'd like to share...may we?"

"Of course," the board president said in a what-else-can-I-do voice. "You have the floor."

The newspaper reporter started writing feverishly and the TV camera started rolling. There wasn't a sound in the room as Jim, a dynamic public speaker, began.

"First, I'd like to say that most of us are here for two reasons. One is the budget discussion but the other, more important reason, is to show our support for Mrs. Reed."

When a burst of applause rang out, Ellie was stunned. Looking around, she began to realize what was happening.

"I've known Mrs. Reed for over thirty years," Jim said. "She was a first-year teacher and I was the class clown." People chuckled in agreement. "I spent more time getting out of things than doing anything productive. But Ellie...Mrs. Reed...took a special interest in me and made me see that I was the one in charge of my destiny. Believe me, that woman changed my life. I can sincerely say she is the best teacher I ever had. Yes, she was tough on discipline; you bet she made us work hard, but we *learned*—isn't that what school's for?" Another round of exuberant applause followed his comments.

"Thank you...that's all I have to say. The next speaker will be Matt Spencer."

Matt rose and went to the microphone. He was clearly nervous, and carrying a paper from which he read.

"Um...Mrs. Reed was my teacher fifteen years ago, but she was more than just an English teacher," Matt said. "She also taught me how to live a good life. Once when I was in her class, I had to write a poem. I had no idea what to write about and then I saw this poem hanging on the wall at home. It said *Author Unknown* so I copied it, thinking since the author was unknown, Mrs. Reed wouldn't know I'd copied it. Well...Mrs. Reed could've used me as a public example of a cheater and embarrassed me in front on the other kids. She could've just given me a zero for plagiarism. But she didn't. She talked to me privately and explained why it wasn't okay to turn in someone else's poem, why it's important to do your own work—even if you may think it's not good enough. Then she gave me another chance to write my own poem. I'll never forget that," he added, finally looking up at the audience.

"Um, some of you guys know me and my wife Janelle...I mean, my wife Janelle and I...sorry, Mrs. Reed...are going to have a baby in a couple months." There was some hooting and whistling from the section where Janelle was sitting. Now Matt looked directly at Ellie. "Well, I just want to say that Janelle and I do have one complaint about you."

Ellie felt her face flush as she waited for Matt to continue.

"Our complaint is that you're going to retire in a few years and you won't be here to teach our baby when he or she is in seventh grade," Matt said. Then he winked at Ellie.

Ellie's relief was expressed with a warm smile.

"But I know I'll be a better dad because you taught me

how to handle things when my son or daughter makes a mistake. By the way, in case anyone was wondering, the poem I turned in was called *Footprints*." Matt paused for some good-natured chuckling from the audience.

"Ellie Reed has definitely made a footprint on my life, and my wife's. I'm sure there's more of you in this room, and hundreds more who couldn't get here tonight, who feel the same." A huge swell of applause rose from the audience as Matt returned to his seat beside a beaming Janelle.

Several speakers followed, including parents of current students who praised Mrs. Reed's curriculum and close colleagues who stated they had never seen Ellie misuse her influence as a teacher. They all stressed Ellie's hardworking habits and her devotion to her students. Ellie listened intently, but found herself in a daze several times, in shock over the heart-rending tribute from so many.

By the time Ellie's "exoneration" ended, her face was bathed in tears, and the meeting was well behind schedule. The board president called for a five minute recess, and she was finally able to look over to where Mrs. Nielsen and Henley were sitting. She stared at the two empty chairs and wondered when their occupants had slipped out.

Janelle and Matt came over to hug Ellie. "Matt, you were terrific," Ellie said. He just blushed and looked at his wife.

"That part was his idea," Janelle said. "Getting all these people here...that was mine. It was pretty easy though; all it took was the power of email."

Matt's friends were calling and he clearly wanted to rejoin them so Janelle said quickly, "Let's get together next week. Call or email me...I have MAJOR news. If we don't get together real soon, I'll email you the whole story." Janelle noticed a look of concern in Ellie's eyes. "Don't worry, the baby's fine; the news I have is about Bradley's wife."

"Oh, thank goodness, the baby's okay! Don't tell me he lied to her about something again?"

"No, she read an email I sent him and took it completely out of context. She called me at work today and went off on me about it."

"You're kidding!" Ellie leaned closer to Janelle so the people crowding around waiting to talk to her wouldn't hear. "Do email me. I'd love the details now; it sounds too interesting to wait, but there are so many people I need to thank for tonight, including you!" Ellie hugged Janelle again before she left to catch up with Matt.

Ellie thanked the many people surrounding her until the meeting was about to resume and then thought it best to leave. "Let's go home, honey," she said to Jack, "I think they're done with me." As they walked up the aisle she overheard Tom telling one of the reporters, "Of course we supported Mrs. Reed a hundred and ten percent from the very beginning, she's one of our finest."

Another reporter Ellie recognized, but couldn't name, shoved a microphone in her face and said, "That was really something in there, Mrs. Reed. How does it feel to be such a hero?" Ellie looked to Stacey for approval.

"Go ahead, you waited long enough," the lawyer said.

"Of course it feels wonderful to have such community support," Ellie began, "but if I'm a hero, then there are hundreds of thousands of heroes in this country. They are the educators in communities across this nation who get up every day and go to schools to teach our kids, no matter how difficult the challenge. Sadly, over half of all teachers who began last September will be out of the classroom in five years. Too many fine educators quit each year, not because of the difficulty of dealing with students, but because of parents like the one who brought this complaint. I want to encourage them to stay, to stand their ground, because an individual teacher's impact is not seen in the short run; it takes decades to bloom and flourish."

"Thank you, Mrs. Reed," the reporter said, taking back the microphone. She then turned to the camera and added: "Tonight at this school board meeting-turned-tribute to middle school English teacher Mrs. Eleanor Reed, one couldn't help but think of the famous words of Christa MacAuliffe. I think what happened here tonight proves that Christa was right when she said, 'I touch the future; I teach.'"

CHAPTER 22

Not the camping type, Janelle and Matt always used Memorial weekend to get work done around the house and to spruce up the yard for their annual Memorial Day Picnic. As usual, by Monday, Janelle was exhausted.

Why do I forget from year to year how much work it is to host this picnic? Oh, well...at least it's less work than walking on eggshells around Bradley all day at the office.

She'd been up since 7:00. The first item on her list was to prepare Spanish hamburger, and the kitchen was already bathed in the scent of browned ground beef, onions, and garlic simmering in a tangy tomato sauce. Next she cut watermelon into bite-size pieces and added it to her festive fruit salad. *Yumm...I would eat fresh fruit every single day...if someone else cut it up for me. God, my legs ache from standing on this floor.* She shifted from one foot to the other to relieve the pressure.

Strategically placing luscious strawberries as garnish on the fruit salad, she turned her attention to her world-famous beer cheese pretzel dip. She pronounced it perfect after several taste tests to adjust the seasoning. Next came Matt's favorite: fat dill pickles rolled inside deli ham slices slathered with cream cheese. Going into the pantry to fetch the toothpicks that would serve as finger food spearing sticks, she noticed the crackers. "Oh, that's right," she said aloud, "I forgot about the venison sausage in the fridge downstairs and there's cheese to slice yet." Each time she crossed an item off her list, she added one or two more things to the bottom.

Janelle looked at the clock; it was 10:30. Matt was gone to the store, so she decided to take a shower. *It'd be rude to excuse myself to take a shower once everyone gets here... but if I'm still busy preparing food, people will either offer to help or think nothing of it.*

Janelle hadn't realized just how sore her legs were until the hot pulsing water hit them and relaxed the aching muscles. She lathered shampoo into her hair and then massaged her head, paying special attention to her temples. *Please, not another headache. Not today.*

Janelle rinsed thoroughly and turned off the water. As she was wrapping herself in a big fluffy cotton towel, she heard noise in the house. Peeking her head out the bathroom door, she called out, "Matt? Is that you?"

"Yup. Back from the store! You need me?"

Janelle's eyes lit up. "Yes, come here, Matt."

"Hey, babe," Matt said, walking into the bedroom. "I put the beer and soda in coolers. Anything else I can help with before I go get the lawn chairs out of the shed?"

"Uh huh," she pointed to the sheets in the laundry basket. Still wrapped in her towel, Janelle felt relaxed and refreshed as they finished spreading clean sheets, still warm from the dryer, onto their king-size bed.

"Now I have another thing you can help me with," Janelle said, circling her arms up and around Matt's tanned neck and kissing him full on the lips.

"Mmmm, Janelle. What's gotten into you?" Matt asked. "I saw your to-do list on the counter..."

"Oh, well, sometimes less important things don't get done," Janelle said mischievously, reveling in the joy of catching Matt off guard.

"Oh, okay," Matt said catching his breath. "Then let's take care of the important things right now."

Eat your heart out, Beverly, I'm seven months pregnant and I can still seduce my husband. What makes you think I need yours?

Lingering afterward, Janelle recalled the first time they'd been together after she'd "popped." She was pleasantly surprised to find Matt wasn't in the category of husbands who couldn't make love to a pregnant wife, yet she was grateful he wasn't drawn to other pregnant women like Beverly said Bradley was. Matt was very gentle, but that made it all the more intimate. Every time since then, as she lay in Matt's arms afterward, she wondered if this would be the last time they'd make love until after the baby was born. *What will sex be like when we aren't trying to conceive or not hurt a baby?* True, they'd had their days of carefree lovemaking before they decided to start a family, but that seemed so long ago…she just couldn't remember.

Janelle's musing was cut short by a voice at the door. "Yooo! Whooo! Anyone home? Janelle, it's Mom. I came early to help!"

Janelle threw on her lightweight summer robe, kissing Matt one last time when he promised to remake the bed.

"Hi, Mom!" Janelle hurried to the kitchen. "Jeez, it's twenty after eleven!"

"Well, that's why I came early. Put me to work."

"Do you want to slice the cheese and venison for me?"

"Sure, I can do that. You go get ready. Where's Matt?"

"Getting dressed."

"He just got up?"

"No, Mom, we were *busy*."

"Oh," Claire said with an slight giggle, trying not to look at her daughter's expanding belly. "I'm so sorry. I shouldn't have come early."

"Mom, it's okay, really. We were…you didn't interrupt. I'll go get dressed. Be right back."

Janelle and Claire made amazing progress in forty minutes. Aunt Christine and Uncle Rick were the first to arrive——promptly at noon.

"I said hi, Janelle, dear. I haven't seen you since Easter." Christine set her taco dip tray on the snack bar. "You're looking good. I was just going to say, how's the baby?"

Here we go again! "Well, I was just gonna tell you the baby's great," Janelle replied. *I can't help myself; maybe if she hears me imitating her she'll realize how she sounds.*

"In fact, I said I can show you a video from the ultrasound later if you want."

"Really? I said that would be so nice. I'd love to see it." Christine was obviously clueless, but Claire, who was sprinkling paprika on the deviled eggs, wasn't. She elbowed Janelle when Christine wasn't looking.

"I said is there anything I can help with?" Christine asked as she sat down at the table.

"Christine, I was just going to say you could empty these crackers into the bowl," Claire replied, suppressing a giggle as she handed them to her sister-in-law. "And set it out on the banquet table on the patio. I said we'll be out with the rest of the food in a little bit."

Christine was unfazed, apparently oblivious to the fact that she was being imitated. As she took the crackers out to the patio, Janelle heard her say, "I said Happy Memorial Day, Matt. I said you sure got nice weather again this year for your picnic. I was gonna say yesterday was so miserable and today it's just beautiful."

"Jeez, Mom, that is soooo annoying," Janelle said in a hushed voice.

"Janelle, she's done that for as long as I can remember. Mimicking her isn't going to make her change."

"Well, I can hope, can't I? I wonder how Uncle Rick handles it."

"Oh, I think he stopped listening to her years ago."

"I don't know why I pick up on things like that and they bother me so much. There are some people...when they say the word column if they're working on a spreadsheet, they pronounce it like there's an "i" in the word—'col*li*umn.' If we're having a conversation and I repeat the word and pronounce it correctly, kol-lum, in the very next sentence they say 'col*li*umn' anyway!"

"What about when people say zink instead of sink?"

"Ouch, that stuff hurts my ears. I wonder if there's anything I say or do that annoys other people like that."

"Well, you say jeez a lot. It doesn't bother me, but it might bother other people. And let's see, I remember when you were in grade school you pronounced the word open with an "m" in it," Claire replied.

"Oh, yeah, I'd say om-pen. I never even realized it till Cassie told me. Now, every once in a while, I'll hear someone say om-pen and that makes me cringe too."

"Maybe it's all Ellie Reed's doing. She was always picky about that stuff."

"Could be. Ellie still corrects my grammar. She says she can't help it. I bet she'd be climbing the walls if she had a conversation with Aunt Christine."

"I'll have to make a mental note of that. We can seat them next to each other at your baby shower." They both grinned. "I really hope Ellie can make it," Claire added, sounding sincere.

"Didn't she reply?"

"Uh, no, not to me. Maybe she called Cassie or Sandy."

"That reminds me, Mom, Cassie and Jeff might stop by on their way home from camping, depending on what time they get back."

"She's been such a sweetheart. Can you imagine helping with someone's baby shower back when you were trying so hard to get pregnant?"

"It would've been hell, Mom, but I would've done it for Cass...she's been my best friend forever."

"I know you would've, Janelle," Claire said, rubbing her daughter's shoulder affectionately.

After Claire and Janelle took the rest of the food out to the patio, Matt insisted they both sit down, relax and have a drink. He made Janelle a Virgin Mary and poured Claire a berry wine cooler. Rick and Christine already had a drink in hand.

"Heellloooo," Sandy's voice called from inside the house.

"We're in back," Matt yelled. "C'mon out."

"Happy Memorial Day everyone," Sandy said, making a grand entrance with a tall, graying, quite attractive man who looked as if he'd spent all winter on a Florida golf course. "I'd like to introduce you all to my friend, Roger."

It was always hard for Janelle to enjoy herself at their picnic, not just because she was busy catering to everyone's needs, but also because it was uncomfortable for her to mix their families. This year, with Sandy's promise to shape up and the two expectant grandmothers working together on the baby shower, Janelle had hoped the situation would improve. Unfortunately, she had not factored in the possibility of Sandy bringing a date and reverting to her old self.

Sandy made her way to Claire, with Roger following close behind, and handed her the cake pan she was holding. "Here, Claire, I better give these brownies to you. We don't want Janelle to eat too many."

Aahh, I knew my new and improved mother-in-law was too good to be true. A handsome guy on her arm and all bets are off. She's definitely in her element when she has a man. She's like a peacock with all her feathers fanned; her makeup flawless; not a single tinted hair out of place. And that burgundy sundress…tightly fitted to show off her slim figure. And jeez, anyone familiar with Wisconsin spring weather would know that her tan came from a tanning bed.

Claire took the cake pan and quickly made room for it on the food table. One thing was certain, even if the mixed company wasn't the best, the food was. As everyone grazed leisurely at the banquet table, Janelle could feel Sandy watching her so she purposely took a second brownie, making sure she took the biggest piece left in the pan. As they made eye contact, Janelle took a huge bite, daring her to say something derogatory.

Instead it was her mother who asked with concern, "Janelle, what's wrong with your eye? Did you bump it?"

"What?" Janelle shoved the rest of the brownie in her mouth, only half listening to Claire.

"Your eye. It looks puffy and red."

"Uh, no. I got this a couple weeks ago," All eyes were on Janelle as she chewed her brownie to empty her mouth so she could finish explaining. "I think it's a mosquito bite."

"Does it hurt?" Uncle Rick asked. "Maybe it's infected."

"Sometimes. Not right now though," Janelle said. "My eye's been twitching a lot lately…that's annoying."

"Maybe when you cut your forehead at work you hit some nerves around your eye," Claire suggested.

"That's probably it, Mom," Janelle said, satisfied with the explanation. "I'll have to ask at my next appointment."

"I said how is work going, Janelle?" Christine asked.

Janelle rolled her eyes and Matt started to chuckle.

"I said what? I was just gonna say what's so funny?"

Matt, Sandy and Claire encouraged Janelle to tell the Beverly story so she did, to a very captive audience.

"Unbelievable," Roger said. "What'd you do after you hung up?"

"I went right to Bradley's office to tell him."

"I said really? What did he say?" Christine asked.

"He's the one who transferred her to my private line!"

"Are you serious?" Uncle Rick asked in amazement. "Then she even had the nerve to call Matt?"

"As my boss would say, 'as serious as a heart attack,'" Janelle replied. "The last two weeks have been horrible. I am soooo ready to get out of there."

"Yeah, she called twice that same night," Matt said, "but we saw her number on the machine and didn't answer…I'm just glad she didn't leave a message."

"You should've answered, Matt," Sandy said. "You could've told her that you trust Janelle *implicitly*."

"I emailed my friend Ellie the whole story and she thinks we should've answered too. She had some great ideas for things Matt could've said."

"One was to tell her the reason Janelle and I are so happy is because we have an open marriage where we allow each other to date." Everyone laughed at the mock-serious expression on Matt's face.

Around 2:00 in the afternoon, the next-door neighbors, Bill and Martha, walked over and Cassie and Jeff arrived.

"How've you been, Cass?" Janelle asked when they went in the kitchen to refill the snack bowls.

"Doing much better," Cassie said with a big smile, twirling her shiny dark brown hair into a bun on the back of her head before letting it fall naturally onto her shoulders.

Janelle wondered if Cassie's demeanor meant she was pregnant. "Much better? How much better?"

Cassie must have seen the look of hope in Janelle's eyes, and she held both hands up like stop signs. "No, I'm not pregnant. I got my period last week."

"Oh, Cass. I'm sorry. I thought maybe..."

"I know, don't worry. I'm okay. I looked up that SOS Group you told me about and I went last week."

"You did?"

"It was absolutely fantastic! I learned that what I read on an inspirational calendar once is true: we all want to trade our problems until we listen to other people's; then we prefer to keep our own."

Janelle smiled wryly, remembering some of the stories she'd heard when she attended the group.

"Jeff and I talked a lot this weekend and we've decided to explore adoption. We want to be parents, and there are so many children in this world who want to be loved. It feels like a perfect fit for us." Cassie's hazel eyes sparkled like sunlight dancing on a northwoods lake.

Janelle hugged Cassie. "Cass, you're going to be such good parents. I'm so happy for you."

"I'm happy for us too, but we're taking things one step at a time. We know adoption can be its own roller coaster of emotions so we're not going to get ahead of ourselves."

"The nurse I had before we switched insurances had infertility problems and she adopted her oldest son," Janelle responded. "A pregnant teenager chose her and her husband, then while they were waiting for the baby to be born, she got pregnant—now she has two sons only five months apart!"

"Oh my gosh, I'm not ready for that," Cassie said, gesturing stop signs once more. "Jeff and I want two or three, so if we do get pregnant down the line, great, but we'd like our little blessings to be more than five months apart!"

They laughed and hugged. Janelle's heart soared as her baby began playing football with her ribcage. "It's so good to see you happy and hopeful again, Cassie."

Ellie turned her oven down to warm, noting with satisfaction that everything looked perfect. Her famous cheesy potato casserole bubbled in its baking dish next to a large pan of Settler's baked beans that promised to be the perfect sweet and spicy side dish. A seven-layer lettuce salad and a light dessert—strawberry angel food torte, were chilling in the refrigerator. A cooler filled with a nice variety of specialty beers and several kinds of soda had been taken out to the four seasons room where her family had already begun their annual Memorial Day celebration.

Ellie lifted the lid on the over-sized Dutch oven containing several pounds of bratwurst and polish sausages that simmered in an onion and beer bath. At least a half-hour before eating, Jack would place the meat atop a very hot charcoal fire, grilling the sausages quickly. Fat dripping onto the charcoal would raise a cloud of smoke that imparted an indescribably delicious flavor. Ellie inhaled and thought, *Mmm, smells good, but anyone who ever smelled brats cooking over charcoal must agree that the aroma is one of the most pleasurable sensations a human being can experience, especially a hungry one.* The sausages would then be returned to the beer bath to marinate.

"Is the fire ready to go?" Ellie asked when Jack came into the kitchen.

"Uh huh...we can start it whenever; Jonah said he'd do the brats when he gets back...you just relax." Jonah had gone to pick up Helen. Although Ellie was surprised when her son offered, she understood clearly when Jonah requested Blackbird for his "mission."

"Everything sure smells good in here," Jack said as he took a deep sniff, smiling approvingly at his wife's culinary achievements. "Come on and join us, honey," he said. "You worked all day yesterday so you could take it easy today."

Ellie didn't need persuading and followed him out to the four seasons room, accessible only through the dining room patio door. The addition, done five years earlier, was really three walls of windows and a roof attached to the house. Jutting out into the backyard, it took up a substantial part of their half-acre lot, but it also gave them much-needed space for entertaining. Earlier Jack had put on the screens—with sunshine and temperatures in the 70's forecast, he felt it was time to open all the windows and let in the spring breezes. Jonah, who had obviously inherited his father's green thumb, cut the lawn and tended the flowerbeds while Ellie cooked.

"Thanks for letting me sleep in, Mom," Rebecca said as she came over to hug her mother. "Good thing we're having the party today; what a perfect day."

Ellie basked in her daughter's affection before leaving her embrace to get them both a diet soda. She hadn't seen Rebecca since the Brewer game and just having her home for the entire weekend was a treat.

"Saturday it was so foggy in Minneapolis that flights were delayed," Rebecca explained, as she opened her soda, "and yesterday was so cool and rainy here."

"I'm glad you decided to drive this time, sweetie," Ellie replied. "Memorial Day weekend is always so iffy, weather-wise. We usually seem to manage one nice day though and today's it. Guess we must be living right this year."

Hearing the unmistakable purr of Blackbird's engine in the driveway, Ellie sent Jack out to help with Helen, allowing her a few more precious moments alone with Rebecca.

"By the way, Mom, I did extend your invitation to Stacey and Dave for this weekend, but they already had reservations at a romantic bed and breakfast in Door County."

Ellie nodded. "I understand all too well; I miss those days with your father. We'll just invite them for our big Fourth of July celebration instead; that's always such a great time."

Jonah interrupted the conversation by appearing with Helen on his arm. "May I present my grandmother, Mrs. Helen Lowe," he said with an exaggerated, chivalrous bow and a big grin on his face.

"Go on, Frank," Helen said, nudging him with her elbow. "You're always such a clown."

"You called me Frank, Grandma," Jonah said, somewhat surprised. "I'm Jonah, remember?"

"Oh, yes,...of course...I know who you are, Jonah. I just forget small details every now and then. I do have a good memory, it's just short," she said, giggling. Then, abruptly switching subjects she asked, "Who else is coming today?"

"The neighbors...and Josie and Carl should be here any minute...well, speak of the devil..." Jack said as Ellie's sister and her husband came into the room. "We didn't even hear you drive up."

"We parked in the street. Don't want to even come near your T-Bird, Ellie," Carl said, half-joking. "I saw the look on your face Mother's Day when my car door just kissed your precious Blackbird."

Ellie knew she should say something to contradict Carl's comment, but she didn't. Instead, she turned to Jonah. "Why didn't you park Blackbird in the garage?"

"Sorry...I'll do it now," he said in appeasement. "You know, Mom, you taught us never to get too attached to things, but you and that car..."

Knowing he was right, Ellie felt a twinge of guilt but still couldn't help from using one of her mother's hard and fast rules. "When you borrow something, put it back where you found it, please." She pointed to the driveway and pushed her son in that direction.

Jonah left with another exaggerated bow and the moment of tension eased. While Jack went to fetch beers for Josie and Carl and a glass of milk for Helen, Ellie went to the kitchen. She returned with a colorful vegetable pizza she had made the day before and a cheese sampler tray. Rebecca followed, carrying a platter of chips and salsa, and the whole family sat down on the rattan furniture to enjoy the finger foods and each other.

"Is my Frankie coming today?" Helen asked.

"I haven't heard from him," Ellie said. *I don't care to see him after what happened on Mother's Day.* Unwittingly, Ellie's mood turned black and her thoughts were bitter. She remembered how her hand had trembled with anger as she wrote out the seven thousand dollar check to pay off Frank's credit card debt. She only hoped that her attempt to keep her brother from doing anything like that again would be successful. Unable to bring herself to tell Carolyn what Frank had done, Ellie asked her to shred any credit card applications that Helen might receive. Carolyn reluctantly agreed after Ellie stated that it was in her mother's best interest.

"Well," Helen said from out of the blue, "when Frank took me to put flowers on your father's grave yesterday, I told him about the party and he said he might drop in."

Ellie worked hard to conceal her surprise...and her fear. *Frank was here yesterday? I wonder what he's up to now? Whatever it is, it can't be good.*

Jack jumped in with a question to divert everyone's attention. "Think the Brewers will win this afternoon, Mom?" he asked Helen.

"You bet," she said, but her expression was blank. She obviously didn't know what Jack was talking about.

"Aren't they playing the Cubs at Wrigley today, Uncle Carl?" Jonah asked.

"Correct. Should be a good game, too. Anyone care to place a small wager on the outcome?" Carl asked. He took a couple of twenties from his black leather wallet.

"Yeah, I think I can put a ten-spot on the Brew Crew," Jack said.

"Okay, count me in for five bucks," Jonah added.

Rebecca and Ellie each found a five-dollar bill to add to the total, and Josie put in five for Helen and a ten for herself.

"Done," Carl replied. "I sure do hate to take money from my favorite relatives this way." He gathered the bills and put them in a basket on the coffee table.

They all laughed and Jack asked, "Think it's okay to cook the brats now so we can watch the game, Ellie?"

"Go ahead, we aren't eating until around three," she said. "It doesn't hurt them to soak..."

Carl, Jonah and Jack each grabbed a fresh beer from the cooler and went out to start the grill as the four women went to look at some wallpaper books Ellie had borrowed from a local paint store. For the first time in her career, Ellie was planning no school-related work summer. Instead, she was going to redecorate her house. She planned to repaint every room and replace the outdated wallpaper and carpeting in the living room and hall. Cooking more meals, taking advantage of leftovers, and using coupons faithfully, Ellie had saved an average of twenty-five dollars on groceries every week during the past two years and she had a little over two thousand dollars—more than enough to finance the project.

The doorbell rang and their next door neighbors, Chuck and Jackie, arrived with a luscious-looking fresh fruit tray. A minute later, toting a pasta salad, Steve and Sue, their neighbors from across the street, joined the party. When Bob, the widower in the house that adjoined their back yard arrived midafternoon, it made it an even dozen for dinner. Each of the newly arrived guests threw money into the "pot" and Carl didn't seem at all worried that he was on the hook for an even hundred dollars if the Cubs lost.

Spending the afternoon snacking and talking amiably was just what Ellie needed. She watched the baseball game, though not closely, because the Brewers weren't exactly tearing the cover off the ball. By the top of the ninth inning, with the snacks nearly gone and the Cubs leading 5-2, Carl was gloating. When the first two Brewer batters managed only weak ground balls, he was already counting his winnings.

But baseball is a game of 27, not 26 outs. Carl reacted with disgust when the Cubs' shortstop booted an easy grounder and their pitcher walked the next two batters. As Hillard Brant strode to the plate with the bases loaded, Carl breathed a sigh of relief. The big guy was in a rare 0-22 slump and had struck out in his first four at-bats. Then, Carl sat in stunned disbelief as "Hilly" sent the first pitch sailing over the historic Wrigley Field fence. The Reeds and their neighbors cheered so loudly that Helen put her hands over her ears. When the game ended 6-5 in the Brewers favor, everyone agreed the money in the pot should go to Ellie's redecorating project. Her protests were futile and Carl good-naturedly handed the money over to his sister-in-law, muttering something about how Brant would probably never again hit two grand slam homers in one season——let alone one month.

As dinnertime approached, Ellie noted with relief that Frank was a no-show. Deciding not to ask if anyone knew if he was planning on coming, she served dinner on the table she had decorated appropriately with red, white and blue.

Memorial Day always had a special significance for Ellie since her father had been a veteran. This year——due to September 11 and the Iraqi War——the day held additional meaning so before eating, everyone joined in a prayer honoring all who serve in the military, especially those who had made the ultimate sacrifice.

Over dessert, Josie turned to Rebecca. "How do you like your new law firm, Rebecca?"

"I love it! The pay's a lot less, but at least I get to do meaningful work."

"I suppose meaningful is important," Josie said with a touch of sarcasm, "but so is money, sweetness." Rebecca just nodded. She knew Aunt Josie would never understand someone taking a job that paid less just because it was fulfilling. "We do miss you in Chicago though. I know we didn't get together that much, but it was nice thinking we could see you when we wanted to."

"So what made you decide to leave McKinley and Sholdy?" Carl asked.

"Just call it a difference in philosophy."

"Philosophy?"

"Well, when they hired me, they said I could spend at least twenty percent of my billable hours doing pro-bono work, then one of the partners demanded I spend more of my time on her cases. That left me with very little time for the only work I enjoyed."

"Still a bleeding heart liberal, huh?" Josie asked in a patronizing tone.

She looked at her husband who smirked and added, "You know what Frank says, Beck, a conservative is a liberal who's been mugged. Let's hope you don't find out the hard way what he means."

"Why Uncle Carl," Rebecca said in as sweet a tone as she could manage, "at the office we say a liberal is a conservative who's been arrested. Let's just hope Uncle Frank doesn't have to find out the hard way."

Helen had been silent during the meal, but now she spoke up. "Please stop talking politics; it just upsets everyone." Then she added in a petulant voice, "I'm tired and I'd like to go home, Eleanor."

Helen's pointed comment broke-up the party. *It's probably just as well, before any more feelings get hurt.* The women insisted Ellie drive Helen home while they cleaned up. Figuring she'd be back in an hour, Ellie agreed and they were soon on their way.

Upon arriving at her mother's house, Helen and Ellie walked next door to say hello to Carolyn and her husband who were sitting outside watching their two children ride their tricycles up and down the sidewalk. Taking Ellie aside, Carolyn slipped her a white business envelope she said had been taped to Helen's front door that afternoon. Ellie hid the envelope in her pocket and escorted her mother home. She was surprised to find the inside front door unlocked and made a mental note to scold Jonah for not checking to see that Helen's house was secure before leaving. Ellie was relieved to see the house was tidy and in order. Recently she had insisted on paying Carolyn to check on Helen several times each day, thus giving Helen's young neighbor some much needed income and Ellie much needed peace-of-mind.

Helen took her medicine and told Ellie to go home because she wanted to watch some television and then go right to bed. While her mother was using the bathroom, Ellie opened the white envelope. Inside was another small envelope, a pawnshop business card, and a note.

While cleaning that jewelry you brought in yesterday,
we found two pictures inside the antique locket.
Thought you might want them back.

Ellie opened the small envelope, which contained tiny baby pictures of her Grandpa and Grandma Jackson. Helen had often said these were the only baby pictures of her grandparents that still existed.

Fearing the worst, Ellie crept quietly into Helen's bedroom and tiptoed over to her jewelry box. She opened it and could not stifle the guttural sound of rage that escaped her throat. *All of mother's jewelry is gone! Frank! You dirty, rotten son of a...*

Forcing herself to be calm, she found a picture of Frank her mother kept in the guest room, got Helen settled, said her goodbyes and returned to Blackbird. Fishing the business card from her purse, she immediately dialed the pawnshop on her cell phone.

A gruff voice answered after two rings. "Easy Cash Emporium, Ernie speaking."

"This is Helen Lowe," Ellie said. "You left a note and some pictures from a locket at my house today?"

"No, that was my wife, Francine, she did that."

"Do you still have the locket and the rest of my jewelry?"

"Yeah, I think so. Haven't been very busy today, holiday and all. Business usually picks up after seven when the casino buses roll in."

"I've changed my mind about selling my things," Ellie said. "I'm coming over right now so please don't sell anything. I want to buy it all back."

"Suit yourself," Ernie said in a disinterested tone.

Ellie asked her next question with trepidation. "How much will that cost?"

Ellie could hear an adding machine working in the background. "Twenty five hundred," Ernie said. Ellie gasped, a gut reaction she immediately regretted. However, Ernie had already hung up and didn't hear her dismay.

Ten minutes later Ellie was entering the pawnshop. On the ride over, she had decided to tell the truth. The shop was deserted except for a short, balding man with a huge belly and serious five o'clock shadow that no electric razor was going to touch. She presumed him to be Ernie and walked over to the counter where the man was working his way through a jumbo box of snack cakes.

"Ernie?" Ellie asked. She took his grunt for a yes. "I just spoke to you on the phone, but my name is not Helen Lowe. It's Eleanor Reed...I'm Helen Lowe's daughter. I need to know if this is the man who pawned her things." She showed Ernie the picture of Frank.

"Yup," Ernie said after glancing at the photo. "Said his mother asked him to pawn her stuff...acted kinda nervous...but I don't make any money askin' questions."

"Ernie, you have no reason to care if I tell you this or not, but I am going to anyway. My brother took these things without my mother's permission. She has Alzheimer's and he's been stealing from her for a long time."

At the mention of the word "Alzheimer's," Ernie perked up. "She got The Big A, huh? My old man had that. Put my old lady in the grave takin' care of him."

"I'm so sorry," Ellie said. Ernie just shrugged so Ellie carefully changed the subject. "I know you said it would cost twenty-five hundred to claim Mom's jewelry...I'll level with you. All I have is two thousand dollars. So I'm asking..."

Ernie looked at her with a modicum of pity. "Say your brother filched this stuff off his own mother who's not in her right mind?"

Ellie nodded.

"Well, other than my wife cleaning up the stuff, I ain't got that much into it. And who knows how long it could take to get my money out." It sounded like he was talking himself into something. There was a long pause. "Okay, I guess if you take it all, I can let it go for two grand."

Ellie wanted to hug him, but she resisted the urge and wrote out a check that would virtually clean out her "redecorating" account.

Ernie did the paperwork and Ellie left the store with her mother's jewelry safely tucked in her purse in a manila envelope. *There has to be something I can do. I can't keep letting Frank get away with this...it's criminal!* She called home to tell them she was going to be delayed for another hour. Then, with her mouth set in grim determination, she drove straight to the police station.

CHAPTER 23

Monday, June 2nd

Janelle decided it was time to connect with Ellie—it had been almost three weeks. She wondered how her mom was doing and wanted to share with her all the crappy stuff she'd been dealing with.

Dear Ellie,
It's been forever since we talked.
So much is happening…and I NEED ice cream!
Love, Janelle

Janelle pressed Send. *Oh jeez, I wonder if Ellie's coming to the shower? I forgot to ask Sandy and Cassie.* She was considering sending Ellie another email to ask, when Bradley appeared at her doorway.

"Janelle, can I talk to you?"

"Are you sure your wife doesn't have any informants here? We wouldn't want her to know you actually talked to me, would we?" Janelle knew she was being snotty, but she didn't care. She was still seething about Beverly's accusations and she was angry because she'd basically lost Bradley as a friend. Plus, she was beginning to worry about her job getting done during her upcoming absence.

"Janelle, please. It's important."

"Have a seat," Janelle said indifferently.

"I just wanted to let you know that I'm turning in my resignation. Today's my last day."

"What? You're not quitting because of *me*, are you?" Janelle was shocked.

"Not exactly because of you...because of Meredith——my little girl means everything to me. Bev hates the fact that we work together, and she's been threatening divorce."

"Bradley, this doesn't make any sense. Your wife is a jealous delusional; quitting isn't going to change that."

Bradley ignored Janelle's slam. "Well, I have other reasons too."

"What?"

Bradley hesitated so she added, "Oh, come on! I consider...consider–ed...you my friend...can't you at least give me an explanation? First the phone calls from your wife, then this suffocating atmosphere, now you're quitting?"

"It's...well...it's just that I do have...feelings for you." Janelle blushed a deep purple.

"A friend of mine saw us dancing at the hotel and when she confronted me, I admitted as much. She promised not to tell Bev as long as I quit."

"Sounds like blackmail...what kind of *friend* is that?"

"Actually she's more Beverly's than mine."

"How can you stay married to someone you're afraid of?"

"I'm not afraid of Bev."

"Then why not tell her the truth?"

"It's complicated, Janelle. Let's just say it probably would be best for everyone if I leave." He looked at her as if he wanted her to talk him out of it.

"Fine...you're right, it would," Janelle said, anxious to put the whole sordid situation behind her.

"There's also the virus...the Fool-virus..."

"What do you mean? What's that got to do with this?"

"I wasn't going to tell you, but it's only a matter of time before everyone knows," he said quietly.

"Knows what?" Now Janelle's curiosity was piqued.

"I was the one who created it...that's why I knew how to write the fix so fast."

"You're joking right? Why would you do that?"

"I did it when things between us were...well, I guess I wanted an excuse to spend more time with you."

Janelle just stared at him, speechless.

"The original file was supposed to go off on April Fool's Day. I wanted to impress you with my ability to fix a problem. I didn't think it all through, because after Beverly started badgering me about my new look, saying that she thought it was because of you, I figured I should delete the file..."

"And?"

"Well...somehow the virus survived..."

"You're kidding...right?" Janelle asked in disgust. She leaned back in her chair and crossed her arms, remembering the grief Bradley's prank had caused.

"I wish...I really messed up! And since it got out to your mom and a few others, and we...I, in good conscience, sent the fix to everyone infected...it's only a matter of time before someone puts two and two together and traces it back to me."

Janelle rolled her eyes at the words *good conscience*. "Then what?" Janelle wasn't sure what he was saying.

"Then their IT Departments will bill Creative Solutions for damages. You don't want to know what some IT Techs charge per hour. Not to mention the non-productive time of all their employees while they waited for the fix for the virus. Unfortunately, there could even be lawsuits involved, so of course Larry will fire me...if I'm still here."

"This is all too weird. Why did you want me to be the first to know you're resigning?"

"Because I like you and I was enjoying our new-found friendship, and I wanted you to know how sorry I am...about Bev and everything."

Janelle remembered what Cassie had said about trading problems and decided whether Creative Solutions found a temporary replacement for her or not was small potatoes compared to the shambles Bradley's life was in.

"Thanks for the apology," Janelle said, deciding to be kind. "I enjoyed our friendship too...you're a great listener, and in spite of everything, I hope things work out for you."

Until Frank's latest fiasco, Ellie had so looked forward to today—the first day of summer vacation, but not now. Using her savings to reclaim the pawned jewelry meant her redecoration project would have to wait. She could barely afford the paint and wallpaper, let alone scrounge up the ambition to start working on either one. Despite her going to the police, there was no hope of recovering her money. The officer she spoke to had been polite and sympathetic, but he said he could not proceed with a complaint unless Helen— the actual victim, filed it.

By the time Ellie returned home that night, the neighbors had already left. She had made up her mind it was time to level with her family about Frank's behavior. She told them all of it—the purloined checks...the credit card advances...the theft of Helen's jewelry...everything. Rebecca's professional opinion concurred with the police: their hands were tied because Helen had not yet been declared legally incompetent. After a lengthy—very animated— discussion, they made the unanimous decision not to put Helen through the ordeal of having Frank arrested.

It struck Ellie as almost funny that Josie seemed more upset that she had paid the pawnbroker two thousand dollars for some "worthless" jewelry than the fact that Frank was a pathetic, despicable thief. At one point, Ellie had even thought her sister might actually offer to cover some of the cost of redeeming the jewelry, but Josie had merely commended Ellie for her "unselfish decision to reclaim Helen's things" and *generously* told her to keep the jewelry as it had *sentimental* value. When it was all said and done, the responsibility still fell entirely on Ellie's shoulders.

The next morning, it took the phone ringing six times to get Ellie—usually an early riser—to drag herself out of bed. *Who the heck can that be...for God's sake?* She groggily answered the phone only to be jarred into the present by a very distraught Carolyn. "Dear God, Ellie, I thought you'd never answer! Can you get over here right away? Your mother...everything's fine...she's okay...anyway...there was a fire...a *little* fire...your mom's okay, but the smoke...the kitchen was so full of smoke, you couldn't see a thing...your mom...she's okay...she'd managed to get to the back door just as we got there...we called 911..."

"Omigod...Mom..."

"The paramedics said she is going to be just *fine*. She was coughing... gasping...we helped her get outside..."

"You're sure she's okay?

"They...the paramedics...they say she's fine..."

"What happened?"

"Apparently she'd been trying to bake cookies in her toaster oven and forgot to remove a batch..."

"Where is she...is she still there?"

"She's here, but she's really upset."

"I'll be there as soon as I can. Thanks...thanks...I'll be right there!"

Ellie threw on some jeans, hurriedly ran a comb through her hair and bolted out the front door. *Ellie...breathe...she's okay...now just breathe...she's fine...*

Flipping on the radar detector, she decided this was the time to test Blackbird's wings, pushing the accelerator well beyond eighty. In no time at all, she was screeching into Carolyn's drive.

Ellie rushed headlong into the already open door. "Oh, Carolyn...thank you...thank you so..." Then, seeing her mom, she enveloped her in a life-giving hug. "Mom! What did you think you were doing? You could've been killed!"

Pouting and defensive, Helen responded. "What's going on? I was just baking some cookies...your favorite, Eleanor! After all, you're getting so thin. I need to go get them out of the oven...they'll burn and you won't like them...I have to go home now!"

"Oh, Mom..." Ellie had to think fast. Knowing her mother usually acquiesced if a male opinion was involved, she replied, "This nice man, the fire chief, he said it's not safe. You'll have to stay with us...tonight." To Ellie's relief, it worked and Helen backed down. She asked Carolyn to watch Helen for a few more minutes; she needed to pack some of her mom's things.

"Sure...we can do that," Carolyn said. "Ellie, I almost forgot, here's a few things I've...uhmm...from your mom's mailbox." Carolyn retrieved a plastic bag full of papers and envelopes from her front entry closet.

"What in God's name?"

"I don't know...it's weird, last week, during the day, she started making several trips to the mailbox. We thought we'd better check it out...this is what we found."

Seeing the ratty-looking envelopes, Ellie's heart fell. "Oh, Carolyn...this is all happening so fast...I'm sorry! Thank you for looking out for her...we...I, was hoping this wouldn't get to this point so soon...I'll be right back."

The firefighters had opened all the windows before leaving, but it still reeked of burned cookies. Even though it was June, the house felt chilly to Ellie. *Please God, I don't want to remember it this way. This house was always so warm and inviting. I can still remember how it used to smell when Mom baked. Please God, I don't know what to do...I guess I'll just have to do whatever it takes.* Ellie quickly sorted through Helen's clothes, selecting things she had seen her mother wear recently, laying them on the bed. She took an empty container from the pantry and filled it with her medications and personal hygiene items. Then she went back to Carolyn's to pick up Helen.

As she drove slowly away, she was flooded with unbidden thoughts. *Maybe it would have been better if Mom had died. They say dying from smoke inhalation is relatively painless. At least it would have spared her from what's to come...losing her memories, her identity.* "Ellie! Shame on you," she chastised herself aloud, "you have really lost it. You recite the Act of Contrition right now to ask God to forgive your sinful thoughts!"

CHAPTER 24

Sunday, June 8th

M att was cutting the lawn, so Janelle decided to sit out on the front porch to write in her journal.

Sunday, June 8th
Dear Baby,
   I had another doctor appointment on Friday. This one was LONG. The nurse made me drink some really sugary stuff and wait for an hour so she could test my glucose levels. Only six weeks left!
   Last night I sent your daddy out with the guys because once you're here, that won't be so easy. Your daddy's being very protective of us right now, just like he should be. You and I are so lucky to have him! He's even going to start working shorter hours so you and I get to see him a little more. See how much we love you? I can't wait to hold you! Love, Mommy

Just as Janelle signed the journal, the cordless phone on the lawn chair next to her rang.

"Hello, it's Sandy...you want to come over for supper?"

"I guess so. Matt's cutting the lawn now. What time?"

"Five-thirty, six o'clock. By the way, how did your doctor's appointment go?"

"Good." Janelle knew Sandy really wanted to know only one thing, so she decided to just spill it. "I've gained a total of eighteen pounds so far. The doctor thinks it's not enough, so when I go back in three weeks, he wants me up at least two more pounds."

"Really? I only gained fifteen pounds *total* with Matt."

"So you've said, but my doctor wants to see me gain another five to seven pounds anyway."

"Trust me, you'll be a lot happier after the baby's born if you don't have to lose all that extra weight," Sandy said, sounding like an authority on the topic. When Janelle's response was icy silence, she changed the subject. "What about the lump on your eye?"

"Oh, he said it wasn't from the bump on my forehead. He seemed a little concerned, but since it wasn't very puffy when I went in, there wasn't much for him to look at."

"Well then, I guess that's...that. See you and Matt in a couple hours?"

"Oh, jeez, Sandy, I keep forgetting to ask you. Is Ellie Reed coming to my shower?"

"I meant to talk to you about that. Don't you think it would be...awkward...to have a former teacher at your shower? Showers are for close friends and family."

"Ellie *is* a friend...a very good friend!"

"Doesn't it seem like you're just asking for a gift by inviting a teacher you had in seventh grade?"

Janelle was incredulous. "What do you mean by that? Didn't you mail her an invitation?"

"Calm down, Janelle. I meant to ask you, but I forgot."

"Ask me what? Mom wanted a list of my friends...Ellie's name was on the very top. Why do you have a such a big problem with Ellie being my friend?"

"I don't...I simply forgot..."

"I don't think you *forgot* anything. For some reason, you simply don't want Ellie there. Let's just *forget* supper tonight!" Janelle slammed down the receiver.

Twenty minutes later she was knocking on Ellie's front door. She'd been there only one other time—to pick up a letter of recommendation for a college scholarship. Except for her own reflection in the window of the storm door, everything looked exactly the same: the bushes meticulously trimmed, the thick lawn perfectly manicured and edged along the front walk, Ellie's summer flowers vibrant with color.

"Janelle! What a wonderful surprise!" Ellie said as she opened the door, inviting her in. "Mom and I are out in the sunroom enjoying the weather. Would you care to join us and have some fresh-squeezed lemonade?"

Janelle followed her out to the bright airy sunroom and sat down as Ellie handed her a frosty-cold mug of lemonade. She'd taken only a few sips when finally, unable to contain her anger any longer, she blurted, "Ellie, I'm so damn mad at my mother-in-law...I could just spit!" Feeling the burden lift from her shoulders as she related everything that had happened, Janelle finally began to relax.

"I received your 'need ice cream' email just this morning. Even though school's out, I've had my hands full with Mom. It's almost impossible to even get my regular chores done, much less find the time to get online. I *really need* to go to Paradise Island soon. I have so much to tell you." Ellie nodded in her mother's direction.

"Janelle, I need to take my neighbors' mail across the street. They were on vacation last week. I hate to ask, but would you mind staying with Mom for just a few minutes?"

Janelle looked at Helen who sat staring unresponsively out the large sunroom windows. "She'll be fine," Ellie explained. "She likes to watch for birds or squirrels. When she doesn't see any, she thinks they're playing hide and seek or peek-a-boo."

"Sure," Janelle said apprehensively. "I can handle it."

"Great. I'll only be a few minutes. It's the blue house right across the street." Ellie grabbed the designated stack of mail off the kitchen counter and hurried out, leaving Janelle and Helen in silence. Janelle grew uncomfortable and tried to talk to her. "Hi. Remember me? I'm Janelle, Ellie's friend." Helen didn't even acknowledge her.

As they sat there in complete silence, Janelle realized she needed to get to the bathroom...*fast*...the pregnancy and her nervousness, combined with the lemonade, were too much for her bladder.

Helen, I'll be right back. I'm just going to go potty."
Helen continued to stare out the window, still as a statue, so
Janelle hurried to find the bathroom. She quickly relieved
herself, then washed her hands with cold water to get back
sooner. She couldn't have been gone two minutes, but when
she returned, the sunroom was empty!

"Helen?" Janelle called out, looking around frantically.
"Helen, where are you?"

She ran to the front door, thinking maybe Helen had
gone outside to find Ellie. No, Ellie was still across the street,
standing in the driveway, talking with her neighbor. *Oh my
God, what've I done? How am I supposed to take care of a
baby? I can't even keep track of Ellie's mother for three
minutes!* Janelle was beginning to panic. She began
searching the house. Every room was empty and showed no
signs of recent activity. Feeling more and more desperate.
"Helen...Helen...where are you?" *Oh my God, I have no
idea...she could've fallen or something! What if she's hurt
and can't answer me?*

Janelle decided to check the basement and the garage.
The basement was cool and damp...no Helen. The garage
was hot and stifling...no Helen. Janelle returned to the house
in tears, positive that something terrible had happened on her
watch. *What am I going to tell Ellie?*

Almost hysterical, she was headed to the front door to yell
for Ellie when she heard something that sounded like a fart.
Janelle stopped to listen. "Helen, is that you? Where are you?"
She heard the noise again; it came from the front closet.
Before Janelle could move, she heard Helen giggle and say,
"Oops...I tooted." Janelle rushed to the closet and opened the
door. There sat Helen in a tangle of coats, shoes and boots.
"Peek-a-Boo!" she squealed when she saw Janelle.

Helen laughed uproariously at Janelle's frightened
reaction. "Helen, you scared me," Janelle chided her, then
quickly wiped her tears and offered her hand to help Helen
out of the closet and back to the sunroom.

"You didn't tell me where you were going. I thought you
were lost," Janelle said, breathing a sigh of relief.

"I'm not lost, you are. Who are you?" Helen asked, pulling her cold hand from Janelle's.

"It's okay, I'm Janelle, Ellie's friend, remember?" Janelle could see the fear in Helen's eyes.

"Where's Ellie?" Helen asked, sounding very bewildered. "I want Ellie!" she demanded angrily.

Thank God! That has to be Ellie at the front door. I was beginning to think she was never coming back!

"Mom, are you giving Janelle a hard time? I'm right here. I just took the neighbors' mail across the street." Ellie went to comfort her mother. "Thank you, Janelle. She wasn't too much trouble, was she?"

"Oh no, she was fine," Janelle lied as she got up to leave, "I better go. Matt's expecting me. See you next Saturday?"

"I'll do my best. I really want to come; I'll see if Jack can stay with Mom. If not, I don't know who else to ask."

Good thing I'm busy and you can't ask me!

After Janelle left, Ellie wrote the date of the shower on her calendar. If people asked how it was going with Helen living with them, Ellie always said it was "working out." This was nothing but "spin" because the truth was that Ellie had basically lost control of her life. At first, Helen asked several times a day when she could go home, and each time Ellie lied, saying "soon." Actually, she had no intention of ever taking Helen back. Jack had secured Helen's house for an extended period of vacancy, and they had discussed consulting a real estate agent to put it on the market. Ellie's house was Helen's home now.

The first two days, the hardest part had been keeping Helen busy. Then, inadvertently, Ellie came upon the perfect way to occupy her mother's time. She had been going through some paperwork and Helen offered to help. Just to give her mother something to do, Ellie pointed to a large box of old receipts and told her mother to sort them. Helen spent hours happily arranging and rearranging the useless documents into piles. After her mother went to bed, Ellie threw the papers back into the empty box. The next day Helen saw the box, took out the papers and started making piles again, never realizing she was doing exactly what she had done the day before. Ellie did the same thing again that night, and the next day Helen began contentedly sorting away. This meant Ellie could actually get something done while Helen was busy "organizing" her papers.

Still, Ellie was unable to trust her mother alone. It was worse than taking care of a preschooler because with children one can see gradual growth toward independence. With Helen, each day was another discernible step in the downward spiral of retrogenesis.

Helen's next appointment with Dr. Randolph was at 2:00 on Thursday. The follow-up assessment would shed definitive light on Helen's current condition, but Ellie thought the difference the medication had made in the beginning was rapidly wearing off. She calculated Helen's downward progression to be somewhere between ages five and eight, depending on the day, sometimes even the time of day. At least her mother was not a "sundowner," an Alzheimer's patient who becomes agitated and hyperactive in late afternoon, making the caregiver's task even more daunting.

"Alzheimer's is the cruelest of all diseases," she had written to Janelle in a recent email, "because Mother's living life in reverse. At least when the kids were little and required this much care, I knew they'd grow out of it."

Helen slept soundly from nine at night until eight in the morning, allowing Ellie an absolutely necessary good night of sleep. As she had done during her first pregnancy, Ellie did research to help her cope with an unfamiliar situation. She read everything she could find on Alzheimer's Disease. One theme ran through all the literature: an Alzheimer's caregiver's most dangerous enemy is sleep deprivation—get help, get support, but most important—get some sleep!

The rest of Monday, after Janelle's visit, and Tuesday and Wednesday passed uneventfully as they all settled into an acceptable routine. Helen spent Thursday morning with her "paperwork," and after an early lunch, Ellie supervised while Helen got ready for her doctor's appointment. Her mother no longer bathed or changed her clothes unless specifically directed, so Ellie took charge. With specific instructions each step of the way, her mother dutifully showered and put on clean underwear, socks, and a pair of black slacks with matching red and black light sweater.

The only advantage to their new living arrangement was that Ellie didn't have to pick Helen up to take her to her appointments. If Ellie provided a wind bonnet for her hair, Helen got a kick out of riding in Ellie's convertible, so they put the top down and left an hour early to go for a drive. It was an exhilarating June day, seventy-five degrees with blue skies and fluffy cumulus clouds flying. Ellie decided to take a look at the new houses being built in a nearby subdivision and she and Helen laughed out loud when a construction crew whistled at them as they drove by. When Ellie had learned Ford was suspending production of the retro Thunderbird due to disappointing sales, she was actually delighted. That meant Blackbird was a potential collector's item and even more valuable if she took good care of it.

They arrived several minutes early for their appointment and Ellie recognized "Vange" as they entered the waiting room. *We must be on the same three-month schedule. God, look how much she's gone down hill in such a short time. I'm not sure what would be worse, dealing with the violent outbursts like last time, or this total indifference to everything around her. How sweet it is to see him tenderly wrap his arm around her as if to protect her from the world. For once, I have no words. This disease is so unbearably sad for everyone.*

On the surface, the second appointment with Dr. Randolph was an exact replay of the first. Helen was given the same tests and asked to complete the same tasks. However, it was obvious to Ellie that her mother's condition had drastically deteriorated in just three months. Her short-term memory was virtually nonexistent.

At the end of the session, Dr. Randolph took Ellie aside and told her in her usual business-like manner that she was recommending a new medication that had shown promise in middle to late stages Alzheimer's patients.

"Of course, I'll try anything." Ellie's feelings were very different from the overwhelming sadness she felt after the first visit. Now she felt totally helpless—mentally and physically numb—resigned to whatever the future would bring.

After they had a light, late lunch, Ellie took Helen to the grocery store nearby to get a few things for dinner. As usual, she parked her precious Blackbird in the far end of the spacious parking lot. As they entered the massive front doors, Helen said she was too tired to walk so they found a battery-operated cart the store made available to handicapped shoppers. Helen was delighted by the little electric vehicle and scooted up and down the aisles like a happy preschooler on a kiddie car ride. By the time they had what they needed, Ellie was exhausted from trying to keep up with her mother. At the check-out Helen whined, "My legs are still too tired to walk all the way back to the car," so Ellie told her to stay in the cart by the front door while she took the two bags of groceries and went to fetch Blackbird.

"You are not to move from this spot, Mother," Ellie instructed firmly. "Did you hear me? Stay right here, Mom."

"I heard you, Eleanor," her mother replied, sounding annoyed at her daughter giving her orders. "I may be old, but I'm not deaf."

Ellie shook her head at the comment and walked to the car. As always, after putting her groceries in the trunk, she took a moment to inspect Blackbird before leaving. She wasn't sure she would have the nerve to confront anyone if she ever did find a dent, but she quickly walked around the car while she dug in her purse for the keys. Knowing she had to get back to her mother, she wasted no time buckling up and starting the car. Carefully backing out of the parking space, she went to get Helen. Coming around the front row of cars, she heard horns beeping. It took her a moment to realize what was happening.

"What the…" Then it registered. Tooling right down the middle of parking lot two aisles over was Helen, full throttle with the motorized cart buzzing at top speed! Shoppers in stopped cars were beeping, some yelling and some laughing as her mother whizzed by. Ellie slammed on her brakes, shoved Blackbird's transmission into park, let the engine idle and ran across the lot to cut her mother off. "Mom, what are you doing? I thought I told you to stay put!"

"I got a chill and I wanted to go to the car, but I can't find it. Have you seen a tan car? One with four doors and a St. Christopher medal on the dashboard?" Helen looked as pathetic, confused and disoriented as Ellie had ever seen her. "Where is my car, Ellie?"

"Mom, we have my car today. It's black, remember? Come on, let's get you in the car and then I'll take the electric cart back to the store."

Luckily, as she was buckling her mother in, she spied a young attendant coming out to get stray shopping carts. She waved him over, explained the situation, and apologized profusely. The young man laughed good-naturedly and happily volunteered to return the cart to the store. Ellie felt relieved, even more so when she saw that Helen must have drained the battery because the cart stopped abruptly, and the young man had to drag it the last twenty feet into the store.

As they drove away, Ellie replayed the scene in her mind. The incident could well have been tragic, but now that she had time to think about it, it was going to make a really hilarious family story. She wondered if the store's security cameras caught Helen's stunt on tape so she could send it to one of those silly video contests. She was sure an audience would roar at the sight of her mother racing that cart up and down the parking lot. *I bet Janelle could even edit the tape to dress Mother in a leather jacket, Snoopy helmet and Red Baron scarf, and maybe some goggles.* Ellie chuckled softly to herself all the way home.

CHAPTER 25

Saturday, June 14th

"Wake up, sleepy head," Matt said as he rolled over to tickle Janelle. "You have a baby shower to go to today."

"Aww, Matt," Janelle groaned. "I slept like crap. It can't be morning already."

Matt reached over her to hit the snooze button and then tickled her some more. "You told me last night you wanted to be up and showered before I left."

"Matt! Okay, please stop," Janelle laughed and squirmed out of bed. "I'm getting up, just stop already. I hate it when you tickle me. Whoooa, I got up too fast. I'm dizzy."

"You love it and you know it!" Matt called after her as she staggered to the bathroom.

Janelle felt like she was sleepwalking as she went through the motions of showering. *There has to be a way for me to get some sleep...God I'm tired.* She dried off slowly and wrapped herself into the big, fluffy towel, then shuffled across the room to the closet where she gently reached out to touch the high-bodice black brushed-satin maternity dress hanging on a hook. *Thank God I don't have to spend any time trying to figure out what to wear today because I feel terrible. I can't believe this headache is back again.* She put on a robe, made the bed, and then went to lie down for a few minutes while Matt showered.

"What's this?" Matt asked when he saw his wife lying on the bed with her arm draped over her head.

"I don't feel good. I have a headache and my stomach hurts," Janelle whined.

"Maybe you ate something the baby doesn't like, probably green vegetables, just like me," Matt teased.

"Why are you in such a chipper mood?" Janelle asked. "You were up this morning before the alarm even went off. Who are you? And what did you do with my husband?"

Matt grinned. "I'm just excited, that's all. You're having a baby shower today, Janelle. Can you believe that? We're so lucky. Only five more weeks...imagine."

"We still haven't decided on a boy's first name," Janelle reminded him.

"I know. Maybe that just means we're having a girl," Matt said, casually shrugging his shoulders.

"Nice try, Matt. We still need to come up with something we both like. Remember what the Lamaze teacher said, hospitals prefer parents name their babies immediately nowadays for security purposes."

"Ask for ideas at the shower."

"Good idea!" Janelle said, slowly sitting up on the bed. "I can ask everyone to write a boy's name on a piece of paper and put the suggestions in a bag. Then we can look through them together and see if there's one we like."

"Sure, or we could just have a girl," Matt repeated as he pulled his T-shirt over his head.

Janelle rolled her eyes and smiled.

"Maybe you should reset the alarm and take a nap," Matt suggested. "You look pale."

"Another good idea," Janelle said, grabbing the afghan from the foot of the bed. "My head's pounding."

"Give me a kiss," Matt said. "See you this afternoon; hope you feel better."

The nap and a light breakfast of cereal, toast and jelly worked wonders. Janelle was spooning the last of her cereal into her mouth when she noticed an envelope on the end of the snack bar. She read the sticky note:

Janelle, I almost forgot. Your mom asked me to give you this. Hope you're feeling better! Love, Matt

What can this be? Janelle opened the envelope.

Dear Janelle,

I don't want to make you too emotional at the shower, so I'm completing our family ritual by sending you the "my daughter's having a baby love letter" beforehand.

I will never forget the day you were born. Several days before, I began spotting. I was so scared. Grandma referred to it as "the bloody show." I cleaned every closet and drawer in every room of that god-forsaken small apartment we called home. I had everything ready for your arrival, but I certainly wasn't prepared.

On a cold, late November evening, things started happening. I had a horrible stomach ache, like a really painful period. By the time your father came home from working the night shift, I had such terrible cramps I didn't want to leave the bathroom, so he grabbed a TV tray, a deck of cards and the cribbage board. He sat on the edge of the bathtub and we played cribbage!

By mid-morning we were at the hospital. My nurse was meaner than a mad cow and scolded me for not knowing how to breathe. I was mortified and begged for my mommy. (It wasn't my fault; in those days there weren't any Lamaze classes).

My labor didn't take long, but it hurt like hell because you weren't in the right position. The doctor had to use forceps to turn you over. Then, all of a sudden, there you were…wet, warm and screaming your lungs out. At that moment you became the most precious thing in my life. How could I know that one day you would also become the very best friend I could ever hope to have?

Now it's your turn to become a mother, Janelle. You are ten years older than I was when you were born, much smarter and so much better prepared. I know you are going to be a wonderful mother!

Love forever, Mom

Janelle's tear-streaked makeup showed how touched she was by her mother's letter. She had just enough time to fix her face before Cassie arrived to escort her to the shower.

"So, are you nervous?" Cassie asked as Janelle got comfortable and fastened her seatbelt.

"Not really, but I'm excited," Janelle said. "And I'm worried about getting too emotional."

Cassie laughed. "What do you mean?"

Janelle told Cassie about Claire's letter and her visit to Ellie's. "When Ellie got back, I didn't even tell her what happened. I just couldn't get out of there fast enough and I cried the whole way home."

"Why?"

"I don't know. I just did. I can't even tell you how many times I burst into tears this week."

"For what?"

"Dumb things. Like the other night I was making spaghetti and the noodles boiled over on the stove and all I could do was cry!"

"C'mon!"

"I'm serious, my hormones are completely out of control and I keep getting these headaches. So watch out, the waterworks could start any minute. I just hope I don't lose it again with my mother-in-law."

"Stop worrying. I helped your mom and Sandy decorate at the community center earlier, and they were getting along just fine. I'm guessing that means you didn't tell your mom about Ellie's missing invitation?"

"No I didn't, and she'll probably be mad about that when she finds out, but I've managed to avoid Sandy all week."

"Well, you can't avoid her today. What're you gonna do?"

"Keep my fingers crossed and pray."

When Cassie and Janelle arrived at the community center, they entered a pink, blue and white wonderland. The banquet-style tables were draped with alternating soft pink and baby blue tablecloths. A bouquet of pink, white and blue balloons was anchored in the center of each table by a bag of assorted hard candies wrapped in pink and blue netting.

Taller bunches of balloons bobbed and swayed at the entrance, the gift area, the food buffet, the cake table and various other places around the room.

"Wow, I love it!" Janelle said, breathlessly taking it all in.

"Hi, sweetie!" Claire rushed over to give her daughter a hug. "You look really pretty today. Come see the cake. It's lemon poppy seed, your favorite."

"Thanks for the love letter, Mom," Janelle whispered in her mother's ear. Beaming, Claire led Janelle over to check out the cake. Sandy was in the kitchen with her back to Janelle, discreetly keeping herself busy, perhaps to avoid any unpleasantness with her daughter-in-law. *Good, I'm not in the mood for another public apology from Sandy anyway.*

"Oh, Sandy," Claire called into the kitchen, "the corsage for Janelle is in the fridge. Can you grab it and take a picture of us while I pin it on?"

Oh, jeez, here we go. Janelle dreaded the prospect of coming face-to-face with Sandy, but her mother-in-law rushed over with the camera, made eye contact and said sweetly, "Hi, Janelle. You look really nice. Black is such a slimming color."

Cassie, who was artfully arranging party favors on a nearby table, overheard Sandy's comment and piped up. "My best friend looks good in *any* color," she said, giving Janelle a sweet smile that told her to stay calm. "And who worries about looking fat when you're pregnant? God knows I won't!"

Her comment went right over Sandy's head as she snapped a few digital pictures of Claire pinning a blue and pink corsage onto Janelle's dress.

"Okay, now Sandy and Janelle," Claire said, switching places. Sandy obediently handed off the camera and stood next to Janelle.

"Well...c'mon, I'm waiting for a smile from you two," Claire said. "You both look like you're on a first date!" Claire's amusing comment finally elicited two smiles. "There we go, that's much better!"

Cassie went to unstack and distribute the last of the chairs and Claire hurried off to the kitchen, mumbling that she had to finish polishing the silver punch bowl before she forgot again. That left Janelle alone with Sandy.

"Janelle," Sandy began, "I know you probably don't believe me, but I'm really sorry about not inviting your teacher friend."

"Now you're calling her my friend?"

"Yes, and I am sorry. I called her this week to tell her so."

"You what?"

"I called her Wednesday, but no one answered and I didn't want to leave a message. If you don't mind me saying so, I think if she's such a good friend, she won't be upset about not getting invited. Please excuse me, I need to finish rearranging the food. Why don't you help Cassie with the chairs? No sense in you hanging around the temptation of the food table with me."

As Sandy walked away, Janelle gritted her teeth and tried to relax. *I don't need this! I think I liked it was better when she wasn't talking to me. I hope Ellie can make it—I can't wait to see Sandy's face if she shows up!*

Ellie was awakened in the middle of the night by the sound of dishes clattering in the kitchen. *What on earth?* Jack was dead to the world so she threw back the light coverlet and went to the kitchen to investigate.

There was Helen, completely dressed for the day, setting the table with Ellie's best china and silver. Every cooking pot Ellie owned was on the stove. Every last item had been pulled out of the refrigerator and was sitting on the counter. A carton of juice had tipped onto its side and was leaking all over the folder containing Helen's latest test results.

"Mom! What on earth are you doing?" Looking around the room, Ellie felt overwhelmed.

"What does it look like? Making breakfast. Hurry up, get dressed, and wake up Frankie; you'll be late for school."

"Mom...it's three o'clock in the morning...it's summer...there's no school...Frank's not here..."

Ellie's exasperated tone set Helen off—she slammed down a pan and stomped around the kitchen, waving her arms and lecturing Ellie on the "value of eating a good breakfast and the importance of being on time." Ellie heard the bed creaking and saw Jack come stumbling into the kitchen. "What's the heck's going...cripes, what a mess!"

More than a little frightened by her mother's bizarre behavior, Ellie put her finger to her lips to tell him to be quiet. Then she tried a different tone. "Mom, it's summer...we're on vacation. No school today...go back to bed and enjoy your time off. You don't get to do that much."

"No school today?"

"No, Mom...let's go back to sleep."

"I guess I am pretty tired; I think I'll go back to bed."

"Good. I'll help you get into your nightgown."

"Okay, but I'll fall asleep faster if you sing me a song, Eleanor...will you sing me a song?"

Jack could plainly see that Ellie was in no mood for singing, so he made a time-out motion to tell Ellie to say no. But seeing her mother's expression and feeling a surge of protectiveness, she managed to summon the energy and helped her mother back to bed. She could hear Jack muttering as he began putting the kitchen back in order, and her face became a river of tears as she sang: "Sunrise, Sunset...swiftly flow the days...seedlings turn overnight to sunflowers..."

The sun was up by the time Ellie finished cleaning up the mess. Now she sat tiredly at the table, in her once again spotless kitchen, sipping coffee and carefully composing a note to include inside Janelle's baby shower card. She finished writing an upbeat loving message and made out a check for fifty dollars, designating it be used to open baby Spencer's college savings account. After tucking the check inside, she readied the card for mailing. Fighting hard to shake off the depressed, bitter mood descending upon her, she set the card on the counter so she wouldn't forget to send it.

I hope Janelle won't be too disappointed, but I simply can't make it to her shower today. I can't ask Jack to watch Mom...not after last night...I hope she understands.

CHAPTER 26

Wednesday, June 18th

Ellie stirred the dregs of her black cherry yogurt smoothie and read the evening paper as she waited for Janelle at Paradise Island. Looking at her watch, she was surprised to see that Janelle—who was *never* late—was almost fifteen minutes tardy. To keep from worrying, she went back to reading the sports section. When Janelle was overdue almost half an hour, Ellie decided to try her cell phone. She was about to hang up when she heard Janelle's frantic voice.

"Hello, Matt? Matt, is that you?" It sounded like she was fumbling with the phone.

"No, it's Ellie...what's wrong? Are you all right?"

"Oh, Ellie. Thank God...I'm so scared."

"Janelle, what's the matter? Where are you?"

"I'm on the side of the road, somewhere...I don't know exactly where."

Now Ellie began to panic. "Take a deep breath...can you tell me what happened?"

"I started out to meet you, Ellie, and I was fine. Some headlights blinded me...I thought my head was going to split! I could hardly see...I almost hit a car when I pulled over...I don't remember much after that...I'm scared!"

"I'll be right there...you have to help me, Janelle. Think! Where are you? Do you recognize any buildings?"

"I can see the movie theater marquee from here."

"Good girl. Stay right there! I'm coming as fast as I can." Throwing money on the table, she rushed out the door and raced Blackbird across town as fast as she could safely go.

Seeing no one sitting in Janelle's car, she screeched to a halt directly behind it. She jumped from Blackbird and ran to the driver's door, opening it with a jerk when she saw Janelle lying sideways across the seat.

"Oh, Ellie...hi, I'm feeling a little better; I feel like such a fool for worrying you," Janelle said as she sat up.

Shaking with relief Ellie examined her friend's face carefully. "Are you sure you're okay?"

"Yes, I think so, especially now that you're here."

"Thank God...but what's that lump above your eye?"

"I don't know...I think it's an insect bite, but it must be infected. It keeps coming back."

"I want you to promise me you'll have a doctor check it out...and soon. In fact, tomorrow works for me."

"I guess I could call Dr. Felding. He's in on Thursdays."

"No more guessing. Promise me."

"Okay, I promise," Janelle said, although she crossed her fingers secretly just in case she changed her mind.

"Good, that's settled," Ellie said and the mood in the car lightened considerably. "Hungry?" Ellie asked. "I know I am. My stomach's rumbling so loud it sounds like thunder."

"I could eat, I *should* eat," Janelle said, "but I don't feel like driving all the way over to Paradise Island anymore."

"That's okay, I just need food, healthy food."

"How about we get make-it-yourself salads at the deli and go to my place," Janelle suggested. "Matt's out with his friends until ten. That way we can talk and you can see the nursery and my shower presents too."

"Great idea," Ellie agreed. Minutes later the women were at the salad bar, piling their plastic platters high with veggies, protein and packets of light ranch salad dressing. They weighed in, and Ellie paid the freight. She carried the salads out to Blackbird and followed Janelle home.

The excitement over, the women enjoyed the food and each other. Ellie apologized for missing the shower, but Janelle stopped her by thanking her profusely for starting the baby's college fund. She showed her the shower gifts and an album of digital pictures from that day.

"This must be Matt's mother," Ellie said when she saw the photo Claire had snapped. "I guess she is skinny, isn't she? As Jack would say, *she needs some meat on those bones*."

Then Ellie winked and pretended to dump an imaginary plate in Janelle's lap. Janelle giggled, remembering the look on Sandy's face. The baby started to kick and roll, as if it too found Ellie's comment and charades hilarious.

Ellie told Janelle all about Frank's behavior; the difficulty Jonah was having finding a teaching job; Jack's frustration at the effect of the national health care crisis on working families; and Helen's worsening dementia.

"It's crazy, you wouldn't believe some of the things she does," Ellie said. "I have to laugh at most of them; otherwise, I wouldn't be able to handle it."

Yes, I know exactly what you mean. As Ellie described what she and Jack now referred to as Helen's "midnight supper," Janelle shook her head in amazement.

Shortly after nine, Janelle proudly showed off the nursery and then yawned loudly as they walked back to the kitchen.

"Time for me to head out," Ellie announced. "Jack's staying with Mom. I just hope he's not ready for the loony bin by the time I get home," she added, lingering a moment to tidy up the kitchen.

"Sometimes I still marvel at how good a friend you are," Janelle said as she embraced Ellie warmly at the front door. "How can I ever thank you for tonight?"

"Only one way I can think of, Janelle. You can keep your promise...play hookie tomorrow and go see your doctor."

CHAPTER 27

Thursday, June 19th

Janelle had tossed and turned most of the night. *I'll go see a doctor, but there's no reason to worry Matt needlessly.* She sent him off to work without saying a word, then called Larry's voice mail and told him she wouldn't be coming in. She felt guilty knowing Larry would probably be lost. He still hadn't come up with a new plan for Janelle's work while she was off with the baby, and the office buzz was that Bradley was still unemployed and his wife was leaving him. It was only 6:30, and feeling dull with fatigue, she reset the alarm and crawled back into bed. When her radio beckoned at 7:55, she awakened, feeling less rested than before.

Her resolve to call Dr. Felding was strengthened by a pounding headache, plus the mirror revealed that the bump above her right eye was back. *Ellie might be right; this thing is way bigger than a bug bite.* Janelle leaned into the mirror to examine it more closely and gently touched it. It seemed to squish and slide across her eyebrow bone with ease. A dull pain seeped from behind the bump and grew stronger as it traveled to her sinuses and then her ears. More than a little frightened, she went straight to the kitchen phone.

"Hi, this is Janelle Spencer. Can I talk to Dr. Felding's nurse, please?" Janelle impatiently drummed her fingers on the dining room table.

"Hello, this is Trudy."

"Hi, Trudy, it's Janelle Spencer. I'd like to see the doctor today. I've been having bad headaches, blurred vision, dizziness and I think . . ."

"Are you eating?" Trudy interrupted.

"Yes, a lot. I also have a..."

"Headaches and dizziness are common if you're not eating smaller meals five to six times a day. Or you might have low iron. Are you taking your vitamins?"

"Yes...religiously," Janelle said, frustrated that Trudy was trying to diagnose her without listening to her symptoms. *I should've expected as much from her...she never listens to me.* "I don't think these headaches are pregnancy-related. I also have a lump above my right eye."

"A lump..." Her tone finally turning concerned, Janelle could hear Trudy's keyboard clicking. "Does 9:30 work?"

"Perfect."

"Dr. Felding will want to check things out...perhaps order some tests, so don't eat or drink anything except water."

"The tests he'll order will be done today?"

"Yes, if doctor feels it's necessary."

"How long for the results?"

"That depends...why don't we wait and see on that."

Janelle woodenly hung up the phone. *As soon as I mentioned the lump, she started listening...she must think something's wrong too.*

Just to keep occupied, she worked on her thank-you cards until 9:00 and then left for her appointment. Dr. Felding listened to the baby's heartbeat and applied pressure to different areas of Janelle's abdomen. He asked a few questions about her headaches and closely examined the lump.

"I don't like the looks of this, Janelle. It's probably nothing, but I'm going to order an MRI. I want to be sure." The doctor was examining the lump, palpating it with one hand while holding a lighted magnifying glass with the other.

Janelle swallowed hard, "Today?"

"Yes, I'm sure the lab won't be thrilled, they're swamped, but they owe me a favor so they'll squeeze you in," he said with a wink.

Two hours later the lab technician prepared her for a magnetic resoning image test. He slowly slid the gurney she was lying on into the end of a long cylinder. *They're literally going to squeeze me in! This thing is barely big enough for an unpregnant me!*

"Hi, Janelle, this is Heath," the speakers at the far end of the tube crackled. "How are you doing in there?"

"Okay, but this isn't like a tanning bed at all." Janelle craned her neck to look in the direction of the speakers; she saw only a bright fluorescent light at the opening.

"If that's what they told you, they fibbed," he chuckled. "It's *very* important that you lie still during the test. Remember, the Emergency Stop button is near your right hand. Use it if you have to, but try to stay relaxed because if you stop the test, we'll have to start it all over." His voice was calm and reassuring. "What kind of music do you like? I'll turn on the radio."

"Country or Top 40." The platform stopped moving and the speakers crackled again as Heath tuned in—a deep baritone voice filled the chamber almost immediately.

"Okay, Janelle, remember; lie still."

As if I could move! My tummy is almost touching the top of this thing. "Okay, I'm ready," she said with more confidence than she felt.

"That's good," Heath continued, "then let's get going. When the camera starts, it'll be noisy; you'll be hearing the magnets moving around the machine. Just try to concentrate on the music and stay relaxed."

"Okay," Janelle took a deep breath and closed her eyes. *Mind over matter, I can do this.*

The machine started moving and Janelle's eyelids jolted open. She didn't feel any physical pain, but the assault on her body was no less severe. A jackhammering sound bounced and echoed inside her cocoon, like a machine gunner shooting bullets inside the walls of a metal chamber.

What was I thinking? I can't do this! Oh, God, I have to get out! Jeez…I wonder if they ever make the techs have one of these so they know what it really feels like—or rather sounds like. What makes them think you can hear anything in here at all. This is worse than those jack-hammers they use to tear up the road. I'll just close my eyes and try that breathing thing. I feel like I'm going to puke. "Hee, hee, whooo. Hee, hee, whooo. Hee, hee, whooo." *Well that works just swell—not! When will this be over? I need to move, move, move!* She clenched her teeth and curled her toes. Bullets of sound ricocheted endlessly all around her, exacerbating the dull ache in her head into a crescendo of excruciating pain.

It's so loud! The baby must be scared too! Great, I didn't tell anyone I was coming here today. What if Mom tried to call me at my desk when she didn't get me in my car? Why didn't I check my cell phone voice mail on the way here? What if she tried to call me at home? She might've tried to call Matt...they could be worried sick about me. I should've told Matt. I have to get out of here! No, I have to do this, if not for me, then for the baby. I have to calm down. I can do this.

Since she could barely hear the radio, she decided to try counting the thrusts of sound being shot at her. They were coming so fast, that to keep up, she rhythmically abbreviated some of the numbers: "...twenty, one, two, three, four, five, six, seven, eight, nine, thirty, one, two, three, four..." When she got to one hundred, she started over and marked her hundreds with her fingers which where tucked closely to her side. Amazingly, concentrating on the source of her aggravation began to distract her and she began to relax. She had seven fingers marking the thrusts when she lost count because the baby started to kick. *I know sweetie, this is no fun. Mommy's sorry. It's almost over...I hope.*

Finally, mercifully, the machine stopped as abruptly as it had begun. Now the absence of sound was deafening, and her head still pounded the rhythm over and over.

"You did great, Janelle," Heath praised as he slowly pulled her out.

"I feel like a butterfly hatching from a cocoon. I'm so happy that's over," Janelle said. At first her eyes couldn't focus and her body was stiff from the cramped quarters and tension. She felt overwhelmed by the abundance of space available to her now. Heath smiled as he came over to help her up.

"I hope I never have to do that again. It was worse than grocery shopping...truly despicable!" Janelle said. She tried to sit up but failed; her head was spinning.

Grinning at her remark, Heath warned, "Take it easy. You're gonna be lightheaded...just rest a little bit more."

She abruptly sat up. "A little bit more? If you think I *rested* in that thing, you're way wrong! It really was despicable, and the baby didn't like it either. Are you sure it was safe? It's not going to affect my baby's hearing once it's born, is it?"

"No, no, no," Heath chuckled, "the baby's hearing'll be just fine. Let's get you back to reality." Heath led Janelle to the waiting area and then excused himself. Janelle used the courtesy phone to call her cell phone, her house phone and her work phone to check for any frantic messages from Claire or Matt. There was only one, from Claire.

Hi, Janelle. I'm running late again this morning. I have
meetings scheduled all morning so my afternoon'll be
crazy. Maybe I'll talk to you after work.
Love ya! Bye!

Good...no one's looking for me. She was about to call Ellie when Heath returned to the waiting room. "I just talked to Dr. Felding. He said you should go home and he'll give you a call later this afternoon."

"Go home?" Janelle hadn't expected to leave without getting some answers.

"Yeah. It's 11:30 now. The lab will start on your pictures right away, but even a rush order takes a few hours."

Janelle was terrified to ask what the doctor was looking for and why he put a rush on the results so she agreed to go home and do something she hated to do...wait.

Thursday evening Jack and Ellie took Helen out for dinner. She was lively and talkative and had one of her best days in weeks. They came home, watched the news, then went to bed. Sometime near dawn, Ellie was jarred awake by a loud thumping sound. Then a strange, burning odor tickled her nostrils. Still groggy, she tried to identify the smell...she settled on a summer fruit pie bubbling over in the oven. She lay in bed for a full minute, desperately trying to convince herself she was dreaming.

At the very moment she was finally awake, Jack rolled over. "Ellie, something's burning," he said crossly. "Why the hell would you start breakfast and then come back to bed?"

"I didn't," Ellie replied sharply, forcing herself to get up to investigate, "but I think I know who did." As she hurried to the kitchen, she called back, "Please get up, Jack. I might need you."

Ellie was astonished to find the kitchen deserted and the stairwell light to the basement on. Baffled, she waited a moment until a very cranky Jack joined her. Together, they descended the stairs, Jack in the lead.

"What the hell...?" Jack said.

Then they both stared at the source of the noise. There stood Helen, clad in her nightgown, calmly watching the dryer rotate, some sort of heavy object clunking away as it spun round and round. The thin black smoke rising from the exhaust pipe was the obvious source of the burnt pie odor.

Helen turned to them and said sweetly, "Hi, children. I didn't want to wake you up until breakfast was ready. I found some jelly donuts in the freezer...I'm warming them up. They'll be done in a minute."

Ellie's immediate reaction was to spank her mother like a naughty child. Instead, despite Helen's objections, she led her firmly back to bed. As they ascended the stairs, she heard Jack curse as he opened the dryer door. "Look at this god-awful mess. I've frickin' had it; I can't take this anymore!"

CHAPTER 28

Friday, June 20th

Janelle and Matt arrived at the doctor's office at 8:00. Trudy had called late Thursday, saying Dr. Felding wanted to see them both first thing in the morning. A shocked Matt had taken the call. He interrogated Janelle and she told him about the MRI and her reasons for keeping it a secret.

"Matt, I didn't...I still don't know how serious this is. I didn't want you to worry if it's nothing."

Not completely satisfied by her explanation, Matt had taken her in his arms anyway and kissed her forehead. "Well, I'm guessing it's *not* nothing, but let's not worry until we know for sure." Uneasy and unwilling to speculate, they had skipped Lamaze class and gone to bed early.

When Janelle went to the desk to register, Trudy appeared at once. Uncharacteristically warm and friendly, she immediately led them through a maze of halls to a very plush office area Janelle had never seen. "Dr. Felding's waiting for you," the nurse said as she knocked on the solid mahogany door. Without waiting for a response, she opened the door and announced, "Mr. and Mrs. Spencer are here."

"Thank you, Trudy," Dr. Felding said, extending a hand to indicate Janelle and Matt take the pair of burgundy leather chairs opposite his massive desk. Another physician Dr. Felding introduced as Dr. Myommar sat in a side chair.

"Jeez, I feel like we're in the principal's office," Janelle said, nervously tucking her hair behind her ears.

Dr. Felding smiled at her comment and asked, "How are you feeling this morning, Janelle? Any headaches?"

"No, maybe a little nausea. All this waiting and worrying is really getting to me," she admitted.

"We didn't sleep too well last night," Matt concurred. "Let's cut to the chase, doc. What did my wife's MRI show?"

"Well, since this isn't my area of expertise, I had a neurologist look over Janelle's pictures." Dr. Felding paused and turned to the specialist.

"And?" Janelle asked. She saw the two medical men exchange a look and felt a surge of panic. "What...what's wrong with me?"

Dr. Myommar, whom Janelle guessed to be a Middle Eastern immigrant, spoke exquisite English, with a European accent. He pulled out a set of MRI films and hung them onto the lighted wall board facing the couple. As if he were a professor lecturing medical students, Dr. Myommar said, "Your MRI shows a pylocytic astrocytoma of the inferior trigone of the fourth ventricle fundus."

"What the hell does that mean?" Matt asked.

Dr. Myommar looked at Dr. Felding who took his cue. "In layman's terms, you have a brain tumor, Janelle."

Dr. Felding's face seemed distant and misshapen; the only thing she could focus on was his mouth. She hadn't noticed his bottom teeth were crooked until now. She just stared as he went on. "The usual manifestations are headache, blurred vision and dizziness, sometimes nausea or perhaps even seizures. And, as in your case, patients usually feel well between episodes."

Janelle felt Matt's hand grasping hers, pressing it into the cushiony leather of the chair. Her mouth felt like sandpaper and she could hear Ellie's voice in her head, "Janelle, I've had two babies, your symptoms are NOT normal. See a doctor."

"What about our baby?" Janelle voice cracked. She felt as small and defenseless as the child she carried inside her.

"The baby hasn't been affected at all so far. However, Dr. Myommar and I agree we need to take it soon. No doctor would risk this type of surgery on a pregnant woman."

"What the..." Matt's feet stomped on the floor and one swift motion hoisted him from his chair. "Brain surgery?"

"Unfortunately, we must remove the tumor, Mr. Spencer. There is good news though," Dr. Myommar answered. "Grade one astrocytomas have well-differentiated astrocytes and well-defined margins. Your wife's clinical course indicates a complete cure is possible if we can operate... *if* we can operate within the month."

Janelle squinted and robotically reached up to touch her right brow. *A complete cure is possible*... She forced herself to concentrate as Dr. Felding translated. "Fortunately, the lesion is benign and encapsulated, meaning it's not malignant, *not* cancer. Unfortunately, these tumors can become aggressive, and yours is already pressing on the optic nerve. Dr. Myommar and I agree if we remove it soon, there's an excellent chance of full recovery."

"Are you saying you want to cut into my wife's head?" Matt's nostrils flared with anger. "What if something goes wrong? Isn't there any other way?"

"Not operating will jeopardize your wife's sight and possibly her life. I assure you, Dr. Myommar is a very skilled neurosurgeon. His success rate is phenomenal. Waiting also increases the risk to your wife..."

"A risk I am prepared to take," Janelle interrupted resolutely. "The last month of pregnancy is crucial to my baby's development." Her voice sounded eerily calm. "I refuse to have the surgery until after my baby's born...full term!"

Matt opened his mouth as if to argue, but Janelle cut him off. "After everything we've gone through, I'm not putting our child in harm's way, even to save myself!"

"What about me?" Matt asked bitterly. "Doesn't my opinion matter? Maybe my mother and your religious Aunt Christine were right!"

"About what?"

"We shouldn't have messed with Mother Nature. We should've adopted like Cassie and Jeff. If you weren't pregnant, you wouldn't have to gamble with your own life!"

"Matthew Adam Spencer! Take that back right now."

"I will not. You're letting our baby hold you hostage! Babies are born a month early all the time and do just fine."

"Whooa, you two," Dr. Felding had obviously decided it was time to play referee.

Matt sounded just as determined as his wife. "I'm sorry doctor; as much as I love our unborn baby, I cannot risk losing Janelle."

"You're not going to lose me, Matt. Right, doctor?" Janelle sat stubbornly on the edge of her chair waiting for Dr. Felding's response.

"Let's not worry about that right now, okay?"

"Please don't tell us what to worry about, Dr. Felding," Janelle said. "Just tell us what we need to know."

"Well...as with any major surgery, there are certain risks...in this case...the sooner we operate, the more we minimize them."

"Minimize...not eliminate?" Matt challenged.

"That's right." Dr. Felding folded his hands together and cracked his knuckles one at a time. "I will accept your decision," he said to Janelle and then turned to Matt, "but if Janelle was my wife..."

"What do you mean...what would you do?"

Realizing the decision was ultimately Janelle's, Dr. Felding turned back to her and continued, "I'd make an appointment to take the baby C-section right after the Fourth of July weekend. How about Monday, July 7th? That would give the baby sixteen more days. Dr. Myommar will be able to operate during our window of optimal opportunity. Does that sound like a fair compromise?"

Janelle buried her face in her shaking hands. She took a deep breath and brushed two big tears from her cheeks before facing Matt who looked at her expectantly.

"All right," she relented. "Monday, July 7th will be our baby's birthday. I can live with that."

As soon as Jack left for work, Ellie got started on her to-do list by putting Helen to work. The sorting papers gig had grown old; now Helen spent many hours each day mending.

Ellie had been re-sewing a loose button on one of Jack's dress shirts when Helen offered to help. In a brainstorm, Ellie gave Helen an old torn pair of Jack's workpants and a threaded needle. Helen spent three hours happily mending the garment, and just like that she had a new pastime. Each night, Ellie ripped out the stitching; each day, Helen picked up the mending and set to work. Her short-term memory was totally gone now, and while she could recall with crystal clear detail things that happened seven decades ago, she couldn't remember a thing that happened seven minutes ago. It infuriated Ellie to have to repeat herself so often; she had to constantly remind herself that anger was useless, trying to laugh it off whenever possible.

Since Helen was now occupying Rebecca's room, Ellie's daughter had called Tuesday night to say she had reserved a suite at the Downtown Hotel for the Fourth of July weekend. She also extended the invitation to Stacey and Dave and was pretty sure they would accept since they had no other plans. If so, Dave and the girls would spend their days with the Reeds and their nights relaxing at the hotel.

After the "dryer-done donuts" incident, as Jack called it, Ellie promised she would look into institutional placement for Helen. She reluctantly went online for some haphazard research, half-heartedly asked around about assisted living facilities, and called the local Alzheimer's Association. However, since Jack wasn't really pressing her, or more likely because she was in denial, she didn't follow up on any level.

It seemed that the new medication stabilized Helen's erratic behavior so Ellie convinced herself that they had weathered the "adjustment period" and were now entering a more comfortable holding pattern.

Thinking about donuts made Ellie's stomach begin to grumble. She ignored the hunger pangs as long as she could, finally giving-in to them around noon. She had lost twenty-three pounds and knew she looked great in her summer clothes—especially the soft yellow cotton capri pants and coordinating striped top she had bought recently. She always had good legs but tended to be thick-waisted and chesty; she had beamed widely when Jack commented that the weight loss showed most around her middle.

As she bent over the sink washing celery for a low calorie tuna salad, the phone rang. Ellie picked up on the first ring and heard the wonderful deep sound of her son's voice saying excitedly, "Hi, Mom, I'm glad you're home. I have some great news. I'm not coming home for the Fourth."

Ellie's heart sank. "I'd hardly call that great news, Jonah. You'll miss the fireworks, the picnic..."

"I know, that all sucks, but I have a *very* good reason."

"What?"

"I got a job!"

"You did? That's wonderful, honey! Where?" With statewide school budget cuts, Jonah had almost despaired of finding anything before school started the end of August.

"In an Indian village thirty miles from Nome."

"You don't mean Nome, as in Alaska?"

"That's the one, Mom. I heard about this opening from Emily, this girl I met a couple months ago. On a whim, I mailed them my credentials. They called me Wednesday, interviewed me on digital photo phone yesterday and faxed me the contract this morning. It's for two years. And you'll never believe this, I'm going to be the only secondary teacher in the high school, and acting principal too."

"But Jonah, Nome..."

"Emily says it's really a great job; you feel so needed there. Do you have a piece of paper? Write down the school's website so you can do a cyber visit. That's how the Superintendent showed me around the place. You have to check it out...it's great...I can hardly wait to go!"

Ellie wiped her hands and recorded the information on the message pad next to the phone.

"Emily...is she a girl friend or a girlfriend?"

"I guess you'd call her a girlfriend. I really like her, Mom. She reminds me a lot of you. Her favorite color's yellow and when she smiles, her face lights up like the sun."

Ellie smiled, flattered that her son wanted someone who reminded him of her, though her heart ached at the thought of losing her son to the Alaskan wilderness. "And how does this Emily feel about you going off to the end of the earth where the sun never shines?"

"That's more good news, Mom. Emily's going too."

"She is?"

"Uh huh. So you might say I'm taking my own private source of sunshine with me."

"What?"

"She's going to be the only primary teacher, so I'll be her colleague and her boss. Isn't this just sweet? Doesn't it remind you of Grandma? She taught in a one-room country schoolhouse when she was young, right? And you and Dad always said we should try to make a difference..."

"Yes, but thirty miles from Nome..."

"Mom, just be happy for me, okay? And ask Dad to do the same, please?"

"Of course, Jonah. We're so proud of you, honey. This is just so sudden, I don't know how to react."

"Well, then look at it like this...now you have a perfect excuse to finally come see the Iditarod for real. I'm already making plans to see you and Dad in Nome the second week in March. We can all be at the finish line when the first musher comes in."

Still shaking her head in disbelief as she hung up the phone, Ellie looked into the living room where her mother was still busy mending. Her appetite gone, she put the tuna salad in the refrigerator and went to check out the website Jonah had given her.

She logged into the Internet and checked her email first. She had only one new message, from Janelle.

Hi Ellie,

I'm emailing you from home. I'm not at work because I'm on forced medical leave. There's no easy way to say this except to spit it out. I kept my promise (part of me wishes I hadn't) and went to the doctor. They did an MRI and I have a brain tumor. Don't panic! It's benign and "encapsulated"—apparently good things. They believe a full recovery is possible.

They have to remove the tumor, but they want to take the baby by C-section first. That's scheduled for July 7th at 7AM, the seventh month, the seventh day at the seventh hour...7-7-7...how's that for tilting the odds in my favor?

Matt doesn't like it, but we've agreed not to tell anyone but you. I'm having a hard enough time dealing with my own worries and fears, much less everyone else's...especially my mom's.

In my mind I can already hear you asking, "What can I do, Janelle?" You're such a good friend, Ellie; you've come to my rescue so many times. Now I need you to pray that none of my worst fears come true. Ironic, isn't it? For so long, I asked God to let me become a mother, but I never specified how long I wanted motherhood to last. Pray that it isn't just a few hours or a few days.

I'm trying to stay busy. So far today I've watched a glorious sunrise, organized the peg board in the garage, cleaned a closet, finished the shower thank-you notes (that was a challenge because my vision blurs and I get headaches doing close work), and started sorting my photographs. After the baby's born, I'm hoping to start scrapbooking the baby's pictures. Right now I'm just trying to get all the pictures I have in chronological order...not a very easy task, let me tell you!

It'd be nice to meet you again for ice cream at Paradise Island, but I'm really not up to it. Please don't call me, it's just too overwhelming, and writing is easier for me right now. We can keep in touch via email and be cyber-friends for a while, can't we?

Love, Janelle

Ellie slowly re-read Janelle's shocking email. Her head was spinning, and she was trying to make sense out of the senseless when the doorbell rang. She felt a tinge of anxiety as she heard Helen open the front door. *I've told her a hundred times, but she still opens the door before checking to see who's there.* Ellie hurried to the living room.

"Why, Frankie," Helen cried as she reached out her frail arms to her son.

"Hi, Mom...how're you doing?" Frank set down an oversized suitcase and bulging leather satchel in the foyer to lift his mother off the floor with a big bear hug, then set her back down and disengaged himself from her embrace.

At the sound of Frank's voice, Ellie's heart started pounding; and at the sight of him, her stomach churned. Although she fought it with all her will, she was powerless to stop the ensuing physical reaction. She felt her face flush and her mouth go dry. *First, Jonah's moving to the Alaskan frontier, then Janelle's email, now Frank's sudden appearance...I guess bad news does come in threes.*

"Hi, Ellie," was all her brother said, his demeanor and tone more polite than Ellie had experienced in years. She couldn't help but wonder what he was up to.

"Hello, Frank," she said as she watched Helen lead him over to the sofa and then sit down beside him, lovingly brushing a lock of his hair up off his forehead as she had done ever since he was a toddler. "You've gotten so thin, Frankie," she cooed. "You need to eat. Good thing Ellie's making lunch."

"That'd be great," Frank said. "I'm starved." Ellie took a good look at her brother and realized he did look extremely thin—thinner than she could ever remember.

She excused herself to prepare the meal and listened as Helen and Frank watched a game show re-run on television. She was still at a loss as to why Frank had come, but she set a nice table and fussed a little more than usual. After putting the tuna sandwiches and a summer fruit tray on the table, she added a bowl of chips to round out the meal. She poured a small glass of milk and two large glasses of iced tea and carried the beverages to the dining room. Helen and Frank came as soon as she called and her brother dug right in, eating three large sandwiches, an extra-large helping of fruit and the entire bowl of chips. He complimented her on the food and chitchatted as though they were old friends. Baffled, but caught up in the "new Frank" personality, Ellie asked no questions. When he asked if she had any dessert, she even apologized. "No, sorry. I did mix up some chocolate chip oatmeal cookie dough yesterday, but it's been so hot—I wasn't going to bake them until tomorrow."

"Guess I'll have to wait until then," Frank replied.

Surprised that Frank believed he would be there tomorrow, she wanted to ask him what was going on, but didn't. Suddenly, out of the blue, Helen announced, "I have work to do, children." She got up from the table and went back to her sewing.

Ellie took the opportunity to assuage her curiosity.

"What's going on, Frank?" she asked quietly.

"Well. . .I guess it's time to put my cards on the table," he said ruefully. "That's the whole problem I guess, cards. Blackjack to be exact. The truth is, I was evicted from my apartment, my car's been repossessed, and I'm flat broke. I spent a week with Carl and Josie, but I guess I wore out my welcome. Yesterday they gave me a couple hundred dollars and a bus ticket. I planned to stay at Mom's, but the house was all locked up. At first I was going to break-in, but that nosy neighbor saw me and came over. She told me you had moved Mom out and that she had strict orders to call the police if anyone tried to get in."

Ellie held back a smile. She had told Carolyn no such thing, but she made a mental note to thank her for her bit of quick thinking.

"I thought I could turn the couple hundred into more so I headed out to the casino. . .I lost the money inside an hour and spent the rest of the day walking around." He paused as if he didn't want to tell the rest, then plunged ahead anyway.

"I slept in the men's room last night, took the shuttle back to the station this morning, and hopped the 9:30 bus here. I didn't even have the buck and a quarter city bus fare so I had to walk all the way here from the depot, two miles, carrying my luggage. You can't imagine how humiliating that was." He looked at her with desperate eyes and added, "You and I both know I would never have come here if I had anywhere else to go."

Ellie looked at her brother with a mixture of pity and disgust. Though he looked dejected and lost, his face deeply lined and his hair gray, she struggled not to see the arrogant, spoiled brat she had come to detest.

"I'll beg if I have to, Ellie. I have no pride left," he said. "Please... I need a place to stay until I get back on my feet."

CHAPTER 29

Tuesday, June 24th

Janelle couldn't find a comfortable sleeping position, so at dawn she finally gave up and went out on the front porch, taking her pregnancy journal with her.

Tuesday, June 24th
Dear Little Miracle,

So much has changed since I last wrote...I should be getting ready for work, but instead I'm watching the sun rise and listening to the birds sing. The sun is painting the sky a million shades of pink right now. Red in the morning, shepherd's warning? The doctor told me I had to go on medical leave so now I have all kinds of time to get ready for you! Someday, you'll realize that people always want more time. Christmas always comes too soon. Summer's always too short. Weeks just blend one into another and weekends fly by. When a new month starts, I turn to a clean calendar page and cross off the days as they pass... before I know it, it's time to turn the next page! I know, I'm rambling. What I'm trying to say is I know I should be grateful for this "gift of time." I'm trying. I'm not feeling very well, so after you're born, Mommy needs to stay in the hospital for a while so they can make me better. Don't worry; your daddy will take good care of you until I get home.

Janelle stopped writing to watch a mother robin deliver a worm to the top of a spruce tree. *She's feeding her babies. Please God, give me the chance to do that.*

While Helen watched television, Ellie sat down at her computer on Tuesday morning. Although her response to Janelle was short, finding the right words was almost impossible and it took a while to compose.

Dear Cyber-Friend Janelle,

I got your email yesterday; I've decided there are no words to tell you how sorry I am! It's good that you kept your promise though…now, let's let modern medicine ensure there are many happy Mother's Days in your future! Janelle, are you sure you want to keep this from Claire? I know if it was Rebecca, it would break my heart, but I'd still want to know. Just think about it…

You're never going to believe who's staying with us. Frank. I know, I'm crazy, right? He showed up yesterday. I wanted to say no, but he's desperate. Mom wouldn't let me "turn Frankie out on the street." She said if he went, she was going with him. It's only for a couple days, but Jack is livid! Good thing he's out of town most of this week.

You're in my prayers, Janelle. Please take care of yourself. I'll try to check my email every day so if you need to "talk," I'm here.

Love, Ellie

CHAPTER 30

Thursday, June 26th

God it's hot for June, Janelle thought as she waddled from the air-conditioned Medical Center to her stifling car. Under normal circumstances, she couldn't take the heat, and now she was just plain miserable. Her ankles were swollen and she felt as big as a church. Her headaches were increasing in frequency and intensity, but, for the baby's sake, she was determined to endure the pain. She cranked the air conditioner to high and headed home. It was a short drive, and just as she was starting to cool off, she had to navigate their oven-like garage. She was drenched in sweat before she got to the kitchen. Checking her machine, she saw a red "0" and wondered briefly why her mother hadn't called. *I suppose it was a lot easier to email me when I was at work than it is to call me at home now.* Glancing at her computer across the room, she grabbed a bottle of water from the refrigerator and sat down at the desk.

> *Hi Ellie,*
>
> *I just got back from the doctor. Thank God the baby's growing normally, probably about six and a half pounds now. I'm losing weight, a couple of pounds since last week. The doctor says I should eat more even if I'm not hungry, but the only food I really enjoy now is Paradise Island smoothies, so Matt's been running over there every day for me.*
>
> *I had another MRI; it was worse than the first! I got so claustrophobic. I'm told they have an "open MRI machine," but it doesn't do as good a job so I went into*

the "tunnel" again. *The tumor is a little bigger, but my doctors feel it's safe to wait until July for the C-section.*

How is everything with your brother? I admire you for taking him in. You always look for the good in people…if there's any good in Frank, you'll find it.

I have piles of pictures all over the dining room table. I'm still trying to get them sorted. I'm going to buy matching albums once I know how many I need. Matt refuses to discuss it, but I want to make sure that if things don't turn out the way we want, he can use the photos to tell our child about me. I guess you could say I'm getting my affairs in order.

Speaking of that, I got out my living will and durable power of attorney papers; the doctor wanted copies. I'm glad we had them drawn up last spring; who would have thought I'd need mine so soon?

About telling Mom, for right now it's actually good that she doesn't know. Yesterday she brought over lunch and she's so excited about the baby's arrival, it's contagious…I actually let myself forget about my troubles for a while and that felt so good.

Love, your cyber-friend, Janelle.

P.S. Any major plans for Independence Day?

With blistering sunshine radiating down, Ellie endured another hot and humid summer day in northeastern Wisconsin. Thundershowers were forecast for later in the week, promising blessed relief as a massive high-pressure front with cooler, drier weather moved in for the weekend. She hoped the weather forecast was right for a change. *Too bad I don't have a job where you can be wrong at least half the time and still call yourself an expert,* she mused as she pulled down the cellular shades on the south and west sides of the house to save on cooling costs.

Some half-wit down the block had failed to call Digger's Hotline and had done quite a hack job on the neighborhood media cable, so Ellie's Internet broad band service was down all day Thursday. She thought about calling Janelle but decided not to go against her wishes. It was early evening before she got to check her email. Ellie read Janelle's message and shuddered. She'd always thought her young friend had grit, but Janelle's courage and devotion to her baby was proof positive. She fought back tears as she composed her response.

Dear Janelle,

Your photograph project sounds wonderful. I believe with all my heart that your child will look at those albums in a few years with Matt and YOU!

I thought the kids were coming home for the Fourth, but no such luck. Jonah and his girlfriend, Emily, are flying to Alaska (I'll tell you all about that later) and Rebecca just called to tell me her plans have changed dramatically. Remember my WEAC lawyer, Stacey? She set Rebecca up with Greg, a friend of her fiancé, Dave. They're all corporate attorneys and put in grueling hours. Anyway, for some reason the four of them decided to redeem frequent flyer miles and say Happy Birthday to America in Boston. The fireworks there are supposed to be spectacular. I don't know how they could be better than what we have here! I'll miss the kids, but I'm also relieved they aren't coming. With Mom and Frank demanding so much of me, I just have no energy left for anything else.

About my brother...I don't know how long he'll be here. He doesn't seem too motivated to do much except take up space and watch TV. I know you're having trouble eating, but he isn't. Last night I made a huge pot of beef stew for Jack to take on his fishing trip this weekend. I put it out in the garage fridge to cool and this morning when I went to adjust the spices, half of it was gone! Frank said he was "hungry." I just got back from the store—I have to make more because if Jack finds out, well, it's already way too hot here!

Love, Ellie

CHAPTER 31

Sunday, June 29th

Janelle was miserable most of the weekend. She managed to work on her photo project, but passed a lot of time on the couch. She was irritable and depressed, unable to sleep, eat or even write in her journal. Matt was equally on edge and they ended up having an argument over, of all things—money. Matt was clueless when it came to family finances. He also found refuge in denial about Janelle's condition, so when she insisted they go through their financial obligations together, he grew sullen and uncooperative. When he angrily stalked off to the garage, Janelle surmised it might be better to just write everything down. She went to the computer, thought of Ellie and decided she needed to vent.

> Hi Ellie,
>
> Sorry I didn't email you this weekend. I wasn't feeling too well until this morning. I tried to go over our finances with Matt. He flipped when I said I want to make sure we don't get behind on our bills while I'm recovering and he should know all this stuff anyway...just in case. He stomped off to his safe haven (the garage!) to change his oil and "cool off."
>
> Matt's not doing very well, Ellie. He never was one to display...how did you tell me Ernest Hemingway put it? Grace under pressure. It's like there's this huge black cloud of anxiety crushing him. I insist he go to work every day; there's nothing he can do for me here anyway, and Lord knows we need the money. Plus, having the two of us around being miserable together

makes it worse. Matt's actually lucky; I wish I could be at work. I talked to my boss two days ago and he said they're doing okay, but they miss me (that means they're just getting by).

I got an email yesterday from Bradley. It seems the office rumors are true; he's still job hunting and his wife is leaving him. Oddly, he doesn't seem too upset about it; he's more interested in us being friends again. He said he wants us to "pick up where we left off." I'm not really sure where he thinks that was, but it's obvious that it's a different place than I thought. I can't even begin to tell you how shocked I am, and it's just one more thing I don't need in my life right now so I didn't reply to him and I'm not telling Matt either....he has enough to deal with.

Why is it that when you're waiting, time goes so slowly? Aside from the mess of pictures on the dining table, I doubt our house has ever been so clean. It felt good to throw the junk away. Funny how "things" don't mean so much to me anymore.

I think I'm finally starting to learn that I can't control everything. All my planning, predicting, analyzing, forecasting, and worrying...look where it's gotten me. You told me once that worrying is useless because ninety percent of the things you worry about never happen and ninety percent of the bad things that happen to you happen so fast you don't have time to worry about them. How right you were! During my entire pregnancy I kept waiting for the hammer to fall, for something bad to happen to the baby...instead it's me who's in jeopardy.

I better go. Cassie's stopping by in a few minutes and I need to pull myself together.

Take care, Janelle

P.S. Great news about Jonah and Rebecca...maybe there'll be a grandchild (or two) in your future after all!

Violent thunderstorms rolled through Sunday night, lighting up the sky with jagged bursts of blinding light. High winds and hail pounded the southeast side of town, and massive oak trees, some over two hundred years old, were uprooted on the nearby university campus. Ellie's own backyard looked like a disaster area, with broken tree limbs dangling and her flowerbeds whipped into a tangled mess. She and Jack spent all day Monday cleaning up the damage.

Frank sat on the couch with Helen, watching the weather channel, while outside Jack seethed, "That lazy son-of-a-bitch is long past wearing out his welcome." Ellie ignored her husband's justified ranting, content to let Frank watch over Helen while she tended the remnants of her vegetable garden. It was Tuesday before she got to her email.

Tuesday, July 1st
Dear Janelle,

Happy July 1st! Your waiting is nearly over, sweetie. In one week you will be a mother! I pray every day that everything goes well for you, and I trust with all my heart that God will protect you AND your baby. As far as time slowing down is concerned, I'm sure most pregnant women feel that way during the last month. I know I did... it's probably the anticipation of being so close to finally meeting the little life that's been snuggled up under your heart for months!

It's really not that odd that Bradley is attracted to you, you are such a beautiful girl, but I think it's good you didn't reply to his email. If I were you, I'd tell Matt about it though... maybe not right now if he's having a tough time with everything else, but as soon as you can. If Bradley doesn't get the picture and leave things as they are, it will only be harder to explain things to Matt later.

You asked about my brother. Unfortunately, he's still here. Yesterday Jack was home, helping clean up after the storm, (did you have any damage?) and he caught Frank snooping around the curio where I keep my grandmother's Hummel collection. I haven't told Jack, but Frank's been stealing money from my purse. Not a lot, but he sneaks off almost every afternoon, and I can smell alcohol on his breath when he comes back. I know I should confront him, but I'm just so glad to be rid of him for a few hours that I prefer to consider the missing money "an investment" in my sanity. I never realized how "exposed" a person can feel by living under the same roof with someone who can't be trusted.

Jack's trying to be patient, but between Mom's "episodes" and my brother's obnoxious behavior, our privacy is non-existent. Something's got to change soon; things can't go on like this much longer.

Love, Ellie.

P.S. Does your mom know yet? She's going to find out eventually…don't you think it would be best for her to hear it from you?

CHAPTER 32

Thursday, July 3rd

With a cooler, less humid weather pattern making its way into the Valley, perfect summer days were forecast for the Fourth of July weekend. Exhausted from working long hours in the scorching sun, Matt was so sound asleep that he didn't hear the alarm blaring. It took Janelle a full ten minutes to get him out of bed. Even then, he stumbled around the bedroom like an inebriated fool. After she had finally shoved him, still groggy and grouchy, out the door, she took her glass of tomato juice and journal out to the porch.

Dear Baby,

It's a beautiful morning. I think someday you're going to love our front porch as much as I do. Daddy took this afternoon off work because I go to the doctor again. He's so tired, he needs some rest, and he hasn't heard your heartbeat in a while.

We've finally decided on names. At your baby shower everyone gave us suggestions and we looked through them last night. If you are a boy, you will be Benjamin Owen and if you're a girl Dana Marie. My teacher friend Ellie says your name affects your self-concept more than any other word in the English language, and parents need to choose their children's names very carefully. I hope you like yours!

I'm getting so excited to meet you, but I have to admit I'm apprehensive too. I've had some pretty sharp

*pains lately and some of the signs they told us about in
Lamaze class started happening last night. So I wonder
if I'll be having that scheduled C-section or if you have
plans of your own. Will you tell me? I'm betting these
cramps will pale in comparison to actual labor…and
that scares me! Right now my entire body hurts, but
mostly my arms ache to hold you…in that moment
our lives will be perfect.*

    Love, Mom ✎

Janelle read over what she just wrote. Satisfied, she went
inside to refill her glass. As she put the tomato juice back in
the fridge, she noticed she had left the computer on last night.
Before shutting it down, she sat down to email Ellie.

Hi Ellie,

    *Guess what! I lost my mucus plug last night! Isn't
that the grossest term? When they talked about it in
Lamaze class, I thought they could call it something
else…now I realize there's no other way to describe it!
I called the nurse and she said it could be another two
weeks or I could go into labor in the next 24 hours! I'm
so lucky, Ellie! Dr. Felding is the one on call for the
holiday weekend, so if I do go into labor, I'll have my
own doctor. He thinks it would be great if the baby
comes naturally (then I won't have to have two major
surgeries back-to-back). I ache all over and I'm feeling
really uncomfortable, but I've been headache-free for
two days and I'm high on life. Everything's going to be
okay…it has to be! We'll be in touch!*

    Love, Janelle

Ellie rose early, made coffee and read the paper before
going back to bed. Jack had taken the day off and she
snuggled contentedly in his arms. It had been weeks since
they had made love, so she turned up the volume on the clock
radio in case Helen or Frank got up early, and then made up

for lost time. As was often the case, Jack fell back to sleep afterward, and Ellie crept quietly from bed. She went to her office to check her email. Reading Janelle's upbeat news made her spirits soar. After a light breakfast, she talked Jack and Helen into taking a walk to a nearby park. When Helen stopped to smell the "flowers," so did Ellie. *We take so much in this world for granted...why haven't I ever noticed the simple beauty of a dandelion before?* When Helen got tired, they sat on a black metal park bench and leisurely watched the children scramble all over the play equipment while their mothers hovered nearby. *This time next year Janelle could be one of those mothers. Please, God, let her...and the baby...be all right.*

When they arrived back at the house, they found Frank sprawled in the recliner, watching an old movie. He didn't bother to acknowledge their presence, so they went out to the sunroom to relax with another cup of coffee. Helen, who no longer recalled if she had eaten recently or not, drank a large glass of milk and ate the two pieces of whole-wheat toast with strawberry jam that Ellie brought to her. After her second breakfast, she said she had "mending" to do and settled herself on the sofa with her sewing. On a whim, Jack persuaded Ellie into asking Frank to watch Helen so they could go out alone together. He had forgotten to put his pickup in the garage the night before so they climbed into the truck to go for a ride, just like old times.

They went to their favorite ethnic restaurant for a Mexican omelet, ran into a number of people they knew, and time passed quickly. They talked about Jonah flying to Nome early Saturday morning, about life's ironic little twists...like Rebecca's and Stacey's rekindled friendship leading Rebecca to find a boyfriend, and about how they had refused to let Frank's presence in the house ruin their relationship.

"Speaking of Frank," Jack said. "He's been with us what, ten days? What's he done except eat, sleep and watch TV?"

"Nothing...except for staying with Mom so I can go grocery shopping and run other errands...he's done absolutely nothing."

"How long is this going to go on?"

Ellie was just as sick of her brother as Jack was. "His vacation is over as of Monday. I'm going to demand he get up off his butt...get out of the house, and go look for a job and an apartment!"

"I'll believe that when I see it."

"Well, believe it, Mr. Reed, because as much as it's not exactly fun caring for Mother, having Frank around is much, much worse. Plus a third of the summer is over, and I can't imagine teaching and having to come home to that after a grueling day at work. I just wish this would all go away."

Seeing the opportunity, Jack asked tentatively, "Ellie, why don't we stop by Senior Village this afternoon to see if they have an opening?" The Village had an exemplary dementia unit and Jack was very familiar with the staff there because his union represented them.

"Let me take care of getting Frank out of our lives first, please, Jack?" Ellie pleaded.

"Okay, Ellie, I've been patient, but now I'm putting my foot down. We'll talk to him together, and we'll do it today."

Ellie felt her stomach turn over and wished she hadn't eaten so much. "All right, let's go before I lose my nerve."

As they walked arm-in-arm to Jack's truck, Ellie's heart was heavy. She had to admit that Frank's presence in her home had turned her life into a living nightmare. He had immediately commandeered the remote control, cleaned out the liquor cabinet, regularly emptied her refrigerator in bizarre nocturnal eating binges, refused to let her into Jonah's bedroom which had begun emitting a strange sickening odor, not to mention his occasional tavern escapades funded by pilfered money from her purse.

As Jack drove toward home, Ellie had an uneasy feeling that something was amiss. When he pulled into the driveway, she thought, *Strange...the service door to the garage is open.* Jack obviously didn't notice and pressed the button on the door opener. The heavy door moved up slowly on the rollers, and it took them both a second to realize the garage was empty. Ellie cried out in disbelief, "Jack, my car's gone!

Someone stole Blackbird! I'll bet money that someone is Frank. That's it! I'm calling the cops!"

Incensed, Ellie threw the truck door open and ran into the kitchen. The house was absolutely still. She picked up the phone in her shaking hand, and was about to dial 911 when she saw the note on the counter.

Ellie, Such a beautiful day…I decided to get Mom out of the house. Went for a drive. Hope you don't mind.
Frank.

Jack, who had quickly parked the truck in the garage, came into the kitchen to find Ellie re-reading the note, pushed beyond rage.

"That bastard…" she kept saying over and over. "If anything happens to my car…he's going to wish he was dead. I'll probably kill him myself!"

"Want to go out looking for him?" Jack offered.

"Now wouldn't that be a wild goose chase. We've no idea where he'd go. All we can do is sit here and wait for him to come back. If I had any doubts before about kicking him out, they're certainly gone now!"

Still beside herself, Ellie went into the living room. The newspaper was strewn around on the floor, and Helen's mending lay neatly folded on the coffee table.

"What a slob! Well, I might as well *read* the paper since I have to pick it up," Jack said. "Why don't I turn on the Brewer game? Maybe it'll make the time pass a little quicker."

No, just like Janelle always says, time is going to crawl by now because we're waiting.

The Brewers couldn't hit, pitch or field that day, so with the score 9-2 in the seventh, they turned off the television and sat in silence. Hearing sirens in the distance, Jack said, "Ambulance. I hope it's nobody we know."

"It's always somebody *somebody* knows," Ellie replied automatically as she jumped up. "Jack. I can't sit here any longer. I'm going to take a walk, want to come?"

"Sure, maybe they'll be home by the time we get back."

Jack had to quicken his step to keep up with Ellie.

Unwilling to go too far from the house, she insisted they walk up the block and back. As they paced their street, they encountered little tykes riding big wheels down driveways, friends gathering in front yards to chitchat, teenage boys throwing a football around on a quiet side street, and an elderly couple sitting on their front porch, soaking up the afternoon sunshine. Ellie sniffed the air: "Someone's cooking hamburgers over a charcoal grill."

"Ordinarily that smell would make me ravenous, but I'm still digesting that omelet and I'm impervious to sensory stimulation," Jack said in a failed attempt to humor his wife. She gave him a wry glance, then grudgingly laughed at his silliness. After a half hour of pacing and with no Blackbird in sight, they walked back to the house, opening the door just as the phone rang. Thinking it might be Frank, Ellie answered immediately.

"Hello, yes, this is Eleanor Reed," she said. "What? Yes, I'm the registered owner of a Black Ford Thunderbird."

The sound of Ellie's voice and the look on her face made Jack come close. "What? Ohmigod, Oh, God, no...we heard the sirens...no...it can't be...it just can't!" Ellie cried. Then she went limp and the phone fell out of her hand and crashed onto the floor. Jack just managed to catch her as she collapsed into his arms.

CHAPTER 33

Thursday, July 3rd

Matt and Janelle navigated the drive-thru at 11:43 for a quick lunch on their way to the hospital. Matt ordered the double cheeseburger meal, while Janelle had the yogurt parfait, only because Matt insisted she eat something.

"I'm really not hungry, Matt. Honestly."

"Are you still…ummm…leaking fluid?" Matt asked, concerned and looking a little embarrassed.

"Yes, I have a pad on right now."

"Well, maybe your water did break then."

"I don't know. I expected it would be more…dramatic. I didn't think I would just start…dripping."

"We're skipping your 12:15 appointment with Dr. Myommar," Matt said, pressing harder on the accelerator. "If your water did break, they'll postpone your MRI until after the baby's born. We're going straight to emergency to check in like they told us in Lamaze class."

"Sounds like a plan," Janelle said. "Hurry up and eat." She put her half-eaten parfait in the cup-holder and reclined in the passenger seat, then closed her eyes and held her stomach. "Awww, Matt. I don't feel good. This could be the real thing."

"We're just about there," Matt drove with one hand while he inhaled his sandwich and then shoveled in a few fries. "I have no idea why I'm eating this. I'm so nervous, I can't even taste it," he said washing it all down with a huge gulp of soda.

"Matt don't forget our mortgage has to be paid by the 10th or we'll get a late fee," Janelle said as Matt pulled into the hospital parking lot, scraping the underside of the front bumper on the cement.

"Damn!" he cursed for not noticing the steep incline. "Will you please forget about that, Janelle?"

"Matt, I just want to make sure..."

"Janelle, stop it! Can't you just trust me? We went through it all last weekend and you wrote it all down. I'll figure it out, I promise."

Suddenly, Janelle was overcome with tears. "I'm sorry, Matt. I do trust you, but I'm scared."

"Janelle, honey, it's okay to be scared. I didn't mean to snap at you. Everything's gonna work out. We're gonna have a handsome son or a daughter as beautiful and precious as you." He shifted the car into park and lovingly stroked her hair. "Did I ever tell you I love how soft your hair is?"

Janelle blushed and wiped away her tears. "Yes, and I love it when you say that, but what if they have to shave it all off to do the operation?"

"Then it'll all grow back." He got out and came around to open her door. "How does that Randy Travis song go?" he asked as he helped her from the car, then began singing in an exaggerated nasal tone: "I ain't in love with your hair...if it all fell out, I'd love you anyway."

Janelle couldn't help but laugh and punched his shoulder to stop his teasing. "And then we're going to live happily ever after," Matt exclaimed as he took her hand.

Janelle kissed her fingertips and gently placed them on Matt's lips. "From your lips to God's ears, Matthew Spencer. I love you."

"I love you too...both of you," Matt said, touching Janelle's tummy tenderly.

They made their way quickly into the hospital, and she didn't even object when an attendant insisted she use the courtesy wheelchair.

"Hi, I'm Maggie. How can I help you?" a nurse asked Matt and Janelle as they approached the registration counter.

"I'm Matt Spencer. We think maybe we could, I mean, maybe my wife Janelle could be in labor."

"I think my water broke, but I'm not sure..."

"Okay, Janelle, why don't we get you to a room," she replied with a twinkle in her eye, then added, "and we'll see if that little firecracker in your tummy wants to put a little extra excitement into your Fourth of July this year."

Matt waited outside while Maggie helped Janelle into a gown. She handed Janelle a new sanitary pad and white pair of fishnet underwear.

"I know, these are really awful. No one likes them, but when you're in heavy labor, believe me, the last thing you'll want to do is shimmy to get your undies off."

"They're definitely not designer lingerie, that's for sure," Janelle said, still able to find humor in the situation, even though she was feeling increasingly uncomfortable each minute. The nurse helped her to the bathroom and Janelle noticed with alarm that she was bleeding.

"That's okay," Maggie assured her. "Your water probably did break. We'll check when you're ready. Don't worry. Everything'll be fine." Janelle climbed into the bed and put her feet in the stirrups as instructed. For some reason, she was expecting the procedure to take a while and maybe even hurt. Instead, Maggie simply took a piece of paper that looked like the test strips Janelle had seen diabetics use and barely touched Janelle's vaginal area before she held it up and announced, "You'll be staying. It's amniotic fluid."

Maggie asked Matt to come in, and Janelle instructed him to call Claire and then get her overnight bag from the car. The nurse started an IV and put a plastic strap around her tummy to help monitor the baby and her contractions. Being hooked up to the machines and confined to the bed, Janelle remembered her MRI appointment. *Saved by the baby,* she smiled to herself. "Does Dr. Felding know I'm here?"

"If he doesn't know already, he will soon. Don't worry, he'll be in direct contact with me or your new nurse at shift change," Maggie said, looking at her watch.

Janelle had lost all concept of time and glanced at the wall clock, wondering where Matt was, surprised that it was already 1:30. "What time is shift change?"

"Three o'clock." Maggie arranged different shiny instruments on a tray next to the bed. Janelle was just about to explain that she had missed an MRI appointment when the door opened and Matt and Claire walked in. *Thank God, I could've been talking about the brain tumor when Mom walked in!*

"Hi, honey!" Claire's voice was brimming with hope and excitement. "You nervous?"

"A little, I'm really uncomfortable," Janelle answered. "I just want it over."

"Okay, Dad and Grandma," Maggie interrupted as she put her rubber gloves on, "I'm going to see if Janelle's dilated. You can stay in the room, but would you both move up near the head of the bed?"

Janelle had to laugh because in one swift motion they were out of her way—it was as if Maggie had lit a small firecracker under both of them.

Maggie checked Janelle and announced: "Three centimeters dilated and seventy percent effaced."

"Only three centimeters?" Janelle was disappointed. "Now what?"

"Well," Maggie said, "now we wait."

Ellie sat by her mother's bedside, holding one frail hand in hers. Helen had not regained consciousness since the accident, and Josie and Carl had gone back to the hotel to get some sleep. It was nearly midnight and Ellie was exhausted, but she refused to go home in case her mother did awaken.

Sitting there, she thought again about the last eleven hours. The police had been kind, speculating that Helen had survived the accident only because she was buckled in. They had had to use the Jaws of Life to free her and she was barely alive when they got her out. Helen had instructed in her living will that no "heroic measures" be taken to save her life, and the hospital staff acquiesced. Her condition was critical and the doctor was not optimistic about her chances.

This time Frank's irresponsibility had led to a terrible tragedy. Investigators at the scene determined that he had been traveling at a high rate of speed down the deserted country road, failed to negotiate a sharp curve, and rolled Blackbird over into a cornfield. There was no trace of him at the scene other than blood spatters that matched his rare blood-type: AB negative. The police had posted a statewide search alert for him, but Ellie wasn't at all sure she wanted them to find him. *If they do, I just might be the one who goes to jail. . .for homicide. . .I could kill the bastard!*

When Josie arrived around seven and asked for some time alone with Helen, Ellie had demanded that Jack drive her to the scene of the crash. It was getting dark and there wasn't much left to see. *Highway crews are so efficient at cleaning up after traffic accidents. I wonder if there's a crew who could come and clean up my life?* She then insisted on going to the junkyard where Blackbird had been towed. Of course, the car was unrecognizable, a pile of twisted, mangled steel, its tires turned at obscene angles to the chassis. The only salvageable item was the case that held her CD's—amazingly they were still intact. *You failed to take your own advice,* she berated herself as she walked away. *You know better than to get too attached to things. . .after all, it was just a car. . . .* Then she couldn't help but think of a stupid song she'd always hated: *Bye Bye, Blackbird.*

As the rest of the family gathered at the hospital, one by one they went in to see Helen. Unable to watch as Jack comforted Rebecca, Ellie went to the cafeteria for a cup of coffee and bumped into Sharon Kelly. The entire story was related quickly.

"I'm so sorry, Ellie," Sharon said sympathetically, and then added as if she was reading Ellie's mind: "But you are not to ever consider any of this your fault."

"No, I'm pretty clear on who's at fault here. . .my beloved brother," Ellie responded bitterly. *As usual, he creates the crisis. . .leaves me to deal with it. Josie doesn't seem to give a damn that he's missing, so why should I?* "Whatever happens to him from this point on, he's on his own!"

"Good thinking, my friend. Best to let it, and him, go," Sharon advised. They hugged and promised to keep in touch.

Upon returning to Helen's room, Ellie saw Jonah with his grandmother. *Thank God Jack was able to reach him before his flight left.* She stood quietly in the doorway, her heart breaking as she saw her son kneeling by Helen's bed.

"Grandma? Grandma?" he said through his tears. "Did Mom tell you? I got a job teaching in a one-room school just like you used to. It's in Nome. I was supposed to leave early tomorrow morning, but that can wait."

Consumed by his anguish, Jonah was not aware that Ellie was standing there listening. "I met a girl—Emily. She's going too. I think we're in love, Grandma. Please don't tell Mom and Dad. They'll think it's some kind of sin...the two of us living together, but I have to do this. If my life is going to mean something, I have to make a difference, not just for the kids but for myself too. I know you understand."

Jonah leaned closer and spoke animatedly, as if he had more news he couldn't wait to share. "You know what else? The Brewers are starting to play some awesome baseball. You always said someday we'd see the Brewers win the World Series. Wouldn't that be sweet? Good thing my school's online in Alaska. I can listen to the games on the Net and won't miss any of the excitement."

Tears flowed down Ellie's face as she watched the tenderness with which Jonah kissed his grandmother. And she wept for another reason too. She had known the moment Jonah told Helen about Emily that she had lost part of her son forever. *A daughter's a daughter all her life; a son's a son until he takes a wife.*

Sitting by her mother's bed, and not knowing what else to do, Ellie prayed, not sure exactly what she should pray for. Emotionally exhausted, she found herself dozing off. Then suddenly, she felt pressure on her hand and her mother moaned. Ellie rose and put her mouth close to her mother's ear. "Mom, can you hear me?" she asked softly.

"Mama?" Helen said faintly.

"No, Mom, it's me. Ellie."

Helen seemed to hear but not comprehend. "My head hurts, Mama. Make it stop hurting, please?" Her voice was small and weak, like a little girl with a scraped knee.

"I'll call the doctor, Mom…"

"No, don't go. Sing me a song, Mama. That'll make it better. You always make things better when you sing."

"What should I sing?"

"The one about sunshine, Mama."

"Do you mean *Sunrise, Sunset*?" Helen didn't answer but squeezed her daughter's hand, so Ellie began to sing, "Sunrise, sunset, quickly go the years…one season following another, laden with happiness and tears." Her voice cracked and tears streamed down her cheeks.

"That was nice," Helen said. "I love it when you sing." Then she added, "I love you, Mama."

Ellie couldn't believe her ears! Her mother had said, "I love you." Even though the words weren't exactly intended for her, it made her heart swell just to hear her mother say them. "I love you, Mom," she said.

Helen opened her eyes and looked directly at Ellie. "I love you too, Ellie," she said clearly, squeezing her daughter's hand. Choked with emotion and unable to breathe, Ellie thought her mother was going back to sleep. Then Helen sighed deeply…her hand went limp…she just slipped away.

Ellie had a momentary urge to scream for the nurse, even though she knew there was nothing more to do. She wanted this moment for herself, to gather herself and bask in the warmest affection she had ever experienced from her mother. Ellie knew her mother's final words had been spoken in a moment of unmistakable clarity. "I love you too, Mom. Good bye," she whispered. "Go with God, you know Dad's waiting for you. See you in Heaven."

When the nurse came in about an hour later, Ellie was all cried out, but still holding her mother's hand tightly. The nurse gently untangled their entwined fingers, unhooked Helen's IV and covered her with a sheet. She took Helen's chart from the wall and asked Ellie if she knew what time Helen had passed. Oddly enough, Ellie had looked at the clock and was able to tell the nurse that her mother's exact time of death was 1:23 A.M. The nurse finished Helen's chart and quietly told Ellie she would take care of Helen so she could go home and rest. Stubbornly refusing to leave, Ellie said she would not allow her mother's body to be taken down to a cold storage room to await the funeral home attendant. "I don't care if you think I'm crazy, I'm not leaving my mom."

The nurse was too busy to argue, so Ellie kept watch over her mother's body the rest of the night. She did fall asleep for a little while, waking with a start at dawn. She went over to the window to watch the sunrise. It was breathtakingly beautiful this morning—as if Helen's flight to heaven was lighting up the sky with a special glow.

As the sun rose higher in the sky, she decided it was time to call Josie. "Mom's in a better place," was all her sister said. "At least she doesn't have to suffer anymore."

Then she called Jack. "Of course," he said when she asked him to tell the children. "We'll be right over. Hang in there, honey...you know we love you and we'll get through this like everything else...together."

Later, after the family had arrived and said their goodbyes, Jack called the mortuary where they had pre-arranged Helen's final wishes. On impulse, just before the attendant took Helen's body away, Ellie pulled back the sheet and kissed her mother goodbye. Helen's cheek felt cold, and the sensation sent a chill through Ellie's heart. *I'll go to hell for this, but I hate you, Frank. Not because you killed Mom or wrecked my car, but because, despite being a worthless piece of crap, you were always her favorite.*

Suddenly, Ellie felt very tired. "Let's go home, Jack," she said softly. She went over to the window sill to pick up her purse, and out of habit, looked out. Her drooping eyes opened wide when she saw Cassie and Jeff Kingsford carrying a huge stuffed teddy bear into the hospital.

"On second thought, would you wait for me down in the truck, honey?" she asked, her heart once more transformed by the gift of a special friendship. "I'll just be a few more minutes. I need to make a quick stop in the nursery."

CHAPTER 34

🍂
Saturday, July 5th
Dear Baby Dana,

   Holding you for the first time was more amazing than I ever imagined. You were so warm and wiggly. When you opened your little eyes and stared up at me, you looked straight into my soul and I was powerless. I'd dreamed about you for so long, but I had no idea what one look from you would do to me.

   You are too young to understand this now, but someday you will—usually the things in life that make us feel powerless at first are the same things that we gain strength from later. The image of your little face is going to give me strength in the next few days and for the rest of my life.

   Love forever, Mommy 🍂

Friday, July 11th

A week later Ellie sat beside another hospital bed—this time Janelle's. Matt had called late last Friday, just after she had returned from making funeral arrangements. "Mrs. Reed? It's Matt Spencer. I'm at the hospital and we had the baby! Wait until you see her...she's so beautiful! Dana Marie Spencer, 6 pounds, 9 ounces. She has blonde hair just like Janelle and..."

   "Matt, that's wonderful...congratulations! I actually did see Dana when I was at the hospital with my mother."

"Well, you should've stopped in to see Janelle. She'll be upset to hear you didn't."

Ellie realized that they didn't know about the accident and she explained briefly. "Matt," she then said probingly, "what about the tumor?"

"Dr. Myommar's scheduled the surgery for Monday morning at seven."

"Does Claire know?"

"Yeah. Claire's pretty worried, but on cloud nine about Dana. Janelle's upbeat now that the baby's here. She babbled something about her surgery being on the perfect month, the perfect day at the perfect time, whatever that means."

Ellie smiled. "Please give Janelle my best and tell her I'll come next week...with the funeral arrangements and all..."

"That's fine, Ellie. Don't worry about us. Just give us a call when you can. And I'm really sorry about your mom."

Monday night Matt had called again. The neurosurgeon had removed the tumor and declared the operation a total success. However, when it was time for Janelle to come out of the anesthetic, she remained unconscious. The specialist said the situation was rare but not unheard of and there was cause for some concern—each passing day could mean physical or neurological damage. He stressed that round-the-clock stimulation might bring her back from the land of shadows.

Unbelievably, it was Sandy who took charge, making a schedule. Sandy would take the seven to three shift at the hospital while Claire cared for the baby. Then they would switch places for the three to eleven shift. Sandy would fix supper for Matt, do the dishes and leave when the baby was bathed, fed and ready for bed. Ellie had volunteered to take the night shift at the hospital, which allowed Matt to be with Janelle during the day and the baby at night.

So here was Ellie, exhausted yet loyally sitting at her young friend's bedside. Janelle lay pale and still—as she had done the past four nights. Tonight, Ellie's voice was urgent as she tried to coax her friend back, "Janelle, Janelle, honey, wake up. You have to wake up. Your baby needs you. Matt needs you. Your mother needs you." *I need you.*

There was no response. A moment later, restless, Ellie got up to open the curtains and let the faint morning light in. She looked over at Janelle who had not stirred and then out the window again. The sun had begun to peek up over the horizon. The sky's dawn-face, like a virgin's, blushed in a rose-colored glow of anticipation. Ellie watched in silence as the sun inched its way up over the horizon, sending streaks of radiant light to rekindle the fire of life for another day. *Reminds me of a picture in the seventh grade literature book, the one with Apollo driving across the sky in his golden chariot. Most of the time we take the rising and setting of the sun, and life, for granted. But like the sun, the cycle of life just goes on. . .or does it?*

"Dear God," she prayed aloud in the same words she had said thousands of times before for herself: "You need only to say the word and *she* shall be healed."

Ellie walked over to the bed and reached for Janelle's left hand, noticing it was still bruised from being poked repeatedly for an IV. Ellie examined it. *They must have tried four or five times before they gave up on this one.* She massaged Janelle's hand as she talked, repeating much of what she had already said every previous night. . .things about Matt, the baby, Helen's funeral, Cassie's plans to adopt. She told her about the mysteriously silent young man who had come in quietly one night and left a bouquet of red roses with a card that said, *Please, come back soon, I miss you.*

Releasing her friend's hand, Ellie whispered something that she knew Janelle would understand. "Did you know my mother went to heaven just a few minutes before your baby was born? You know, Janelle. . .I think when someone dies, a part of his or her soul stays here. Not like reincarnation. . . more like recycling. I think Dana Marie Spencer needed a soul and Helen Miriam Lowe was chosen as her donor."

Janelle stirred and Ellie took her hand again. Without realizing it, she started twirling Janelle's wedding ring around on her finger, rubbing it with her thumb. "Mmm. . .mmh, Matt, stop. . .it tickles." The corners of Janelle's mouth turned up slightly as she pulled her hand from Ellie's.

"Janelle! Wake up! Wake up, honey...talk to me!"

Janelle made a murmuring sound, wrinkled her nose, and slowly opened her eyes, forcing herself to focus. She rubbed the bandage on her head. "Jeez...my head hurts."

"Just rest, honey. Everything's under control. And don't worry about Dana. Sandy and Claire have been taking turns with her so Matt could concentrate on getting you better."

"Dana?" Janelle touched her head again gingerly and then felt her flattened stomach. A look of total bewilderment came over her face. "My baby? Was it a girl?" Her voice took on a panicked expression. "Ellie, why can't I remember?"

"It's okay, honey," Ellie said calmly, reassuringly, using the same tone that had always soothed Helen's anxiety. "After all this time, it's perfectly normal for you to be confused. Look here," Ellie said, holding a photograph for Janelle, "as of July 4th, you were officially somebody's mommy."

Janelle managed a slight smile and the fear in her eyes softened as she focused on her baby's first family picture. Then another puzzled expression passed over her face. "Wait, you said...after all this time? What day is it, Ellie?"

"It's Friday, July 11th. Dana's a week old already."

Janelle tried to comprehend but winced as she again touched the bandage on her head. A deep breath turned into a yawn; she wanted to go back to sleep. Ellie wasn't alarmed. Her young friend had been through so much.

"Honey, you don't need to fret about anything." She looked over at the book propped on the hospital bureau. "I bought you a new journal and I gave myself the task of writing down all the important details of what's been happening to you. The rest of the assignment is up to you."

Janelle smiled weakly, "Thank you, Ellie, you're such a good friend."

Looking at her friend
with a heart full of affection,
Ellie added softly, as Janelle drifted off,
"So are you, honey...so are you!"

296

About the Authors

Kathie and Heather met in 1986 when Heather found herself in Kathie's seventh grade classroom. From the first time Kathie graded one of Heather's writing assignments, she knew this student had remarkable talent and made an extra effort to encourage and direct her prize pupil.

As an eighth grader, Heather served as Kathie's student aide and their relationship grew into a true friendship. They kept in touch periodically over the years, often communicating by letter and email.

While having lunch together in 2001, the two shared their burdens: Heather's infertility issues and Kathie's mother's recent diagnosis of Alzheimer's Disease. A few months later, they met again and decided to chronicle their experiences. At a third meeting that year, they decided to collaborate on a novel and their "baby" was conceived. It took two years, but they have now given life to this heart-warming and unique cross-generational novel, *Sunrise Sunset*.

A Special Note to Teachers:

If you are an educator, I forward and dedicate Heather's letter on page 298 to you. Never forget that teachers enrich the lives of their students in ways that cannot be anticipated. To paraphrase Christa MacAuliffe, "You touch the world, you teach."

    —Kathleen Marie Marsh

Kathleen Marie Marsh

Kathleen Marie Marsh was born the third of eight children and grew up on a diary farm in northeastern Wisconsin. A scholarship took her to Mount Mary College, Milwaukee, where she majored in English and History. She later earned an MA in Education from Marian College in Fond du Lac. Kathie had an award-winning teaching career at the secondary level in Kaukauna where she taught English for 35 years before retiring in 2002. She has operated a free lance writing business for the past 20 years and is CEO of Otter Run Books, LLC. She is the founder of the UpNorth Author's Circle, a group of local writers dedicated to the support and encouragement of fledgling northern Wisconsin authors.

Kathie serves as a staff development specialist for several colleges in Wisconsin, teaching courses in writing, educational psychology, classroom management and desktop publishing. In 2004, with the help of Goblin Fern Press, she published the widely acclaimed *Portly Princess of Thynneland*, a grown-up fairy tale that addresses the critical role of parents in preventing childhood obesity.

Kathie and her husband, Jon, cherish their delightfully blended family of four children and four grandchildren. They currently live on the Townsend Flowage, a lake in northern Wisconsin where the wildlife abounds and a breathtaking lake view inspire her to write on!

Kathie is currently working on *My Mother Kept a Scrapbook, the Story of a World War II Prisoner of War*. This must-read book chronicles the POW experiences of Wausau, Wisconsin resident Gerhard Johnson, and will be released April 16, 2005, the 60th anniversary of Johnson's release from Nazi captivity.

Heather Sprangers

Heather Sprangers was born and raised in Kaukauna, Wisconsin, and is currently employed at August Winter & Sons, Inc. in Appleton. She discovered her passion for writing in Kathleen Marsh's seventh grade classroom. She earned straight "A's" and volunteered the next year to be her student aide, thus beginning their life-long friendship. That year she also won a writing contest; the prize: a coveted ride in the local news channel helicopter.

High school classmates shook their heads in disbelief as Heather actually welcomed composition assignments. But it paid off. She won a partial college scholarship with "The Gates of Heaven," an essay depicting the last moments of her beloved stepfather's life after his eight-week battle with cancer.

To earn money for college, Heather spent her nineteenth summer working rotating shifts in a paper mill. She used every spare moment to create characters and develop plot ideas for *Transplant*, her first novel, which she completed that summer. Even though *Transplant* was never published, it provided her with valuable writing experience and stoked her friendship with Kathleen who provided suggestions, support and encouragement.

She married her high school sweetheart in 1997 and two years later they decided they were ready to start their family. To their surprise and disappointment, they learned that "family planning" wasn't so simple. With the help of IUI, Heather eventually got pregnant in November of 2001. She and her husband, Adam, are now the proud parents of Benjamin Owen Sprangers.

Dear Kathie,

Co-writing this novel with you, the woman who introduced me to the art of creative writing and then nurtured and encouraged my writing years and years after I left your classroom, has been an unparalleled experience for me. Throughout the process, you complimented me several times on my writing and editing ability. Thank you for that, but please always remember it was you who gave birth to my desire to write.

Life is so strange…as a young teen I sat in your classroom and listened to you dream about writing a novel when you retired and I made a promise to myself that I would own a signed copy of the first novel by Kathleen Marie Marsh…I had no idea then that my name would appear in print next to yours because we wrote it together!

Kathie, I don't think I can ever express what our friendship and this journey we've traveled together means to me. If our readers can't experience a friendship like ours firsthand, then my hope is that Sunrise Sunset *and the story of Janelle and Ellie will be a page turner that will portray at least a glimmer of what our friendship is like and will linger in their hearts and minds for years to come.*

    Love, Heather

Musical Acknowledgements

Sunrise, Sunset —Joseph Stein, Sheldon Harnick and Jerry Bock *—Fiddler on the Roof*, 1965

Letting Go —Doug Crider and Matt Rollings, Voices in the Wind (Suzy Bogguss) Liberty-Capitol Records, 1992

Love Grows Best in Little Houses —Mickey Cate and Skip Ewing, The Best of Doug Stone (Doug Stone) Epic Records, 1995

I'm Gonna Wash That Man Right Outta My Hair —Rogers and Hammerstein *—South Pacific*, 1958

If Ever I Would Leave You —Frederick Loewe and Alan Jay Lerner Camelot, 1967

Someday There'll Be a Place for Us —Stephen Sondheim and Leonard Bernstein *—West Side Story*, 1956

Love Shack –B'52's Cosmic Thing, Warner Brothers, 1989

Lady in Red —Christopher DeBurgh Very Best of Chris DeBurgh–Ark 21, 1991

Forever and Ever, Amen —Paul Overstreet Always and Forever (Randy Travis) Warners, 1987